CALL OF THE FATHOMS

II

ALSO BY EMMA HAMM

Deep Waters
Whispers of the Deep
Song of the Abyss
Echoes of the Tide

Seven Deadly Demons
The Demon Court
The Demon Crown
The Demon Prince
The Demon Mark

Dragon of Umbra
Fire Heart
Bright Heart
Brave Heart
Torn Heart
Taloned Heart

and many more...

Every foreword of every book in this series so far I have
reminded people -

This is not scientifically accurate.

I think ya'll get it so I'M GONNA TALK ABOUT WHAT I
WANT TO TALK ABOUT.

Which is Humboldt squid.

Right now, you don't know why this is so important for you to
know. All you know is that they exist in real life.

I'm going to put a little real fact in here (because in case you
didn't know, some of this is actually scientifically accurate and I
did use this book to lock you in a room with me so I could rant
about the random ocean shit I know from Nature and Nova).

These squid species are the ONLY ONES that divers actually are
scared of.

You'll find out why soon enough.

Chapter 1

"Alexia! Thank goodness you're here. I am certain I am about to die."

Even though she knew Original Harlow would not expire any point soon, Alexia still moved into the room with more purpose. She'd been seeking out new towels in Tau since her Original was certain that her own were not the same softness as before. She couldn't guess what might have happened in the time between when she left and when she had returned.

Still, it was her job to ensure that Harlow lived the most comfortable and safe life possible. So she set the bundle of towels down on the nearest surface and strode into Harlow's bedroom.

The room was elaborate in an understated way. Many of the Originals clung to old grandeur that made their rooms almost stuffy to be in. They preferred gilded edges, carved figures poured in molten gold, and paintings that had been saved for hundreds of years. But not Harlow. She loved to live in the new ages of their world. So instead of hiding that she lived underneath the sea, Harlow luxuriated in it.

Every surface of this room glistened. The floor was mother-of-pearl, crushed and inlaid into the tile. The furniture was dusted with iridescence, each arm and leg gleaming in the chandelier light from overhead. Crystal cylinders hung from the ceiling, sending dancing rainbows throughout the room whenever the light was on.

Three of the walls were entirely glass. Harlow had spent a good amount of money making sure that every single wall was strong enough to hold the sea at bay, while also giving her a view of the sea beyond. Of course, there was another glass wall about forty feet farther away, just to make sure no undine got ideas to come close to one of the Originals.

In the space between her glass wall and the second, fish and flora flourish. Coral and tiny schools of fish gave pops of color to the otherwise desolate space. But at one point, there had been a dolphin trapped in there. Harlow liked to make it do tricks until it had died.

That memory still made Alexia feel strange.

"What is the matter?" she asked, walking toward Harlow, where she stood near the glass.

Harlow was a stunning woman, always had been, and would continue to be. The Originals were ancient, and Harlow was one of the oldest, although only by a few years. She looked very much to be a stunning fifty-year-old woman. Though her hair was still a warm, golden brown, her skin was still pristine and her spine straight and strong. She was lean, with the slightest of curves in her hips. But beyond her physical presence, she had a way of looking into a person's soul with a glare so severe it had leveled lesser men.

Now, she stood with the shoulder of her dress drooped down to her elbow, displaying unblemished, lightly tanned skin. She spent hours a week in a tanning bed, making sure she still looked like she lived

Above, and then hours fixing that sun damage through other means.

"See this?" Harlow said, pointing at a faint red patch on the highest peak of her shoulder. "Look at it."

She looked. Alexia had to do whatever Harlow said, even if it felt a little foolish to be looking at a slightly flakey patch of red skin. "Yes?"

"It's a rash. A rash! One of the reborns must have slipped through the security checks on their genetics." Harlow scoffed. "To think this would happen to me and not one of the others."

Well, it was unlikely that the scientist in charge of Harlow's reborns would make any mistake like that. However, if that was what Harlow wanted to think, then that's what she was allowed to think.

Carefully, Alexia shifted Harlow's dress over her shoulder again. "Come. Let's get you tucked into bed. A rest will make you feel better."

Harlow sighed. "I forget that having you around instantly eases me. You are a wonderful companion, Alexia."

It was a lie. Alexia was a good guard, and that was all she had been created for. She towered over Harlow's diminutive form, but then again, Alexia towered over everyone if they weren't like her. At six foot seven, Alexia was a massive woman created for power and strength. She would put her body in between anything that attacked Harlow and had many times. Harlow was still very much alive, and thus, she was damn good at her job.

Guiding the Original over to her massive bed that was the color of sea foam and filled with so many pillows, it was hard to imagine how she slept at all. She helped Harlow into the bed. "Would you like me to brush your hair before you sleep?"

"Oh, would you? You know you're the only one with a touch delicate enough to do so. The others always pull at the strands and I only have so many."

Some part of Alexia stirred at that. She went to the nightstand, pulling out the brush that was also inlaid with mother-of-pearl, and stared down at her own reflection in it.

What had Harlow said? Years ago? When Alexia was finally ready to serve her, the first thing the Original had said at the sight of her was, "Damn, you're a big brute."

There was some part of her that believed those words still. Her dark hair was pulled back severely from her face, tight against her skull and making her eyes appear slanted like a fox. She wore no makeup, not like the Originals, but her dark slashes of brows needed no addition to make them obvious. The permanent scowl on her face was intimidating to most, and then there was her height, of course. Bunches of muscles made her neck seem even thicker than it already was, and her shoulders even broader. As Harlow had once said, she was a brute of a woman.

But then again, she'd been made like this. It was hard to look away from her own reflection sometimes. She caught her own gaze and was sucked into it as thoughts that didn't feel like her own suddenly jumbled in her mind.

She hadn't been born. She'd been created in a test tube. Genetically engineered to be the person they wanted her to be. There were still thoughts in her mind, memories of a time when she had been growing. Blips of a history when she had been just a child, learning how to be strong, how to fight, how to not cry. All the things they told her she had to learn, but no one else did. Some part of her had resented that, then. But now, she could hardly feel a thing.

"Alexia!" Harlow's tone was sharp now. "You were going to brush my hair."

Of course she was.

Alexia ripped her gaze away from her own reflection and turned her attention back to Harlow. She walked over to the bed and knelt beside it, her knees already aching on the hard floor but easy enough to ignore. How many times had she done this? Kneeling while Harlow sat, brushing through the long strands of her Original's luxurious brown hair. There were threads of gold in it, a fact that Alexia had commented on multiple times.

Usually, now was the time that she would lavish Harlow with compliments. She'd tell her how beautiful her skin was, and that she surely was the youngest looking of all the Originals, even though she had been one of the oldest when they had first come down here. The strands of gold in her hair caught the light prettier than anything Alexia had ever seen.

But tonight... tonight she didn't feel like telling the other woman all that. A strange mood had overcome her, and she wasn't sure where it originated from.

Harlow huffed. "Can you believe the geneticist missed something with the last reborn? Really, it's not that hard to do his job. I could replace him just like that."

The snap of her fingers made Alexia flinch.

The reality was that the Originals could replace anyone they wanted in this city. Unfortunately, replacing someone usually meant killing them. Alexia had done it herself with the last geneticist who had disappointed Harlow. The man's neck had been all too easy to snap and the snap of Harlow's fingers sounded eerily similar to the sound his bones had made.

Swallowing hard, she nodded. "I can give him a warning, ma'am."

"Do you believe a warning will make him listen?"

"He's been your geneticist for nearly ten years now. I do believe replacing him would be very difficult."

There was a long pause as Alexia realized she'd given an actual opinion. Harlow didn't want someone else's opinion about anything. Her Original wanted Alexia to just agree with everything that Harlow said and parrot it back to her. That was their relationship, and it had worked for years.

What was she doing? Why was she even saying anything about this?

"Right," Harlow said slowly. "You're probably correct that I should give him another chance. But make sure you have him prepare another reborn. I can't have a blemish like this for long."

"Prepare—"

She felt herself freeze.

The reborns were identical to Harlow and the others. They were clones that were only awoken from their stasis when an Original needed them. There were hundreds of them deep in the heart of this city, surrounded by geneticists who made sure that every single one of them was a pure-blooded creation that was ready to be used for almost any illness or injury.

It was how the Originals had stayed alive for over two hundred years. They took pieces of themselves whenever they needed a replacement.

She hated going into that eerie place. All those bodies in various states of age, hanging there. Suspended in giant test tubes, nude, with their eyes closed. The first time she'd gone into the reborn center, she noticed that their eyes were still moving underneath their lids.

They were dreaming. And it had been hard to think of them as anything other than people when she recognized that small detail.

"A reborn?" Alexia finally managed to cough out. "Is a reborn necessary for this? I can get a doctor and have them prepare you a cream."

Harlow stilled underneath her hands. A fraction of a second. That's all it took for the Original to whip around on the bed and grab Alexia by the throat. She was surprisingly strong for an older woman, but it wasn't her strength that Alexia feared. No, it was the rage in her eyes.

At any second, any Original could choose to have someone removed from Tau. It would only take a single moment for Harlow to bite down hard enough to activate the warning signal that every single Original had affixed to their teeth. Within seconds, an entire entourage of soldiers would appear at her door and they wouldn't ask questions. They would kill any person who was near Harlow.

Because at the end of the day, even though she had served this woman her entire life, Alexia was dispensible. There were hundreds of other genetically enhanced guards ready to take her place. Some were more willing and biddable, and perhaps even more qualified.

"You're thinking an awful lot for yourself today," Harlow murmured. Her eyes flicked back and forth between Alexia's. "Why is that?"

"I don't know, ma'am."

"When did it start?"

"This morning." It was the first thing she'd noticed when she looked in the mirror.

She'd woken up, looked at her own reflection, and wondered why she looked so different. It was like she was looking at a stranger. Her reflection wasn't her. That hardened woman who had seen too much surely couldn't be her.

"Interesting," Harlow said. "What happened?"

"I don't know. My thoughts are very foggy and I have been trying to understand them."

"You're trying to understand your own thoughts?" Tilting her head to the side, Harlow seemed to peer into her mind. "What kind of thoughts?"

"I have yet to put a name to them, ma'am. It's hard to follow them when there are so many. They're quite jumbled." It was the best explanation she could offer, even though she knew it was the opposite of what Harlow wanted.

All the Originals preferred hard truths and logic. But human thought was rarely that.

Harlow hummed under her breath before loosening her grip on Alexia's neck. She rubbed her thumb along the carotid artery there, as though in threat. "You have been thinking too much. That is a burden, my dear."

Alexia didn't think it was a burden. More of a blessing, really. She had a feeling that free thought wasn't something she'd been afforded for a very long time. And now that she had it, she wasn't all that certain she was willing to give it up.

"You shouldn't be thinking on your own." Harlow released her with a sigh and then stood from the bed. "My dear, I have told you that you are my very favorite guard, haven't I? All these years, going through your kind over and over again, it's so easy to think of you all as one being. But you've always stood out to me as my favorite."

That didn't feel like a compliment. And yet, she couldn't free herself from her kneeling position on the floor as Harlow opened her night table and drew out a syringe.

Her medicine. Or at least, that's what they always told her it was.

Alexia had been injected by people her entire life. Needles full of chemicals became so normal it was hard to imagine life without them. When she was a child, they were full of vitamins and all the other pieces and parts that made her body grow bigger and stronger. Maybe if she hadn't been tested and poked and prodded, she would have been a normal sized woman. Maybe she wouldn't have stretched and had such growing pains that she was up late at night screaming as her legs grew faster than they should have. Maybe her hands wouldn't have been the size of a human head if they hadn't stuck her day in and day out, injecting her full of poison that twisted her body into something unrecognizable.

Her heart rate sped up as Harlow came closer with that needle in her hand. A voice she didn't recognize in her own head screamed at her to run. She shouldn't just wait here, kneeling, for all that poison to yet again affect her thoughts.

But there was another part of her that only listened to Harlow.

"Wouldn't it be easier to no longer have those thoughts?" Harlow murmured. "I would hate to lose you. You know you are, and always have been, my favorite."

She stayed where she was, watching that needle come ever closer. Because it would be easier to not have any thoughts. Especially these thoughts. These whispered words in her head that nothing was actually fine, and that everything was wrong, and if she wasn't careful...

"Shh," Harlow whispered as she wrapped an arm around Alexia's neck, holding her head to the side. "Let me take care of it for you."

She shouldn't. She should fight this. But instead of struggling, she tilted her head to the side and allowed it to happen. The sharp prick of the needle pierced through the muscles where her shoulder and neck met. A long time ago, she would have winced at the pain, but now it was so familiar she didn't react at all.

Instead, she remained frozen in Harlow's arms as she felt her emotions drain away completely. Disappearing into the ether of darkness at the back of her mind where all bad thoughts gathered to be tossed into the sea.

"There we go," Harlow said with a tight squeeze before releasing her. "You don't have to think, Alexia. All you have to do is be here for me."

And that was easier than thinking.

"Thank you, Harlow," she replied, standing. "Would you like me to speak with the geneticist now?"

"Yes. I will rest and you prepare the reborn for me. Oh and, Alexia? You are ever so good at your job."

She was the best at her job.

Alexia turned and walked out the door, leaving all those dark thoughts in the room with the Original who had caused them all.

Chapter 2

Fortis waited in the depths, watching as the ships zipped overhead, illuminating the sea with great spears of light. He had come here on his own at first. Just to see what the great city of Tau would look like. And he was not disappointed.

Massive spirals sank into the depths, each of them winding around each other as though the entire city was a giant knot. There were bulbous ends where he regularly saw people, but those were uninteresting. Workers meandered about their day, slaving away as they should not for the people in power. They were not what he was here for. He was here for an opening, a weakness, a way into the city through the shield of energy that protected it.

He had not trained his entire life for this moment, only to let it slip through his fingers. No matter how long it took, he would find a way into this city.

His son floated beside him, surveying Tau with a keen eye. "Are you sure today is the right time? The ships appear to be in far greater numbers. Surely if there are more of them, then they will be more aware."

"Yes, it is the right time, Aulax. The goddess has told me." He took a deep breath in through his gills, tasting the scent of the city.

Metal and biting chemicals. The same scents that had covered his son when Aulax had been released from the clutches of Alpha. There was more in this city than any of them could guess. These people were using medicine, as Anya called it, to do something terrible within that twisting labyrinth.

"How can you be sure? Prophecies are difficult to read at the best of times."

"The sea has provided me a time and a place. I will know when to enter this city because I am where the sea tells me to be." He truly believed that, and he wished his son was more prepared to believe it as well.

Fortis had been raised in a time when the sea was revered. The gods of their people had come out of the depths more often, although these days they did not leave their home at all. So few of the younger depthstriders had trembled in the presence of the ancients deep in the abyss. His son would benefit from doing so, because Aulax was far too likely to deny that the sea was a god.

Soon enough, he would learn. The sea always contacted depthstriders in one way or another. His son would be faced with the reality that there were massive creatures somewhere in this ocean that controlled them all. And that if he closed his eyes, he could feel the connection with the same beasts that breathed with every single one of their kind.

Aulax let out a huffing breath. "I do not believe that you are meant to die this year, Father. It is foolish to seek death simply because your wife saw it long before I was even here."

And therein lay the problem.

He should have guessed that his son was struggling with the truth of what was to come. Fortis himself had seen his father die before him when he was very young. It was a hard part of life, one that everyone had to deal with eventually. It was a unique situation for the two of them, because they both knew when and how he was going to die.

"Your mother was gifted a prophecy by the gods. It was both a warning and a detailed message so that we could all stay safe," he replied. "I have known my place in this sea since I was a very young man. Your mother was the best vision seeker of the depthstriders. She saw many peoples' deaths, including her own."

And not a single one of those prophecies had been wrong. He had seen every one of those people die, exactly as she had described it. So he knew he was going to die the same way she'd claimed.

Aulax's gills flared, and a few of his colors burst to life before he calmed them. "I do not wish for your death as you seem to."

He should soften himself for his son. Fortis often disappeared into the connection with their gods, but right now, his son needed him.

He wasn't always the best father. Still, he tried.

Flexing his fluke, he propelled himself toward Aulax and caught the young man in his arms. Wrestling for a moment, he managed to get his son to still so that he could actually hold on to him in a grip that was as punishing as it was comforting. "I forget you are grown sometimes. I still see you as the boy who used to tug on my tail and beg me to swim with him."

"I fail to see how that is helpful on the topic of killing yourself."

"I am not killing myself. I have had many years to come to terms with the fact that I will not live as long as the rest of you. I also know that my sacrifice will bring about a new age of people who will guide our own kind into a future with less fighting. It is a sacrifice I will gladly make so that your life will be easier." He leaned back, releasing his son so that he could look him in the eyes. "Not everyone is given the chance to become a martyr. My death is the answer to all our suffering."

"And so that means you can be reckless?"

"It means I cannot die before my time, because I already know my end." He flicked his fin, moving back again to his post against a jutting rock, and looked toward the city. "My fate has been decided. I will not die before that time comes, and the sea will protect me to ensure that is so."

"I still think this is a fucking stupid idea," his son muttered.

"Fucking?" Fortis repeated dryly. "You have been spending too much time with Ace's sister."

It wasn't the first time he'd heard one of the People of Water using achromo vernacular. Many of their people were adopting phrases as they spent more and more time with the other kind. He found it to be a disgusting practice, unfortunately they were all more than welcome to waste their time on foolish words if they wished to do so.

Another ship blasted past them, sending dust scattering up from the sea floor and obscuring his vision. This was the moment when he would antagonize them. The sea had already told him that he needed to get inside of Tau. That was where his opportunity would present itself.

He wasn't sure what that opportunity was, though. Apparently, there were many options for him to discover. The sea was helpful, though not very clear at the best of times.

Perhaps that was what his son found so disagreeable. Aulax

liked things to be black and white. He wanted to know everything and anything about a plan long before he would indulge himself in pursuing it. It was a good trait that would make him an even better warrior in his later years.

Fortis had learned long ago that opportunities always presented themselves to those who had their eyes open. His son had yet to learn that, and it would take many years still for him to learn such things.

"I am proud of you," he said, looking back at his son one more time. It wasn't the last time he would see Aulax, even though his son feared that it would be. Perhaps it was a good idea to give his boy something to remember him by. Even though he would return soon enough. "I always have been, you know."

"Father—"

Leaving no more time for discussion, Fortis darted out into the sea. He took a deep breath through all four of his gills and illuminated his entire body. Every tendril that hung from his sides turned bright yellow, so vivid that it would be impossible for the achromo ships to miss him. If any did, they were a worse predator than he thought they were.

And then he stayed there. Floating in the water, and waited for the next ship to come by. When the strange, oblong shape came close, he illuminated his lights even more. He was a blinding, ethereal creature from the depths and the achromos would surely feel terror the moment they saw him.

It did not take long. The achromos in Tau were smarter than the other cities, and they were far more used to dealing with his kind. They knew how to attack his people. They knew exactly what would harm him, but that wasn't what Fortis knew he would see happen today.

"Don't make it easy for them, father!" Aulax called out with a haunting, whale call. "Make them hunt!"

That was exactly what he had planned on doing.

He turned at the last moment and sped through the water. His tail was larger than most of his kind, and so was his body. It took longer for him to get up to speed, and that was likely not what the achromos were expecting. Soon enough, they would realize that he was difficult to catch.

The water parted around him, easing his way so that he could go faster. Then he curved his body and dove ever deeper. Farther into the depths of the sea, where eventually he came across a massive warship that had long ago sunk. He took the achromos past this ancient vessel as a reminder of their failures. They had weapons that could harm his people, but the achromos were the species that had always fallen.

Time and time again. Their reckoning was coming. They had no idea that he would be the catalyst.

They fired their first weapon at him, white hot and searing as it bubbled through the sea. He evaded it easily enough, although it was curious that they only fired the one shot. Usually, they fired at least twenty of them all at the same time. The massive amount of bolts were far harder for his people to dodge when they covered so much space.

The warning shot was soon followed by something he had not seen before. A net.

Spears attached to the ends stretched it wide, and he realized a rope attached it to the underbelly of the ship. The sea had been correct. The humans didn't want to kill him today. Instead, they would want to capture him.

So Tau really was another facility that experimented on his people. Good. The sea had claimed he needed to get inside of Tau, and he intended to listen. Allowing the humans to bring him in was much easier than finding a weakness in the impenetrable city.

The net missed him. It seemed they were not very good with this new weapon of theirs. Perhaps the achromos needed practice.

How hilarious it was to see them struggling. With his son's voice in his head, he turned to look at them. He was far enough away now that he wondered if they would give up. He couldn't have that. Fortis was having fun, and there was a point to all this.

He wasn't so far away that he couldn't see their silhouettes within the ship. The achromos were staring at him as well. Surprised he would turn to even look at them. With every ounce of hatred in his heart, he flicked his fluke and started toward the ship.

If he was going to be taken by their kind in any believable sense, then he needed them to feel fear. Already he could see them scrambling. There was terror in their expressions as they struggled to find the right button. Perhaps one of them wanted to send out a bolt that would surely kill him. Others were saying to send out the net. And then he was right in front of them.

He reveled in their fear. Fortis soaked it into his body even though he could not smell them through the metal. If he struck the ship at this speed, he would damage it beyond fixing. They would all sink to the bottom of the ocean where the ancients would eventually feast upon their corpses.

He looked forward to seeing what fate the sea chose for these achromos.

The water parted around him, sending him careening ever faster toward the panicking humans. He was so close he could hear them shouting when the weapon they chose fired. Closing his eyes, he let peace surround him as he waited for the sea's judgement.

And there it was. Not the burn of a laser. The sensation of a net wrapping around his body. It twined around all of his fins, pinned his arms to his sides and sent him swinging below the ship. They needed to believe they had caught him. They needed to believe that he was just another undine they had found in the sea. Not a single one of them would believe he had allowed them to catch him.

The net twisted one of his side fins hard. He bared his teeth in a snarl, hoping that if there were cameras on the bottom of the ship that they would see his pain. He could hear them all cheering in there, celebrating that they had caught the feral creature who had nearly killed them.

Hilariously, they had no idea they were transporting a shark into their home. A shark who intended to hunt the first moment he could.

As they traveled past the shield, he saw a few flickering lights on the sea floor. He knew that was his son. Aulax was letting him know that he would return to the others and tell them that Fortis had started his mission. Soon enough, they would know that he had succeeded.

He wasn't sure how, yet. The sea hadn't told him that much.

Fortis allowed himself to fall into that liminal place between reality and the future. The place where the sea held his hand and guided him without fear.

These achromos were weak, basic creatures who were in a world that they were ill-equipped to handle. All he had to do was bide his time and everything would fall into place.

It always had.

He stayed quiet and did not struggle as they approached the lights of the city. Soon, he would be within those walls. Soon, they would try to break him with medicine and sharp weapons. What they did not know was that he was ready and prepared for such things. They would not break him.

He would break them.

21

Chapter 3

She found Doctor Barker the next morning. Harlow had plenty for her to do in the meantime, as the woman's mind moved a mile a minute. Before Alexia went to find the reborn, first she had to make sure that the Original's clothing was still perfectly pressed, that someone had seen to the servant who had made her feel slightly uncomfortable the day before, and that her breakfast would no longer contain whatever it was that she was allergic to. Just in case the next reborn didn't fix this unbearable issue.

Throughout all of it, Alexia meandered through life in a fog. The medicine made it so much easier to handle everything. And yet... there was still a voice screaming in the back of her head. Like a ringing in her ears that she couldn't get rid of.

By the time she was standing in front of Doctor Barker's office, it was getting hard to ignore again. Which was ridiculous. She was not supposed to feel like this. The medicine existed so she could get ahold of these thoughts and cast them aside, not struggle every single day.

Knocking on the door in front of her, she tried to quiet the screaming in her head.

This area of Tau was easier to be herself in, anyway. The doctors and the guards all lived in the same wing. There wasn't beauty here. Only cold steel, utilitarian cots to sleep in, and medical equipment lying beside weapons just in case the Originals needed to be protected. Even from their own people.

Barker opened the door quickly. He was a tiny man in comparison to her. Barely five foot five, he came up to her chest and had to crane his neck to see her face. The bottle thick glasses perched on his nose didn't help, although they did magnify his wide brown eyes. Silver hair topped his head like someone had blown a cloud on top of him and spun it into a cotton candy like twirl. His white lab coat hung from his lean shoulders, because the man was always forgetting to eat no matter how many people were on the job to remind him.

"Alexia?" he asked, a question in the word.

"She wasn't happy with the last reborn. There's a rash on her shoulder now."

"A rash?" he muttered, turning back into his office to gather his things. "That shouldn't be happening. Rashes are exceedingly hard for the Originals to get, unless the reborn isn't perfect. But I check them. I check every time we use one."

"Perhaps a mistake was made."

"I don't make mistakes."

But he was human, and therefore, he did. She had seen him make mistakes before, although they were rare. He was a good man, this doctor, but that didn't make him perfection personified. Still, she kept her mouth shut as he gathered a white medical bag and started down the hall.

She did look around his room while he gathered his things, though. Alexia liked to look at how people decorated their private spaces, because it gave her a small glimpse into the life of the person. Barker's rooms were all plastered with old images of Above. He particularly liked pictures of the land around the sea. White sand beaches and bright fluffy clouds that danced above the waves.

The land wasn't like that anymore. No one could go up there, and if they could, they definitely wouldn't find white fluffy clouds. Only angry tempests that threatened to kill anyone who was out in them with shards of ice as big as her head.

She stalked down the hall with him toward the reborn center. The hallway they were in was shaped a bit like a tube, and she was suddenly struck with a wave of dizziness. The entire room was moving, like the tube was rotating.

What was going on with her?

Alexia reached out a hand and touched the wall, anchoring herself as she walked after him. She would not show weakness. She would not let him know that something was wrong.

But he looked over his shoulder and frowned at her. "What's going on with you today?"

"Nothing," she muttered.

"You're holding onto the wall like the sea is sending you tumbling into a vortex. Are you dizzy?"

"No."

"I'm a doctor. If you have something going on, then you should tell me." He didn't have time to say anything else before the reborn center was right before them.

Glass walls fitted with twin glass doors showed everything beyond. All the frozen tubes, kept in a cryo genetic state once the bodies were finished growing. All the cylinders were filled with goo and contained various stages of humanity.

Her gaze caught on the tubes filled with the faint orange liquid. The color was due to the vitamins to keep the fetuses inside alive. She hated looking at those strange little worms that eventually turned into children, knowing that she herself had grown in that same kind of vat. Except they had purged those tubes regularly, testing all the genes in every baby and picking the ones that were worth something.

The ones like her. With genetic mutations that had been carefully cultivated and injected and pushed into a little life like that.

The doors hissed open into the area that wasn't as cold as the rest of it, and Doctor Barker headed in. That was her cue. She was supposed to follow him into the room. She was supposed to be a good personal guard and do everything that she needed to do for her Original. It was the reason she had been made.

Just like all those people hanging in those tubes, frozen, created to live for only a few moments before their gasping breath subsided and they were used instead for someone else's immortality.

"Alexia?" Doctor Barker asked, his voice now filled with concern. "Would you like to come inside with me?"

Shit. Why wasn't the medicine working?

She'd taken these drugs her entire life. They always made life easier. She'd always been able to inject herself and forget everything for at least a week, if not longer than that. Were these thoughts stronger than the drugs?

Heading into the room, she audibly swallowed as the doors hissed shut behind her. "Sorry, doctor. This room always makes me uncomfortable."

Even admitting that was strange. She'd been bred to be impossible to shake. Anxiety and fear weren't something her body could feel, those chemicals just didn't exist in her brain. At least, that's what she had been told her entire life.

"Uncomfortable?" Doctor Barker repeated before pointing to a leather chair beside him. Countless metal arms behind the chair were used to determine the health of people like her. From blood pressure cuffs to injectables, the chair was as much as of doctor as the man in front of her. "Before we gather the reborn, why don't we do a quick workup of your physical state?"

That definitely made all these feelings worse. Stiffly, she sat down in the chair. He sat at a desk opposite to her, typing away into a computer that commanded the metal arms to move forward. They quickly did all the work that was necessary. Blood pressure? Perfect. Heart rate? Normal.

Maybe this wasn't fear. Because her hands weren't shaking and her heart rate was exactly how it should be. Yet, her mind was racing, and she thought, for a moment, maybe this was anger. Was she supposed to be able to feel that, though?

Doctor Barker muttered something under his breath and started the reborn algorithm that would pick the next clone that was ready for harvesting. The computer did most of the work these days, but the doctors were all required to look over the genetic sequence even after the computer chose it. Then he turned his wheelie chair and looked right into her eyes.

"Your vitals seem normal."

"As I assumed they would be."

"But you are uncomfortable in this room? That is unusual behavior for someone of your origins."

She knew that, damn it. She knew it was strange for someone like her to think on her own. She hadn't before this. At least, she didn't think she had. There were a few years where they had put her back in training, but she didn't think that was because she had been thinking for herself.

Fuck. Was it a bad thing to think for herself? Was it really all that bad if she looked into that room with all the reborns just hanging there, growing, and for her to think it was a little morbid? She wasn't going to do anything about it. Alexia knew better than that. The Originals had this entire place locked up so tight that someone like her couldn't get the reborns out, and even then, what would she do with them?

They weren't real people. They didn't have a life or learn as they were growing. They were popped out into the world as fully formed adults, with brains that still fired correctly for someone of their age, but who had no experience even breathing on their own.

Besides, she didn't have a death wish. And death was all that would happen if she tried to move against the Originals.

Doctor Barker took his glasses off and rubbed the bridge of his nose. "You know what they do to guards who start thinking for themselves, don't you?"

She rattled off the information she had known since she was a child. "Guards who are no longer capable of performing their function are decommissioned."

"Decommissioned, yes, that's what they call it for you all." He shook his head. "They kill them, Alexia. You can try to make it lesser if that's what you want, but the reality is that someone like you who is thinking for herself will end up killed. We'll reuse the pieces of your body that we need, take your genetic sequence, and make another you. A version who won't have the flaws that you had before. There have been countless Alexias through the years, but none of them were as powerful or as perfect as your design. And the next one will be even better. Do you understand what I'm saying?"

She didn't, although it sounded like a threat and maybe something she didn't want to understand. So she remained where she was and stared at him with what she hoped was a blank expression and not one of utter rage like it felt like.

He cleared his throat. "Don't let them see that you're different. That's what I'm saying. In the meantime, I'm going to update your file with a different formula of your daily medication and that will help with these feelings. If they continue, come to me first. Not anyone else."

"I have a doctor." One specifically had been given to the guards, and he put them through rigorous testing regularly to ensure they could do their job correctly.

"You will come to me," Doctor Barker said as the computer barked that the sequence was ready. "Now, I need to look over this reborn and make sure it's ready for harvesting, since the other one apparently wasn't. A rash, you said? Was it a food she was allergic to?"

Alexia jumped into the same job she'd always been doing. Protecting Harlow.

She rattled off all the food Harlow had eaten yesterday, making sure that she listed every ingredient in every recipe. She knew all of this information like the back of her hand. Every day she poured over everything that the Original ate, and she was good at her job. She was always better than the others, no matter how much work it took.

It took the better part of an hour to go through everything that might have made her allergic, but then Barker nodded. "Found the issue. Computer, terminate all reborns with this genetic mutation." He clicked a few buttons and then she could hear the sound of glass shattering. Icy bodies fell to the floor, tubes whipping out of their mouths. Soon enough, people would enter the room and drag those bodies out. They would be tossed out to sea without harvesting a single one of those organs because Harlow might now be allergic to shellfish.

Wrong, a voice whispered in her head. This is wrong.

But she turned her attention from the glass and instead looked at Barker. He stood, twisting side to side to crack his back before hitting the final button on the computer. "Come on, the reborn should be in the right room. It won't take long to get the right serum to inject her with. This will all be over by the end of the day."

Thank goodness. An angry Original wasn't what any of them needed in their lives.

She left all her complicated emotions in that room and stalked down the hall with him. No one would hold on to these thoughts willingly. She was not going to hold on to them, either. It was not her place to think about the reborns or the ethics of even having them. She had to shake this off.

At least, until they passed by the first surgical suite. Alexia slowed to a stop, staring through the glass at the creature they had laid out on the table. "Is that—"

Barker stopped as well, freezing in place as his eyes widened even more behind those strange glasses. "An undine?"

"Why would they bring an undine into Tau?" she snarled, already reaching for the device affixed to her wrist that allowed her to speak to all the other guards. "Code Red. There is an undine on the premises."

Another voice came out of her wrist, this one from a guard named Hyperion who was a personal guard to one of the oldest couples of the Originals. "Understood. Where?"

"Surgical suites."

"We will stay clear of that area and shut it down for all the other Originals."

Doctor Barker was looking at her strangely.

"What?" Alexia asked.

"You're uncomfortable in the reborn center, but you aren't uncomfortable looking at that?" He gestured toward the massive body on the table.

She was. She was very uncomfortable looking at the massive, limp fish who had been laid out on two surgical tables and still his tail was somehow drooped onto the floor. His pale purple skin was odd to look at, not to mention the darker shades of his tail that ended in little bulbous yellow tentacles that dripped down his sides like beads. His hair was long and tangled over his face, obscuring that from her view, at the very least. There was something wrong about looking at a creature like him.

He still had a human form. His chest was familiar enough, although there were no nipples to speak of. His hands were webbed, and one of them had fallen off the table and nearly trailed along the floor. The black tipped claws on that hand were intriguing, but there was something wrong about staring at a creature who was unconscious and thinking about the veins on his hands.

"Let's go inside," Doctor Barker said, before putting his hand on the door and starting to push it open.

"Excuse me?"

"There's plenty of time. They have to thaw the reborn, anyway. I haven't ever been given the opportunity to see one of these beasts in person." He looked over his shoulder at her, mischief glinting in those massive eyes. "Unless you're afraid? I thought you weren't having those feelings?"

Damn it. He had her, and he knew it.

Sighing, she followed him into the room, which already smelled distinctly fishy.

Chapter 4

The sea had not warned him about all of this. Fortis allowed the second membrane over his eyes to close, leaving the world slightly foggy but convincing the idiot achromos who surrounded him that their drugs had worked. He had been preparing for this moment for years. Of all the depthstriders, Fortis was the one who had taken the most sulfur. He'd inhaled a significant amount of numbing mist in the deepest sea. He'd even punctured his skin with lionfish barbs.

No achromo drug would make him sleep. But he wanted them to think that he was resting, because he wanted them to make a mistake.

Already they were speaking, giving him more information than any of them likely wanted him to know. He knew this place was Tau, that he had found the correct city to infiltrate. He knew the Originals were the ones living here, confirming all the achromo mates' theories.

This place was run by ancient achromos. Achromos who had been alive for much longer than was natural. The Originals, as they called themselves, were unnatural beings who had designed all these cities underwater. They were the ones who had brought the metal to life underneath the sea, and somehow, they had not yet died.

He needed to see this for himself. Or at least find proof that this was possible. So he stayed quiet. Even when they hefted his body with six men out of the net and onto a wheeled table. Even when they brought him into this room, that smelled like antiseptic and metal.

He kept his eyes looking like they did, kept his breathing low and still. What were they going to do to him? Were they going to tear into his body exactly as they had planned for his son?

A flare of anger burned white hot in his chest. Aulax had suffered as no depthstrider ever deserved to. He had shared his son's memories after he had gotten back, taking some of the anger onto himself so that Aulax could function without rage determining every single choice that he made.

Fortis hoped they would try to experiment on him. He wanted the pain to ground him when he knew that there was a part of himself that could fracture at any point. He hoped they would give him a chance to destroy them.

Instead, they did nothing. The groups of achromos stood around him, looking him over and murmuring thoughts to themselves.

"I wonder if the gills are capable of breathing in air?"

"No, we tested on one before, remember? They have a set of lungs as well. He must have expelled the water from his gills already, because he's still breathing. See? You can see his chest moving. That is a good sign. He's not dead."

"How would we know if he died? Is the only sign of life its breathing or do their colors change as well? Some fish do that. Their scales lose their luster after we bring them in."

"Good question. We should try it on this one and see if the colors dull."

He heard the door to the room open and close. More achromos coming in to peer at him like he was a spectacle just for them to leer at. He would never understand these creatures. They were so interested in his people, but they also did everything they could to eradicate his kind.

Frustration brewed and he could already feel some of the electrical signals in the tips of his fins aching to burst. He wanted to glow and terrify them. He wanted them to see how large he was, and how the sight of his lights made him seem even bigger.

But he wasn't in the water, and those electrical lights wouldn't make him look larger here. So he kept them off as these newcomers walked over to him.

The first one reeked. He could just barely see the man as he strode into the room, but his lip nearly curled at the scent that clung to him. Blood, drugs, and the strangest scent of something sweet underneath all of that which gave him a rather rotten smell. He was a small male. So small that it was, perhaps, concerning. He should have been able to be larger. How was he supposed to protect a mate when he looked like... that?

And then the second person walked up behind his head. He couldn't see who this was, but he was suddenly blasted with the scent of the sea. Saltwater, the fresh sea air that so rarely cleared his lungs when he was above the water. And something else. The comforting scent of sea grass and vetiver, a scent he'd only smelled once in his entire life. When he was young, he'd traveled throughout the entire ocean and he had stopped at a marshy area. That place had smelled like this person.

Whoever it was, they smelled good. They made him want to fill his lungs with their scent.

He hated them for it. Immediately.

"Where did you find a specimen like this?" the metallic smelling man asked.

"He was right near Tau, off the deep sea ledge. I wasn't expecting to see an undine there, but here we are. Bastard tried to ram us in the sub, but we netted him and then brought him back here." The soldier seemed proud of himself. Fortis wondered just how proud he would be when he found out that Fortis had planned this entire thing.

"Interesting..." A cold, dry hand touched his side, gently lifting one of his hip fins and fingering the bulbous end there. "Strange. This one doesn't look like many of the others I have seen."

Movement over his head made his eyes flick to the hand that touched his hip. A hand that was now covered by a significantly larger one, gently peeling the man's fingers off of Fortis's fin. That hand was massive, but it wasn't masculine at all. Long fingers, tapered nails that were filed short, and callouses on the palm. It was a working hand, a hand of a warrior.

Who was this person who smelled like the sea and had hands larger than any achromo's he'd ever seen?

He'd made a mistake. His eyes had moved underneath those lids. There was the faintest intake of breath from this massive person leaning over him, and he knew that whoever it was, they had seen him move.

"Are his eyes supposed to do that?" A deep voice, but feminine. Rough around the edges, like she didn't talk very much.

He let his eyes limply return to the center, but that meant he was looking right up at her.

Fuck, he hadn't realized achromos got this big. She was a massive woman. Mira was tall, and he'd seen some taller male achromos as well when he had spied on their homes. But this woman? She was huge.

She towered over him and all the other people in this room. Her strong features were carved from marble, cut in sharp lines and ragged edges. This was a woman made for battle. He could tell that from the hard set of her eyes and the sharp clench of her jaw while she stared down at him as though she knew he was faking.

The metallic man beside her chuckled. "He's very much out, if that's what you're concerned about. The drugs we use would kill a human if we even got a whiff of it. It's perfectly normal for their bodies to react to touch. They are very unique creatures, Alexia. Would you like to touch him?"

No, she shouldn't want to touch him. None of them should want to touch him. As far as they knew, he was unaware of anything that was happening. It was wrong to touch another person like this, and yet, none of these creatures cared. To the achromos, he was just a sea creature who had no thought or reasoning.

So when the woman walked over to where he could no longer see her, he wasn't all that surprised. Though she was bigger than the others, she wasn't different from them. She'd just been given the opportunity to explore an undine when he could do nothing in response. Why wouldn't she take that?

Her fingers glided over his gills, a rather sexual touch that she likely didn't understand. No one had touched him there since his wife, and she'd been long dead. The sensation was... not entirely something he hated, but given the circumstances, he wanted to flinch away from her. Her fingers weren't even gentle about it. She touched him like she had a right to do so.

And then she leaned over his eyes again, looking right into his dead gaze as though she knew what she was doing. And damn it, maybe she did. Because she sank her fingers a little deeper into his gills.

It took everything in him to not grind his teeth. She'd notice the bouncing muscle in his jaw if he did so, but damn it, that was not what she was supposed to be doing. If she kept fingering his fucking gills, then he would have a reaction none of the people in this room would likely expect. He wanted this woman to stop testing him, when she damn well knew that he wasn't actually asleep.

"Gentle, Alexia!" the short man beside her scolded. "It's a live specimen. You can't just jam your fingers inside of it. If you harm it, then the other scientists will never let me hear the end of it!"

"Sorry, doctor," she muttered.

The slow glide of her fingers out of his gills was something he wouldn't likely forget any time soon. A shiver nearly traveled through him. Those broad, strong fingers had skimmed through the natural slickness of his gills with far too much ease. Like she'd done that before and knew every single nerve ending to tempt him with.

Rage bloomed in his chest. This achromo might be different from the others, but he would kill her with even more rage for touching him. He would see her eyes widen in fear and shock, then he would bathe himself in her blood. He would coat himself in her pretty scent and glory in the sounds of her drowning.

She stepped back, and the doctor moved closer again. He flashed a light in Fortis's eyes, and yet again, he just barley managed to keep himself still. They really were trying everything they could to make him angry.

"No reflexes to light. I'm sure it's all fine. I'd like to research him more if you don't mind, Alexia? We'll have the reborn brought in here to thaw so I can keep an eye on both specimens."

"I don't think that's very safe, doctor." The woman was smarter than everyone in here. If there was some creature they wished to hide from him—this "reborn"—then they really shouldn't bring it in this room.

But they did.

He laid there, unseeing, as noises filled the room. The sound of wheels as another table was brought in. More lights as they illuminated the space even further. At one point, a metal arm extended over his head, this one seemingly full of needles before it disappeared again. Their murmurings voices were saying things that meant absolutely nothing to him.

Something about calcium levels, genetic mutations, and letters and numbers mashed together like that was a language on its own.

All throughout, the big woman loomed above his head. She never moved. Not once. Those dark eyes stared down at him with distrust.

She knew he wasn't asleep. Or at the very least, she suspected it. So she was more aware than any of the others in this room, and that meant she was the one he needed to watch out for.

Fortis waited until the right moment. A scientist bumped into his table on their way over to the other, and he allowed his head to flop to the side. It perhaps looked harmless to most, but he noticed the way the big woman stiffened at the movement.

Now he was staring at the other table. They'd laid out a woman there. She was young, with pretty long hair and a proud nose. Completely nude, she also seemed to be slightly damp. Her pale skin was nearly white, as though it had never once been touched by the UV lights that filled these rooms and helped the achromos not die in their long time away from the sun.

A hulking machine surrounded the woman, and they were jabbing her with long needles. He had no idea what this reborn was, but he did see that there was something attached to her mouth. It looked a bit like the rebreather Mira had created, although this one also had a heavy device wrapped around the woman's torso. As he watched, it inflated and then deflated. Continually.

Whatever was attached to the woman's face was keeping her breathing, and that was all he needed to see.

Timing this right was important. But he knew the sea had planned to provide him with an opportunity, and this was that opportunity. The woman lying on the table might be ill, but she was the only one weak enough for him to grab and disappear into the ocean with.

The scientists turned as one at the sound of a noise outside of the glass. Likely another person reacting to the sight of a massive depthstrider laid out on the table.

It was the right time. He could feel it. Almost as though the sea itself swelled in his chest and bid him to move. So he did. Using his arms, Fortis shoved himself off the table and onto the ground, twisting as he did so. He landed on his forearms, which made it all too easy to slither over to that table, lunge for the woman, and drag her onto the ground with him.

Shouts echoed in the room, and he knew there were plenty of people reaching for weapons. By the time they got those weapons drawn, however, he was already out the door.

So many achromos underestimated him because of his size. They thought something big like him would be lumbering and slow, especially on land. But Fortis was quick. Dragging the strange creature with him wasn't all that hard either, considering the woman weighed less than he expected. She was so thin, so small…

He turned down the hallway they'd brought him in and immediately heard a shout of rage. He took only a few moments to look over his shoulder, delighted to see the big woman was following him.

"You will never catch me," he tossed over his shoulder as he headed toward the room with the large moon pool. He'd watched them lock it, and he knew how to open it now.

They were all fools. Every single one of them.

Slamming his hand onto the panel, he mimicked the complicated pattern, and it was that easy. Buttons to push and a door opened.

He watched the floor parting, ready to flee into the sea with this weak little creature who would hopefully stay alive in the freezing waters just long enough for him to get some information out of her.

But at the last second, a harsh spike of pain zinged up his tail. Baring his teeth in a snarl, he turned to see the woman had plunged two blades into his fluke. She held them against the ground, or perhaps she'd stuck them into the floor itself, and glared back at him.

"You will not take her," the woman hissed.

"I find it hilarious that you think two little knives are going to stop me."

He watched her eyes widen, perhaps in recognition that he was talking to her, before he ripped through his fluke and disappeared into the dark waters with his prize.

Chapter 5

That bastard had just stolen her reborn.

She had no idea how he wasn't passed out, but she'd had a bad feeling from the moment she'd walked into the room. The scientists were always overconfident in what their drugs could do. Look at her own situation. She was thinking and feeling for herself when that shouldn't be possible. It wasn't out of the realm of possibility that an undine would be able to do something similar.

His breathing had been too shallow. She'd seen people under anesthesia before, many times. The reborns were usually under some concoction of drugs to keep them calm and quiet while they were in their tubes. None of their breaths were so measured. It was like he had been counting between inhaling and exhaling. Too perfect. Too regular.

That was why she had stayed so close to the doctors. The last thing she needed on her record was the death of an entire room of people who were not as easily replaced.

But to lose a reborn? She'd never done anything worse than that.

Reborns were worth more than the lives of every single person in that room.

So when she stared down into the black waters that still churned with the weight of him striking them, she knew there wasn't another choice.

The doctor ran into the room behind her, his breath sawing through his lungs. "Did you catch it?"

"No," she hissed. "It learned how to lock and unlock the door, likely by watching our own soldiers."

"Impossible. They made sure it was drugged."

"It wasn't."

Spinning, she hit the button on her wristband and started barking out orders. "The undine has escaped with one of Harlow's reborns. Turn all exterior lights on in Sector 251. Every single one of them. I want to see where the bastard is going."

There was a scratchy sound on the other end, but then she could hear the city coming to life. Tau wasn't just a fortress that should have been difficult to break into. It was also a living machine that could do whatever it took to protect those within it. The arms extended outside, weapons engaging as powerful lights turned on that would turn the entire sea into a summer's day.

Stalking to the back of the room, she slammed her hand down on one of the panels to open up a wall. Metal suits were lined on the other side. Suits that would withstand almost any pressure of the sea, just like her body could with all her genetic enhancements, and keep her alive even more than her own genetic enhancements could. The thin metal looked like ribs that would cover her own, stronger bones in the arms and legs that would prevent her own from being snapped if he caught her.

"What are you doing?" Doctor Barker asked, his voice shaking as he repeated himself. "What do you think you're doing?"

"I'm going after them."

"You can't go after them! You want to dive into open water with an undine? That's suicide, Alexia."

No, it wasn't. Because she had her suit. Because they had spent countless years teaching her how to fight, how to tear apart the world with her fists, and how to learn from other people's fighting tactics to see just how much she could push herself. She was one of the few people who could do this.

The red button on the wall opened the suit like a clam. She stepped into it, turning around so her back was pressed where it needed to be and then slotting her hands through the arms of the suit. Hissing sounds filled her ears as the suit reacted to her being inside of it, carefully closing and then sealing her within.

It wasn't a suit that covered her entire body. More like an exoskeleton that would help her move faster and swim farther. The metal was light, barely adding over twenty-five pounds to her figure, but strong. Flexing her hands, she reached above her head and pulled down the face mask that would give her oxygen while she was down there.

"Is the reborn still alive?" she asked, shifting her feet in the boots.

"The temperature of the water... and we don't even know why the undine grabbed her..."

"Doctor Barker!" Alexia shouted his name in his face, stepping out of the wall and advancing on him. "Is the reborn alive?"

He stammered, but finally answered her question. "It's entirely possible, yes. The water is cold enough to perhaps put her back in stasis and as long as he did not remove her breathing tube, then yes. It is entirely possible that the reborn is alive."

"Good enough."

She hit the button to heat the suit up, enough that it would help her in the freezing cold temperatures of the depths. She'd trained in below freezing temperatures for hours. She knew what her body could take. The genetic enhancements were good for something, she supposed.

Alexia hit the water hard, sinking straight to the bottom of the plateau that surrounded Tau. Her boots hit the ground, silt and dust puffing up around her body as she shifted before hitting the button that would propel the boots. Suddenly, she was flying through the ocean.

Everything was illuminated, so it was easy for her to see where she was going. There wasn't much of a hint of where he went, but she could follow the lights. The other guards were surely leading her toward the undine, so she didn't go in the direction where there weren't any lights. The speed with which she cut through the water was almost maddening.

But rage made her not think straight. This undine had taken something from her. It had made her look a fool, and even then, no one was allowed to come into Tau and take a single thing from the city that was meant to be impenetrable.

Lifting her wrist, she hit the button to speak. "The men that brought the undine into the city? Kill them."

"Should we confirm with Original Harlow first?"

"Inform Harlow that they are the reason her reborn is currently in the depths of the sea, and then kill them. I don't care. Mistakes like that will not be tolerated."

And then she caught sight of him. The undine. The bastard who had stolen her greatest honor and made her seem incompetent. The flicker of a tail as the lights followed him through the depths of the sea that he called home. Hitting the buttons on the thumbs of the suit to go even faster, she pursued.

At first, it didn't seem like he knew where he was going. Tau was a labyrinth. The entirety of the city wrapped around itself, like some kind of churning whirlpool of a building. It was easy to get lost. If he went straight up, which she almost hoped that he would, then he would run into the most powerful of all of their weapons. The lasers were very accurate. They would target only him, and not the reborn.

But the creature did not go straight up. Instead, he continued winding through the tunnels and through the difficult areas of Tau where he might accidentally get caught.

Was he trying to lose her? She knew the layout of this place far better than he could ever hope to. Surely he had to know that he would not escape her.

But he was heading toward an area that would make it more difficult for her to follow him. There was an abyss at the edge of Tau, mostly where they dropped all of their garbage and the bodies that they needed to get rid of. That would disappear into the depths of the sea and she definitely would have a hard time keeping up with them then.

If he made it through the shield. If he struck that with the reborn in his arms, they would both die. And she would still be at fault for the death of a reborn.

Lifting her arm, she shouted, "Drop the shield in Sector 254."

"What?"

"Drop it now!"

She watched a shimmer of light ripple in front of them and swore the undine looked back and grinned at her. As though he knew she would drop the shield.

The lights of Tau only stretched so far. Of course, he went right over the edge of the cliff and down she followed him. Faster and faster, until she swore there were eyes on her from above, from the sides, from everywhere.

Alexia had learned to listen to her own intuition. Even when she was doing all of her basic training as a kid, she knew when someone else was going to hit her. She'd learned to read other people's bodies, knew that when her gut said something was going to happen, that she had to listen to it or something terrible would happen to her. Right now was one of those moments. She knew, without a doubt, that the undine wasn't below her anymore. He was somewhere in this water with her.

So she turned the suit and stopped. Clicking on the light at her shoulder, she peered through the darkness that was only pierced by tiny filaments of white dust. The small jets on the bottom of her boots kept her in place, making sure she didn't move when she wanted to remain still. She needed to listen. To look through the water when she knew he was hunting her now.

But there was nothing to even see in the water like this. Just the darkness that surrounded her. Breathing slowly, she connected with that part of herself that could sense when someone was looking at her.

Unfortunately, she was too late.

He barreled out of nowhere, just barely catching in the light attached to the suit before she felt the first slice of his claw. He dragged the long tip of it down her arm, and blood bloomed in the water as he disappeared. She had no idea where he had gone, but he wasn't with her any longer.

Then again, he came, suddenly, and out of nowhere. Alexia reacted better this time. She reached for the knife at her side and lashed out at him. She swore she caught onto something, but he didn't react like he'd been struck. Instead, that massive bulk slid along her side and a knife punctured through her torso.

Letting out a low groan, she turned with him. But that only made things worse. Not a knife after all. They were serrated spines and part of him, she realized. He had spines all down the backs of his arms, down his back and his tail. All of those spines were the sharpness that had scraped along her, tearing open her side and ripping through her flesh with so much ease.

She'd never fought against something like this. Never in her life.

Alexia should have been better at fighting him. She should have been more prepared after all of her training, but right now, she realized she was very much the weakest one in this battle. She was in his domain, and she should have respected that.

But she would not give up. Not when there was still a chance that she could win her honor back.

Hitting buttons on the suit, she turned on the rest of the few meager lights she had and then called out, "I know you can understand me! You're the first of your kind that I've seen with a translation device."

The waters seemed to still. No, not still. He was circling her. Like a shark. Twisting and winding around her, but slowly now as he stalked her.

"Give me the reborn," she said, knowing her voice was carrying through the water to his ears. "And I will let you go."

A long, low chuckle echoed in the water. She had no idea what direction it was coming from. Instead, the sound seemed to surround her. Wrapping her body up in that deep, achingly powerful voice. Since when had she ever thought a voice was interesting like that? But she wanted to listen to him talk about anything.

As if that wasn't an insane thought when she was currently bleeding out in the water.

Then he spoke, not just a chuckle, but words. "You will die here, achromo."

"I'm not going to die unless I take you with me," she replied.

There was a long pause. She had to imagine she had surprised him. After all, he clearly thought that he was getting away with whatever he wanted, considering her people weren't supposed to know that his could even speak.

"Allow me to trade you information. I can understand you," she said. "Tau deciphered your language a long time ago, the first year we all moved down here. The Originals knew you existed and that your people would meddle if humans were to bring an entire city down here. It was one of the first things they did. Learn your language, so just in case, they would know what was being said if your kind continued to hunt ours down."

And she'd known he had spoken to her when he'd taken the reborn. But she also knew that his people were bloodthirsty and battle hardened. She knew how to deal with people like him, because she was the same way. She wanted to fight, to prove herself, and more than that, to reach some kind of glory in her life.

All she had to do was bait him. Just get him a little closer and then she might level the playing field.

That low voice rumbled again. "I knew you could understand me. That is not something I expected from your people."

"No, I'm sure you didn't." She turned, trying to figure out where he was in the water. "Why don't you show yourself, undine? Fighting from the shadows doesn't seem very honorable, and your people do so love their honor."

"You know nothing about my people."

"Not really. I can't imagine it would be difficult to discover, though. Fish are easy to understand when you just watch them. I imagine it is the same for undines."

A quick movement from the shadows, a slight flash of yellow light. "Fish? I shouldn't be surprised that's all you think of my people."

With a quick movement, she reached for the gun that was always attached to the suits and whipped it up. A single laser, just enough to figure out where he really was, blasted toward where she had seen the movement. And there he was. It illuminated just to the right of him, and the pale figure of the reborn still clutched limp in his grasp.

She kept firing. Over and over again, lasers that would have seared him if she hit him, but she chose not to. Not once. Instead, she kept the scatter shots all around him, over and over until the gun was so hot in her hands she nearly dropped it.

Only then did she give them both a breather, where he clearly understood she could find him even in the darkness. "Give me the reborn," she said again. "Give her to me and you can leave. No one needs to know that you failed."

"I didn't fail," he replied. Something in his tones made all the hairs on her arms stand on end. "But if you want your... reborn back, then you can take her."

This felt too easy. He wasn't just going to give the woman over to her, no matter how easy that would be for the two of them. He could hand the body over, and Alexia would honor their deal. She would bring the reborn back to the city far faster than she would fight with him again. But she could tell that wasn't how this was going to go.

And then suddenly, the entire sea lit up. His body had lights, she realized. Individual, yellow flickering lights that glowed from deep within his skin. Hundreds of them, all leading to the larger globes that were attached to the tips of his fins.

It was... strangely beautiful. Haunting in the darkness to see all that bright yellow light lingering on the edges of the limp, nude woman in his grasp and the nightmarish form that surrounded her. He was a creature that most would only ever see in their nightmares. A deep sea monster with sharp teeth and long claws that had already damaged the reborn. Fine ribbons of blood covered her sides where he had held onto her body.

"If you want her," the undine said with his sharp teeth bared in a grin, "Catch her."

And then he dropped the reborn.

The heavy weight of the breathing apparatus dragged the reborn down into the abyss. It was swift and fast and almost impossible to stop. She had to make a split second decision. Fight the undine before her, or plunge into the darkness.

It wasn't a choice.

Cursing, she hit the buttons on her suit and sent herself careening down into the abyss after the one thing that might allow her to live when she returned to Tau.

53

Chapter 6

The hunt burned within him. It had been a long time since anyone had chased him. He knew how the other People of Water's mating rituals went. The males hunted their much larger prizes, and then they would kidnap them. Trapping a massive female they enjoyed was hard enough, but then providing her with enough food and gifts for her to decide that they were worthy of a mate? That was no easy feat.

But the depthstriders were a little different. His people knew the future, and their mating rituals were easier because of it. He had long known his wife would come to their pod and that he would mate with her. And from the first moment he had seen her, love had bloomed deep in his chest.

She had been beautiful in a way that so few were. So pale white that she glowed in the darkness. It might have been a weakness to some—it was hard for her to hide, after all—but his stunning bride had never once been afraid of what might find her in the shadows. She'd fought tooth and claw against anything that attacked her. Until all the sea itself knew not to test her.

She'd chased him through the waves for weeks on end. Every time she had given up, he would chase her. Rushing through the waves to taunt her, tease her, get her to turn around in anger and chase him until the very end of the sea itself.

He missed those days. Terribly.

Perhaps that was why the achromo's attack had caused him to remember these things. She wasn't anything like his Astrum had been, but the way she chased him was oddly familiar.

Insane thoughts. And yet, he found himself unable to leave. He needed guidance, because he had been so certain that the sea had sent him to grab one of those reborns. If nothing else, he could have brought the body back to Anya to see what information could be found out about the strange, limp creature.

But then he could feel the whispers in his mind to taunt the big woman. She had worn a skeleton that clearly was made for battle, and his entire mind had told him to bring her deeper into the depths.

Almost as though the sea itself wanted to get a look at her.

It was strange. The sea wanted to know more about this woman, and he wanted nothing more than to kill her. As was right. It didn't matter that her scent coated his gills. She'd smelled just as good in the water, if not better, than she did out of it. It made him want to bite all of her skin off, peel it away so that he wouldn't have that scent in his lungs anymore.

And yet...

After she disappeared into the darkness, all he could do was stare into that abyss. The sea tried to speak to him again. He was certain of that. It wanted Fortis to come into the abyss because it had more for him to hear. More that it wanted him to know.

His lights flickered out, one by one, as he sank into the darkness. The voices grew louder as he got closer to the heart of the sea, although they were in a language he did not understand. The ancients spoke more in emotions and visions than they did in an actual language that could be understood. He had been communicating with them for years, though, and sometimes he caught snippets of what he believed them to be saying.

"Come to us," they whispered. "Come to us and we will show you the future."

He had never been one to deny the future. Not when he knew how helpful it was to know the next step of his journey.

Some part of him feared that he had annoyed them, or perhaps disappointed them. Their orders were never all that clear. They had wanted him to go to Tau. He knew that much. They had wanted him to be caught by the ship and to get inside the city. That was his job. Surely the creature they had laid out on the table, the one who had been tested on just as he was about to be tested on, was the answer.

But no, now he was seeing it wasn't her. He was always meant to grab her, though, that much he was certain. But this entire situation wasn't about that woman called the "reborn".

"Come," the voices said again, this time all merging together into one voice.

But the voice they merged into wasn't the feminine call he was used to. This was a masculine rumble, a deeper sound like the very depths of the sea spoke to him. This one was harder, as though whoever spoke had seen far too much. And it called him into the depths farther than he had ever been before.

Not the goddess of the sea, then. She had not bid him to go to Tau. But who else could it be?

Fortis drifted for a little while, allowing the sea to guide him toward the voice. Because the sea did want him to seek whoever was talking to him, even though it felt strange to wander into the unknown.

Darkness coiled around him, deeply intertwining with his gills, all his fins, even tangling in his hair and giving him a little tug when the currents wanted him to focus.

The voice was coming from close to Tau. The moment he hit the bottom of the abyss, where it was difficult for even him to breathe, he understood why he had been summoned here.

There was a tomb at the bottom of this crevice. It was buried beneath years of silt, dirt, and debris from the ocean, but he could see it clear as the first day it had been built. A monolith of carvings that were clearly etched by clawed hands. It was a depiction of a creature not unlike himself. But this male was not the same as the People of Water who lived today. His fingers were longer, with an extra joint. His face was significantly more animalistic, with a wider mouth that stretched nearly ear to ear. His fins were larger, and he was more massive than any male Fortis had ever seen. Larger even than Fortis himself.

His hair was limp and lank in the carving, as though he was not in water at all. As though he was on land.

But that wasn't possible. Their people had come from the sea and had always come from the sea. But this creature's tomb suggested something different, and Fortis wasn't sure what to do with that information.

Humming low under his breath, he flicked his tail to circle the strange tomb. It was enormous, like a long coffin that had been wedged into the muck. But even then, it was unusual in shape and size. Someone had taken a great deal of effort to ensure that not only was this tomb beautiful, but that it would remain sealed for centuries.

Perhaps even longer.

"Fortis," the voice boomed in his mind. "You have finally come."

"How do you know my name?" Fortis asked, circling the tomb. "How do you exist at the bottom of this sea?"

"I have been alive for centuries." Whoever it was paused to take a long, rattling breath. "I am only now beginning to wake. This world is not how I remember it."

"Many things have changed in the recent years." Fortis paused before the front of the tomb, wondering if he was imagining that the eyes of the statue were nearly... glowing. "When was the last time you were awake?"

"Long ago. Before the storms. Before the... humans."

Strange that this creature used the human word for themselves. His people had always called them achromos, or at least, that's what Fortis thought. He feared this creature would upend all that they knew about their own people.

"Why did you call me?"

"I was awoken by the sea. The cities of these humans are causing far too much damage. The battles beneath the waves must stop." Again, that rattling inhalation, as though the creature's gills weren't properly functioning. "You will start with Tau. You need help to bring the city down and I am the help that you will receive."

"What help can you provide? Unless you wish for me to open your tomb?" Fortis moved to do just that, freezing when the next order was barked.

"No!"

"No?" he repeated, his claws scraping the edge of the coffin. "Do you not wish to be released?"

"It is not yet time for me to enter the sea again." Another wheeze, another gasp, and then the creature continued. "I will remain here until the time is right. Go back to Tau. The woman you saw before, she is the key."

"I don't believe they'll let me anywhere near the reborn again. But I will try if that is the current I must follow."

The voice turned harsh and sharp. "Not that woman. The limp creature you stole has no purpose in this plan. The other woman, that is the one you must convince to help us."

The big woman who smelled like the sea? That was who he was supposed to convince to help them? He wasn't sure it was possible. She had hunted him as only a true warrior would. She would not be easily convinced. She was clearly loyal to her city, and those who ran it. Which only made all of this an even more difficult task.

"How?" he asked. "If you wish for me to do this, then you must help me more than just an order."

"You are a depthstrider. Do your people no longer remember how to ask the sea for help?"

"I have asked the sea for help many times in my life, but never has it been so direct as it gives me the answers I seek."

Another long pause, and he wondered if the creature in the tomb had given up on him. But then there was another long, odd sigh. "Ah, I see. She has grown fickle in her old age. Or perhaps she desires not to meddle as much as she used to. That is fine. I will tell you one secret and one secret alone, depthstrider. Use the woman's memories against her. That is the way you will get her to help you."

Her memories?

The light seemed to fade away from the tomb, and he wasn't sure if that was because it had all been in his head, or if the creature had returned to its slumber. Whatever it was, he now had an answer to his questions.

Find the woman again. He supposed that would be easy enough to do.

Finding the city certainly wasn't hard as he headed out and back to the monolith of the hidden human city. Now that he knew where Tau was, he wasn't sure how his people hadn't found it before. With the lights off, perhaps that was how they had remained hidden for so long. Long, billowing shields hid the city. At a distance, he never would have thought it was anything more than the usual dark dust that spun up at this depth.

But now, he knew what lurked beneath that shield, and its weaknesses. He spent the better part of a day finding a small section not covered by their magic. A small section just beneath the crook of their metal structures had been forgotten, and then he weaved throughout the entirety of the city. There were not many windows. But he wasn't all that interested in the people there. They reminded him of those who had lived in Alpha. Primped and glowing, they were the flashy fish in the sea. The ones who were so small, no large predator would ever attempt to eat them.

Pretty little fish, surrounded by much larger predators, and hadn't realized they were edible yet.

Flicking his tail, he circled the building repeatedly. There were so many weaving tunnels that jutted in this place. He couldn't imagine the achromos within were getting around all that easily. It looked like every few steps they were walking on an undulating floor system.

Every other city was built similar to each other. This one, though, looked like it had been built by a mad man.

Wriggling in between two of the strangely built tunnels, he realized there was a tighter area within. This one had small portholes, large enough that he could peer inside.

Achromos wandered throughout the rooms beyond. Some of these were training rooms. He could see warriors wrestling with each other, all of them grappling and throwing bodies with such force. He paused to wonder if they were actually fighting.

And then he saw her. The big woman who had captured his attention from the start. She was fighting with someone as well. The male was much larger than her, and that was saying something. She was already huge, but while they were of similar height, she lacked the weight of the man who threw her body across the room.

A sensation trailed down his spine, bristling at the sight of someone else attacking her. She rolled onto her side, fingers pressed where the man had wounded her. Blood trickled out of her nostrils when she looked up, and Fortis was shocked to find rage nearly glowing through his body. He didn't like the sight of blood on her.

No, that wasn't right. Fortis didn't like to see blood drawn by another person when he was the only one who should do so. He didn't like being wrong, either. He'd been thinking of her as a warrior, and she shouldn't have put herself in this situation. The male was bigger, stronger. She shouldn't try to fight someone like that. The male would tear her apart.

But then, even with her ribs wounded and blood streaming down her face, her face warped into an enraged battle cry as she launched herself across the room. The man's back hit the wall where the window was, his head cracking hard against the glass before he slid down. Nearly unconscious.

Fortis was too far for her to see him through the darkness, but he swore she could. This woman, with her wild dark hair and blood streaked across her face, stared right into his soul.

63

Chapter 7

"You can't keep pushing your body like this," Doctor Barker grumbled as he stared at the reopened wounds along her ribs. "These will not close the more you fight."

"I need to be ready."

"You need to rest. I have informed Original Harlow that you are not to overwork yourself, or you will have to be decommissioned." He sighed before reaching for the needle and thread on the small table beside him in the exam room.

She'd come here right after her latest training session. The other guards understood she didn't want any of them to go easy on her. She had to keep practicing. That undine had swum around her at an unnatural speed and he'd beaten her far too easily. Her pride stung with that knowledge, yes. But that didn't mean she couldn't get better. Prepare harder.

Next time she fought him, she would make him bleed. She had to.

Everyone assumed the undine escaped and that he wouldn't come back. She was quite certain, in fact, that he would. She'd always listened to her gut. Her body knew the truth long before her mind did, and she'd learned a long time ago to not push away those thoughts. And right now, she knew he wasn't far.

The undine had a plan. He'd taken that reborn for a reason. He'd gotten into the city far too easily, and now they were all on lockdown. The soldiers who had made the mistake and brought him into the city had been executed. But that wasn't enough to keep this beast out. She was certain of that.

Shaking her head, she cleared her throat. "You know I can't stop preparing for his return. None of us can."

"That is one undine you are talking about. One creature who cannot get back into this city. None of them have managed before."

"Just because they haven't managed to get in before doesn't mean there isn't a flaw in our city. We leave this place regularly. There are openings, and the guards need to be aware of them all before we feel safe leaving our Originals alone." She winced. "Harlow is visiting with her ex husband, that's the only reason I was allowed to go to training today. It has been... exhausting."

A little furrow appeared between Doctor Barker's eyes. He turned with the stitches and thread in his hand, but hesitated as he looked her over. "Exhausting?"

Shit. Alexia wasn't to be exhausted or feel anything at all in that matter. She was Harlow's personal guard. Day in and day out. If she was tired, she was supposed to get treatment for such a thing. If she wasn't getting enough rest when Harlow was, then she was supposed to get decommissioned.

"Sorry," she muttered, looking down at her hands and curling them into fists. "A turn of phrase."

"Have you been feeling tired lately, Alexia?" he asked, but the words were slow. As though he was giving her a chance to change her mind. "I have medication I can give you for that."

She didn't want more medication. She wanted to feel this exhaustion. It wasn't like she was physically tired, or that she would fail in her duties protecting her Original. It was more that she was tired of being a personal guard and the monotony of her life. This was all endlessly difficult sometimes.

But she couldn't say any of that to him. Not when she knew how it would look.

"I really am fine, Doctor. I didn't mean to say it like that."

He leaned close. "Alexia, if you don't tell me how you're feeling, I can't help you. And if someone else discovers that you are feeling like this..."

He didn't finish what he was saying, but he didn't need to. She knew what would happen if anyone else caught wind that she wasn't perfection personified.

The doors to the room slid open, the compressed air punching through the space as Harlow strode in with angry strides.

"Why didn't you tell me you went after the reborn in the water?" Harlow snapped. "You chased an undine in nothing but an exoskeleton?"

She looked particularly beautiful today, even surrounded by the stark white of the med room. Harlow's hair was twisted into a lovely low bun, a few strands falling around her pristine face. She wore a strapless white dress that clung to her thin figure and ended just above her shapely thighs. Pretty white heels were on her feet, wrapping around her ankles in delicate silk butterflies that almost looked like they were flapping their wings as she shifted.

The red patch on her shoulder was gone. Likely they'd done the transfer the moment Alexia had returned with the reborn in tow. The clone was good enough to harvest the stem cells they needed to fix Harlow's allergy, and that was that. Another death. Another body to toss out into the abyss and pretend that it wasn't horrifying what they were doing.

Doctor Barker punched the needle through her side, but Alexia didn't react. At least that pain helped to ground her so she wouldn't look tired when she spoke with Harlow.

"Your reborn was taken moments after we found the correct genetic sequence that you needed. I did what any good guard would do, and that was go after the creature who stole the body that would make you more comfortable."

Harlow scoffed. "Oh please, don't give me that drivel. You wanted to hunt an undine and as such, you did so. I understand why. But what I don't understand is how the beast got into Tau in the first place."

"He was brought in by a research team. They thought he was incapacitated." Alexia looked down at the stitching to watch Barker's neat little black rows. "He clearly was not."

It was then that Harlow noticed what was happening in the room. A dramatic little hiccup escaped her lips, and she lunged forward as though the stitches were surely a sign of death in her guard. "What happened to you, dear one?"

Oh, they were pretending that Harlow cared. Interesting. She wasn't sure if this was all for show because Barker was in the room, or if Harlow was having a moment where she realized just how fragile her guard might be.

"I fought the undine," she said through gritted teeth. "I lost."

"You have to be more careful, dear. You are my favorite guard."

"I understand that, Harlow. But I will not live as long as you."

"Unless I have something to say about it. Like I said, you're the only competent guard I've been given in over two hundred years. I don't think you understand how many of you I have gone through." She shook her head before sighing. "You die when I say you die, Alexia. Do I make myself clear?"

Alexia nodded, as a pit grew in her stomach. What did Harlow mean by that? She didn't want to stick around forever. Immortality seemed more like a punishment than a gift. And yet... Was that what she was saying?

"You'll take care of this undine issue," Harlow said. "The other Originals aren't certain how to address this situation, but I am. You already fought him once. We'll give you a better ship, better weapons, and you will hunt him down for me. Bring me his head, Alexia, and you will never have to fear decommissioning ever again."

The Original left the room, and silence burned in her wake. Alexia knew this was supposed to be a gift. A boon. An underlined promise that would give her hope, but all it did was solidify her feeling of drowning and exhaustion.

"I've never heard an Original wish to keep their guard forever," Doctor Barker finally said. He finished with the first row of stitches, and tied off the end with a knot before snipping it with very sharp scissors. "That is a great honor. You've made a lasting impression on her."

"How wonderful for me."

Again, Barker looked at her with a gaze that saw too much. "What was it like being in the water with an undine?"

She searched her memory, trying to figure out what he wanted her to say. Likely, he would expect her to say that it was nothing different from what she had experienced before. It was just another hunt. She'd fought her entire life, and this was a different opponent who had beaten her. But frustration got her nowhere, and self loathing also wasn't what he wanted to hear.

Now that she had her emotions glimmering in the back of her mind, and the meds were wearing off again, it was hard to think of what someone without those feelings would say.

Doctor Barker had never threatened her well being, though. Maybe she couldn't quite trust him, but she could at least be a little more honest than she could with others.

"Magnificent," she finally admitted. "Unlike anything I have seen before."

"Out of the water, he was quite massive."

"They seem even bigger when you're in the water with them. It's odd, because he seems like an overly large human from the waist up… but that tail." She shook her head. "He can even glow underwater. I've never seen any creature like that before. Such power and such control over his own body. There was no way I could fight against him and win."

"What an unusual circumstance you've found yourself in." Doctor Barker wheeled his chair away from her and reached for a needle filled with more drugs that she knew would take her away from this moment. "I have a few more questions before I administer this medication, if you don't mind me asking them."

She narrowed her eyes in suspicion. "Why would you want to ask me questions while I'm obviously not myself?"

"I believe I'll get the more honest and factual answers. But I do ask that you be completely honest with me. No hiding the truth."

He was right. With fewer drugs going through her body, she certainly was more likely to answer everything he asked. And it seemed like he wasn't going to decommission her for having them, at least not right now.

She leaned back in the chair, pressed a hand to her aching side, and nodded.

"How did you feel when you were in the water with him?"

Alexia thought back to those moments, floating there and realizing he was going to continue hitting her out of the darkness. There was nothing she could do. Even if he decided he wanted her dead, there was absolutely nothing she could have done to stop him.

"Small," she replied. "I felt very small, and scared. I didn't know if he was going to kill me or not."

"And when you were faced with him? I assume there was a point where he stopped attacking you?"

He'd spoken to her. She wasn't going to tell the Doctor that, but she was still shocked that the undine had spoken directly to her. Everyone here knew they could talk, but she hadn't thought he would be so bold.

Still, there was something about that experience that had... stuck with her. He had been a warrior, unlike any creature she'd ever met before. A male unwilling to back down, even when she'd pointed a gun at him.

"He was fearless," she replied quietly. "And I suppose I can respect that. It is what you have all designed me to be, and what I have striven to be my entire life. To see a creature without fear and without the help of so many drugs... I'm not sure. It is not an emotion I have a name for."

"Jealousy?"

"No." She shook her head. "Something more like... awe, I suppose."

She had wanted to learn from him. Seek out what had made him so fearless. She wanted a drop of that in herself, because she'd been terrified.

She would not admit there was a healthy amount of intrigue as well in looking at him. She'd never been so close to an undine, and she wanted to know what they felt like. Were his scales rough? What would happen if she tugged one of those glowing tentacles? He'd reacted when she'd sunk her fingers into his gills. No matter how good of an actor he'd been at pretending it hadn't affected him, it certainly had. She'd felt his shiver and seen the goosebumps rise on his more human-like skin.

But it was unnatural to be so interested in an undine beyond the usual scientific curiosity.

Doctor Barker nodded. "Right. I suppose that makes sense. Now, why did you go after the reborn?"

"It's my job to bring her back."

"That's not what made you go after it."

She cleared her throat. "I was angry that a creature bested me. I wanted to get her back to prove a point."

His brows were still furrowed, though. And she had to admit, it didn't sound convincing to her either. At the moment, that was exactly what she had wanted. She was enraged that the undine had bested her. She wanted to prove a point to herself and to the creature that Alexia was not someone to fuck with.

And yet... The longer she was out of the water, the further she was from the situation, the more she thought maybe she was wrong. It hadn't been rage that had fueled her.

Doctor Barker moved the needle between his fingers. "You continue throughout this conversation to use pronouns such as he and she for both the undine and the reborn. I find this interesting terminology to use for creatures we do not consider to be... people."

She sighed and looked toward the door. The more she talked, the more uncomfortable she became. And the more she looked at that needle, and wanted him to inject her. "They look like people. Both of them talk, too, you know. I was in the room where someone didn't give the reborn the right amount of drugs to keep her quiet. She woke and tried to speak. I didn't think they were intelligent enough to do so, but she did. She looked right at me and asked me for help. I had to step back and let them continue on with the procedure even though I knew she was in pain."

"Was that the first moment when you started feeling emotions that were outside of your normal range?"

Alexia shrugged. "I have no idea. It wasn't like there was an instant where I suddenly knew that everything wasn't the same. It's been a gradual change, and now... I'm here. Looking at reborns with sorrow and at undines with intrigue."

Doctor Barker wheeled closer to her and reached for her arm. He smoothed his thumb over her bicep, which was bruised where she'd been grabbed and thrown on the sparring mats. "These are highly unusual emotions for one such as yourself. I wish to understand, before I... well."

The needle came closer to her skin, and she knew exactly what he meant. Before he took all those emotions away again. Before she returned to that numbing state she was beginning to hate more and more every time she came out of it.

But it was safer for her to be numb. She would remain alive a lot longer if she wasn't emotional like this, and was able to do her job without questioning what she was ordered to do.

Barker hesitated. The needle was poised right over her skin, and then he looked up at her with an expression of concern. "Stay safe, Alexia. I worry the longer you bury these emotions, the more you will feel them."

She placed her hand over his and stuck the needle a little too far into her arm. Her hand was so much larger than his, so it was easy to put her thumb over the depressor and inject herself. Emotions drained out of her quickly as she stood. Mere seconds and she was back to herself.

"It's all right, doctor. It's the right thing to do."

75

Chapter 8

And so the hunt began.

His wife's prophecy had been correct. She had been the first to see it, and then spread the news among many who had confirmed her suspicions. Fortis remembered her words as though she were floating right beside him.

"You will be chased by a silver beast. You will lead it into the depths and from there, you will win a battle of flesh without blood."

He never understood the last part until the god beneath the sea had clarified. He needed her memories. And now, as he watched as this achromo prepared herself to hunt him, all he could think was that she must be mad. They must all be afflicted by insanity, because there was no reason an achromo should ever believe they could hunt one of his people. Not in these waters.

Perhaps achromos were more capable in shallow waters. The People of Water were unused to the sun, and they used shadows to their benefit. Fortis himself had been raised in the depths. He knew all the parts of the abyss that could hide him, and all the areas that would help him. He would lead her ship into the deepest part of the ocean and then sink it until she would never see the light again.

The thought had merit. Perhaps it would teach this little warrior that she should never have fought against him.

He could only see so much from his position attached to one of the longer arms of the city. The tangled nest was frustrating to get around, but he managed well enough. Other achromos were ushering her into a ship, it appeared. Plenty of weapons and boxes were shuttled into it by droids that were lumbering along beside every single person in that room.

Soon enough, the door to the sea would open and it would release her into his world. He would lead her on a merry chase, just as the sea wished for him to do. He would destroy every ounce of her bravery, but first, he had to fulfill his own prophecy.

A chase. Just like he had been promised.

A silver beast that would test his own mettle and every ability he had spent years developing. Already his tail vibrated with the need to show her the kind of monster she hunted.

Had she been training to fight against him better? No training on land would ever prepare her to face a depthstrider like him, no matter how big she was compared to all the other achromos.

His mind wandered as he watched the ship get filled with even more supplies. If he had given her the time, she likely could have been an impressive fighter. The metal skeleton she'd worn had helped that. With the right training, she could likely use it even better to her advantage. The problem had been how she was fighting against the currents. He knew she could feel them. Mira and Anya both had gotten very good at feeling them. So this warrior could also learn how to find the currents and use them as she fought.

It was foolhardy to even think she could learn, though. Their kind were incapable of such things. Only the select few were worth his time, and honestly, even then, he wasn't all that certain her kind had the capacity to learn.

Then the achromos were ready to leave the safety of their home. The ship came to life, all the lights turning on brightly and filling the moon pool with a blinding ray. He covered his eyes, hissing out a sound as all his gills flared wide. But he had to drop his arm. He had to see what their plan was.

They wouldn't be so foolish as to send their best warrior after one of his kind alone, would they?

There she was. Stunning in her tall and powerful stance. She'd twisted her hair into a braid, and it swung nearly to her hips as she strode through the crowd of people to the ship. Armor covered her body, but he'd expected that. After all, she would need everything they could give her to keep her alive fighting him.

She entered the ship, and then... yes. They were so foolish. They were going to send her to her death hunting him.

A series of complicated panels opened in the floor. The first would send her down onto the loading dock area where they had kept him for a while and injected him with their useless drugs. Then she would descend into a second area with mostly glass panels, a waiting area, he supposed. He knew there must be devices to watch what happened in that room as well, because they hadn't opened their last defense until he'd stopped struggling. Perhaps assuming he had tired himself out in the net.

Then finally, she was released.

He moved his tail from where it was wrapped around one of the looping antennae and darted out into the open ocean. He didn't have to hide himself. Not from her. She was hunting him, after all, and he wanted to make it easy for her.

The metal beast of her ship rose out of the darkness and stirred the silt into a gray haze that was broken only by the twin beams of light in front of it. She was in a much smaller ship. It was clearly made for only one person, and that much he appreciated. It would be easier for her to move it around and to dart after him when he proved to be much faster.

Fortis positioned himself in front of the beams, waiting for her to notice him.

Of course she did quickly. He could see the determination in her expression through the glass. That glare on her face should have peeled his scales right back from his tail. Ah, he so enjoyed the hatred that burned in her features.

"Come, warrior," he snarled. "Let's see how fast your ship is."

And off he went. He could hear the engines of her ship roar to life, and then she was speeding after him. Impressive. He hadn't known their ships could go that fast, but the longer she chased him, the faster he got. But she'd known that from the beginning. He knew deep in his gut that she hadn't taken this mission lightly, because she'd seen what he could do already. She'd only wanted to do this to get her revenge.

He wouldn't give her that.

Flexing all the muscles in his tail, he curved down toward the abyss and knew the shield would part for him. Perhaps she would think that he was bringing her to the same spot where they had originally fought. But then he twisted around a rocky outcropping, waiting to hear the crunch of metal on the stone.

Instead, he swore he could hear her curse before she managed to not hit the stones. Interesting. She was a better pilot than he'd thought she was, but then again, she was good at surprising him.

"All right," he muttered, "Then let's try this."

Off he went to the right. This time curved her towards volcanic vents that opened up and blasted hot water. He wasn't certain if her ship could withstand that, but he was surprised to see that it could. The heat was blistering to him, but her ship didn't slow in the slightest.

Curious. Then he brought her out into the open ocean. The darkness there was easier for him to slip away. Her beams of light could only hold on to him for so long before he just... disappeared.

All he had to do was flick his tail and roll beneath her ship that was rapidly gaining on him. He let her, of course. He wanted her to think that perhaps she could catch him. Surely she had weapons that were all pointed right at him. All she'd have to do was hit a button in this darkness, but he realized she didn't want to do that.

If she shot him here, then his body would disappear just as easily as he had fled from her now. If she wasn't careful, she'd lose her prize.

The damned woman wanted her trophy. He only knew this because he would want the same thing if he were her.

Gills opening wide and filtering through as much air as he could stuff into his lungs. He hovered above her ship as she slowed it. The whole thing pivoted, moving in a circle with a single engine still going as though she was listening for him.

"Achromo," he called out, the word long and low. He knew she could hear his whale song.

The ship turned, but he needed her to get out of her ship. Out of that protection that would only give her a barrier between him and all the memories that he knew he needed to gather from her.

Swimming slightly closer, he sang his taunts louder, knowing she wouldn't be able to deny him.

"The little achromo arrives in a ship. Terrified of what the massive undine could do to her. You are afraid."

Again the shipped turned, but he did not hear her speaking within that metal contraption. Not yet.

So he swam even closer to the top of it, knowing she would not look above her until the last second. "If you're not careful, I will believe your people are even less capable than expected. You don't want to get into the water because you know I will kill you if you do."

Then he heard her small scoff. "I have no fear of you, undine."

"You are deeply afraid. But you don't want me to smell it on you again." Then he was close enough to her ship to trail his nails down the glass on top of it. All she had to do was look up.

And then she did.

Those jet-black eyes, as deep and endless as his own, looked up at him. He knew the lights from below illuminated his face. He must look terrifying to her, all flared gills and floating hair. Slowly, he grinned. Spreading his lips so all she could see were the sharp points of his teeth and a mouth that was a little too wide.

Her nostrils flared. He wondered if that was fear or anger, but that was the best part of all this. Perhaps, if he was lucky, he would get her out into the water so he could tell.

They were so disgusting to him. Fortis had never looked at achromos overly much, because they were stomach churning. Except he wanted to look at this one. He wanted to know every single feature of her face that moved and changed when he taunted her, because his hatred ran so deep that he needed to know these details about her.

Her hand slowly stretched forward, fingers steady as a rock, he noted, and then she hit a button.

There it was again. That exoskeleton. Stretching down from

somewhere above her in the ship and wrapping around her body like a second skin. She held his gaze the entire time, her body jerking with the movements to get it settled in the right places that should have protected her from him.

But the suit hadn't the last time, and it wouldn't this time.

"I have thought long and hard about our last fight," she snarled. "I know where I went wrong, and I know how to fight you better."

"Is that so?"

"This time, I won't hesitate to shoot." Her fist slammed into a button next to her at the same time, she dragged a face mask over her mouth.

He could so easily rip her air away from her and kill her. Surely she knew that. These threats weren't scary to him in the slightest.

Maybe she had always wanted to fight him again in the sea. Maybe some prideful part of her believed that she could fix her own honor by winning this time. She wouldn't, but he could respect the desire to do so.

She landed in the water and he sucked her scent into his lungs. It was fresh and light, but acrid this time.

So she was afraid. Good. She wasn't an idiot.

Fortis breathed her into his gills, coating them with the exquisite taste of her fear as much as he could before darting forward. She yanked a gun out just as fast, and he wasn't surprised to feel the pulse of pressure as her gun fired right through his side. Black blood bloomed in the water like ink, but he was already upon her. There was nothing she could do to stop it.

Perhaps she thought she could take him with her. If she was going to die, then at least she could kill a depthstrider on her way out of this realm.

He had no plans to kill her, though. The sea had given her to him. He was going to rip through her memories and use them all to his advantage. He would tear her apart, memory by memory, until she was nothing but a drowning mess.

As he wrapped his arm around her waist, he couldn't help but notice how tight the muscles were there. Yes, the metal skeleton wrapping around her was bitterly hot and searingly distracting, but he could feel her beneath all of it. Strong, wiry muscles, a body made from years of fighting. Her abs flexed against his palm as he reeled her back against his chest, pinning her there.

Leaning down, he pressed his lips against her throat just to feel her swallow against his teeth. "If I wanted to kill you, virago, I would have done it the first time I had you trapped in these waters."

Her ship floated just below her feet. She kicked them, clearly trying to get purchase so she could shove back against him. As it was, he had her tangled up in him. She couldn't kick. Couldn't fight back. She had to stay in his arms, struggling in slow motion as he coiled his tail around her.

"You bastard," she hissed, hitting a button that made her suit even hotter. It singed his scales, but he'd suffered worse pain.

Fortis turned her in his arms, feeling his gaze turning from the usual black to swirling colors that would allow him to peer through her resistance and straight into her soul. She struggled, those strong arms coming down on his tail and trying to thrust him away from her. She wanted to flee, to run, to get away from her own past that soon he would walk through without her permission.

Some part of him felt like a god when he did this. Fortis was one of the few depthstriders who could. Most of them only saw the future, but he could see the past as well. All he had to do was reach for it.

"What are you doing?" she asked, her voice already sounding drugged.

"Seeking the truth." And then he dove into her memories.

85

Chapter 9

What the fuck was he doing? He should be killing her. All he had to do was squeeze the vice of his tail and soon enough, she would be dead. She could feel the power in his muscles as he tightened that tail around her. The fins on the sides of his hips kept them from falling, so they just hovered where they were.

And what was going on with his eyes? She had looked into them enough now. They were pitch black, without a hint of white in them. But now they were an oil slick. Black water covered by a thin film of beautiful colors that shimmered the more she looked into them.

Her gut rolled with the knowledge that she shouldn't be looking into his eyes. Some inner part of her screamed to look away, and that she was losing her chance to do so. But she couldn't tear her gaze from his. Those colors had caught her in their grasp.

"What are you doing to me?" she tried to say, but the words came out slurred.

She plummeted. She wasn't sure if they were falling through the ocean or what was happening, but all of a sudden she wasn't floating in the dead center of the sea with a monster holding her in his tail. She was standing in Harlow's room.

Alexia shook her head in confusion. Was she losing her mind?

Looking around the room, she tried to ground herself. Everything was the same as she'd always seen it. Opulent, beautiful, maybe a little different from normal, with the drapes the wrong shade of pink and the bed was more rumpled than usual. She couldn't feel her feet on the floor, either. Or even react when she looked right up at the bulbs of light. Her eyes didn't water, and she didn't get the burned orbs in her retinas.

What was happening?

The doors opened and in walked Harlow and... herself. Alexia stared at her younger version, back when she had first been gifted to Harlow. Not a single ounce of nerves showed on her features, and she remembered how numb she was then.

She'd been just out of training when she'd been given to her Original. Everything had felt so new and wonderful and she'd eaten up all the attention without an ounce of shame. She had been one of the first in her class to get her own Original.

How magical it had seemed. How honorable it had been.

"You are going to live in the room beside mine. I hope you will be satisfied with the size." Harlow chuckled. "The last one wasn't happy with how small it was. You behemoths never seem to be comfortable, though."

"I will be fine," her younger self said, with zero emotion in her voice at all. "Thank you for the honor, Original."

"Please, call me Harlow. I don't like all that Original nonsense. It makes me feel old."

And then a voice whispered in her ear. A deep, echoing voice that sounded like the rumble of a sea, "So you serve one of the Originals."

Alexia spun toward the voice, but there was no one behind her. She was alone in this memory. But it didn't feel like she was alone.

Furrowing her brows, she searched for where the voice had come from. While the other two women in the room continued to talk about expectations and how Alexia would be essentially a slave to the Original, she looked for that voice.

Finally, she paused in front of a mirror that didn't have her own reflection. Instead, she was staring into dark, swirling eyes and a wide open maw that spread wide the moment their gazes met.

"Good job finding me," the undine snarled. "Now show me more."

She was spun out of this memory and thrown deeper into the recesses of her mind. She tried to push him toward memories she didn't care if he saw. Memories that were easy enough for her to live through again. Training where she fought other genetically enhanced soldiers. The mundane parts of her days where she didn't have to think about Harlow or anyone else. The commissary, or the other guards. Anything he could see other than the reality of her life.

She didn't like to think about the times when she was a child, but that was immediately where he took her.

Alexia stood there and watched as she was pulled out of the test tube where they grew the children. Tubes that were filled with a viscous liquid that was breathable, but not really. It was enough to keep the specimens alive, but she remembered waking up from it. The small version of herself, still nearly five feet tall at only six years old, landing on her hands and knees.

She vomited up all that yellow goo, watching as it splattered onto her hands where she crouched on the ground. Not a single scientist had helped her. They just left her on her hands and knees as they moved to the next genetically enhanced child, and the next. They were all disposable. No one had cared that there was a little girl in front of them. Because to them, she wasn't a little girl. She was a product they had designed.

"I wondered what was different about you," the undine murmured in her ear. "They made you, didn't they?"

"I am not having this conversation with you," Alexia snarled, turning away from the sight of herself that still stung. "Get out of my head."

And then... She could feel it. A power in her that he didn't control. This was her mind. Her memories. If she didn't want him to see what he was seeing, then she could make him get out.

She thrust against the presence in her mind, shoving at him with all her might until she felt him move. The bulk of him wasn't knotted around her mind as much now, and she could at the very least change the memory. It was still warped, still felt like striding across sand, but it worked.

Suddenly, they were back in Harlow's room. The Original was prattling on about something to do with her hair, and that was better than watching herself as a child.

"No," the undine snarled, and the tension around her mind knotted yet again.

Then she was standing in the med bay. She had been a little girl at this point too, although she was fourteen and over six feet tall at that point. They'd sat her down in a chair and strapped her arms into it.

"Just for protection," the doctor had said. She didn't remember who it was that administered her first shots, and as such, all she remembered was a faceless man in white who had injected her.

She turned her eyes away from it. It was the first time she hadn't felt like a person. Even when they were training her, brainwashing her, telling her who to be and how to protect, she had still felt like herself. Alexia. An individual with thoughts and desires and hopes and dreams.

This memory made her remember that she used to draw on her arms. Weaving patterns that looked like waves. She'd steal pens from the doctors and redo them every time they scrubbed her skin clean of the black etchings. She'd always wanted to tattoo the patterns onto her skin. She didn't know where the thoughts came from, only that she liked to look at them.

"What are they putting in you?" he asked, his voice deep and cajoling. "What do your people give someone like you to keep you under their thumb?"

"Get out of my head!" she cried out, crouching and putting her hands over her ears.

Her heart was racing. She could feel her breath sawing in and out of her lungs, and some rational part of her mind remembered she was still underwater. She couldn't keep breathing like this. Her air was finite and soon enough, she would run out of oxygen. She needed to control her emotions.

She needed her medicine.

Struggling to get through the memory, she turned away from the sound of her own struggles. Back then, she'd fought it. The memory warped into the next time they'd given her the drug, and she could hear herself begging to not have them put whatever it was in her body.

"Please," she had screamed. "Please don't. Don't do this!"

The doctors never listened. She was injected, and then all her struggles disappeared. Memory by memory, she argued with them less and less each time until finally they handed her a box of needles and told her to take them back to her room.

And she'd done it ever since. It had never changed. Every morning she injected herself with the medicine that kept her quiet and composed, no feelings to interrupt with the job that was meant to be done.

"How strange," he muttered in her ear. "You have never sought freedom on your own."

That wasn't true, though. She'd been seeking it lately, and no one knew it yet.

The moment she had the thought, she was suddenly sitting in front of Doctor Barker again. Not watching the memory as she had with those older ones. Time had given her the ability to see all those old memories through another lens. Or perhaps she had simply become a different person since then.

This memory was new.

Fresh.

Aching.

She sat in front of him and remembered how he'd asked her why she was feeling. His words still echoed through her mind, but worse, it was her own thoughts that seemed like they were real people speaking all around her.

"You're broken. You're feeling. You're thinking."

The worst one was the quietest, but she could hear the tiny murmur, "Maybe it's time to go."

Rage burned through her. She was not a weak-willed woman who would listen to these foolish thoughts and the folly that came with them. She was a warrior who would fight until her very last breath and she would not give up this easily.

With a cry of rage, she thrust him out of her mind and staggered back into reality. The cold hit her first. At some point, he must have turned the heater off of her exoskeleton. Her entire body was freezing, icy in a way she hadn't felt for ages. Teeth chattering, she glared at the undine who wasn't hiding in the back of her mind now. He was still coiled around her, looping his tail like a snake around her entire body until she couldn't even move her arms.

"Fuck you," she spat out. "And stay out of my head."

Already his eyes were glowing again. That whirling kaleidoscope of colors that had called to her originally, but now she knew what it was.

Alexia turned her face away from him, hissing out a breath when a clawed hand cupped her jaw. He was trying to force her to look at him. He wanted her to have to stare into his gaze because he wanted to steal even more of her memories. But they weren't for him. They were for her to suffer through alone.

A voice chirped in her ear. "Oxygen at fifteen percent."

If she didn't get back into her ship, he was going to drown her. And he knew this. He understood her language. His hearing seemed far too good to not have heard the warning along with her.

She wiggled her fingers. Her arms were pinned by his tail, but she thought if she could get her hand to just rotate, then she might grab her knife. It was heated, just like the rest of the exoskeleton. She just needed to distract him long enough to grab it.

"You like to paw through my memories?" she said. "Seems like something an undine would have to do. You damn well know I'm not going to tell you a single thing, not even if you torture me."

That clawed hand moved up from her jaw to the mask attached to her face. Alexia struggled a little harder as he squeezed it and the glass creaked.

His hand could crack through her only oxygen and he would drown her right here, right now.

The undine leaned ever closer, that open maw of his sharpened teeth coming ever closer. "Do you want to see how long you would last with me torturing you, virago? I think we both might enjoy it."

There! She grabbed onto the handle of her knife, hit the button to heat it, and twisted it into his tail. He let out a little sharp sound, but then his tail only tightened even further. Thankfully, that worked in her favor. The heated blade sank deeper, bubbles rising from where it was boiling through his flesh.

Finally, he relented. The coils dropped from around her and it gave her just enough time to hit the other button on her suit that fired up the shoes. Propelling herself away from him was easy. But she was so frozen it was hard to get back to her ship. She overshot the entrance and nearly ended up on the wrong side before grabbing onto the opening with an achingly cold hand.

An echoing roar of rage seemed to shake the very ocean itself as she hauled herself into the ship.

Water dripped from her body in a river as she sealed the door. Coughing, she yanked the mask off her face and breathed in the stale air within her ship. It would get better as the filtration was used more. They hadn't used a ship like this in a very long time. Breathing heavily, she avoided hitting any of the important buttons as she struggled to stand.

It was a small battleship. Just enough room for her to walk five steps to her bed, five more steps to storage, and five other steps to the pilot's chair. A tight space, no doubt, but it would do well enough.

"Computer," she called out. "Turn the exoskeleton offline."

"Affirmative."

The suit opened, and she staggered out of it. Soaking wet in her skintight black suit and shivering, she rushed to the pilot's chair and sat down.

"Now, where are you?" she hissed. "I'm going to light you up with as many lasers as this ship can shoot."

But she couldn't find him. Again. He was so good at hiding in these murky waters and there was only so far her lights could break through. Somehow, it seemed almost more dusty than it had been when she'd first exited the ship. She narrowed her eyes, ignoring the drip of saltwater from her hair down into her eyes.

"Come on. Show yourself, you big bastard."

A small flicker of a tail. That was all the warning she got. Then she opened fire. Over and over she shot into the darkness, hoping that at least one of them would catch him. She'd already shot him once, stabbed him, but she really didn't know if that was going to be enough to take him down. He didn't seem easy to kill, that much was certain.

When she stopped shooting, she inhaled in the sudden silence. There was no way she'd killed him. He was too strong.

A thud echoed throughout her ship. She looked up just in time to see his grin once more where he was attached to the roof of her ship. He gave her a little smirk and then seemed to yank on something.

The lights in her ship flickered. Was he...

She screeched as he yanked again and all the lights on her ship went out. He'd taken the damn batteries off the ship. How he had managed to yank them off, she had no idea. The amount of power it would take to forcefully remove welded metal was a shocking display of strength.

But she didn't have time to think about that once her ship started a slow decline through the sea.

"Computer!" she shouted, spinning to press the buttons that would display the ship's life support, power supply, and ability to move. "Why are we sinking?"

"The ship cannot sustain life support and continue idling."

"Then send the ship home."

"We are too far with only minimal battery life. Docking ship."

"Docking ship?" she repeated, screaming now with anger. "Where the fuck are you docking the ship?"

"The sea floor."

She was sinking to the fucking sea floor. As she watched the undine disappear into the darkness above her, she flipped him off while he gave her a little wave. He'd sent her to a tomb in the darkness.

Bastard.

Chapter 10

He followed the ship into the murk of the sea. Fortis had to admit, most of what he'd done had been enraged moments of mistakes. Her memories had given him only the slightest hint at who she was and what information he could use to his advantage. The largest problem arose with the realization that she could kick him out of her mind. No one had ever been able to do that before, certainly not an achromo.

He looked into people's memories and into their future. Once they locked eyes with him, there was no changing that. He looked as much as he wanted, and even then, he would look more if he so desired. No one could stop him.

Until her.

Until she had realized he was there. Maybe that was his fault, he mused as he trailed the slowly declining ship with lights that blinked on and off. Maybe he shouldn't have taunted her while he was in her mind.

That must be it. He would test it out with Maketes, who hated for

Fortis to be in his mind. Perhaps if he was talking to any other of his kind, then they would be able to tell that Fortis was there. Although, perhaps he should wait and try it with his son at first. The depthstriders didn't need other People of Water realizing they could kick them out of their heads. Such a risk was unnecessary, and rumors floated every which way when it came to his people.

Fins flaring, he slowed himself as he saw the ledge beneath the ship. It wasn't as far as he wanted her to sink. The pressure of the depths were more likely to get her to cave to him faster, but if this was what the sea wanted, then he would make do. At least here he could safely get her out of the ship without her exploding into a thousand little dusty pieces of blood.

Not that she was likely to get out of the ship after that entire situation. Maybe he would need to hurry that situation along. At least if he could make her think that she had a chance, he could convince her to come back out.

Because those memories weren't enough. The Originals were who he was after, and the sea had sent him to the perfect person after all. She not only knew about these abominations, but she worked for one directly. If there was anyone who could give him enough information about their kind to make a direct attack, it was her.

He'd been given a treasure trove of a woman and he needed to start treating her like that. He wasn't sure he would get another chance to question someone like her.

The ship hit the ledge with an echoing crunch. He could feel it. The plumes of dust surrounded it as the hull gave a massive groan. He flicked his tail, lunging forward in case the entire thing cracked.

He'd seen that happen before. A ship had sunk from Beta and the moment it hit the sea floor, it cracked in half. The achromos had floated out of it for days, their bodies stinking up the seas for weeks afterwards.

But her ship held. Instead, all he heard was more cursing and clanking from within. A secondary voice, one that sounded suspiciously like a droid, was speaking with his warrior woman.

Virago. He floated closer, making sure all of his lights were out so that he was impossible to see unless he was pressed right up against the glass. He was a fool for giving her a name. Someone like her didn't deserve one.

The lights attached to his fins flickered, as though his own body was calling him out on the lie. She deserved a name. She'd exited her safe ship and faced him with only a small amount of fear that he could taste in the water. Then, when she'd gotten away all on her own, she'd gotten back into her ship and fired at him.

A woman like that deserved a name more than just the one the achromos had given her.

Damn it, he wasn't supposed to respect the woman. He needed to peel her apart, and that was the only option he had.

He swore the ghost of his dead wife would appear any moment to smack him over the back of the head. He did her a dishonor by even indulging himself with this achromo who should have been thrown back to her world above.

Shaking his head, he distracted himself from the complicated thoughts by looking at what was happening within the ship. She held a wrench in her hand and was fiddling with something. Soon enough, she'd gotten one of the panels open and was ripping something silver out of it.

Wait, he'd seen one of those before. That was an emergency blanket. Was it cold in there?

He looked over the lights that were all blinking rapidly outside and within the ship. Yes, it must be cold. She was going to freeze to death if she didn't do something about it. The deep sea wasn't warm enough for her kind.

Interesting.

He floated closer, letting his lights blink on one by one. He could hear her talking, likely to the droid that controlled the ship. She'd wrapped the silver blanket around her body and was muttering something that he couldn't quite hear.

"Cold?" he asked.

Part of this worked into his plan. She deserved to see the wounds she had inflicted upon him. Perhaps that would make her believe that if she exited the ship again, she could continue to harm him. Over and over again, eventually she would wound him enough that he would die.

Or at least, that's what he hoped she would assume. Already the sea was closing the stab wound, although the laser wound would take longer to heal.

She whipped around, her wet hair tangling in front of her eyes at the movement. "Fuck off, undine."

"I don't think I will."

"You've trapped me down here. Come to gloat?"

"I'd rather make a deal." He swam past the front window, making sure his injured tail slid against the glass so she could see what her work had done. It wasn't much in the grand scheme of his body, but it was still an injury.

He heard her intake of breath at the sight. Good. Let her think she had bested him and that he was hurting. He barely even felt the tiny slit in his side.

Circling back around, he laid himself on top of the ship so she had to stare up at him. Only his torso and a small portion of his tail would be visible to her. Hopefully she would think he was less of a monster because of it. She couldn't see all the massive length of his tail or the lights that were flickering back on, one by one.

"I don't want to make a deal with you. Somehow, I have a feeling I would be on the losing end of that deal." She wrapped the silver blanket around her a little tighter. "Computer, how are we doing on that battery?"

"I have turned off all portions of the ship that are unnecessary. You have two hours and sixteen minutes to remove any food from storage before it freezes."

"Thank you," she hissed before stomping toward the back of the ship, which had no windows.

But he wanted to see what she was doing. This woman was clearly very capable, and she had a plan for surviving this deep in the ocean. What would she do? The curiosity in his chest burned, and it hadn't done that in a very long time. He couldn't just look into her future, either. She wasn't meeting his gaze any longer.

Frowning, he crawled over the top of her ship, dragging himself along it. Claws clinking as he moved, he waited until he could hear the faintest banging beneath him, and then started tapping back.

"What are you doing, virago?"

"Go away!" she shouted, but there was a slight strain to her voice.

No, that wouldn't do. He needed her alive and well, not possibly hurting herself. He had yet to see into her future because he'd been the fool so interested in her past. Grinding his teeth, he spat out, "Come where I can see you."

"You sank my ship into the bottom of the ocean. You don't get to tell me what to do." Another grunt, and this time he could hear her moving again.

Crawling the opposite direction, he moved back to the glass to see her place down a crate that was so massive, he was shocked she could pick it up. And then she disappeared back in the other direction.

It wasn't that big of a ship. He could stay where he was if she was going to keep coming back. And she did. Crate after crate, she placed on the main section of the ship and then tapped the side of it.

"Computer, close off the living quarters."

"Affirmative."

The living quarters? The ship was hardly large enough for that. But then she stepped out of the way and a massive wall sank down from the ceiling. It closed off the rest of the ship, leaving her with enough space to maybe walk five or six steps. And considering she'd filled the space with crates, she could barely move as it was.

"What did you do?" he asked.

"I made it so that I can survive a few more days," she muttered. He watched her take a deep breath before rummaging through the crate on top of the pile. "Leave."

"I have no plans to do that."

"Why are you hanging around?"

"I'm curious to see what you will do now. I want to know if you'll let yourself starve." She'd have to, after all. It wasn't like she could hunt fish from where she was in this tiny contraption.

"I'm changing. Unless you want to be disgusted by my human body, you should leave."

He was certain it would be disgusting. He'd seen bodies like hers before. Their two boney tails were the most disturbing things he'd seen. But of course, there was also the opportunity to enrage her. If only he could get her mad enough, she might look at him and allow him to peer into her future this time.

Baring his teeth, he took the opportunity that was presented. "I am certain you are ridiculously ugly. Just look at you now. I've never seen an achromo who looks like you before, and certainly that was by design. They did not care to make you pretty and functional."

"It was entirely by design." She carefully folded and placed the silver blanket in the pilot's seat at the front of the ship. And then she peeled that wetsuit off her arms. Though her back was to him, he could already see there was much he could talk about.

Not a single scale on her body protected her from the elements, and she was far too muscular. The shoulders she revealed were rounded, far too large to be attractive to her kind. After all, they were such foolhardy people that they liked their women to be smaller than they were. Ridiculous.

"My kind seek out larger woman than they are," he informed her. "We desire a woman with bite. A woman who can protect herself, with claws and sharp teeth, who would make even the greatest of sharks flee from them."

But then that wetsuit slipped down the impressive muscles of her back and he forgot what he was saying. By all the gods in the sea, this woman was strong. He could see all that power in the way her back moved as she shifted the material away from her skin. The hollow of her spine trailed down to a trim waist, even though her shoulders were broad and strong.

Dotted all along her back were scars. He could tell they were old, as many of them were pale. So many of them. Some in long lines, some deeper and ropey textured, suggesting that they were mortal wounds. Some of them were little, though. Tiny pinpricks that looked almost like lines of stitches, the same as his people would do. Hundreds of them, scattered all along her skin and circling to her ribs.

She didn't seem to care that he was looking. Instead, she just peeled the wetsuit off her body. Now she was nude. Standing there in the middle of the room with her back to him as she pulled dry clothing out of that top crate, completely unaware that she had rendered him mute.

He hated their legs. Always had. Achromo had two tails that were both useless at swimming, when they should have had at least one working tail. But this woman's legs were powerful. Thick thighs with defined muscles that flexed with every movement. Her glutes were...

Why was he staring so hard at her ass? There was no reason for it. He had never been someone who cared what an achromo's ass looked like. His people barely had them. Their muscular tails were clearly powerful, but glutes were something that just developed. And they certainly didn't look like that.

Was he calling it an ass even in his head? He'd been around their kind too long. He didn't need to know the nicknames for their anatomy. They were her gluteus maximus, they were…

The globes moved as she did, and then his eyes widened as she bent down to slide pants over her legs. Goddess, how was it even better when she bent down like that? The view was stunning, remarkable, and he was staring at an achromo like he'd never seen one before.

Growling, he forced himself backward over the ship so he wasn't looking at her anymore. At least the lack of sight would stop him from thinking all these terrible things.

Stupid depthstrider. He knew better than to get interested in a person. Already he could feel himself desiring more and more to look into her future, and it wasn't because he wanted to find out anything about the Originals. He wanted to find out more about her.

What made her the way she was? She was massive compared to the others of her kind, and he had seen that she was made, not born. But how? Why had that they done that? The achromos were a confusing lot at the best of times, so why had she served those who created her?

Perhaps he didn't need to look into her future. Perhaps he could get her to talk to him. All he had to do was steal that medicine, which clearly controlled her.

Peering back over the edge of the glass, he frowned as she sat down in the pilot's chair and opened a small box. Within it were a myriad of needles. She took one of them and then stuck it into a bottle full of some kind of fluid.

Was she going to give herself the drugs? It appeared she was, because she very quickly filled the needle in her hand and then plunged it into her arm. No reaction. Not a single one. She just stared into the darkness of the abyss as she did so, and then placed the needle back in the box once she was done.

That was what he needed to get, then. Whatever medicine she was giving herself, that was the barrier he had to tear down.

Chapter 11

Time passed strangely in the abyss. She would never have known how long she was down here without the computer informing her it had been eight days. Eight days of her rationing food, drugs, and time spent staring into the darkness that seemed to look back at her.

Alexia was stuck here. She knew that. The ship's AI would not let her override it and manually drive the ship home. She'd argued she could get them closer to Tau before the whole ship shut down. But the AI only said she didn't have high enough clearance to force it to do what she wanted.

Slumped against some crates where there was still meager amounts of food, Alexia told herself not to look into the sea. The lights above her head still blinked on and off. They were driving her crazy. Sometimes she asked the computer to turn them off entirely and just sat in the pitch black. She understood the reasoning for the warning lights. Many systems didn't have enough battery power to continue for much longer. The ship only reminded her that they were in dire circumstances.

Life support would last the longest. But some of the filtrations were already blowing. She only had a few more days under here without those batteries, and that meant she had to get her shit together.

Not to mention her food supply was dropping. She looked down at the tablet in her hand where she had been keeping count of everything. The food she'd been sent was enough to last a week. She'd spaced it out enough that she knew it would last double that. But even then, two weeks with that little food was going to weaken her.

And then what was she going to do?

Her eyes found the box of medicine that she'd left in the pilot's chair. The drugs were stronger than her usual dose, thanks to Doctor Barker realizing she needed a lot more than normal. But because she'd been rationing all of that as well, she'd been using the same amount of medicine as she always did.

She had too much time to think. Her mind wanted to wander back to memories that she knew were dangerous to linger on. Memories of how Harlow had never really appreciated her or how Harlow had gone through more guards than any other Original, and that's why Alexia had more generations than the others.

Her mind always rounded about to what Harlow had said when she'd seen Alexia hurt. She would not let Alexia die until she said she could. What did that mean?

Would she be forced to live an unnaturally long life just because Harlow wanted her around? She didn't want to do that. She wanted to die early, if she had a choice. This life wasn't the one she wanted to endure forever.

The swishing movement of a tail beyond the front windows of her ship caught her attention, and she was ashamed to admit it made her heart lurch. A week of silence with nothing but the sea to keep her company was making her mind do strange things.

With the right amount of medicine, she wouldn't have been having these thoughts at all. Back in training, they'd put her in isolation for months on end. They'd made sure that no one could ever torture information out of her, and even staying alone wouldn't make her think differently.

But now, she wanted someone to talk to. Even if it was the undine who thought nothing of tormenting her for hours on end. At least that was still a conversation, as fucked up as it was.

He appeared on the other side of the glass, lighting up bit by bit. He always did it in the same way, and she wondered if that was on purpose. First the lights on his massive fluke, and then they trailed up his entire body. Every time it was shocking how big he was, no matter how far he was from the glass. His arms would glow. Then finally, the fins around his face would glimmer with a strange purple that filled the darkness of the water.

He was like a god, illuminating out of nothing. But those were stupid thoughts she never would have had if he hadn't stuck her in this predicament.

He floated a little closer, that grin on his face already angering her. "Are you ready to give up yet?"

Of course, that's what he asked. He knew she had been in the darkness, enduring the abyss on her own for a week. This had been part of his plan. "Not yet, undine. I'll let you know when you've bested me."

He seemed frustrated by her response. His brow wrinkled, and the muscles on either side of his jaw jumped. "I'll make you a deal, virago."

She hated that he had a pet name for her, and something in her snapped. "Alexia," she hissed. "My name is Alexia."

All of his fins flared out around his face. In shock? She thought that's what it was. She'd been watching him just as much as he watched her. It was easier to read him now.

He hadn't expected her to tell him her name. And now he was wondering what to do.

She stood, taking the three steps to the pilot's chair and sitting down in it. "I told you my name, soldier. Usually this is when you'd tell me yours."

"I'm not telling you my name."

"Then we are not bargaining if you are unwilling to even make yourself seem like a real person. I could continue calling you fish man, but I don't think you like it when I call you that."

Again, those flared fins. She wasn't sure if he enjoyed it when she talked back to him, or at least, that's how she was taking that reaction. Alexia wanted to scream at him all the time, though, and at least barbs thrown like this wouldn't get her killed.

At any point, they both knew he could flip this ship right over the edge of the cliff she was wedged on. Alexia was well aware her situation was precarious.

He floated a little closer, his tail flicking with what she was certain was annoyance. "I am called Fortis."

"You're not like the other undine I've seen before. I mean, I've seen some that look like you, but not a lot. Why is that?"

If he had eyebrows, that expression would have arched one. "This is not a chance for you to ask me about my people. I have you trapped. You are the one who will answer my questions."

"I suppose that's fair. What if I answer a question and you answer one of mine?"

"No."

She blew out a frustrated breath and slumped back against the chair. "You are the worst person to bargain with. Are you sure you don't want to just give me an ultimatum and get this over with?"

"I don't understand your words."

"You could just tell me you're going to kill me unless I do what you want. Get it over with, considering we both know that I'm going to die a slow death in here, regardless." She waved her hands at the air around her. The hollow chamber wouldn't last much longer.

"I'm not going to do that." All of his lights flared a little hotter at her suggestion that he threaten to kill her.

Interesting. Clearly he didn't want her dead, which went against everything that she assumed. Here she had been believing this was all in retribution for taking the reborn back. But as she watched that discomfort rolling through him, she realized that this situation was entirely different.

She leaned closer to the glass again. "You want something from me."

He sighed as if she was exhausting. "You only figured that out now? I could have killed you long before this. Why else would I keep you alive?"

"What do you want?"

"I want to know everything about your city. About Tau. I want to know what the Originals are planning to do and how they control the other cities. I want you to betray your people in retribution for all the damage they have caused in this sea."

The speech was noble. But it was foolhardy. "No one can rise against the Originals. If I were to betray them, I would be signing my own death warrant."

He swam close enough to touch the glass. Those webbed fingers spread wide, claws scraping in front of her face so hard they left tiny marks. "You are already dead, are you not? You are at the bottom of the sea where no one will find your body."

"My beacon is still on," she replied. "They will find me, undine."

But it was a lie.

The beacon was one of the first things the AI had turned off. Apparently, it was protocol, but she knew that part of it was simply that the Originals hadn't wanted to know if she wasn't coming back. They liked to believe their soldiers got what needed to be done, done. And in reality, a single undine wasn't a threat they considered worthwhile to pursue.

They'd sent her out here on a suicide mission all for their own pride. And they didn't care if she came back.

He just smiled at her, that grin never shifting from his face.

"What?" she hissed. "Why are you looking at me like that?"

"Because I removed your beacon four days ago. It wasn't lighting up anymore, and I thought perhaps you did not need it."

Fuck.

Fuck, of course he had. She'd never gotten the better of this creature. Why did she think she could today? Baring her teeth in a grimace, she leaned forward and asked, "How do you know so much about human ships?"

They were nearly nose to nose now. Her breath fogged the glass in front of her, but she could still see him so clearly. Every freckle that dotted his face and the strange lines that marked down his cheeks like tracks of tears.

"You are not the first achromo I've spoken with," he replied. "But you are not as brave as them if you are unwilling to betray those who harm so many."

Thoughts flickered in her mind. All the people she'd killed. All the reborn bodies that floated down into the nothingness of the sea because an Original had a fucking rash that needed to be fixed. So much death and destruction.

But these were not normal thoughts. Because if they were true... No. She wouldn't even entertain it.

"If they are evil," she muttered, "Then I am just as evil as they are. Why are you expecting me to be better than them?"

"They ordered you to do everything you have done. They drugged you to keep you quiet. You are a product of what they wanted you to be. Nothing more, nothing less. A weapon is not to blame for a death, it is the person who wields the weapon." His eyes swirled with all those pretty colors. "Let me wield you, Alexia."

A shiver trailed down her spine. Heat flushed from her stomach, to her chest, to her cheeks and burned with sudden desire. She thought, if there was a man out there who could wield her, it was this creature who had come from the depths.

These were unnatural thoughts. Unnatural desires and yet, she wanted to encourage them. She wanted to get a little closer to this monster. She wanted to know what it would be like to touch skin so smooth. Or perhaps to see if his lights were warm.

Wrenching herself away from the window, she turned the pilot's chair to the shadows in the back of her ship. "What is your deal, then?"

There was more quiet from beyond the glass. She thought perhaps he had left.

But then he spoke in that deep, rumbling voice that was far too tempting. "Let me into your ship, virago. That is all my deal is. Let me into your ship and I will answer your questions about my kind."

"That's not enough."

"Then I will deliver you food."

She hissed out a long breath. "Why would you do that? You have no reason to care for me. You should let me die."

"I do not wish to see you die. Not like this. You are the same as me, are you not? A warrior who has fought their entire life, trained for decades. You deserve to die fighting. Not in a cage where someone else put you."

Why did that hurt so much to hear? Why was it that a monster understood her better than all the people she'd lived with for years?

Damn it. She could choose to just sit here and die. That wasn't all that difficult to do. All she had to do was refuse his deal, and then eat the rest of her meager food stores. There wasn't much left, but a couple of days were still a couple more days without giving into him.

Or.

She could choose to keep fighting another day.

Opening the hatch was so little. She didn't know why he wanted her to open it, but she could.

So she stood, against her better judgement, and hit the button. The small door on the floor slid open. It was maybe large enough for him to wedge himself into, but unlikely that he'd fit into the space. Still, if he wanted to, he could kill her now.

Maybe it was better if he did. He could end this all, and the complicated feelings she was having would be over. So when he appeared in the water just at the edge of her toes, she didn't react. Not even when she noticed how broad his features were with his hair smoothed back from his face or the droplets of water that ran down his neck to the hollows of his collarbone.

His arms reached up through the hole and then he leveraged himself upright. He was almost eye level with her, staring into her very soul as he just... remained there. Frozen. Looking into her gaze without all those dangerous swirling colors.

She swallowed hard. "Well?

"You are the warrior I thought you were," he murmured. A single claw stroked down the side of her face to the sharp edge of her jaw. "How interesting it is to see you not in the water. I cannot sense if you are frightened."

Should she be honest? No. She would not show weakness to this creature. "I am not afraid."

"Is that you speaking? Or is that the medicine you keep injecting into your arm?"

She didn't know. Maybe that should have been a warning sign in her mind that something was about to go terribly wrong. Why was he even asking?

But she was so mesmerized by the creature in front of her. All his pale lavender skin, the dark purple at the edges of his face and the tear tracks down his cheeks. She wanted to trace those marks with her fingers. She wanted to disappear for a few moments, and for some strange reason, it felt like he knew how to do that.

She was honest when she replied, "I don't know."

"I think perhaps it is time for us to find out."

He lunged forward before she could even process what that meant. Their chests bumped, and she tripped over one of the stupid crates behind her. As she toppled backward, he grabbed onto the box that contained all of her medication and disappeared into the water.

It all happened so fast. She stayed where she was, dumbfounded and sitting on top of three boxes while another had fallen over behind her and spilled all the clothing and weapon contents on the floor.

"That bastard," she muttered. "He just took all my drugs."

What was she going to do now?

Chapter 12

Fortis darted away from her ship. He knew there wasn't a weapon she could send after him, and if there was, it wasn't working. But he still wanted space to look at what he had stolen. This box of needles held some of the answers he had been searching for. He was certain of that.

The sea guided him. He barely even focused on swimming as a current caught him and thrust him away from the ship. Instead, he looked at the box in his hands. It wasn't even locked. He could open and close it easily, although he kept it closed enough that the needles didn't fly out. He wanted to know what this medicine was, and just how much of it she was dosing herself with.

If there was anyone who knew how to endure substances, it was a depthstrider. He had grown up in the sulphur fields, deep in the sea. He had spent years inhaling those fumes that would give him the ability to see into the future. It was partially why the achromo medications didn't work on him.

Although, his son had succumbed to them. The achromos in

Alpha didn't realize they had caught such a young one of his pod. They'd given Aulax far too much for one his age, and that had been enough to keep his boy still and quiet.

It still enraged him. Fortis had gone back to Alpha with the others and he had torn through every achromo who couldn't make it to the ships. The others knew their job was to save the people of Alpha. They didn't want to fill the ocean with red blood just to prove a point. But Fortis had wanted to.

They'd taken his son. They'd experimented on him, intended to kill him just to pull apart his pieces and find out what was inside. He needed some of them to die for that. The scientists had been far too easy to find, and he made good on his threat.

The ocean deposited him on a rocky outcropping a little way from her ship. He could still see the meager lights, but they were nothing but a twinkle some distance away. Nothing could find him here. Not her weapons, and certainly not her rescue party that wasn't coming for her.

He wrapped his tail over the lip of the rock, holding himself in place as he turned the box and opened it. Needles floated out, some of them empty, some half empty, but others were full. He let all but one float away into the sea. They would be buried in the depths with all the other refuse in the ocean.

The one he caught was so tiny in his hands, barely useful at all. He couldn't imagine that this amount would do much to her. Still, he depressed the end and let whatever was within the small plastic container float into the sea. With a deep breath, he inhaled some of it into his gills and instantly knew this was a potent dose of whatever drug it was.

Within an instant, he could feel it working. It flowed through his body and made him almost numb. The medication seeped emotion from his being until he could only think without emotion and without an ounce of the heart that had guided him his entire life. His connection to the sea was severed immediately. No wonder the soldiers from Tau were so good at what they did, other than the fools who had brought him into the city itself.

Usually, they were tactful. They took their time seeking their opponents, and they fought with precision. Like she did, in a sense. But he could sense her anger that sometimes got the better of her, and also a need to be the best at what she was doing.

This drug was stronger than it should need to be, he realized. If he was feeling even an ounce of it at his size, at five times her weight, if not significantly more than that, then this should have knocked her out completely. But it hadn't.

She'd been taking it a long time, he remembered. Since she was little more than a child. These people had been creating children, drugging them into oblivion, and then training them to be soldiers who did what they were told without asking why.

Horror made all of his fins flare wide. He hated that he was pitying this woman, but... Then he remembered the next part of his wife's prophecy.

"From the silver beast, you will find your salvation."

He wasn't certain if he'd done that so far. But there were more of Alexia's memories to tear into, more of her lived experiences to decipher. But first, he had to win her trust. Which meant he had to at least pretend to like her.

Sighing, he dropped the last needle into the abyss. Fortis didn't want to pretend to like her. He already respected her, and that was far too much emotion for one of her kind. He should just kill her and be done with it.

But some part of him didn't want her to die. Not unless she was fighting him to the bitter end.

The sea coiled around him, and he could feel the pressure of a vision sent by the goddess. It was the same one his wife had seen. The same one that he'd learned to live with. A cold metal table beneath his back. Dark eyes and dark hair leaning over him, and the numbing sensation of death curling around his body.

Was it her? Was she the one who was going to kill him?

Visions were rarely so clear, but as the sea gave him the same vision he'd seen throughout many years of his life, he realized... it was her. She was the one who was going to kill him, and he had finally reached the end of his story.

Breathing out, he allowed that knowledge to seep underneath his scales. Soon, he would die. She would be the one to wield whatever ended him, and with that came some sense of peace. He'd fought a long time to get here. And now? Now he knew the end was soon.

Flicking his tail, he darted through the water back to her ship. She would not kill him today, he didn't think. There was still time for him to gather all the information he needed. Still, he hoped one of his people would find them soon so he could share what he'd learned thus far. Just in case.

The ship's lights were dimmer than they were before. He'd placed her batteries not far from the wreckage, but somewhere she would never see they were hiding. At least he knew she wouldn't get to them without his interference. Her power levels didn't allow her to do much other than stay where he had put her.

But as he got closer this time, he could see the opening into her ship was still... open. She should have closed that when he left. But she didn't. What game was she playing here? Did she want him to come back inside after he'd stolen all the medicine that she clung so desperately to?

Frowning, he circled the bottom of her ship. Small metal poles attached to the ship gave him just enough room to get underneath it, but this all felt like a trap.

She was too good of a warrior to leave an opening without a plan.

Narrowing his gaze, he listened for any movement within the ship. Nothing. Not even the faintest scrape of a foot on the metal. Had she been foolish enough to leave? He wouldn't put it past her. She was determined to save herself, but she hadn't done it in the many days that she'd been down here so far. Why now?

Or she was waiting within, expecting him to come look for her. And she would bludgeon him to death in the small space.

Picking up a rock, he tossed it up into the ship and waited to see if anything would move. Some part of him hoped he had hit her, and yet, no sound. Nothing to give away that she was inside or not.

"She wouldn't be so stupid," he muttered, but he also wasn't certain that was right. She might be that stupid.

She was reckless about her own safety. That much he knew. He'd already seen her throw herself into the water after him.

Carefully, he poked his head through the hole and into the ship. He surveyed the room, but there wasn't a lot to see. The crates were all neatly stacked from where she had knocked them over. The chair was still turned the way he had left it after grabbing her medication. But it was darker, like she'd turned more of the lights off to preserve even more energy.

No woman, though.

"Alexia?" he called out, coming farther out of the water. Bracing his elbows on the floor, he peered around the crates as though she might be hiding there. No woman. Maybe she had left.

Then he made the mistake of going just a bit more into the room. With his hips braced on the floor, Fortis realized that he hadn't looked behind him. He didn't have a reason to because the door had been closed to preserve heat, and had remained closed for the past week.

Or so he thought.

The weight of her struck his back so hard he struck his chin on the floor. Then a sting erupted in his right hip fin. When he tried to turn, he realized it wasn't as easy as it should be. Looking down, he realized she'd fired a rivet through his fin and through the metal floor. That would puncture a leak in her ship. Didn't she realize that?

He was forcibly flipped, the nail tearing at his fin enough that he bared his teeth at her in anger. "That hurts," he snarled.

"Good." She placed the tip of the rivet gun against his other hip fin and fired again. "It was supposed to."

She straddled him now, and it was far too easy for him to grab onto her hips to hold her in place. This wasn't what a depthstrider would feel like in the slightest. He was used to cool scales meeting his palms and the slick glide of his fingers making it hard to grasp a female.

But this woman was warm. Even in the frigid room and how cold she'd been for days, she was warmer than him. Her hips were so soft to grab, the muscles in them flexing with power as she held him still with just her thighs. Her pants were a strange texture, and easy for him to grab onto for leverage. His claws sank a little deeper, likely digging into the soft skin beneath her clothing.

It made her stay in place, though. And that was where he wanted her. He wanted to stare up into that angry gaze as she thought she had him pinned. Fortis wanted to revel in her anger, as this was a creature who had never felt it so powerfully before.

She lifted the rivet gun and pressed it to his forehead. "You said you would bring me food. You didn't."

"You haven't given me a chance to hunt for you yet, virago."

"I don't want you to hunt for me. I want the food here, now. When you make a deal, it's usually with something you already have." She pressed the metal tip harder into his forehead. "I'm so fucking over being disappointed in you, undine."

"Fortis," he reminded her.

"I don't give a shit what your name is right now. I've decided I'm not going to die down here. You're going to bring me back to Tau, so I can get more of my medicine, and then everything will be put to rights."

Fortis grinned at her. This wasn't where he died. He already knew that. The metal beneath his back wasn't the right temperature, and there weren't any swinging white lights that made it hard to see her face. So he was certain she wouldn't kill him.

He pressed harder against the tip of the rivet gun. "If you want to kill me, then kill me."

She let out a shriek of rage that echoed in the room, but still pressed harder into his skin. Hard enough that he felt a little bead of dark blood drip down his forehead. "I can't kill you without killing myself!"

His hands squeezed her thighs harder, his large fingers somehow touching the softness of the same ass he'd been staring at only a little while ago. That... did something to him. Something he hadn't felt in a very long time.

She stared down at him with her features shaking in rage. But then she dropped the rivet gun onto the floor. It clanked next to his head, just missing the fins behind his jaw.

Rage shook through her. She lifted shaking hands and wrapped them around his throat, slowly. She gave him every opportunity in the world to fight back against her, but he didn't. He just let those long fingers glide through the gills there, just as she had done while he was on the table in Tau.

"I hate you," she said. "I hate what you have done to my life. What you have forced me to become."

"Good. Hold on to that hate. It'll keep you alive down here."

But then they both... froze. Staring at each other with heat blooming between them. It wasn't a heat he recognized. It seared through his scales, lifting them slightly like the bumps that rose on her arms.

Their eyes met. And he realized he didn't want to use the power inside of him to see into her future or past. Not right now. He was far too interested in the striations of darkness that split through her irises. They weren't entirely black, not like his eyes. Instead, she had fissures of deep, earthy brown and stunning gold that filtered throughout her vision.

He could stare at her eyes all day. What a strange thing to even think, but he did. There were secrets there he wanted to discover without the use of his power.

He wanted to hear her tell him all her secrets. And what a dangerous game that was to play.

Taking everything he could from her was the only choice he had. Yet, all he wanted to do was linger here with her legs spread over his scales and his hands on her ass. He envisioned rolling his tail up against her just to see what would happen. Perhaps she would gasp.

Maybe she would put that rivet gun to his head again. Both reactions were just as good.

But then he realized what he was thinking, and the heat in those thoughts was wrong. So wrong. This woman hated him, and he hated her. Their kinds fought until their last breaths.

And she was going to kill him.

What was he doing? Fortis palmed her thighs and tossed her off of him. She launched into the air, flying through the door that had previously been closed, and landed on her back. He could hear the "oof" of breath that escaped her lungs. Perhaps he'd been too rough.

He didn't have the time or patience to check on her. He ripped his fins free from the rivets, leaving the metal in the floor so they didn't cause a leak, and then hissed out an angry breath.

"I will return with your feast, virago." Sliding into the water, he waited until the last second to add, "But if you try that again, I will toss you out for the sharks."

Chapter 13

She was losing her mind down here. The darkness was getting to her without her medication, and the anxiety was getting worse with every moment that passed. Alexia had never felt fear before. She could freeze into a block on the floor and with her medicine, she wouldn't have cared. Her mind would have continued to figure a way out of the situation, of course, but that didn't mean she would have been afraid of death.

But she was now. She was terrified of it.

Every bit of her, every fiber of her being was frightened about what was going to happen. She'd run out of food before the reserve energy died. But there was no way of knowing that. Life support systems continued to fail. The filtration to her water was next to turn off, and after that, she was a goner.

Alexia never had the time or ability to think about death. When she had her medicine, she understood it was just a lights out situation. Some part of her that the drugs couldn't reach was a little relieved by that. She didn't want to think about an endless life with Harlow.

But now? Now she wanted to live. That lizard part of her brain had awoken, and all she wanted was to live for every moment that she could. She didn't want to be stuck down here in the deepest part of the ocean, wondering when an undine might return with a scrap of food.

"Computer?" she asked, pacing back and forth in the meager space as she could. "Update me on the life support, please."

"Life support was updated thirty minutes ago."

"Again."

"Life support is at three percent. All non functioning facilities of the ship have been turned off. Water storage will be depleted shortly. Oxygen levels will remain as the last function onboard."

"What's the next function after water that I will lose?"

"Heat."

Of course it would turn the heat off next. That's the only logical next step. But she'd likely freeze to death before she would notice that there was no more air. A quiet death awaited her then, but why did that make her heart race?

Staring out into the darkness didn't help. There wasn't anything she could look at in this ship that helped. At least the blinking lights had kept her adrenaline up. It was hard to think with those constant blinking lights. But those were all gone now. Every single one of them. All that remained were the few console lights that were still in front of the pilot's chair. The blue light turned everything dreary and, frankly, terrifying in this meager space.

She could lie down and just let it happen. She could situate herself on the floor and tell the computer to turn off all the heat and oxygen. The remaining battery could likely be used for a message to Tau, who would eventually want to recover this ship and understand what had happened to one of their trained guards. But a voice inside her screamed that she wasn't done fighting. Not yet, at least.

Grinding her teeth, she grabbed the rivet gun that was only meant for emergencies and started banging it on the outside of the ship. She'd learned a day ago that if she shouted for hours on end, he still wasn't very likely to hear her. But if she banged on the walls, then he could. The metal sound apparently traveled much faster than her own voice.

It didn't take long until there was a flash of a tail outside of the front window. He never took that long to show up. It was almost like he was as starved for attention as she was.

Or maybe he was just curious about her. He watched her, she'd realized. When she was sleeping, sometimes she'd open her eyes in the middle of the night and swear he was right outside of the window. She'd become some pet for him to stare at. No matter what time of day it was, he was likely somewhere beyond that glass. Watching her every movement.

Already her body was starting to atrophy. Alexia could feel her muscles aching to be used and now, two weeks later, they felt like they weren't even there. She'd tried to do pull ups and pushups for hours on end, but without food, she couldn't do them. She was forced, instead, to linger here. Staring into the darkness and hoping that an undine would show her mercy.

He didn't. But of course, his kind rarely did.

The fins flashing in front of her window were a warning that he'd chosen to lay himself on top of the ship. He liked to do that. She wondered if sometimes it was only because he wanted her to look up at him in some power play that was supposed to make her feel small. It worked, if that was his plan.

Looking up at the massive creature that seemed to float above her, she found it was harder to notice their differences. Yes, he was strange.

The long tail wrapped around almost the entirety of her ship, and he still had long claws that he loved to trail along the glass. But there were other parts of him that were familiar now.

The strange, toothy grin usually meant he was up to something. The way his fins flared when he was surprised. Sometimes she even noticed that his glowie bits would light up in a particular pattern if he was angry or hungry. She'd been observing him just as much as he'd been observing her.

"How far away were you this time?" she asked.

"Not far."

"You haven't brought me any food." She gestured at the ship with limp hands. "Hilariously, my batteries are running out every moment we wait. So you better try to get what you want from me sooner than later or I'm going to die in here."

His brows furrowed. "You're not going to die."

"I have three percent left." To drive her point home, she said, "Computer? How many more days will the ship be functional?"

There was a long pause before the tinny voice replied, "Two days and sixteen hours. First, water function will be turned off—"

"Thank you, computer." She interrupted before it would run through every situation and make her chest seize up like it did last time. Instead, she tried to be brave. Just like she'd trained her entire life to be.

Alexia crossed her arms over her chest, widened her stance, and stared up at him.

"What?" he asked, playing dumb. "You're giving me a look."

"You have less than two days to make up your mind."

"About what?"

"Whether you're going to kill me or not."

He tapped a long nail on the glass. She could see he was pretending to think. Usually, when he was actually considering her words, the lights on his forearms lit up. It was almost like he didn't realize they were doing it. And she'd used it to her advantage thus far. But this time, the lights remained dormant, so he had already thought about this.

His hair twisted in a stray current that toyed with the strands. While he thought he was tormenting her, she looked at the delicate way his gills flared open when he breathed. His body was remarkable this close. She had never seen anything like him before, and now that she had, Alexia wasn't sure how she would go back to a normal life.

Who else in Tau had experienced this? Sure, there were plenty of scientists who had experimented on an undine. There were a lot of them who had seen undine up close and far more personal. But none of them had talked to one. None of them had spent days on end watching their graceful movements and the way it seemed like the sea accepted them in a way that it never would humans.

Finally, he tapped his nail on the glass harder, getting her attention away from the gills on his ribs and instead on his face. "What do you have to offer me?"

"You were the one who wanted to make a deal for food in the first place!"

"What would you offer me for a battery?"

She froze. What did he mean a battery? He'd ripped them off her ship and then likely thrown them into the depths of the sea. He wasn't smart enough to... keep them.

He was.

He was smart enough to keep the damn things, and he had done exactly that. He'd just been waiting until the very last second to barter with her.

"You have the batteries?" she hissed.

"I have a battery to trade with you for information about your city." He shrugged. "And if you give me more information at a later time, I may have the second battery as well."

Rat. Bastard.

He was going to keep her on the threshold of death for however long he wanted her to. He was going to continue with this torture until she snapped.

She squeezed her eyes shut and tried to find that numb place the medicine brought her to. The place where her thoughts weren't running red and she could focus on what was being said in front of her, rather than wanting to get that rivet gun and empty it into the ceiling above her, flooding be damned.

"What information would you consider to be good enough to get the batteries back?" she ground out.

There was a lot she could tell him about Tau that wouldn't be dangerous for him to know. The layout of Tau was obviously off limits. She wasn't going to tell him—

"I need a way into the city that others of my people could use."

"Absolutely not." That was the last thing she was going to tell him. "You trapped me here, undine. That doesn't mean I am willing to sell out my entire city."

"You'd rather die?"

"I would."

He leaned closer until his face was nearly pressed against the glass. She could see the anger in his gaze boiling underneath the surface of those black eyes. "Your people stole my son. I thought he was dead. But he was just in Alpha with all their scientists, who were preparing to tear him apart so they could catalogue his insides. Did you know that? Just before Alpha was destroyed by my people, yours almost killed the only child I have."

She wanted to argue that Alpha wouldn't have done that without reason, but she had seen it herself. No one in the cities treated the undine like they were people. And that killed her, because she could so easily see that he was a person.

He had a family. A reason to fight.

Damn it, he had a son. She leaned against the wall of the ship and crossed her arms over her chest. "I'm sorry to hear that. It shouldn't have happened. No one deserves to lose a loved one like that, it's…"

There were no words. Not for something like this.

She could apologize a thousand times over, but it wasn't her who had done it. She hadn't made the choice to kidnap his son, nor had she been one of the scientists who had experimented on the boy. But she knew deeply what it was like to be a child in the hands of a scientist.

Her heart ached for Fortis's son. She looked down at the floor and whispered, "No one deserves that. And I hope that he has found some peace since."

As if those words would ever be enough. As if she could wipe away the wounds that his son had sustained.

"He's better than he was when I found him," Fortis replied. "Making friends with achromos as we speak. How he's doing that, I will never know. After what your people did to him, he should hate you."

Her head lifted at the words, shock allowing her to look him in the eyes again. "Making friends?"

He shook his head. "This is not information you get without betraying your own people, virago."

"My name is Alexia." And for some reason, it was important for her to hear him say it. It seemed like the nickname he had given her tore her away from that humanity she still clung to. The humanity that wasn't here in a tiny ship with nothing but the vast, endless sea to watch her.

"I don't like the name."

"You don't get to name me."

"It looks like I do." He paused for dramatic effect, then eyed her. "Virago."

Her nostrils flared with anger. Yet again, she wanted to punch a hole through the ship just so she could throttle him. But she didn't. She was good. She controlled the anger that was flaring so white hot in her stomach that it was almost impossible for her to focus on anything else. A medal was needed for the sheer force of will it took for her to grit out, "Alexia."

"Virago," he repeated. "You have no idea what an honor it is for me to gift you a name other than what the achromos have given you. Your name means nothing to me or my people. But virago has a purpose, a meaning."

"And yet, it is still not my name. You're purposefully trying to distract me from the fact that you refuse to do anything about my circumstances. I will not tell you anything about my city if you are unwilling to at least give me something to eat. Or batteries, so I don't freeze down here and die."

He scoffed. "I will not have this conversation with a woman who refuses to even get into the water with me. You are so terrified I will kill you that we cannot even have this conversation without you becoming so angry you cannot see straight."

"You want me in the water?"

"I think you're afraid to get in the water."

Her temper would get the better of her, it seemed. Because the moment he said that was the moment she lost all control over the situation. Her face burned with anger, something it had never done before. Her hands curled into fists, and she snapped.

"Fine!" she was shouting, and she didn't even know why. "You want me in the water that fucking bad?"

"You can't get in the water. You cling to the safety of your ship, because without the medicine they gave you, you are weak."

That stupid, sarcastic smile on his face hadn't budged. And she couldn't let him win.

Chapter 14

Fortis couldn't believe it had worked. Taunting her like that had thus far ended in nothing. He knew she had her emotions controlled and was capable in her abilities as a warrior. She would realize that he was being a flipper head to get a rise out of her.

But this time it worked. This time she stomped over to the exoskeleton, muttering under her breath the whole time. Every single movement was rushed and angry, a foolish choice in this situation. Surely she understood that acting in anger would always lead her in the wrong direction?

Apparently, he'd said something that had gotten her so angry she didn't care anymore.

Or the meds had worn off entirely, and she wasn't sure how to focus when her mind was new. He could work with that. He could use her weakness to his advantage in this hour of need. But something else bloomed in his chest and made his gills flatten against his skull.

He was taking advantage of her in this state. Peering into her memories without permission was different when they were fighting as equals. He didn't mind as much when she'd battled and lost to him. But this? This wasn't the woman he knew. Her frantic, angry movements weren't right for the cold-hearted warrior he had seen in Tau.

Had he broken her?

The exoskeleton wrapped around her and she struck the button to open the door into the water. Down she went, plunging into the sea like the stones were far away from her. They weren't. He heard the crunch of her feet hitting the ground and knew that must have been a bone jarring landing for her, especially with the exoskeleton's added weight. All throughout, he could hear her swearing.

She wasn't in control over anything right now; it seemed. Somehow, guilt made his fins flatten even further to his scales. He'd wanted to win her trust so that she would tell him everything. He hadn't wanted to do… this.

The sea ruffled through his hair as though it were pleased with him. "Is that the path you wanted?" he murmured as Alexia figured out how to get out from underneath her own ship. "You are a fickle beast. She is the one who will kill me, and yet you wish for me to pity her."

In a way, at least. He didn't quite pity this woman, but now he wanted to help her. She deserved his help.

He'd stolen everything that made her who she was. The scientists in Tau had developed her into being this perfect, unfeeling machine of a warrior who had done everything they wanted her to do. But in doing so, they had suppressed everything she was. She deserved to know what it was like to fight with rage burning in her heart, to know what it was like to choose to fight for something she believed in.

He'd been a warrior his entire life, but he'd also taught many people how to fight. This would be no different from that.

Floating around the edge of the ship, he peered down to see her ripping herself free. The bubble around her mouth fogged with all her exertion, but she didn't seem concerned.

No, her cheeks were still bright red with anger. Another easy giveaway to notice that she was not in control, nor would she likely be in control any time soon.

"You relied on medication to make you a good guard," he said. "How strange it is to see you lose your way."

"I have not lost my way, undine." She floated up in front of him, those boots giving her the boost she needed to look him in the eyes. "I can fight just as I did before. I am not any different than I once was."

"Are you not? I can smell your anger, Alexia."

A little cry of rage escaped her lips, and then she darted toward him. Those boots did make her swim a lot faster in the water, but even that wouldn't give her the advantage she thought it would over him. He flipped over onto his back and let her glide right past him. She could stop with the boots quickly, it seemed. But even that was a little clumsy.

"Who trained you?" he asked, curious about her people at this point. What he didn't expect was for her to rant and give away far more than she likely knew she did.

"I have spent half a lifetime training to keep the Originals safe," she hissed. "I have trained on land and in water. There is nothing and no one I do not know how to fight. I have torn people limb from limb. I have killed hundreds of people. I know death well, undine."

"Hundreds?" He flicked his tail to move out of her way again, slowly gliding backwards so she had to follow him out into the abyss. "Where did Tau even find hundreds of people for you to kill?"

"You'd be surprised how many humans are down here, and how many Tau deems unworthy of the cause." She paused in the water, her eyes widening even as she said the words. "I shouldn't have told you that."

"No, you shouldn't have. But it is interesting to me that Tau has a cause. Which means they are training you for something other than just keeping your Originals alive." When she reacted a little to that, he narrowed his eyes. "Or they are training you to keep only your Original alive, but there are others who will make it difficult for that to happen. Is that what is being planned?"

"You see too much, undine."

"What would make that even occur? There won't be a war between the achromos. Tau already makes sure they control every single city. We've discovered your outposts within each one, and it was far too easy to find it within the ruins of Alpha. So it is not your own people you expect to fight."

She raced for him, but he already knew why she was doing that. A distraction. He was getting too close.

Annoyed, he grabbed the bony arm of her exoskeleton and tore it off the suit as she passed. It was so easy to do. The metal was thin and brittle, so it shattered with an audible pop before he tossed the metallic bone into the abyss.

She froze where she was, staring down at her arm that was now exposed to the frigid sea. With only one useful hand now, the exoskeleton was significantly less helpful.

He grinned. "So it's my people. Tau is planning to attack the undines."

She hissed out an angry noise. "It has always been known that this sea is yours. Even before we came down here, the Originals were aware there was another species in the water. They weren't sure how you would react to so many new faces in what had historically always been yours."

"We didn't like it."

"No, you didn't." She shook out her still working arm and then curled the fingers. "And because of that, and two hundred years of fighting between our kinds, the Originals have had enough."

He wasn't all that surprised. The attacks on his people had been getting worse recently. He had seen the way ships were following the People of Water in the shallows. Even Beta, a city they should have had under their thumb at this point, was reacting a bit differently when his people swam by. Of course, there were only three cities still standing, and one of them was a prison.

There would be no allies amongst the achromos, other than those who were already helping them. If it came to a true battle, they would be far too easy to wipe out of existence.

"Damn it," he hissed. Then he lunged for her.

Grabbing her other arm, he tore the metal skeleton off of her, leaving her only in just those useful boots and the spine piece. She barked out a swear and then swiped at him. At least this time, she actually connected. Her fist hit hard enough to leave a bruise, something he was rather surprised about. Even without the skeleton, she'd hit him hard.

But he wasn't interested in continuing this fight with her now. She'd given him so much information. So much more than what he had ever expected he would get this soon.

On her next angry pass, he grabbed her by the back of the skeleton's suit. There were a lot of cords and metallic pieces in his grasp now, so it was so very easy to just snap it. Her entire body jerked with the movement, but then he pulled the headpiece off and most of the spine with it. With one hand, he held her shirt, and the other, he dangled the rest of her last weapon in the water beside her. It left her bare, and the booted pieces of the suit entirely without power.

The silence that came after his rather violent yank should have warned him. But he dropped the rest of the pieces into the sea as well, still holding onto her by the front of her shirt.

Fortis waited until she looked at him. That glare stirred something inside of him, and he hated how he responded to just that look. Because he hated her. Every bit of her and no matter what she did to reveal truth after truth, he would always hate her.

Grabbing her by the neck, he let her dangle in the darkness that surrounded them. With a flick of his tail, he brought them farther out into the sea. Soon, the only light that surrounded them came from his body.

She grabbed onto his wrists, but she wasn't struggling now. Almost as though she knew she had been bested, and easily at that.

"You will help us," he told her. "You will betray all that you are afraid to betray, and you will be better for it. If you agree to work with us, I will train you myself. No People of Water or achromo could fight you without losing. But to do all of that, you must trust me, virago."

Her hands squeezed his wrists even tighter. "I will never trust you or your kind."

He dropped her. It was that easy. He just released his hand on her neck and let the weight of her boots and her body drag her into the depths. It wasn't a slow decline, even as she tried to swim against the currents, but she wasn't strong enough for that. She fought hard, with her arms pumping and her legs working, but soon enough, even she grew tired.

She hadn't eaten. Hadn't drunk enough water. No one was endlessly powerful. Not even him.

At the last moment, before the currents swept her away, he reached out and grabbed her hand. They remained frozen like that, her falling into the waters below and him, a glowing beacon reaching out to be her salvation.

She stared up at him with those dark eyes, the same color as the abyss beneath her. How many times had he stared into that darkness? How many times had he sworn there were answers for him in those dark waters?

Swallowing hard, he reminded himself that she was not someone who was from the sea. She was not the person he was giving her credit to be. Even though he almost wanted her to be a gift from the abyss.

"Trust me," he said, his voice rough with emotion. "You have no other choice, Alexia. You will have to trust me or I will let you go."

He could see the struggle in her. Some part of her wanted this all to be over with. Perhaps it was the easier choice to have him let her sink into the abyss. At some point, the pressure would kill her. It wouldn't be slow. It would be an instantaneous death that she would not feel, and then the sea would make use of all her parts.

He wouldn't think less of her, but he would be disappointed. Even the sea seemed to pause around them, the currents halting as they waited to hear what she would choose to do.

She looked up at him and didn't move for a bit. She just let him hold her there, dangling over what was certain death until finally she gave him a nod.

"I don't know how to trust you," she said. "But I can promise I will try to learn how to do so."

"That's good enough for me. After all, you told me a secret about your city that will be very useful soon enough."

He drew her up by the arm until he could grab onto her waist. She was such a large achromo and still, her waist felt tiny as he held onto her and swam back to her ship. It was… odd to notice such a thing. He usually didn't care at all about the bodies of other people.

She was very still in his arms. So still that he worried she might have given up. Perhaps she regretted not choosing death.

He swam with her all the way to the bottom of her ship and then jettisoned her up into the opening. But when he noticed she struggled to even get herself into the ship, he realized the problem.

"Are you cold, virago?" he asked.

Her chattering teeth should have been the first warning sign. He was such a fool. His people didn't worry about icy waters, but of course, she was freezing. And here he had been, practically swishing her through the coldest part of the ocean.

Planting a hand on her ass, he shoved her into the ship. She rolled on the floor, but he could hear her trying to get onto her hands and knees. It was a start. At least she was still trying to keep herself alive.

But he also knew there was no heat in this room. The ship didn't have the power to have the heat on any longer, and therefore, she would just freeze to death.

Sighing, he turned to where he had placed the battery packs. One of them wouldn't hurt. Sure, it was one of his few bargaining chips to convince her that maybe, just maybe, she should help him. But if he could keep her alive longer, perhaps that would also win her trust.

This woman held all the secrets of Tau in her mind. And he'd already decided she was much more useful if he could talk to her about what she knew, rather than just stealing it himself and pretending to understand what he had seen.

He got one of the batteries and attached it to the top of the ship. The achromos should make these more difficult to work with if they didn't want his people to figure out how to use them. It was literally attached to the top with just a few seals, and then he could see the connection light up.

It felt wrong for some reason to tease her even more now. She'd already struggled long enough in his presence. Soon enough, the computer would turn the heat back on and then, perhaps, he would return.

For now, though, he would let her mourn the loss of everything she knew about herself in peace.

Chapter 15

The heat turned on not long after he left. Alexia knew she had him to thank for that, but it was hard to give him any credit after what had happened. She laid there on the floor, staring up at the ceiling as the lights blinked on one by one. Some of them were emergency buttons and switches that she was likely supposed to pay attention to. Others were just the lights that illuminated the ship.

He'd given her the battery. After all of that, after the argument and the frustration and the absolute embarrassment of what she had done. He'd given her the battery.

Somehow, that made all of this a little harder to swallow.

Never in her life had she lost her temper like that. Not even when she was a child and frustrated with doctors who were sticking her with endless needles. She'd cried when she was that little. A lot. And often. There were a lot of tears of frustration and sadness and anger. But she'd never flown off the handle and attacked someone without even thinking about why she was doing it or what was the correct way to do so.

All of that and more were reasons he should have just let her die. There was no reason, in the slightest, for her to have done what she did. To argue with him for foolhardy reasons like that? It was stupid. It was reckless. It wasn't like her.

But lying on the floor, staring up at the lights and shivering until her jaw ached... She did feel better. There was no logic in that. Fortis hadn't been kind. He had no idea that while they were arguing, she'd been crying. Every bit of her tears had been swallowed up by the salt of the sea. But she'd been nearly sobbing with effort as she tried to hit him, to do anything that would prove she was still the same woman.

Time had passed long enough to make her realize, without a doubt, she had made a mistake in choosing this path. She should have stayed comfortable in Tau. Nothing had to change if she'd done that. Nothing at all. Her entire life would have been numb and void all of the potential mistakes that she was making right now.

"Computer?" she asked, knowing that this would be recorded, but also knowing that Tau was likely not coming after her. "What would happen if I betrayed Tau?"

"Please state your designation and access level."

"Alexia, personal guard to Original Harlow. Access level nine."

There was a long pause as the computer figured out how to answer her. "Immediate termination if information about Tau was leaked to any source. DNA harvested for understanding what flaw caused the issue."

"Right," she muttered, blowing out a long breath. "That makes sense."

Of course they would harvest her, just like they did all the time. That was the whole point of Tau.

Rolling, she crawled toward the crates and pulled out the last pieces of dry clothing she had. The anger that had made her rush out of the damned ship like an idiot without even a wetsuit on was the greatest folly of her life. Now her exoskeleton was broken, and all she had were the metal remains of boots that wouldn't work without a power source.

A sob broke through the silence. She tried to stifle it, but all that did was shove the emotion down into her chest, which ached so fiercely even a good brisk rub didn't take care of it.

Alexia struggled to take the boots off. Her fingers were purple, and they didn't work as well as they should. But the heat was blasting in the room, trying to warm up freezing metal. Biting her lips, she finally yanked the boots off, then her shoes, and then the rest of the sodden clothing.

The whole process took far longer than it should have. And even that was frustrating. She wanted to scream, but all she could manage were little sobs that kept embarrassing her. The fucking ridiculousness of this situation! She was a personal guard to one of the Originals. She needed to get her shit together because she was not meant to be huddled on the floor, naked, clinging to clothing she couldn't put on because she was so fucking cold. Alexia was not weak.

She was, though. She was so fucking weak and tired and beyond exhausted. All she wanted was someone to trust, just like he kept telling her she had to do with him.

But was it trusting someone if she was ordered to do it? Hadn't that been her entire life so far?

Eventually, she dragged her new clothes on and wrapped herself in one of the emergency blankets. It would keep her a little warmer than she was right now, at least. And that was a start.

She headed over to the pilot's chair and sat down in it. Drawing her knees up beneath the blanket, she hugged them tight to her chest. Staring out into the water still felt hard to do. Like there was something wrong with her for enjoying seeing the nothingness that was out there. She hated and loved the sight at the same time. But maybe that was part of what life was for her now. Love and hate.

A fin appeared. He always gave her at least a little warning that he was here. She tried her best to stay still in case the anger came back. But her mind raced. Why was he back? Hadn't he said enough?

Fortis floated up from below the ship, likely anchored beneath it because she couldn't see much of his tail. "You should be resting."

"I don't know what time it is. This ship is not equipped with a day and night cycle, so there's no way for me to know when I should rest." She cleared her throat, wrapping her arms a little tighter around her legs. "Besides, I have nightmares."

Every single night. She had nightmares every time she closed her eyes and tried to rest while she was in this place. All she could think about was what would happen if she stared into the abyss too long. Her mind played dreams of a giant creature rising out of the depths and swallowing her ship whole. Sometimes, though, she dreamt of Tau and what Harlow would say when she returned.

Her nightmares turned what had been a relatively safe home into a waking serpent's nest. Once she got back, they would decommission her. They'd stick her full of needles and pull her brain apart while she was still awake. All the shocking things she'd seen them do to someone else were suddenly a possibility for herself.

Fortis rolled, looking like he was lying down outside of the window. That gave her his profile, so at least he wasn't looking at her. "I have nightmares too."

"I'm not turning this into a pissing contest with you."

"A what?" He glanced over at her with clear disgust on his face. "I'm not doing that with you, either."

"It's a figure of speech. I mean, I'm not going to say your nightmares are worse or better than mine."

"I wouldn't ask you to. Nightmares are nightmares. I'm not trying to be..." He sighed, and bubbles erupted from his gills in a giant wave that obscured his face from her sight. "I'm trying to be nice."

"You're not very good at it."

"I think you're not very good at accepting someone is trying to make amends when they hurt you." Fortis shook his head and then rolled his eyes as though he couldn't quite stand her. "I'm trying here. Tell me about your nightmares."

"I don't want to talk about them."

Again, more bubbles of frustration. "Then why bring it up?"

Why indeed? Some part of her must want to seek comfort, even from this horrible man who had done so much to frustrate her. Their relationship thus far had been one of hatred and pain, but... Well, maybe she could change that.

Alexia bit her lips, rolling them together for a few moments before relenting. "I don't know how you looked into my memories like you did, but I think it was pretty obvious that I wasn't born. I was made."

"That much I gathered."

"In Tau, there are no babies. No one is birthing new humans, and no one is creating families. There are the Originals and there is..." She lifted her hands in a helpless gesture. "Everyone else."

He turned his face so he could look at her. Already she could see the colors swirling in them, as though he wanted to peer through her mind so that he could live what she had lived.

"Don't do that," she whispered. "If I don't want to tell you, then I shouldn't be made to do so. Don't take this choice away from me."

Their gazes held for a few moments longer, but then he looked away. Immediately she could feel the pressure lifting, like a hand had been taken off the back of her neck.

Slumping back in the chair in relief, she took a few deep breaths before continuing. "I was created to guard the Originals. Every part of me, every strand of my DNA, makes me good at that. It's all I've ever known. They made me in a test tube without a single hand of kindness. They flooded my brain with everything I was supposed to be from day one. And then when I was not exactly as they wished for me to be, they changed me with medication that made me better."

"I can see how that would be difficult."

"I am not the first Alexia," she admitted. It was hard to even say the words, but that it was the truth. "I'm the seventh. The first six were deemed so unworthy of the job that they were decommissioned. My model has always been... willful."

That's what they told her, at least. The previous Alexias were too opinionated, and that always got them in trouble. They'd been decommissioned quickly, but then some scientist figured out what had made them so willful and they changed that genetic strand. This version of her was much more biddable.

"My genetics were taken from the very first guard that Harlow had over two hundred years ago. Apparently, she was much smaller than me, but capable of learning how to fight and protect Harlow. That's all I was created for and now..."

There wasn't any reason for her to be spewing all of this to him. Maybe she was just feeling raw. Every part of this experience had stripped away who she was. Her medication was gone. Her safety was removed. Even the knowledge that she would have regular food was gone. She was adrift, just like he wanted her to be.

"And now?" he prodded, making her talk more about this awful sensation in her chest. "How do you feel now that you are freed from all that?"

"Broken," she whispered. "If they are as bad as you claim—and I am certain they are—then I took part in that. I helped them create monsters like me and I helped them hurt people."

Memories flooded forward, pressing against her mind so fast she hardly had time to even think about them all. Holding down a young boy so they could extract DNA from him and then send him out into the abyss. Hundreds of reborns, all of them destroyed because of stupid things like a rash or a cold that would have gone away on its own in mere days. Training children to fight when they should have just been held.

Because that's all she had ever wanted when she was their age. She'd just wanted someone to hold her.

When had she closed her eyes? By doing so, she'd locked herself inside her own mind with those memories. The moment she opened them again, she looked into dark eyes that saw straight through her.

"You were protecting someone," Fortis finally said. "You were doing what you thought was right. What they told you was right."

"No one in Tau is doing anything because it is right," she whispered. "Not a single person in that place. They do it because they want to do it. The longer I am away from that place, the more I see that kindness offered to even the Originals is often veiled. Everyone wants something from everyone else. I don't know how to be the person you're asking me to be. It is nearly impossible for me to be kind. All I know is how to protect the wicked."

"Protecting anyone is kind, even if they are not good people. You saw what others could not. Even if that was the merest glimmer of light in the darkness." He shrugged. "I'm sure even Harlow has good moments."

A startled laugh erupted from her lips. "Good moments? Harlow has nothing like that. The woman is a menace."

"Is that so?"

"She's a spoiled brat. Everything is about her, but it's always about the Originals. The mere idea of the world existing without her in it is just foolish to imagine. She hates everyone else and is so jealous when someone gets anything that she does not have. She'd rather murder than allow another person to have any gift or item that she couldn't get her hands on."

Now that she had opened the tap on what she thought about Harlow, she couldn't stop spewing all the hateful words. "She once had me murder a scientist because he said blonde hair was his favorite. Just because she didn't like it that his favorite color wasn't the same color as her hair. She told me to snap his neck and then waited while I did it. That's who Harlow is. A petty, jealous child who never had to grow up and likely never will."

Taking a deep breath, she opened and closed her fists. "It feels better to say that, though. I've thought it for years, but who am I to say anything about an Original? They created all of this."

"Did they?" Fortis asked, rolling upright once more. "Or did other people create it for them after they paid them with more useless achromo trash?"

Fuck. He was right. The Originals weren't gods. They were barely even people these days. They were just spoiled children with so much money and notoriety that no one knew how to tell them no.

Blowing out a breath, she shook her head. "Thoughts like that are dangerous."

He hummed low under his breath, starting to float backward. "Yes, they are. But you aren't in Tau anymore, and if you want to think like that, you can."

Fortis left with those parting words and it was so hard for her to argue. Yes, they were thoughts she could have now. Thoughts that were her own and no one else had put them in her head but herself.

So why was it so hard to believe them?

Chapter 16

There was honor in her, and Fortis hated that he saw it. The more he spoke with her, the more certain he was that this was a dangerous current to swim. She was an unusual specimen of an achromo. He hesitated to even call her one.

Though she shared the same looks and the same body that many of their kind had, she was so different that it didn't seem right to lump her in with all those monstrous creatures. Alexia's experiences made her singularly different. She struggled with the choices she made, just as he did, and that was something he could appreciate.

Because she had done terrible things. Just the few glimpses he'd gotten and the few things that she'd told him, her life had been filled with brutality. They were memories that would haunt her for the rest of her life, as they should.

But he had the same kind of memories. A city that fell because of his intervention, so many deaths that he had prophesized and there was nothing he could do to stop them. Countless memories that had made him question if he was a good person or not. He understood the struggle she was going through and it angered him that he could identify with someone of her species.

Fortis floated through the sea, sinking deeper and deeper into the depths where he could find some peace.

The sulfur fields were mainly used by his people. Not the rest of the People of Water, but specifically the depthstriders who could glide through the noxious waters without passing out. Of course, there were some who lingered deep within the yellow fields in the hopes that they could disappear from the world for a while. He'd even encouraged Daios to be here for a while as he struggled with his own choices.

Anger could not exist while a person was floating through the sickly smell. Nothing could exist. It was a place where the sea spoke directly to the soul, and no other thought could survive.

He needed that.

Desperately.

Because he was softening toward an achromo that he could not leave alone. He hated their species. Always had.

So why, when he closed his eyes, did he feel the curves of her hips in his palms? Why could he see the perfect image of her when she'd taken her clothing off and he had stared at her? He had no permission to do so. And why... why did he care that she had promised to try to trust him?

This was wrong. He needed to get his mind back on the mission. He didn't need to think about the way she'd been curled up in that chair, strangely small when he'd always thought of her as a towering pillar of strength. But she'd been so little outlined by blue light, even with her muscular arms wrapped around her legs. That moment of weakness had nearly destroyed him.

He hated to see her like that. Hated to acknowledge that he had anything to do with it.

So he sought out his goddess. He had to know that he was doing the right thing, and that he wasn't making the same mistake so many of his friends had already.

The first hint of sulfur tickled his nose, and he knew he had found a hidden vent. There were more frequented fields on the sea floor, many of them were extremely large. They were easy to find with the lava flowing underneath them. This one appeared to have not been disturbed for many years. It was only him and the sea.

The yellow coils spread up into the water, sending sparkling motes that floated all around him like chips of gold. He breathed in deeply through his gills, allowing the particles to slide into his bloodstream and calm his mind.

He sank deeper, close enough to the lava vents that he could feel the heat against his body, and then hovered there. Frozen in the sea, with all of his gills spread as wide as he could, his fins holding him in place, and his tail limp in relaxation.

Here he was home. Here, he was held in the warm grasp of the sea and he could release all his tension and worries.

"Show me," he whispered. "Show me what you wish for me to see."

It wasn't usually that easy. The sea was a fickle mother and impossible to control. She did not like to tell anyone anything. Not when she could teach them a lesson instead of speaking it.

He blinked his eyes open, staring through the sparkling gold as it appeared a fin flickered in the water. At first, he almost yelled at the new depthstrider to leave him in peace. He'd found this place in the hopes that he could commune with the sea goddess without being interrupted by another of his kind, but he also realized that no depthstrider owned any of the sulfur fields.

It was, however, surprising that one of his kind would be this close to Tau. Usually his people avoided this area of the ocean. It was a desolate place with very little food and even fewer resources. There was no reason for anyone to come here.

But then he blinked, and the depthstrider came closer. She was large and therefore must be female. Easily the same size as him. Her tail stretched on forever, it seemed. She dragged it behind her, as though the weight of it was too heavy for her. Not unusual in females of that size, but he wanted to shout and warn her that the vents here were hotter than most.

Until she came close enough that he could see her coloring.

White, he realized. White as the belly of a whale or the pale beasts that hunted in the depths. White as a pearl, and he knew now that this wasn't just any depthstrider who had found him.

"Wife," he whispered, the word broken as it escaped his lips. "Why have you come?"

The ghost of his dear one floated ever closer. And he looked his fill.

Fortis was a starving man as he looked her over. This woman who had captured his heart from the first moment he had seen her. Now, she was right before him again, and never had her spirit visited him. Not once. Not even when he had seen so many people who had passed on. His wife's soul had never found him in the sea.

She was still so beautiful. Those fins around her face were small, delicate even as they accentuated how pronounced her cheekbones were and the harsh the angles of her jaw. Tiny speckles dotted around her cheeks and spread down to her chest where there were starburst lines that spread all around her ribs.

"You are just as beautiful as I remember," he croaked, remaining still as though a single movement might banish her from his sight.

"You never found me beautiful," she replied, her voice carried to him by the currents. "You found me sturdy, strong, and powerful. These are the things that you loved about me, Fortis."

Her words broke him. His wife. His beautiful, wonderful wife.

"Astrum. You know I thought more of you than that." He reached out his hands, feeling his fingers pass right through the image of her. How he would have given anything to touch her. "I miss you," he whispered.

"No, you don't."

"How could you say that? Every day I swim in your wake, hurtling toward you in the hopes that soon enough, I will join you in the afterlife."

"Oh, my sweet love. I don't want you to hurtle towards me. What a terrible end to our story that would be." Astrum swam around him, her tail so long that it was able to wrap around him in a giant circle twice before she stopped with him tangled up in her spirit. "You remain here for a reason, Fortis."

"I remember your prophecy."

"You remember your death. You have been chasing the end for all these years, and have forgotten to live." Her hand reached for him, just barely touching his cheek, and he swore he could still feel her cool touch. "I released you all those years ago, my love."

"There is no life without you." Even to his ears, the words sounded broken. "I raised our son as you would have wished. Aulax is capable and wise. He is one of the few depthstriders who sees through a person and into the soul deep within. He is more than ready to be here alone without me."

Astrum's shoulders curved in. "My dear. I never wanted either of you to suffer for the lack of me."

"How could we not? You were the light in our life. The guiding beacon that brought us to safety and happiness. Without you..." He looked down at his empty palms and clenched his fists as though he could grasp even the slightest bit of what they once were. "There is nothing without you, my love."

"You have spent all these years since my death searching for something in the sea that would bring you peace." Astrum laid her cold hands over his chest and he swore he could actually feel her touch. "But what you seek is in here, Fortis. The sea has been reminding you of that for years on end and you have willfully ignored her message."

"I ignore nothing. Of all depthstriders, I am the closest to the sea and all her messages. I listen. I learn. I seek the answers that no others will." He looked up at her helplessly. "What have I missed?"

"Everything," she replied. And then her form started to fade. "You have missed everything from the prophecy, from what the sea wants, even what I want, dear husband."

"What do you want, then?"

The desperation in his voice was aching. He didn't want her to go. Not yet. Not when he had just been filling his soul with the sight of her and every memory that had brought him so much peace.

But she was leaving already. Even he knew that the spirits of the sea weren't allowed to stay for very long. Not when there was so much for them to tend to. They were the guardians of the ocean, the ones who guided all the living through currents and away from danger. She was more important now than she had even been when she was alive.

A small smile crossed her face, and he remembered this was when he had found her the loveliest. "I wanted you to live, Fortis. I fear you've been half dead since I left, just waiting for when you could let go."

"Yes," he whispered reverently. "That is exactly what I have been doing. I wanted to honor your memory."

"Then live, husband. Live until the end of my prophecy and you will understand why it is so important."

He reached for her, his claws disappearing through the remaining image of her tail, but he wanted one last moment. One last second to hold her in his arms and tell her all the good that had happened since she'd left. Every proud moment he'd had as a father. When Aulax had killed his first fish and looked so proud of himself holding the long dead creature. He wanted to tell her about the first time their son had swum on his own, and how graceful he'd been for one so young. How their boy had been one of the few to survive the achromos and their torture.

There was so much for him to be proud of, and his wife deserved to know what an incredible being their son had become.

But she was gone, and there was only him now. Lingering in the sulfur vents where there were few answers and only more questions.

He sighed, readying himself to leave. Shaking out his fluke, he tried to understand why the sea had sent his wife. Was it because the sea wanted him to remember why he was doing what he was doing? He remembered. His family and his... friends needed him.

A low, echoing chuckle rocked through the vents. Quite literally through the vents. It was like the depths of the sea rumbled with the sound, echoing with that ancient voice who had called him deep into the abyss not all that long ago.

"You aren't very good at listening," that god-like voice boomed. The vents bubbled with the force of it. Giant lava bubbles erupted from within the vents, disturbing the sulfur and sending more of it cascading out toward him until he expelled it all from his gills because it was too much, even for a depthstrider.

Was he hallucinating? The sea floor could not speak.

"I listen well," he said. "I hear you."

"As you must. But you speak with the dead and you do not listen. What an interesting depthstrider you are, Fortis. I am greatly enjoying watching your journey."

The spines along his back and arms rose. "Who are you?"

"I did not tell you then, and I will not tell you now."

"Why are you hiding yourself? You were in that tomb, were you not?"

"I am everywhere and nowhere. I am part of the sea and part of the land. I am beyond your understanding."

Who was this voice? Fortis had spoken with the ancients before, but this was different. This creature did not sound the same as those lingering giants in the depths.

His guts twisted with fear. He hadn't felt like this in very many years. Fear wasn't something a depthstrider often felt in the sea, and even when he had discovered his son had been captured by those in Alpha, all he had felt was rage. It was rare for Fortis to lose control like this.

But the creature who now spoke to him was unlike anything he had met before.

"Oh Fortis," the voice chuckled. A few lava bubbles popped with the laugh, spraying out sizzling molten pieces into the sea. "You think too much. I can feel those thoughts rumbling in your head. I'm not going to ask you to do much."

"What are you going to ask me to do?"

"That thick skull of yours is impeding my plan. I need you to take the woman out of her ship. Look through her mind again. There has to be some information that will get you and your people inside of Tau."

"I do not wish to force her." He hated that it was the truth. Even saying the words felt like a betrayal to his wife, who had just been right in front of him. "If she has information to share with me, then I would have her tell me through her own volition."

It was the least he could do. After everything Alexia had shared, and after everything he had seen himself, he didn't want to force her. Not when there was still a chance she could make the right choice.

A low hum echoed through the water, and the lava stilled. "You believe you can win her over."

"I do."

"You believe she will choose to help us."

He hesitated only a brief moment before sighing, "I do."

Another low hum. "If that is so, then you need to do it faster than you are now. She said she has never seen kindness, Fortis. Show her kindness."

What a terrible idea. She was a warrior woman, a creature who responded only to violence and fighting. She wouldn't care if he was kind. But the more he thought about it, the more he thought perhaps this strange, unknown voice was right. Maybe Alexia did need to see a different side of him.

Chapter 17

What a fool Fortis was for even believing a voice under the sea that had absolutely no reason to help him. He didn't even know who the suspicious voice was, but that was a fear for another day. Right now, he had a plan.

A plan that would help her open up to him. Because the voice was right. She had never seen kindness, not from anyone in her life. If he could show her that, or perhaps convince her that kindness was worthwhile, then he could push her in the right direction. A nudge. That's all she needed.

Fortis could sense she was close to helping them. She wanted to do something good in her life and if he was the one who convinced her what "good" meant, then all the better. Perhaps it was still manipulation, but at least it was manipulation for the better.

Swimming to her ship, he was pleased to see she was still conserving energy. She wasn't about to waste what he had given her. The lights were still not on in her ship, and though she had the heat on, it did not appear that she had even tried to fix the function that would allow her to send messages back to Tau.

These were all good signs.

She was sitting in the pilot's chair again, staring out into the sea. She did that a lot. At first, he thought it was in defiance of her own fear. He had smelled it the few times that she was in the water. His little virago wasn't as good at hiding that as she thought.

He froze just outside of her range of sight. She wasn't his, he corrected himself. She had earned the name, but that did not mean he had any claim to her.

The damn sulfur fields hadn't helped his unreasonable line of thinking. And he wasn't all that certain taking her where he wanted to bring her would do so either.

"Fool," he muttered, shaking his head. "This might be a bad idea."

But he was compelled to get her to open up to him. He knew there was a chance that what he was going to do would bring them closer, but also, he wanted her to be closer to him. He needed her to see that there was a reason to help his people.

Fortis was so tired of forcing others to do what was right. For once, he just wanted someone to make the right choice because it was what they wanted to do. No prophecies. No peering into the future. Just people doing what they must for the betterment of the sea.

He lit up all the bioluminescent parts of him. Each one of them flickering from the tip of his tail all the way to his stomach where dots scattered across his ribcage in bright, vibrant yellow. Her eyes moved toward him, but that was the only part of her that moved.

Was that a good sign? Or not?

He knew achromo minds were very fragile. He worried that keeping her this deep alone for so long was going to break her.

"Alexia," he said as he swam close to the window. "Put your wetsuit on."

"Why?"

"Just do it without arguing."

"You're not bringing me home," she replied with a snort. "So why not stay here for a little while longer and rot?"

So she'd been staring into the abyss too long. He'd seen this happen with others before. There was something about the abyss that lingered in people's minds, like the barbs of some malicious fish. It was hard to crawl out of it.

"Wetsuit. Now, virago."

She glared, but at least she stood up and went into the back of her ship. She'd opened the entire thing up, thankfully. So he wouldn't watch her undress, although some part of him whispered that he should look. All it would take was for him to crawl over the top and he'd be at the right angle to see those long legs again, and those glutes that...

No. He had better control than this.

Fortis smoothed his hands down his sides, pushing the fins at his hips flat. They were not fluttering. They were keeping him still and if it was anything other than that, he would cut them off himself.

She made quick work of it, at least. Alexia appeared once more with the wetsuit on and her face mask in her hands. "I assume I will need this?"

"Yes."

"Why do I feel like you're taking me somewhere to kill me?" she muttered.

He wasn't sure she wanted him to hear that part, but it inflated his pride. This was the first time the warrior woman before him had admitted he was stronger than her.

Damn, that shouldn't feel so good.

He knew it was dangerous to be thinking these thoughts. But the spirit of his wife had told him to live. The only reason he could think for that was that she knew the end was close. He was with the person who was going to kill him, and for some strange reason, that did make him want to live.

Alexia stared at him through the glass, unknowing of what was going on in his head or the alarming thoughts bubbling in his mind. Though she gave him an odd look when he didn't speak.

"Well?" she asked. "I assume you want me to get into the water?"

He cleared his gills with a quick expulsion of air. "Yes. Yes, I do. I'm bringing you somewhere to get away from the ship for a while."

"Thank god," she muttered, before turning and hitting the button to open the area of the floor where she could escape. "Not that I'm happy about this, mind you. But it will be nice to get out of this cramped space."

He waited until she made her way out from underneath the ship and into the open water. This was different. Somehow, looking at her without any of her armor or weapons made it seem like they were going on some adventure together, rather than fighting like they always did. It made something twist inside of him.

No, he thought to himself. You will not react like this. She is not yours. You just saw the spirit of your wife, whom you have longed to join for years. Your body is merely reacting to the mating urges that are... are...

Primal. Raw. Aching.

She swam toward him with strange flippers attached to her feet, and he marveled at how smoothly she moved through the water. Her wetsuit was black as night, completely different from his wife, who had been so pale even in life. Alexia's hair was black as well, smoothing back from her face with every movement and then billowing in front of her eyes as she paused before him.

"Well?" she asked, her voice muffled by the contraption over her face that allowed her to breathe.

He couldn't speak. Not with thoughts like this dancing through his betraying mind. He reached for her, his arm snapping out a little too quickly as he dragged her close to him.

Her hands smacked his chest hard enough that he felt the air expel from his gills. She would not let him throw her around, but then she did something that he hadn't expected.

She wrapped those long legs around his waist. The sensation of them was equally intriguing as it was odd. Two of them twined stiffly around his body but holding onto him with surprising strength. The same position they had been in when she'd shot rivets into his fins.

For a moment, they both stared at each other. Her eyes were narrowed in suspicion, and he was likely staring at her with a wide-eyed gaze because he'd never thought he'd feel like this. No other achromo had touched him. Not like this, at least. And to feel her against him, so warm even through the wetsuit, was... was...

Her hands came up, and he let her touch him. Her fingers stroked the gills along the side of his face, feather light but still calloused from years of fighting. It took everything in him to not roll his eyes back into his skull.

"These are so pretty," she murmured, the touch far more intimate than she knew. "It's strange that you have such delicate appendages when you are so brutal."

He had no words. Only pleasure that ached down to his bones as she continued to touch the very sensitive edges of his gills. He wanted to bite down on her fingers, then draw her closer so he could burrow himself in her heat.

Why was she so warm? Why was he letting her touch him when he knew how risky this was? She shouldn't be allowed to touch him. Not like this. He should toss her away from him, but by the gods, it felt so good to have someone touch him.

He was suddenly reminded that it had been a very long time since he'd been touched. Sure, he'd hugged his son and made sure that Aulax knew how much he meant to him, but that was the extent of it. How long has it been since he'd let another person touch him with kindness and tenderness?

Years. Nearly twenty years, if he thought about it. And it felt so good.

He was a fool to entertain this. And yet, his arm curved around her a little more tightly as he flicked his tail and they were off. She braced herself on his chest, holding herself up while they flew through the water.

Alexia thought she was fast with those boots? She was anything but. This achromo was going to learn just how fast his people were, if only so he could entertain her. He knew she liked to travel quickly. The way she'd piloted that ship gave that away. The woman enjoyed taking risks.

Just as he'd hoped, she tilted her head back and let the water run over her features. There was no fear scent now. Just pure enjoyment of the water rushing by her.

They darted through the currents, and she had no way of knowing that he was bringing her toward the surface. Not all the way, of course. Tau happened to be in the heart of where many of the storms brewed. There were so many hurricanes in this part of the sea that it was deadly to be at the surface at all. But he wanted to head somewhere he could potentially summon his son.

Aulax would know that his father was within reach. There was much he wanted to tell his boy, so the others would know to prepare. They were so close to getting Tau under their thumb, and he would not waste time wooing this woman. But he would try to get her on their side.

It was complicated. His feelings were difficult to parse through, but Aulax wouldn't ask him anything that he didn't want to answer.

Soon enough, they hit the right temperature of water for the creatures he sought. This time of year, the ocean put on a show, and he wanted her to see it.

The first sign was the brightening of the water. Soon enough, he could see her face without the light from his own body illuminating her features. Her pupils were still blown out, not used to the brighter light yet. Now he could see her eyes. The few times he'd seen them before, he had been so certain there was gold in them. And he'd been right. Pretty gold strands that were so lovely.

Fuck, he was having the wrong thoughts again. He couldn't. Not with her. Not with any achromo.

Rather than stare into those lovely eyes, he turned her so her back was pressed against his chest. He lifted a hand, pointing for her to look at all the sparkling particles around them.

"See these?"

Her mouth dropped open inside the mask. What would she look like in the water without it? Already he could see the red lines on her skin around the plastic. It hurt her face to wear such a thing, and yet, she had to wear it when she was in the water.

He could reach under the long length of his own hair and attach a tentacle to her neck. He could breathe for her, although he had no idea what she would do if he pricked the side of her throat and then ripped the mask off her face. She'd lose her mind. She'd try to fight him again, and he hated how much he wanted her to do that.

He enjoyed it when she struggled in his arms, but he was finding this wasn't all that bad, either. Limp and trusting, she leaned against his chest and stared up at the silver edged particles floating all around them.

"One time, Harlow brought me into a room that is off limits to everyone but the Originals," Alexia said quietly as she stretched out her hand to touch one of the silver lights. "She said it used to be called an observatory, before they'd all come underneath the sea. We walked into a room and the entire ceiling was sparkling lights like this. She called them stars. I didn't even know something like that could exist."

"I've seen the real ones before." It broke his heart that she didn't know that. What kind of life had she led that she didn't know stars existed? "There are still evenings where the sky is not so angry. You could see them too, if you stayed with me."

She had quieted at the words. "Stay with you?"

Shit. That wasn't the right way to say it. She would not stay with him, she was just going to leave Tau. "If you wish to stay with the other achromos working with us, that is. You don't have to. Beta is a perfectly suitable place to live. Albeit, a little cramped now."

"Since Alpha was destroyed."

"Correct."

He swallowed hard, trying to clear the lump in his throat that he had gotten from the mistake. "Right, we keep going."

"Where are we going?"

"Somewhere beautiful, virago. You said you had no kindness nor beauty in your life." And everyone deserved that. Even an achromo like her.

Chapter 18

Tiny sparks filled her vision in stunning numbers. She'd never thought to see the ocean look like this before. All she knew was what surrounded Tau, and there was very little there. Only the few meager plants that grew around the edges of the city, and of course, Harlow's small section of false ocean.

As Fortis drew her through the sparkling lights, she caught one of them in her hands and stared down at the little glow. "Harlow had a space beside her bedroom. She liked to fill it with all manner of creatures."

He tensed at her back, all the muscles of his chest hardening. "I saw them. The creatures she has within that cage will not survive long. They were not meant to be trapped so deep."

She knew that. She'd watched the dolphins wither and die, even though they had access to air and food. Something in them just gave up. She supposed, in a way, she had done the same. After all, there was only so much she could survive before it just wasn't worth it anymore. Some part of her had wanted to fight, though, and thus she had been nothing more than a tool for Harlow to use. At least, until Alexia had been given a taste of freedom.

Biting her lips, she nodded. No response was right. Those creatures hadn't deserved the fate they were given, and they hadn't deserved to suffer just because Harlow liked pretty things.

Then Fortis rolled with her until her back was pressed against his chest and it felt like she was lying on top of him. For a moment, she struggled. This felt far too intimate, and she liked it a little too much. But he grabbed her forehead and forced her to look above them.

Her mouth dropped open.

Hundreds of jellyfish floated above them. So many that she couldn't even guess at a correct number. They were all glowing bright blue in the light, floating through the water in a current that only barely stirred them. No tentacles floated below them, or at least, not many that she could see. They were little soft balls that appeared to bounce into each other, bumping and rocking through the waves as they tried to settle.

"They're beautiful," she said. She tried very hard to stay still as one came closer. She could see now that it wasn't just a glowing ball of light. There were patterns within it. The outside edges refracted the light, giving it a strange bubble-like quality. The interior had a little flower shaped glow as well. Five concentric circles, all overlapping so they looked like petals.

The outside of the jellyfish undulated in the water, and then it bumped against her chest. She froze, fearing the creature might sting her, even though she was wearing a wetsuit.

"Fortis?" she asked as nerves tingled underneath her skin. "Are these going to hurt me?"

He chuckled and leaned forward. The gills on the side of his neck slid against the top of her head, and she swore she could feel him inhaling against her hair. "Nervous, virago?"

"I don't want to get stung."

"They will not sting you. These are not the kind of jellyfish that harm, although I find it interesting that you believe I would bring you somewhere you would get hurt."

She cleared her throat. Perhaps he was right. There was no reason for her to distrust him at this point, and they were working on that now, weren't they? He wanted her to trust him more, and she...

For her entire life, Alexia had been told to trust no one. She was a pillar of confidence, sometimes even bordering on arrogance, because that was who she was trained to be. She leaned on no one. She trusted no one. She did not speak to anyone about any feelings or fears.

Alexia was a starving woman, and he offered her a bounty that was hard to deny.

Pulling off the glove of her wetsuit, she danced her fingers on top of the jellyfish's bubble. It was soft, just like she'd thought. But rubbery, as well. There was a tension to it that didn't quite make sense. As though the jellyfish itself was covered in a thin layer that was rather thick and sturdy.

"Strange," she whispered, before nudging the little beast back to all the others that were floating in the water. "I didn't think it would feel like that."

"Do you want to feel the rest?"

Yes.

No.

She shouldn't. It would only encourage her to discover new things to experience. Alexia was so afraid that he'd eventually send her back to Tau. Filling her mind with moments like this would only make it seem like she could stay here. Like there was a chance that she wouldn't have to go back to being so cold.

"Are you afraid?" he murmured, that deep voice rumbling through her spine and shaking her entire body.

"No, I am not afraid."

But she was. She was terrified. Not of the jellyfish, but of what this moment would eventually do to her.

Fortis held her loosely as he swam them up through the jellyfish. His arm around her waist was no longer a prison, but there in guidance as he swam with her into the middle of all these jellyfish. Her heart thundered in her chest, although she did not understand why it would. The jellyfish weren't hurting her. This wasn't fear, it was...

"I can feel your heart against my hand." His fingers slid just underneath her breast, and for a moment, something else flashed in her mind.

She wanted him to cup her. She wanted to arch against those webbed fingers, to feel the power of his hand as he touched her, kneaded her breast, flicked those dangerous claws over the hardened tips. Even in cold water, it made her entire body flash with heat.

"It's excitement you're feeling." His deep voice sent her mind spinning. She loved the vibration of the sound that made her entire body tingle with some emotion she couldn't name. "I can smell every single one of your emotions when you're in the water. Achromos always project how they feel. Your fear is acrid and biting, but this is warm and welcoming. You want to seek them out. You want to touch them."

She wanted him to touch her. It wasn't a realization she was proud of, but it was the truth. His hands were so close to where she wanted him. His other hand was on her hip, a branding white hot heat that she wanted to slide down between her thighs.

Alexia had only seen sex regarding other people. Harlow and her many partners still needed to be protected, especially in moments of passion where they were completely weak. Alexia had been trained to be passive in all moments. She kept her eyes on the walls, ignoring the sounds they made and the wet slaps of flesh. But she had never been allowed to indulge in such things herself. Frankly, she'd never wanted to.

The medication they gave her made everything so dull. Sex had never been intriguing. Until now. Until her entire body seemed to come alive all at once and a pressure between her thighs made itself hard to ignore.

And then, mortifyingly so, he took a deep breath.

His hand loosened on her hip, and then clenched so hard she swore she felt the bone creak. "But that," he murmured, his words slow and drawn out. "That I do not recognize."

Fuck. Could he smell her arousal?

This was the most embarrassing thing that had ever happened to her. Not only because he knew she was aroused, but because an undine was making her feel that way. Of all the times in her life when she could have been interested in a sexual partner, right now was the choice her body made? With a massive, finned monster who brought her to see jellyfish?

She struggled out of his arms and this time, he let her go. She didn't look back to see his expression because she didn't want to know if he had figured it out. What if he realized that she wanted him? That the scent he was smelling was...

No, it was too embarrassing to even think. Cheeks burning, she swam away from him through the hundreds of jellyfish that bumped against her sides. Somehow, that helped. The cool water chilling her body grounded her. The rubbery texture of the little creatures around her was a stark difference to the heated thoughts in her mind.

She took a few deep breaths, trying to make it so that her heart wasn't thundering in her chest anymore. He'd said that was excitement, and she definitely understood that now.

Those feelings in her body were so strange. Overwhelming, almost. She hadn't ever thought of someone like that before.

Blowing out a few more breaths, she grounded herself in the water and then turned back toward him. But Fortis was gone. The space where she'd left him was obvious. There were fewer jellyfish in that area, although many were already closing in the gap that he'd left behind.

But where...

A clawed hand dragged down her spine. The tips didn't quite break through her wetsuit, but she could feel them. Icy points that made every hair on her body stand up, and not in a bad way.

"What is that scent, virago? It is not one I have smelled from one of your kind before." His voice was a low, aching growl.

"I don't know what you're talking about."

"I think you do." He circled her, that tail coiling around her until she was surrounded by him. The sight of all those jellyfish disappeared as he wrapped her up in him.

She watched as his gills flared wide and he drew more water through them. Thin gills fluttered like he was quite literally rubbing the scent of her onto them and then they stood out at all angles. Even the fins along his face and hips spread wide, shaking in the water so powerfully that it almost appeared as though air bubbles were being created around them.

She had no idea what was happening to him, but she was lost in that dark gaze.

"Virago," he growled.

There was no arguing with a man like this, not when she could see that he'd lost control. He was an animal at best, a beast at worst. Something about the scent of her arousal had enraged him. Or maybe it had just loosened something deep in his chest so that now he was an unhinged beast.

She swallowed hard. "I'm not going to tell you, Fortis."

A sound rumbled in the depths of his chest. And fuck, he was so big. Bigger than she remembered now that his tail was tightening, twining around her and pressing down on all angles of her body.

But even that felt good. The pressure of his tail, the texture of scales sliding against her wetsuit, even the strange feeling of him moving against the back of her bare hand. All of it made her want to grab onto him. It made her want to draw him closer to her, to see what it would be like if she just pressed her lips to his chest, or if he pressed his lips to many other places on her body like she had seen so many do to Harlow.

He drew her ever closer, and those gills fluttering even harder. For a moment, staring into his black eyes, she didn't even see him anymore. She was used to a calm, collected, perhaps even heartless at times, undine who had pushed her. This was not that man. His black eyes were completely and utterly vacant of recognition.

As his tail tightened even more, she soon was pressed against his chest. Then his hands came up, curling behind her shoulders and holding her firmly against him. The lights of the jellyfish glowed behind him, turning his face into a shadow that stared into her very soul with a hunger that burned right through her.

Another low growl, this one a warning. She remained frozen in his grip as his face descended closer and closer to hers, the fins on the sides of his face vibrating so fast they were a blur.

"What is that smell, virago?" he asked again, although his voice was little more than a nightmarish monster.

This shouldn't turn her on as much as it did. She knew it wasn't helping the situation, but she was intensely turned on right now. She was always the biggest person in the room. Even among the other guards, and the men who had been genetically enhanced as well, she was the same height. Never in her life had she felt small or delicate or even that anyone could overpower her.

But she felt all of those things and more right now.

She couldn't wiggle her hands free, but she could lean forward until her lips almost ghosted against his through the thin membrane of her breathing apparatus. She could feel the heat of his body and was certain he could feel hers. "I'm not going to tell you, Fortis. Now snap out of it."

Another growl.

"Stop. Soon enough, you'll be back to yourself and you're going to be so embarrassed, Fortis. I don't want to know what you are like embarrassed. Please." The last word nearly brought their lips together.

She couldn't stop staring into his eyes until he tilted his head. And then there was a slow glide of something warm, ridged, and slick along her neck. Had he just…

The same time he groaned, she leaned back as far as she could. He chased her with his mouth, as though he didn't want to let her go. Not yet. As though he hunted for the taste he hadn't gotten enough of.

She wanted that, too. Alexia licked her lips as though she could already taste him, and those black eyes followed the movement of her tongue with rapt attention.

"Pink," he murmured, like the word was reverent in some way.

And then she watched it all fall away from him. The madness seeped out into the sea and he settled back into himself. With that came the horror at what he had done.

His tail whipped away from her so quickly that she spun in the water three times before she settled. She was facing away from him again, but maybe that was easier for the both of them. After whatever... that was, maybe they both needed a little time.

A rush of water slapped against her back, as though he had cleared out his gills and was forcibly getting rid of her scent. If that was even how he was smelling anything.

The action made her go cold. Whatever had happened, it wasn't because he had wanted it. Maybe it was some undine thing that made them go a little feral when they knew a woman was... interested. Fuck, this was awkward.

She gestured ahead of her, even though he couldn't see her arms. "I'm just going to explore."

"I didn't mean to... That is... It wasn't..." Another explosion of water against her back and then a flick of his tail beneath her legs. "I will return."

She was sure he would. Otherwise, she'd just let herself sink to the bottom of the sea in the hopes that she would forget all this had even happened.

Chapter 19

Alexia was relieved that he did, eventually come back. But she had an hour or so with the jellyfish all on her own. At first, it had been a bit of a struggle to keep herself upright and swimming with all of them surrounding her. She'd been so afraid of kicking one. They were delicate creatures, and no matter what she did, her flippers always ended up slapping one.

But she got the hang of it. They were so patient with her, too. Or maybe that was just her mind putting emotions onto them. They were jellyfish, after all. She wasn't even sure they had a brain. Not one that she could see, at least.

Transparent and aimless, they floated through the ocean and trusted that the currents would bring them wherever they needed to go. It was a peaceful life, and she envied them for that.

Alexia couldn't even imagine what it would feel like to float through life without worrying about what she was doing or where she was going.

She felt Fortis long before she saw him. Even in the wetsuit, hairs raised on her arms, the same as they always did when someone was looking at her. No one else would be watching her in the ocean. It was a vast, endless place that was more empty than it was full. Until her mind reminded her that there were, actually, a lot of things for her to be worried about in the sea.

Turning toward the source of the gaze, she saw him just beyond all the jellyfish. He was staring at her. Just watching as she floated among the jellyfish, allowing them to bump into her body as they were buffeted by the sea.

Alexia wondered what she looked like. She hoped it was some ethereal moment for him. To see a human, significantly larger than any other of her kind, floating there with the flippers on her feet, making her look even taller. Her hair might be spread out above her, long and graceful, with the ends just barely curling. It was the image she hoped he saw.

In reality, she was certain she looked like some bedraggled horror with tangled hair that flipped in front of her face, a wetsuit that showed every single one of her flaws, and jellyfish that kept bumping her in the face.

With a sigh, she kicked her flippers and headed over to him.

"I take it my time in the ocean is over?" she asked. "You would only be coming back here if we needed to go back."

"You've been out long enough," he agreed. "We must return."

Back to her prison. Back to the tight quarters, the darkness, the unending boredom that was slowly eating away at her mind. It almost made her beg. She wanted to plead with him not to bring her back there. Not now that she had a taste of freedom, and that frightened her.

His gills rippled. "Fear?"

She tried to make the emotion disappear, but couldn't. "I don't want to go back."

"It is where you are safe."

"I can't..." She took a deep breath. "It's so small, Fortis. Everything inside that ship is small. There is only darkness and never ending silence. I sit for hours on end every single day, just watching the abyss. My mind is fracturing."

And she was terrified. So fucking terrified to go back to that tiny room with all those limitations and she didn't know what would happen to her. What if she couldn't stop staring into the abyss? What if one day she just decided she'd had enough and leapt into the sea without her mask on?

She'd thought about it already. But being out here, with all this vast, unending space unfolded before her, she could breathe again.

Alexia was even afraid to get close to him now. Would he lose his mind again? She wasn't sure if she wanted to deal with that again, at least not without understanding what had caused the madness on both their parts.

But at least she knew he thought of her as a person now, and not just a nuisance. So she floated before him, kicking her feet even though her thighs were getting tired. "I am afraid of going back there. I don't like tight spaces."

Something in his expression twisted. His brows drew down a little tighter, his eyes narrowed on her, and his lips tilted a bit to the side. And she thought for a moment that he would deny her this. He clearly didn't want to give her what she wanted. He'd put her back in her cage, no matter what it might do to her mind.

"I do not wish for you to be frightened," he ground out. "It is an unusual emotion from you, and I find I do not like the taste of it."

"Then please, don't bring me back to the ship."

"There is nowhere else for me to bring you."

She tried to think of something, anything, that would be in this area. Tau had many safe houses all throughout the entirety of the sea. But Alexia didn't know where they were, and even then, going to a Tau safe house would alert many people to her whereabouts.

Right now, she didn't want them to know where she was. She had decided that she was going to make the right choice for herself, and that choice was... this. She wanted to find out where this was going, what she wanted to do, and if she even wanted to continue having feelings and emotions and all the other complicated things that were happening to her.

Alexia decided she wanted to know what life was like if she was making the decisions. Not someone else.

Maybe that was foolish. Maybe there was a better plan, and yet... Right now, that was all she wanted.

She kicked her feet to swim even closer to Fortis. "I don't care where you bring me, but I cannot go back to that ship."

He was clearly warring with himself. She could see the thoughts flickering through his mind that if he didn't take her back to the ship, she wasn't contained anymore.

She could take a risk. One that might change the entire course of her life. And maybe, just maybe, that was what needed to happen.

"If I were to entertain helping you," she started, then froze when his entire body reacted to the words.

Spines lifted up and down his arms. Sharp-edged and standing at attention, Alexia knew that if she even brushed her finger along the tip of one, they would make her bleed. As he shifted, she could see the rest of them down his back. Countless spines that had already parted her flesh.

Swallowing, she continued. "If I were to entertain helping you, I would need more proof than what you have provided me."

"You need more proof that it is a worthy endeavor to go against all who have drugged you and used you for their own nefarious desires?" The expression on his face said he thought she was insane.

Maybe she was.

"What you are against is what has defined my entire life. Tau is not the best of the cities, but it is in control. You ask me to go against those with power simply because it is the right thing to do. But I am not convinced that human kind can be better. I am not convinced there is another road to take." She held up her hand when he would have interrupted her. "And I am not convinced getting rid of Tau will fix anything."

In fact, she feared it would send their cities into more ruin. Everything was run by Tau. How much food was dispersed, medication, politics. Every city even looked to Tau for decision making. Without that, humans were capable of great chaos. They needed a firm hand. That was what the Originals had found centuries ago, and nothing about human nature had changed.

"We have to try," Fortis said. "The entire sea is at stake. And I know that means very little to achromo ears, but it is the only home we all have left."

The truth in those words rang true. This was the only place for them. They couldn't live above the water and without the sea... They would all die. It would end in human selfishness. Thousands of people choosing to die rather than admit they might have been wrong.

Her throat tightened. "I feel a great deal of fear in making this decision, Fortis. If I help you, if I betray everything I have ever known, there is no going back. And this choice will have to be made based on the information a single undine has given me after weeks of torture in the darkness and cold of the ocean with the threat of death wrapped around my throat."

His spines snapped back into place. "You believe I am coercing you to make this decision?"

She hadn't wanted to word it that way, but... "I think you did what you believed was right. You took someone who had information, who could give you what you wanted so that you could save your people. I cannot say if I was in your position that I wouldn't have done the same thing."

"But you cannot make this choice and believe it is your own?"

All she had to do was look back into the darkness below them. The deep waters, the abyss that hid so much from her view. "I started seeing things in the darkness," she whispered. "Terrible, awful things that I'm certain were just my mind conjuring up my greatest fears. But any longer in that ship, and I think I might have started to believe what my mind showed me."

The truth was rather painful to admit. She was terrified of what would happen if she went back to those close quarters, constantly worrying about heat and food and the state of her body. She shouldn't even be tired right now, but she was. Weeks on end of her body wasting away had made it so that even kicking her feet for this long on her own had her breathing hard.

She didn't want him to know that. Weakness was the one thing that a guard like her should never show. She was genetically modified so that she would never be weak.

But he noticed, because he was ever so good at noticing everything about her. Fortis reached for her waist, holding her with one hand underneath her armpit as though she weighed next to nothing. "You need more proof," he growled. "Then I will give you more proof, virago."

Alexia's hands were crushed between them and her palms pressed flush to the muscular planes of his chest. Sucking in a deep breath, she flicked her gaze up to his and saw that he was staring at her with an equally confused expression on his face.

Perhaps neither of them knew what to do with the sparks that had been building between them. She hadn't even noticed it was happening. Or maybe it was all in her head because she'd never felt this way before.

Alexia justified the feelings with that thought. She had never once been attracted to anyone. The medication she'd been taking ensured that she wouldn't know what sexual desire felt like. Not even when faced with hours upon hours of an orgy that never seemed to end. All she'd been able to process was that it was rather boring standing around listening to everyone moaning around her.

It made sense that her body would try to make up for lost time. It was unfortunate that he was the only person here for her to lust over. Maybe if it had been another one of the guards, it would have made more sense for her to react like this.

But she tried to think of the other guards who were far more similar in build to her as they darted away from the jellyfish and she just... wasn't interested. She remembered their broad, bulky muscles and the sweat that dripped between their abs. But her body didn't react to the thoughts. Not even when she remembered being pinned by them, with the heavy weight of a man's legs on either side of hers and his face so close after wrestling.

Everyone in Tau talked about how the male guards were incredibly attractive. The Originals had built the men that way. Powerful, perfect examples of male prowess.

Maybe she was just thinking of them wrong. Maybe she needed to think of the Originals themselves, because they were the ones who everyone was modeled after. They were centuries old beings, and that had to count for something.

But every Original she could think of didn't make her body react like it did to Fortis. Not a single one of them. They were all small and weak. They were soft in the midsection, or just soft in general. She didn't like their hair, the way they carried themselves, or their voices. All of it was wrong no matter how many times she tried to slot herself into a romantic thought.

Fortis shifted his grip on her hip, turning her slightly so that she could see more of their journey, and all she could think was that his hands were so large. The webs between his fingers were strange at first, but now she ignored those and instead thought only of the claws that scraped against her skin. And... Fuck. That was all it took, and her entire body lit up like a bonfire.

His grip turned bruising, but if he was struggling with the scent of her again, he did not say. Instead, he just kept his attention ahead of them in the ocean and barreled forward at an impressive speed.

Maybe if she just focused on the destination, all these confusing feelings would go away. After all, she couldn't be that attracted to an undine.

Right?

Clearing her throat, she asked, "Where are we going?"

"Where few of your kind have been before. You wanted proof that this is worthwhile, virago, and I am providing that to you."

Proof. Okay. She could work with that. Proof that there was something insidious that bloomed deep within the heart of Tau.

Perhaps with that proof, she could make her choice without fear of what might come.

Chapter 20

Bringing her anywhere that would prove the depths of Tau's evil was a foolish choice. Fortis knew this. There might be little hope for her yet, but he had seen how hard she had struggled in the depths.

And, in some sense, he understood her hesitation to make a choice after all that he had put her through. He'd just assumed that she would want to fight against those who had wronged her as well. Now that she was clear of mind, it was the easiest choice to make.

He had seen many of his own people addicted to the sulfur fields deep within the sea. He had seen them make choices that were questionable at best, and downright wrong at worst. All so that they could return to those fields and disappear from reality for a little while longer. So he understood her need to be reassured that she wanted this, and not that she'd been forced by the circumstances.

But he was growing impatient.

He sped through the sea, bringing her somewhere he had sworn to himself that he would never reveal to another living person. This was the first place that had shown him what the humans really were. It was the reason he knew Tau existed. And now he was going to share that knowledge with her.

"When I was young, I traveled much of the sea," he started. "I spent many years exploring every corner of this ocean that I could. I discovered a great many things in my travels, but the greatest of them all was the name of your city. Tau. I knew it existed, as did many of my people, but we had no way to find it. I have spent a very long time seeking your hidden city."

"There are signs of us?" She twisted in his arms, trying to look up at his face even though his speed made it difficult for her to do so. "There shouldn't have been any at all."

"Perhaps they are not where you believe them to be." He shook his head. "Too many years have been wasted trying to find your city. But I was the one to find the shrine that revealed all the truth of our world. The truth of Tau."

"A shrine?"

His hands tightened on her body, holding her a little closer. He remembered finding this place and the fear it had caused. For the first time, he had seen what the achromos were truly capable of.

"Fortis?" Alexia asked, her voice shaking with emotion. "Where are you bringing me?"

If only he could tell her. If only he could get the words to come out of his lips, but he couldn't. Speaking any more of that place felt like he was ushering a curse into the world.

So he forced himself to remain quiet and just show her. Because eventually, she would see for herself.

It didn't take very long. Tau was very close to where he had found the original site, almost like the city itself had been taunting him all these years. He had found the first secret, the first sign that there was more than just the three cities under the sea, although at the time there had been four.

It was his greatest failure that he hadn't found Tau on his own. Perhaps he never would have needed to find this woman. He never would have pulled her out of her home, tortured her with darkness and starvation.

But he never would have known how warm she was in his arms, or rediscovered how much he had missed being touched.

Fortis swallowed hard before he found himself back in that hazy place where he was too close to her, too enraptured by her scent. He hadn't even thought about that moment. Instead, he'd stuffed the embarrassing memory deep down.

Unfortunately, he could smell it. Her. Whatever that scent had been. He still had no clue what it was, but he was certain that it had cast a spell over him. One inhalation of that scent and he'd lost his mind.

He needed more of it. More of... her.

Perhaps she wasn't the only one losing her mind. Because while she thought he was just a dangerous beast to be around, he was certain she would be the one to kill him. And yet, here he was, still entertaining the idea that he only had a little while to live anyway, so why not indulge himself one last time?

Finally they made it and he could stop thinking these complicated thoughts.

"There," he murmured in her ear, pointing so she could follow the line of his finger.

In the distance, a strange metallic island drifted. It was wholly unlike anything else he'd seen. The root of it stretched deep into the ocean, balancing land on top. It was mechanical, though. Bits and pieces of it continued to open up and close, constantly shifting and moving under the surface as it filtered out water that was likely necessary for above, along with disposing a long trail of muddy liquid beneath it. Refuse from whatever lived on the island.

"What the fuck is that?" she murmured, furrowing her brows.

"The legacy of Tau," he replied. "Come. We go to the surface."

"The surface?" She seemed to panic in his arms, struggling again even though she knew damn well he would not let her go. "What do you mean we're going to the surface? We can't do that! You said yourself, it's covered in storms."

He was already heading that way, so surely she could see that there wasn't a storm above them. The light pierced through the waves, and long rays of sunlight speared around them. All she had to do was look.

But then again, he had taken away all of her stability. Fortis was learning that this new version of her was far more emotional than the warrior he had met before.

"Alexia," he snapped, holding her even tighter and forcing her to stop moving. "Look."

For good measure, he also grabbed onto her jaw and made her look up. Then, he had the distinct pleasure of feeling her go limp in his arms. She stared up at the surface with awe on her features and wide eyes.

"Is that..." She couldn't even finish the sentence.

"The sun," he replied. "Your sun that all of you achromos are so obsessed with."

He had never understood the love of it. The sun was just there, blinding and overly warm. But when he brought her to the surface and allowed her head to come out of the water, maybe he understood it a little better. Alexia closed her eyes and tilted her head back. Her hair spread out in the sea behind her, but the look of pure bliss was... tempting.

Frowning, Fortis closed his eyes and did the same. Maybe it was the position. The sun still burned even though his eyes were closed, but perhaps it was a little better with the darkness behind his lids. And the warmth was satisfying after being in the sea for so long.

"I never thought I'd see it," Alexia whispered. Her words were quiet, almost reverent. "I never thought..."

He opened his eyes and looked at her. It had been a very long time since he'd enjoyed something like she was enjoying this moment in the sun. He could admit to himself, he wasn't sure he knew how to enjoy things like that anymore. She was so thoroughly invested in this moment. As though no other thoughts existed in her head.

When was the last time that had happened to him? She had seen the monstrosity of metal behind her, and still all her focus was on the sunlight and the feeling of it on her skin for the first time.

Had he ever been so gifted?

Alexia's eyes finally opened again, locking with his. And all that power that existed inside of him surged to the surface so quickly that he didn't have time to grab onto it. One moment, he was here, and the next, he was in her future.

She stepped forward into the sunlight. She wasn't on land, but within the housing that Fortis had seen all the others build for their mates. Her building was closer to the surface than many of them, and that was fine because she wasn't afraid of the storms. He didn't know why he was so certain of that, but he was. Fortis could feel how at peace she was with this life and it was...

Good.

He was pleased to know that after his death, she would still be in a place where there was peace. "The path you walk leads to happiness," he said, the words bubbling from him without control. "Though it may be a struggle to get there, this is the right choice for you."

"Fortis, I don't need you to tell me what to do."

"It is your future." With a rough gasp, he ripped his gaze from hers and shook his head. "I am sorry, virago. I should not have looked without your permission."

"You..." He heard the click of her throat as she swallowed. "You looked? What do you mean you looked?"

"Depthstriders are unique in that we were birthed deep in the heart of the ocean. As such, we have abilities that are beyond that of our other brethren." He'd never felt uncomfortable talking about this before. Why did he feel so now? "I can not only see your memories, but your future as well."

There was a long pause of silence before she suddenly laughed.

He'd never heard the sound from her before. Perhaps a few chuckles of sardonic disappointment, but never a full belly laugh. He was so surprised his grip on her slipped, and she drifted out into the water away from him as she laughed so hard he swore tears were tracking down her cheeks.

"You can see the future?" she cackled.

"Yes, I can see the future." His gills flared wide in anger. "Why are you laughing?"

"That's hilarious that you think I'd believe that." She dunked underneath the water she was laughing so hard, and came back up with a sputtering sound. "The undine thinks he can see the future. That's rich."

"I can see the future."

"Sure." Still laughing, she turned toward where he'd brought her. "We'll go with that."

"I can!" he insisted, but she obviously wasn't listening to him now.

She swam toward the metal island while shaking her head in disbelief. Every now and then as she struggled to the landmass, he heard her mutter, "He can see the future," and snort again.

The damned woman was going to be the death of him. She didn't believe a word he had said, but it was all the truth. He had seen her future, and the future of many others. How did he prove that to her?

He wasn't sure why it was even important to prove it. She had no reason to believe him, because she had never seen the power of what his kind could do. And besides, she didn't care that he was capable of it.

Her laughter shouldn't bother him so much, but it did.

The island before them was less metal on the surface. At first sight, it looked like any other island he had come across. There was a sand beach that led up to emerald green grass, and a small log house in the dead center. It looked like it was all set up there for someone to see it. As though no one had ever lived within those four walls.

But the strangest part of this place was that no storm ever touched it. He had ridden the massive waves for days on end, watching this house that should have been swallowed up by hurricanes or the wind tunnels that would whip everything off the surface of the sea. But not this place.

This place remained untouched by everything.

He would let go of his anger with her for not believing him, and instead, he followed her to the sandy beach. Just like the last time he'd been here, the metal nipped at his tail. He had to get up onto the sand. Which was odd enough of an experience, because Fortis did not enjoy beaching himself.

It was harder to flee, and there were plenty of things on this island that would hunt him. He watched Alexia drag herself out of the water and remove her mask, pausing only when he barked out a warning. "Be careful. You are not the only one on this island."

Her brows furrowed. "Someone lives here?"

"That is not what I speak of."

A horrible cry echoed around them, bursting through the warmth of the sunlight and sending chills down his spine. There it was. The creatures that haunted this place. He had never been able to get inside of that house for long before the hoard of monsters attacked him.

Feathered and small, they appeared to be easy to kill. But no matter how many he pulled into dusty pieces with feathers floating all around him, more always appeared. With talons and sharp faces, they attacked him mercilessly every time he'd come here.

Alexia wore a strange expression of confusion as she watched the tiny beast charge him. She just stood there, as though dumbfounded, when he grabbed onto the beast and tossed it into the ocean.

"Are you—" she asked, then stopped herself before continuing. It almost appeared that she schooled her expression into something that wasn't so obviously stunned. "Are you afraid of chickens?"

"Is that what you call these tiny beasts?" Oh god, more of them were rounding the house. They didn't care why he was here, they just attacked blindly.

"Chickens, yeah," she muttered, before stepping in front of the hoard that were soon to attack him. "They're not dangerous."

"They pick at my scales," he hissed, baring his teeth in a threat as he leaned around her. "I will kill any of them that come near me. "

"There must be a pen around here somewhere. Just... Go back in the water for a bit. I'll let you know when they're contained."

He didn't like it. Fortis wanted to remain with her to see her expression and to know the moment she realized he was right. The last time he'd gone into the house had proven all he needed to know about her kind and how incredibly destructive the achromos were.

But if she wanted to save him from these *chickens,* then he supposed he would allow it.

Chapter 21

A massive undine, a depthstrider, with the ability to kill anyone and anything with just the slightest amount of energy, was terrified of chickens. Now that was something she didn't expect.

Nor was a floating island that was clearly man made. She'd seen the gears and all the strange vents that kept it floating from beneath, but it was the top of the island that surprised her most. This place was eerily similar to pictures she had seen of one of the Original's houses.

Original Jessup was one of the few men who intimidated her. He was the first to kill if anyone disagreed with him, even an Original. She'd been there the day he had killed one of his own in a message that there would be no infighting. All Originals agreed with each other. End of story.

In his wing of Tau, there were pictures on the wall. Lots of pictures. All of them were from Above, and the life he had lived long ago. One of them looked like this. A small log cabin at the edge of the sea. A bed of emerald grass surrounding it, dotted with purple and white flowers that spread in a lush carpet all the way to the waves. It was... stunning, really. A beautiful dream that so many people had shared back in those days.

At least, that's what Original Jessup had always said. To find something like this, floating where no one should ever find it? It was strange, and perhaps a little too convenient.

Eyes and ears open, she ushered the chickens back into a pen that had seen better days. Though the house didn't seem to have aged, the rest of the island was showing wear and tear. The pen for the chickens was made out of wood, and even that material had worn throughout the centuries. Time had taken its toll on everything it should have. At least, if she believed this place was built by the Originals, and she... did.

Closing the gate, she looked around to see there were even more animals. Beasts that shouldn't exist. Three cows were in the field just beyond the house, along with a donkey and what looked like two horses on the horizon. These were animals that had gone extinct long ago, at least according to the Originals.

But here they were. Living on an island that shouldn't exist.

Her stomach churned. It felt wrong to be here, like she was trespassing and just waiting for someone to come on over a loudspeaker and scream at her. Or worse, a bullet to the forehead.

Taking a deep breath, she walked toward the log cabin. She wanted to know what all the fuss was about. If Fortis believed this would make her help, then surely he had a good reason for that. Her people were terrible. She agreed with that fact. But she needed to know what had made him hate them this much.

The log cabin felt like she was walking to her death. Still, she moved forward. She walked right up to the front door, cringing in front of it as she waited for retribution. But nothing happened.

Swallowing hard, she put her hand on the front door and pushed it open.

It wasn't a house; she realized. Stepping inside, she was surprised to see there were only benches lining the floor. No chairs, no kitchen, no living area. There were pictures all along the wall, though. Photographs with little placards underneath each photo that explained the contents.

"A museum?" she murmured, shocked that there was even a building like this.

Who would build a museum floating in the middle of the ocean? No one could come here. There were far too many storms, and no human came to the surface, anyway. But this place was still pristine. Someone had been taking care of it.

Leaning closer, she looked at the first picture on the wall and was surprised to see many familiar faces. All the Originals were in this picture, standing beside each other like old friends. Some of them had their arms around others, some were grinning at the camera or making obscene gestures. Just regular people, long before they became immortal.

It was odd to see them like that. Leaning forward, she read the note underneath, "The dreamers who saw a need and decided to serve."

The story she knew was that the Originals had seen the world ending, so they had created the cities beneath the sea. Perhaps this was the time before the world's end. When they had yet to see the entirety of their lives starting to crash and burn.

The next five pictures were designs that made sense. Each of them was a different version of one of the cities, blueprints that had then been used to create the actual cities. There were also things she had seen before, although the blueprint of Tau itself was different from what they had below the surface.

Alexia traced her fingers over the words underneath. "The safest city in the world."

For them.

It had always been the safest city in the world for those who lived in it, but she wasn't sure if that was a good thing or not.

She turned around, eyeing all the framed portraits here that defined her entire life. There were photos of the first animals that were taken underneath the sea. Cows were deemed far too wasteful, and they emitted too much CO_2. They were dangerous and therefore not worth keeping. After all, the milk they produced wasn't as helpful for those who were lactose intolerant, and quite a few Originals were.

Then there were pictures of the cities as they were built underneath the water. So many people had helped with that. Engineers, architects, artists who had spent countless years developing everything that was needed to save the world.

Another set of photos caught her eye on the far side of the wall. She hadn't seen these before.

Walking closer, she realized this was the start of the genetic program, and a face there made her entire body ice cold.

"Alexia Barron, the first brave soul," she read aloud as she looked at a woman who wore her face in the photo. She was much smaller than Alexia was now, of course. But she was still a hard-looking woman who appeared far more capable than those surrounding her.

That version of herself had willingly joined this group of people. She'd chosen to be experimented on, and all other versions of herself were then forced to do the same. Anger bubbled up inside of her. She wanted to go back in time and slap this woman across the face, because surely she should know what she did to herself and to so many others.

There were so many versions of Alexia who had been tortured and tormented to get to this version. So many who deserved so much more than death on a cold table because they had emotions.

Taking a deep breath, she moved onto the next picture that depicted a strange machine. It jutted out of the coast, metal pieces all gleaming in the sunlight. A single tall pillar, with a ball of electricity at the top.

"The first weather manipulator," she read out loud, the words sticking in her throat. "The first of many. A failed experiment that led to…"

She stopped speaking because the next words were almost impossible to say. Not out loud. She refused to give them breath.

A failed experiment that led to true perfection beneath the sea.

Was this admitting that the Originals had affected the weather? It couldn't be. They were the ones to save the world, not end it. She moved to the next picture, and the next, each one solidifying the truth.

She saw the scientists who worked to create the weather device. Then a photograph of the first hurricane guided to an enemy country. They then created a device that beckoned earthquakes and called about a tsunami that killed thousands. The next photo was of the first storm that got out of hand, a hurricane that stirred up the sea so much that most of the east coast drowned. More and more devastation as the experiment took on a life of its own.

In their quest to create something worthwhile for their egos, the Originals had destroyed an entire planet. They were the reason everyone lived under the sea, and then they had gone even farther with it. They'd genetically enhanced humans, forcing people like Alexia to work for them. Lie for them. Create and enforce stories that other people took to heart.

All because of their own egos. Because they were a group of friends who thought they were better than everyone else.

And then, at the very end of all those pictures, there was a large framed piece of paper. It almost read like a manifesto, and it turned her blood to ice in her veins.

We are the Originals.

We are the few who will survive the end of the world.

We will never die.

We will rule over this new world that we created.

And we will be the only ones who know.

Underneath the words were signatures. Each one familiar to her.

With a shaking hand, she reached out and traced Harlow's name. It wasn't that there was any love lost between the two of them. Alexia hated the woman for everything she had put her through, but also some part of her had hoped the other woman wasn't part of this madness. She wanted to believe, for even an instance, that Harlow had protested this evil.

Pressure built in her chest. Anger, fear, anxiety, guilt. All the emotions she had never been allowed to fear because she had been their puppet. She was built to keep them safe, because they knew without people like her, they had good reason to be afraid.

The end of the world hadn't been caused by natural disasters or unexplained events.

It had been caused by human arrogance.

Tears burned in her eyes. A lifetime worth of tears that had built up inside of her. She had worked for these people. The Originals had convinced her that she was at least working for those who were trying to do the right thing.

But they weren't. They were the reason for the nightmarish existence all humans were now subjected to.

A keening cry echoed out of her mouth as she folded in on herself. This wasn't just their fault, and she knew that. It was her fault too. Her fault for keeping them safe all these years and dedicating her entire life to them. She had spent countless hours trusting that they were making the right choices, and all she had to do was follow their orders.

Her entire life until this point had been a lie. And even worse, it had affected the entire world.

She'd justified her actions by believing at least she was working for the lesser of the evils. Beta was filled with power hungry fools who couldn't make change happen. Alpha was full of beauty and wit, but nothing of actual substance. And, of course, Gamma was a prison city where no power existed. There were so few cities for her to go to, but Tau called all the shots. Tau was the most powerful and therefore had to be the best.

Now she knew even that was a lie.

She mourned the loss of everything she knew, and everything she had been. Shoulder shaking sobs wracked her entire body, purging her very bones of all those dark thoughts and memories that ate at her. And by the end, once she had mourned the death of her previous self, Alexia felt as though she could breathe again.

Because there was another path now. A path that would lead her toward so much more.

Somehow, she felt stronger for it. These emotions, these thoughts, these worries. They had weighed her down even under the cloak of the medication. Now she got to get rid of them once and for all.

Leaving the museum, she stepped out into the sun as a new woman.

She took a deep breath of the fresh sea air, not as stale and stagnant as it was under the ocean. She was free now. Finally, and completely free.

Fortis waited for her in the water. He wasn't close to the sand, but she hadn't expected him to come up here and wait for her, anyway. The chickens were a very real threat to his sensitive scales.

Her chest ached looking at him. This massive, horrible monster had fought her as no other creature ever had, and now everything she had carried for so many years was gone. All the guilt, the weight, the struggle. She could move on with her life.

How did she thank him? He had given her the greatest gift a person could ever give another person. He'd broken her chains.

One foot moved in front of the other. Then she was running across the sands and into the water. The icy waves splashed against her thighs, but she didn't stop until she plunged into the sea.

Alexia nearly laughed at the shock on his features, and then the slightest hint of fear. As though he thought that something in the house was chasing her. Or worse, the chickens.

Ridiculous that he was so afraid of them. And she adored him for it.

She just... liked him. If she was being honest with herself, she'd liked him from the beginning. Even when he'd trapped her in that ship, there was a part of her who had still admired him for what he was.

She swam to his side and threw her arms around his neck. He looked at her in shock, or perhaps like she had lost her mind, but she didn't care. She grabbed either side of his head, his gills sliding through her fingers, and kissed him.

Alexia had never kissed anyone before, but she'd seen plenty of kisses. This was one of thanks, appreciation, and all the good things that bubbled up inside of her now that she had seen the truth. It was a firm kiss, probably too hard considering his teeth were sharp, but she didn't care. His lips were cold and her entire body flared white hot at the touch.

She drew back to thank him for everything, for the truth he had revealed, but then he palmed the back of her head and tugged her back to him. This kiss was hot, his lips sliding over hers before his tongue plunged inside her mouth. He tasted of brine and male, a strange combination that made her head spin.

Suddenly, this wasn't just about thanking him. It was about indulging herself in the feeling of his muscles flexing against her belly, his fingers in her hair, the rough glide of his other hand down her back as he pressed her more firmly against him.

Relaxing into him, she kissed him back. Tentatively. Just a gentle stroke of her tongue against his, but it was like she had lit a fire underneath him. He groaned, the sound long and deep as he pulled her even harder against his body. Any other human and he might have squished them, but she was stronger, sturdier, capable of rough handling.

When a waved splashed over them, soaking her face with icy water, she drew back. Water droplets clung to her eyelashes and obscured the sight of him, but she knew he was staring at her with that dark, almost unhinged gaze once more.

"What was that for?" he asked.

Her fingers slid through the gills on the sides of his face. Gills that intrigued her far more than she wished to admit. "Thank you," she finally got to say. "For setting me free."

Chapter 22

She'd kissed him. And for some mad reason, he had kissed her back.

Fortis wasn't sure what had come over him, only that he knew if he didn't get a taste of her lips, the world might end. She was right there in his arms, holding him around the neck, thanking him for freeing her, and he'd snapped.

The decision wasn't the right one to make. It had been foolhardy and stupid. She was an achromo. And not just any achromo, but one who had worked for the worst of their kind. She'd fought against him and drawn blood as none of her people had done before.

There were a hundred reasons for him to not indulge himself in her.

And one good reason to do so.

He liked her. Even though he knew she was going to kill him soon enough, he found her bravery and the way she faced the world rather impressive. He enjoyed fighting with her, arguing with her, and even just the quiet moments where she found what it was to feel emotions.

Fortis had been so numb for such a long time. He felt himself coming back to life as he watched her experience everything. And maybe he felt his own emotions starting to surface as well.

Helping her place the breathing apparatus over her face once more, he sank into the waves and drew her away from that cursed place that held all the answers but proposed no solutions.

"You found that how many years ago?" she asked, her voice a low murmur.

"Ten, fifteen years ago perhaps? It was the time when I realized I needed to fight against your people with everything that I had in me. You were the villains in the ocean. All of you."

But his arms tightened around her as he said it. Somehow, this woman didn't feel like an enemy. It was the most confusing thought he'd ever had in his life.

She hummed low under her breath. "Right, the villains."

He swallowed, knowing that he had hurt her feelings. When was the last time he'd ever cared if he had hurt someone's feelings? It had been years. He was the one to tell people the truth. To guide them into their future without telling them the why or how of it, only the cold hard facts. If it hurt them, then that wasn't his problem. Their futures were not for him to decide.

This woman was different, though. Being around her made him feel like he wanted to guard her from those thoughts and that terrible mindset that sometimes came over her. He wanted to explain the future in softer tones.

He wanted to be honest.

That clarity pushed him away from where her ship was. Far from where he would bring her back to the dark, and instead, he headed for somewhere they could speak. Somewhere she could be comfortable for a while until he decided what he was going to do with her.

"Where are we going?" she asked.

"You did not wish to return to the ship."

"That…" Her grip tightened around his shoulders and she blew out a breath. "Yes, I suppose I did say that."

Alexia fiddled with the mask on her face, and he wondered just how long that would work. It wasn't like Mira's, where she had created it to filter the oxygen out of the water. Perhaps he should bring her back to the ship to ensure she was safe before he continued onward.

With an audible grunt, Fortis forced himself not to backtrack toward the ship. She was fine. She would let him know if something needed to happen or if she was in danger. He didn't need to take care of her.

And yet, damn how he wanted to.

Frustrated with the thoughts running through his head, Fortis said nothing else until they approached the cave system. It was similar to many throughout the ocean. Achromos had first come down to the sea on missions to find where they could build their cities, and thus there were many abandoned research facilities. Although they were slowly rotting with time, he was quite certain this one was safe.

He approached the tunnel carved into the stone and slipped inside. It was big enough for one of the achromo ships, like the one she had followed him with. So he didn't worry about scraping her along the sides of the stones, although he did reach down to make sure her legs were wrapped around his hips.

Alexia didn't seem to be nervous in the slightest. She straightened an arm and trailed her fingers along the smooth stone walls that had been worn by years of waves and many ships that had passed in the same way that they were passing now.

"Where are we?" she asked.

"An old research facility. Your people used this location to scout where they wanted to place their city."

"Are we close to one, then?"

He thought about her question, unsure if he wanted to give her their exact location. "Close enough to Beta, I suppose. But not so close that anyone from that city would ever find us here."

"Interesting." Alexia wasn't just saying that. She was looking around with her mouth slightly ajar, watching as the tunnel opened up and they were in a docking bay.

He'd seen so many of these at this point in his life that nothing surprised him. But she made a little noise in the back of her throat, struggling to get out of his arms.

He released her, watching in bemusement as she kicked her feet and headed up to the surface. There was an excitement in her that he hadn't seen yet.

"Do you realize how old this is?" she asked as they crested the surface. "This must have been one of the first research facilities they built."

"Perhaps. Everything in here seems old."

Alexia dragged herself out of the water, her hands gripping the rusted rungs of a ladder to pull herself out onto the floor. She scrambled to her feet, spinning to look at the massive room while he looked around with her.

He didn't see what she would be so excited about. It was a singular room, large enough to fit at least ten of her people wandering around. The walls and floors used to be white, but now they were a dingy gray from years of dust buildup. Alexia left footprints on the floor as she walked to the back wall that was entirely glass. Easily four of her high, it stretched all the way up to the stone ceiling.

The light coming in from that wall was natural. Blue filtered through the crystal clear waters. Kelp grew just beyond the glass, and all those waving green fronds outlined her silhouette. She was so pretty. It made every part of him ache to touch her again, and to see if her lips really tasted as good as he remembered.

After everything she had been through, she still stood tall in front of that glass. Spine straight, shoulders back. She looked every inch a warrior woman who was ready to take on the world, and he wasn't sure how to let her do that without him, now.

She turned to look over her shoulder at him, and her dark hair slicked back from her face. "Why are we here, Fortis?"

"I wished to bring you to a place where we could speak."

"We spoke just fine when I was in the ship."

And perhaps he wanted to see that expression on her face. The one of awe where she realized she had found something that she would never see again. The beauty of her soul peering out through her eyes was something he enjoyed immensely.

But he didn't tell her that. Instead, he planted his hands on the cold floor and heaved himself out of the water. It took a great bit of effort. Fortis was too large to move easily on land, but he managed well enough. A wave from his movements helped propel him across the floor, easing his way until he could press his back against the glass and look back at the roiling waves he'd left behind. His fluke was still in the icy cold water, and he left it there as a reminder that he could escape if he had to.

He leaned his head back against the glass. "You laughed when I said I could see the future."

Her lips twisted into a smile. "I did."

"I can see it, though." He met her gaze, already feeling the powers inside of him swirling as though they were also insulted that she doubted them. "You have felt it. You have seen how I can peer into your memories. Why is it so hard for you to believe I can do more than that?"

At his direct question, she squirmed. Alexia shifted her weight from side to side, and her hands opened and closed as she avoided his multicolored gaze. "Looking into someone's mind, forcing them to see memories. That's science."

"Is it?"

"It's believable science. I don't know, I'm not one of the genetic analysts. Look at me! I shouldn't be possible, but here I am. Science made this." She gestured up and down her body as though that was an answer. "But the future? No one knows the future, Fortis."

"I do."

She opened and closed her mouth. "I just... It's hard to believe. That would give you mystical powers or somehow make you..."

He waited for her to continue the thought, but she didn't. "Make me what, Alexia?"

"God-like!" she blurted out. "No one knows the future. It isn't set in stone. It is and has always been something that is out of our grasp. Even seeking to know the future has been the downfall of so many. But you want me to believe that you have access to all that information?"

He shrugged. "Depthstriders are different. We are close to the sea, the waves, the goddess who rules these waters. We dedicate our lives to knowing the future and learning how to find the right path for others. You are correct, some futures are not set in stone. Some futures can be changed and manipulated and guided. That is part of what my role is among my people. I find the futures that will lead us into a world that is better. For all of us."

She leaned against the glass and crossed her arms over her chest. "So you're like a priest, then?"

"I do not know this word."

"A..." Alexia's nose scrunched as she thought. "Holy figure. Someone who talks to god and then relays what god says."

He mimicked her scrunched nose before nodding. "I suppose. It is not the sea telling people their future, though. It's just a depthstrider who has earned that ability by the goddess after years of training."

He could see she still didn't believe him, and that was beyond frustrating. No one had ever questioned his abilities before. He was capable of seeing the future, and that was just how it had always been. Yes, it was frustrating for him sometimes. He would see a future that didn't match up with what he wanted. And sometimes, he would see a terrible future that he could not change. It was just there. For good. No matter how much he wanted to change it, there wasn't a way to save the person.

"I find myself upset that you do not believe me," he muttered.

"I think that's a silly reason to be upset."

Well, now he was offended. "You are questioning something I have been able to do my entire life, and something I have based my entire existence upon."

"You based your entire existence on seeing other people's futures? That sounds voyeuristic."

The amusement on her face warned him that she was teasing, but he was so far beyond that. She antagonized him. "I have based my entire life upon a vision my wife saw of my death. I know how I am going to die, virago, and I never question that truth."

Her eyes widened. "You have a wife?"

That wasn't the way to say it. Clearing his throat, he shook his head. "I had a wife. She died many years ago."

"Ah." For some reason, that seemed to make Alexia uncomfortable. "Well. That might have been nice to know."

Why? Was she thinking about their kiss? As far as he was concerned, his wife had given him permission. Astrum wanted him to live for as long as he could before he joined her in the after life and then... Even if he indulged himself with the woman who would kill him, he had decided that he was going to make use of his last days. Right until the bitter end.

"She prophesied that I would lead our people into a new future. That it would be me who changed the current of time and brought both of our peoples into a new world." He made sure that Alexia was listening to him, dragging his claws on the floor with a sharp screech that had her staring at him. "And then I would die. I have seen the future through her vision, Alexia. I know who kills me. I know when that person kills me, and how. And because of that, I can take risks that others cannot."

"The future is uncertain," she replied. "You said that yourself."

"I did. But some futures cannot be changed."

"You've dedicated your life to something someone told you that you believe will happen. The future can be manipulated, that much I do believe. She made you believe that you would die, and you have fought your entire life to see that come true. No one can see the future, Fortis." Her cheeks turned bright red during the rant, and her chest heaved up and down with anger.

He patted the floor next to him. "Come here, virago."

"Why?"

"Because I can tell you are upset and I would like to talk with you about that."

Her brows furrowed, as though she was suspicious about what he was asking from her. "Since when have you cared how I'm feeling? Historically, you've thrown me in a prison or tormented me. Why are you being so nice?"

Because something was growing in his chest and he didn't know what else to do about it. A voice in his head screamed that he needed to take care of her. He needed her to be safe and happy and no matter what that ended up costing, he would see it through.

She was going to kill him, anyway. The least he could do was make it easier on this achromo, who he knew would carry that guilt for the rest of her days.

"Sit," he said. "I don't have to justify myself to you."

Grumbling under her breath, she at least joined him on the floor. She was quite a distance away, and for some reason, that bothered him. After all the time they had spent together, he'd thought she wouldn't mind being at least a little closer.

She was the one who had kissed him, after all.

Had he done something wrong? Achromos were confusing at the best of times, but he also knew that he hadn't done this in a very long time. His wife had been the one to chase him, as was the depthstrider way.

Achromos were not like that. They were wooed strangely. At least, that's what he had seen with the other three of his people who now had mates. But maybe she would be different. Just like he was different.

Breathing in through his nose, he bumped his head against the glass and stared up at the stone ceiling. "Would you like to hear about my family?"

"Are they all dead?"

His lips twisted into a wry grin. "Not all of them."

"Then you can tell me about the living ones."

The living ones. He snorted and rolled his eyes. "That I can do, virago."

229

Chapter 23

"You what?" Alexia exclaimed with a laugh, trying to keep herself from giggling too hard at the story.

"Aulax was just a boy, and he wouldn't leave the pufferfish alone." Fortis shrugged. "If he wanted to find out why I told him not to touch things, then I decided to just let him touch them. He ended up grabbing onto it in the biggest hug he could and punctured himself in twenty different places."

"Fortis! That's..."

"Cruel?" He looked over at her with a grin. "He learned not to touch pufferfish, now didn't he?"

This wasn't the only story he'd told her that was borderline ridiculous. There were so many. Stories of him and his son meandering through the sea, seeking everything they could that would entertain them. How they fought sharks and rode on the backs of whales. Stories that painted a picture of a single father who loved his son more than anything in the world.

Biting her lip, she shook her head, so she didn't laugh too hard at the hilarity of the story. "It sounds like you love your son very much."

"I do. I am very proud of him."

"Why don't you talk about him more?" Maybe that was her old aches coming through. "I didn't even realize you had a family. Much less that you spent time with them."

"I didn't trust you. Why would I tell you about my family when you could have chosen to return to Tau, or tried to kill me? What reassurance did I have that you wouldn't track down my family if I couldn't convince you to help us?"

It made a lot of sense. Alexia had worked for the people who had hunted undine for ages, and the people in Tau were willing to do anything to get the entire ocean under their thumb.

Blowing out a breath, she reached up for her hair, which was already almost dry. How long had they been talking? Far longer than they should have, most likely. But it was nice to talk to him like he was a person and not just some monster out of the deep.

Taking her tangled hair in her hands, she started to weave it into a braid. "I can't blame you for that. I wouldn't have hunted down your family, though. If that helps."

"I'm sure you would have."

"There's no logical reason to do that."

"Wiping out my people from the sea has always been Tau's plan. That's why they do everything they do. What are you doing?" The last sentence was said so suddenly that she froze.

With her fingers in her hair, she stared at his wide eyes. That expression was far too similar to what he'd looked like the first time he'd lost control in the ocean. Usually there was some kind of emotion in his black gaze, but when he stared at her like that? It was like he turned into a shark. There was no emotion, only hunger.

"Braiding my hair," she breathed.

"Why did you stop?" His gaze never moved from her fingers, he wasn't even blinking, and she wasn't sure what that meant.

Inexplicably, heat bloomed deep in her belly. Alexia didn't know what to do with these feelings, but she knew she wanted him to keep looking at her like that. So she continued weaving the strands together, looping them over and over.

Her hair was long. It took some time to braid her hair. By the end of it where she tied it in a knot that would hopefully stay, the air was thick between them. She was breathing a little harder than before, and so was he. She could see the way his chest moved up and down with some emotion she could not name.

But this feeling awakened another being inside her. A woman who could feel and want and desire, whispered for her to take hold of this moment. It might be the only one she ever got.

Licking her lips, she quietly said, "You believe you're going to die soon?"

"I know it."

"If I were going to die, then I would want to fill every moment with life. I would want to do all the things that I have always wanted to do, and not have a single regret as I left this world."

She realized she was likely prodding him with a stick just to see what he would do, but also, she hadn't felt like this. Ever. Her body had never experienced this warm, liquidy feeling until him and she wanted to explore that more.

"Virago," he said, his voice little more than a groan. "My control is hanging by a thread."

Why did that make her heart thud so hard in her chest? "You took all my medicine, I'm afraid you're the only one with any control left."

A low sound rumbled in his chest. She'd never heard him make that noise before, but perhaps he couldn't in the water. And then suddenly he reached over, grabbed each of her ankles, and spread them both wide. The movement spun her in his direction. She had to plant her hands behind her on the floor as he looked her over with those hungry, scorching eyes.

"You said you felt nothing before you stopped taking the medication," he said, his voice a low rumble. "Does that mean you felt absolutely nothing?"

"Before this? I only had a cold mind. Tactical. Able to see only logic and reason." She took a long, deep breath. "But now I'm feeling... a lot of things."

Somehow those eyes darkened even further. Like he knew what she meant when she said that. He understood that she wanted—no, needed—him to do something, but she genuinely didn't know what to ask for.

"You know what men and women do together, I suppose?" he asked. "It wouldn't surprise me if Tau had removed all pleasure from their city."

"I have seen the Originals doing what they want with each other." Although the idea of that made her wince. "It did not look enjoyable. Their ways are... twisted."

She remembered far too many of them pushing each other beyond limits. It was a game for them all. They liked to see what kind of pain they could cause, how little the other would enjoy it, or how much they suddenly would.

"People who are that old no longer seek pleasure in ways we understand," he murmured, but then his hand curled around her ankle a little tighter. "We are not in the water, Alexia. I cannot scent what you want."

Right. Because he could smell her through his gills. She bit her lip, wondering what he would do if she admitted... "Do you remember losing control in the water with the jellyfish? That scent was that I was interested in you, Fortis."

"You wanted to fuck me?" he asked. His brows rose for a moment before that hungry gaze returned. "That is most surprising."

"You're telling me."

"But you know nothing about... pleasure." He growled the last word and it sent sparks of awareness throughout her entire body. Like a wave of desire, it rolled over her head and crashed down throughout her entire body.

"I know nothing about my pleasure," she corrected.

"Then it would not be right for me to take this first moment from you." The sound of his voice rolled over her. She wanted to feel his skin pressed against hers. A flash of him looming over her, all those teeth bared in threat, made every muscle in her body seem to turn to liquid.

A small whimper escaped her lips, and that was a sound she had never made before.

"Would you like me to walk you through it, virago?" he asked as her eyes drifted shut.

She wasn't sure she would be able to stop him if he wanted to. And she wasn't sure she would ever try on her own. The entire idea of answering this pleasure felt daunting and terrifying. What was she supposed to do? How was she supposed to act? What if she couldn't do it after so many years of people telling her what to do and how to be?

"Virago," he said. With her eyes closed, it was like his voice came from everywhere. "Unzip your wetsuit.

She reached with trembling fingers and pulled the front zipper down. The rattle of it was somehow so much louder because she knew he was watching and all she could think to do was follow his voice.

"Look at all that smooth, beautiful skin," he murmured. "I can see how many battle scars you harbor, virago. So pretty. So many moments where you bested your opponent."

She'd never thought of them like that. But he made it sound like it was a good thing to be marked. She didn't care so much about the scars that dotted her flesh from countless skirmishes and fights. Knife wounds, bullet holes, it didn't matter. All that mattered was his deep groan of appreciation as the backs of her fingers hit her stomach.

Just above her pubic bone he barked, "Stop."

She froze. The warmth of her fingers nearly between her legs was tantalizing. She wanted to slide her fingers between her legs, just to press against the pressure there. She needed... something. Alexia just didn't know what.

"I do not know the body of an achromo," he murmured. "I am learning just as much as you."

She huffed out a little laugh. "That doesn't sound promising. I thought you were telling me how to do this."

"What feels good?"

How was she supposed to know? She'd never touched her body before. She'd never even tried to find out what felt nice or what didn't feel nice.

He seemed to somehow understand without her saying another word. "What I want to do is slide my hands up your ribcage. I want to cup your breasts in my hands."

Alexia followed his words. Her skin felt overly sensitive and warm. Tingles followed her hands as she moved up to her breasts and parted the wetsuit. His sharp inhalation of breath made sparks dance along her skin.

Had her breasts ever felt like this? The cold air made her nipples stiff, but this was even more. The tips were so sensitive.

"Beautiful," he groaned. "Touch your nipples for me, virago. I want to know what noises you make while you play with them."

Her fingers found those aching peaks, and she rolled them between her fingers. It made pleasure spike and somehow, a strange sensation speared between her legs. She was wet and aching, clenching around nothing as though her body wanted to be filled. She couldn't breathe the same as before. All she could do was rock her hips against the floor.

She needed friction. Trying to close her legs, she found she could not. Both of his hands were on her legs, holding them open, forcing her to feel these sensations without doing what she wanted.

"Does that feel good?" he murmured, and she swore she felt his breath on her thigh. "Tell me what you're feeling."

"It feels... incredible." She squeezed her breast harder, imagining it was his clawed hand. "I wish it was your hand."

"What about it?"

"I want to feel your claws." Fuck, it was more than that. "I want to feel them digging into my skin."

The image of sharp little pricks, and how hot the beads of blood would feel slipping down her breast made her whine. That was exactly what she wanted. Not something soft, or delicate. She wanted raw and primal, to feel him rutting into her like an animal, taking what he wanted without asking.

"Careful. I can see you're holding yourself hard enough to bruise." Was that his breath on her stomach? She swore that was a fanning sensation of breath. "Now I want you to reach your pretty hand between your legs. You tell me what you find there."

She swallowed hard. She'd been wanting to touch there, but also had no idea what to do once she did. Everyone she'd seen have sex seemed to enjoy it. What if she didn't?

But the quiet rumble of his growl made it easier to delve her hands between her legs.

"Tell me," he growled, as though it was the most important thing in the world.

"Warm and wet," she whispered, although her voice shook. "It feels... so good."

Another low, echoing growl. "Spread your legs wider, virago."

She did, and then jumped at the sensation of his massive hand touching the zipper. He pulled it down as far as he could. She had no idea what she must look like, her stomach flexed to hold her upright with her legs spread wide and her fingers working between her thighs. All she knew was that this felt better than anything she'd ever experienced in her life. It felt right. It felt as though she was rushing toward something that she didn't know how to grasp.

"Fuck, look at you," he muttered. "Spread out before me like a banquet. I would feast upon if you if you let me, virago. There is nothing I want more than to taste you. Where your fingers are now, I would replace that with my tongue." She swore there was another, wetter sound that followed his words. "I would devour you whole if you let me, until I could taste nothing but you."

She couldn't help herself. She opened her eyes to see that he wasn't as close as she thought. He only had one hand on one of her ankles now, and the other... her gaze traveled down the roping muscles of his torso to see that he had not one, but two cocks. They were fully protruded, a lovely deep pink that melted into the same purple as the rest of him. He gripped the top one in a choking grasp, his eyes between her thighs as he rutted into his fist.

Something about that image made part of her break. Her fingers slid to the top of her pussy where it felt best, and her fingers circled that area faster and faster as her gaze locked upon his massive cocks.

"I can feel you staring at me, virago," he growled, his voice impossibly lower. "Someday, I will make you take both of these cocks. You will learn how they feel inside you."

"I don't know if I can," she whispered.

"Put your fingers inside yourself. I want to hear you."

She did as she was told, and her cheeks flamed bright red. The sound of her fingers sliding inside her body was obscene, but somehow it was even better knowing that he wanted it. The base of his cock bulged, and the sound of his groan sent her tumbling into an oblivion she hadn't realized existed.

With a hissing sound, she saw stars. It was beyond anything she'd ever imagined. One moment she was herself, and the next she was a clenching, needy beast who was seized by every muscle that burned.

She felt ropes of his cum splatter over her wetsuit and even that made her orgasm burn brighter, hotter. She peeled her eyes open again—when had she closed them?—to see him panting over her, one cock in his hand coated with an irridescent liquid, while the other was still very much hard.

Her eyes flicked up to his, and he grinned. "There are benefits to being with one of my kind," he breathlessly said. "Once is never enough."

Chapter 24

Fortis didn't touch her. Not the entire time that her siren song called him with the way her body moved and how her entire being swayed with passion. He'd wanted to. He'd wanted to press his mouth between her legs and taste her passion, but he didn't.

She was an achromo. He had no interest in her kind and he never would. But, somewhere deep inside his chest, he knew that was a lie.

He'd been enraptured from the first moment she'd admitted to wanting him. She'd dragged that zipper down her chest and he thought the world would end right there. The red blush that had stained her chest, the bright pink tips of her breasts, the undulating way she had shifted her hips, all of which made him salivate. He hadn't even realized her people could move like that, but suddenly he wanted to see her do it more. On him. He wanted her to grind like that on his tail, to slide his webbed fingers between her thighs and know what she felt like.

Warm and wet, she'd gasped when he'd asked her. Those words would now live forever in his mind.

Whenever someone said them, he would only think of the way she ground hard against her hand. How her thighs had spread wide, and that wetsuit had parted to reveal her stunning body. All those scars, laid bare for only his eyes to see. He had wanted to lick each and every one of them. To trace them with his tongue and erase every memory of pain that came along with them.

His cocks hadn't ached like that in years. Fortis had planned for the interaction to be short and to the point. An experiment, in his mind, to see what it was that achromos did when they were lost in passion. Another lie he had told himself so he could watch her writhe before him.

He had fooled himself into thinking he could remain separate from her pleasure and then his cocks had punched through his scales so quickly he hadn't even noticed until the top one was in his fist.

And fuck, it had felt good. So incredibly good to watch her while he was thrusting into his fist. She only opened her eyes at the end, but he could feel her gaze on him. Her eyes had widened in surprise at the sight of what he held, and he'd wanted to tell her that soon enough, she would take him.

But he couldn't. She couldn't. They weren't doing this because he was using her as a means to an end. Nothing more. Nothing less. She would bring about a new age with him, then he would die at her hands, and it would all end there.

The plan was simple, and it was one he had to uphold. Fortis knew the end of this, and he knew his path.

But now Alexia's voice echoed in his mind. If she knew she was going to die, she would want to live as much as she could before it was over.

Slipping into the water without catching her eye, he knew very well that he hadn't been living. Not since his wife died. Not since his entire purpose had turned into getting to the end so that he could return to her.

Life was so much more complicated than death.

The icy water helped relieve his mind. As he left the facility to breathe in the salty air, he felt a bit more like himself. Until he scented her in the water and everything went right back to the madness that had claimed him before. He could feel the beast in his chest crying out for him to return to her and plunge inside of that warmth.

"Damn it," he muttered.

It wasn't helping. The ocean wasn't calming the fiery need that burned through every inch of him. He just... wanted. Needed. Desired.

Now that he'd been so close to connection with another living creature, he couldn't stop wanting it. He needed to run his hands along her warm skin. He craved to seek out all the pleasure he'd denied himself for far too long.

Tilting his head back, he breathed in the sea and tried to let the icy waters cool him yet again.

"Sea mother," he murmured, his voice low and quiet. "Please send me a sign that I do not need this. I am tempting myself with what I can only have for a short time. I will find all that I seek in the afterlife once I make it there. And Alexia is wrong. All wrong. Every part of her is that which I hate, and I will not fall apart simply because I have not had the touch of a woman in a long time."

The sea was no help. A current shoved him back toward the building where he had left a panting creature who tempted him more than anyone else had in years. He couldn't go back there. Not when his mind was still so full of her bright red features, how her eyes had squeezed shut, and the sounds she made that rolled out of her throat as she finally discovered what passion meant.

"I have concerns," he told the sea. "So many concerns. She is larger than most achromo, but I am bigger than any of my people. We are not compatible."

On the tail of that thought, he had the image of Daios and Anya pressed into his mind. It was almost like a vision. The sea wanted him to remember that Daios and Anya likely had an even bigger size difference than he and Alexia did.

"But it is wrong," he argued. "Their kind were never meant to be with us. It is unnatural to consider her anything other than an enemy."

More images were pressed into his mind. The memory of Mira helping him find Tau and how hard she had worked to get all the information they could find. Anya patching him up when he'd been scraped by a passing ship, or even when he had just injured himself seeking out this city. Even Ace showing him how to work with droids and teasing him that he deserved to have a little helper. Having one that wasn't alive meant he might actually keep it longer.

There were so many good achromos that were in his life. There were bad ones, but there were good ones as well.

And then one last memory. Of his son and Ace's sister. The two of them working side by side, their heads nearly pressed together as they poured over a projected map of the sea floor that a droid had mapped out.

At the time, he'd thought the image disgusting. He'd taught his son better than to be interested in the thoughts and mind of an achromo. If Aulax wanted to know what she knew, then he should have just taken her memories and gotten on with it. But his son hadn't, because he had seen something in their people that Fortis had never noticed.

Until now.

Until this warrior woman crashed into his life and he realized that maybe he did want to live for a little longer. Ironic, considering he would die at her hands.

Blowing the air out of his gills, he decided Alexia was right. And in some way, the ghost of his wife was right as well. He would live for a little while longer. He would fill his life with as many good things as he could and then, when it was finally his time, he would feel no guilt at leaving this place.

Turning back toward the building, he was surprised to see Alexia had slipped back into the water. In the spears of sunlight, she swam ever so slowly through the entrance to where he'd brought her.

Frowning, he started toward her. "What are you doing?"

"Leaving," she grumbled, grabbing onto the sides of the stones and using her grip to propel herself faster.

Leaving? Why would she be leaving? He just brought her here, and after what they had shared... Taking in a deep breath, he could taste her rage in the water. It was like getting punched in the nose, all metallic and oddly painful.

She had finally reached the end of the tunnel and then used her feet to kick off the edge. He'd thought she might go to the surface, but no. She propelled herself deeper into the darkness of the abyss. She went down, not up.

Frowning even more, he watched her descend. She was an impressive swimmer, he'd give her that. She knew the right cadence to bring her arms up and propel herself ever deeper, not even kicking her legs now, but just keeping her body in a straight line that sank nearly out of sight before he remembered that he shouldn't let her do that.

Flicking his tail, he followed her. "Where are you going?"

"Back to the ship."

"Why?" Or better yet, "How?"

Suddenly, he was angry. They had shared a passionate moment with each other and he was not going to let her disappear into the sea after it. He had questions. Thoughts. Things he wanted to talk to her about.

He'd enjoyed telling her stories about his son and all the mischief the two of them had gotten into. There were more stories he could tell, more pieces of his life that he wanted her to know. And now she was going back to the ship?

Rage made all the lights on his body flicker to life, casting her face in harsh shadows that only made her appear to be even more angry. He wouldn't let her keep doing this. So he moved in front of her, forcing her to stop or she would crash into his massive bulk.

"Fortis," she snarled. "Get out of my way."

"No. Go back to where I put you."

Even he heard how awful that sounded. He ordered her around like he had any right to do so, but he was so angry at her. Her safety was all he cared about. That ship wasn't safe anymore. He could give her the final battery back, but even that wasn't going to power the ship. One battery wasn't enough. She had another week in that cold, dark tomb at most. If the second battery even worked after being in the cold for so long.

This facility was safer for her. It was better. At the very least, until he knew what he was going to do with her.

She'd agreed to help him. That meant he could bring her back to the others, where there were more minds who understood how the achromos worked. She could be back in a city, safe with her own people.

But he didn't tell her any of this. He was so angry, all that came out was, "Or I will make you."

The glare on her face when she turned was enough to set him on fire. "You have nothing to say to me right now. After what you just pulled? I have no interest in you, Fortis. Not in the slightest."

"What I just pulled?"

"You were the one who started all that," she hissed, pointing at him with her gloved finger. "You were the one who made me want... anything at all. Your words. Your plan. Your guidance. And then all of a sudden, as soon as it's over, you up and leave? Without a word. You just slide into the water and pretend that nothing happened between the two of us. I don't care what you have to say or what you want me to do, you giant asshole. You can rot in the ocean for all I care."

And then she kicked her feet and moved around him. But she didn't have her flippers on, so she was damn slow. It was far too easy for him to grab her shoulder and reel her right back into his arms. "Absolutely not. You don't even know where the ship is."

She punched him in the throat. The water slowed her movements, but it was still enough of a jab that he hissed. His gills were sensitive, and she'd hit them hard enough to hurt. It only made him tighten his grip on her, though.

He squeezed her arms down, fighting through the pain. "What was that for?"

"I know where my own ship is! I have a link to it that I can follow. Now let me go."

"Not until we talk about this. I needed to cool off in the water. Why do you think I left?"

"Because you wanted to!" she shouted. Her face was turning red beneath her air mask. He knew her expression when she was angry, and she was beyond pissed.

"Are you listening to me at all? I just told you I needed to cool down." Should he tell her that he wanted to crawl inside of her skin? That he'd left because he feared what he would do to her next, and she deserved to be slowly introduced to the world of passion and desire?

He didn't have time to consider what he would say, because she jammed her hand into his rib gills. Fortis froze as she grabbed a handful of them, pain vibrating throughout his entire body.

"Let me go," she hissed. "I have a beacon. I can get back to the ship without you."

"I did not intend to bring you back to the ship at all," he wheezed, trying very hard to remain still so his gills wouldn't hurt even more than they currently did.

"There are things I need from there. Useful items. If you want me to help you, then I need them." The moment his arms loosened, so did her grip. She kicked off of him to get away, creating space between them that he suddenly realized he didn't like. Not at all.

The space reminded him that he was alone. No, that wasn't even right. It wasn't that he cared about being lonely, because he didn't. He cared that he wasn't with her. He liked spending time with her. He liked pushing Alexia's boundaries and talking with her.

Fortis hated that. He was most upset that he couldn't talk with her more and tell her more stories. The sound of her laughter had been so enjoyable.

And now she was swimming away from him. Heading off into the sea where he could not protect her, or even make sure that she actually made it. So he swam behind her, hoping that she wouldn't notice.

Until she turned with all that rage floating off of her and coating his gills with a metallic bite.

"Fortis!" she shouted. "I need space, for fuck's sake! Get off my ass and go do whatever it is fish do. I'll meet you back at the ship."

"It is dangerous to go alone."

"It's the ocean! There's nothing here." She gestured around her. "Nothing but my own thoughts. So please, for the love of god, fuck off."

He supposed he had no other choice than to honor what she wished. Even though he had no idea what had gone wrong.

Chapter 25

Some part of her knew she was overreacting. Fortis had wanted to explain, and she should let him. After all, maybe that was a normal encounter for his kind. Maybe males were supposed to leave after all of... that.

But for the first time in her life, she had felt connected with another living being. So much so that it had been hard to see him leave. She'd seen men do that to Harlow. She'd been there every time the Original had gotten teary eyed over yet another man leaving after sex, telling herself that it wasn't because she wasn't as pretty as the other Originals or that they found more pleasure in one of the reborns than her.

It seemed to be a universal fear with women, even if Alexia hadn't had sex yet. If she had learned anything from watching Harlow, it was that men left after they got what they wanted. A part of her mind screamed that Fortis had left because he hadn't actually wanted her.

No one could want her. It was foolish to even entertain that someone might. Alexia was a scarred woman. Her body wore the marks of years of mistreatment and she was too big, too much, too everything. She was barely even a woman, as many of the Originals had liked to remind her.

Fortis didn't want her. He was just frustrated, lonely, and anything vaguely female would do.

She was an idiot to get wrapped up in all this. No man should ever be able to affect her, not while she was struggling so hard to even understand emotions. Let alone know what it was like to lean on someone else. He was... frustrating. Annoying. Beyond enraging.

But also she liked him. As she sank deeper and deeper into the water, she knew that was the truth. She liked him a lot, and that was the hardest part of all this. Fortis had wriggled his way underneath her skin, and she wanted more of that. More of him. She wanted to talk to him about his life, to feel his skin against hers, and all the other ridiculous things that made her want to vomit.

The beacon on her wrist lit up, letting her know she was at the correct depth. Now she just had to find the right direction to go. Turning slowly, she kept her gaze on her watch as it blinked on and off, faster and faster until the signal was a steady light to follow. There it was. She was all turned around, but if she kept swimming in this direction, then she would eventually hit the ship.

Now was the hard part. Sinking into the depths of the ocean was relatively easy. She'd learned a long time ago how to dive. All that training was before she'd gotten her emotions back, though. Now that she was finally no longer moving, her thoughts caught up to her.

"Easy," she muttered to herself. "The odds of bumping into anything in the ocean are so small."

She knew the statistics. The ocean was more of a blank space than it was anything else. All she had to do was swim. Even without her flippers, her feet were covered. Her wetsuit didn't have a single hole in it, and its integrity was stable. All she had to do was kick her feet and not stop moving. Perhaps for a very, very long time. But she was proving a point here.

She didn't need him. She didn't need anyone.

Digging deep into her own stubborn pride, Alexia started swimming. Using her arms, she followed her training to maintain a steady movement without depleting too much of her energy. She had learned how to do this from a very young age. She knew how to swim for days on end. She'd trained for this.

Yes, she had also been wasting away on a ship. Weeks on end of not moving made her breathing harder. But she could keep going.

Looking down at the oxygen meter on her other wrist, she realized she was only at half oxygen. That would make things... difficult. She had to control her breathing better, considering she had no idea how long it would take to find the ship.

Maybe this hadn't been smart. Her mind rolled over all the things that could go wrong. She'd had her own personal undine who could swim her all the way to the ship if she wanted. All she had to do was keep her mouth shut. Now, she might drown and he would never know. A shark could find her, of all things, or an orca.

There were plenty of creatures in the sea that would love to find a snack that couldn't fight back against them. Not, at least, like an undine could.

Gritting her teeth, she kept going. Fear did not affect her. She was stronger than that. She was strong enough to continue swimming forward, and she would reach her ship. Even if anxiety made her heart skip beats and her breath saw in her chest. She had just looked at her oxygen. There was fifty percent left. She didn't need to check it again. She was fine. She just had to keep going.

Something glided along her leg. It was a long, slow touch. Hard for her to tell what it was or where it came from. It didn't feel like Fortis, or anything that she'd felt before.

Frowning, she paused to get her bearings. She was still going in the right direction, and maybe her mind was playing tricks on her. Still, her hand was shaking as she lifted it up to her head and clicked on the light attached to her face mask.

She half expected to see a massive beast looming in the darkness before her. But there was nothing. Just the beam of her light and some stray white particles.

"Nothing," she whispered, her voice shaking around the word. "It's all in your head, Alexia. Keep swimming."

But she kept the light on this time. She needed more light to reassure herself that she was, in fact, still alone. Even if she couldn't see all that far ahead of her.

It was only a few more kicks of her legs before she swore there was a current touching her back. Like a creature had swum very close to her spine.

"All in your head," she repeated, but she swam harder. The light on her wrist was a beacon to follow, steady and true.

Until she felt the touch again. This time it tangled around her waist, like an arm had wrapped around her. She reacted, her arms reaching for whatever it was and punching at the creature. It released her, but she swore there was a sticky feeling as it left.

Frantically she looked around, turning her head and light in every direction, but there wasn't anything here. She was alone. She was...

Tentacles and a snapping beak rushed at her. There were more arms than she could count, all of them flaring wide as the squid wrapped itself around her head. All she could see was the strange underbelly, so close now that she could actually see it was bright red. Her light fractured through the thin skin and illuminated the jaws that gnashed near her face.

She grabbed onto it, trying desperately to get it off her head. She'd seen squid before, but never this size. It was nearly five feet in length, she guessed, and the body was so thick it was hard to wrap her arms around.

Eyes. Squid had eyes. She just had to find the damn eyes and then she could push on them as hard as she could. Her hands skated over smooth, slick skin before she felt the bulbous nodes. Pushing hard, she screamed as it shoved off her head and sent her spinning away from it.

Breathing hard, she splayed her arms wide to stop herself. She had to be ready for when that thing came back. And it would come back. Squid liked to hunt, didn't they? She couldn't remember from her training as panic set in. It was so dark. Whipping her head around, she tried to anticipate where it would come from, but she couldn't fucking see.

Tentacles latched around her outstretched arm. She jerked at the limb, only for another to grab her other arm. The first one's beak connected with her wetsuit, biting through the neoprene and sinking into her flesh.

She shrieked, bubbles erupting from around the seal edges of the mask. Her light spun wildly as she arched her neck in pain, and then she saw them.

So, so many of them.

She was surrounded by a hundred squid. All of their ghostly bodies flashing in the sea. There was no light at these depths, which meant all she could do was stare at the haunting images of them tangling above her.

Another latched onto her right thigh, biting deep. She screamed again, writhing to get out of their grip, but they were so incredibly strong. One biting her arm, the other her leg, they were all latched onto her with impossible strength.

Wisps of her blood darkened the water. It looked black in this light, flashing red as it got close enough to her light. Strangely, she could hear them. Bumping into each other as they all rushed forward, fighting against themselves before moving as one as they shifted and moved like a pack. They were hunting together, she realized.

Humboldt squid. She'd heard of them before. Her mind fractured, trying to get away from the pain that was seemingly unending. They bit into her again and again, the bites digging beyond her skin and severing through tendons and muscle.

She should have stayed with him, she thought. Alexia had let her anger get the better of her again, and now she was going to pay the ultimate price. She'd never thought she would die being feasted upon by squid, but she supposed it might be fitting after everything she had done with Tau. Maybe this was just the ocean finally getting back at her for everything.

A flash of thick, rubbery bodies. They moved as one, revealing a glimpse of yellow in the distance. She was already weak, and it seemed like the tentacles wrapped around her arm were going to break it now. She wasn't even sure which arm.

Cold water had rushed into her suit. Her heart beat was slowing down considerably until she could hear it like drums in her ears.

That flash of yellow came again, so bright it blasted through the ghostly squids, revealing their red colorings in bright orange as the light moved closer. Many of the squid gave up. They all turned as one, their long tentacles flaring as they hovered near enough to watch what was happening.

With a single tail flick, Fortis rose through them, approaching her with an expression of pure rage on his face. Of course, he was angry at her. He was always angry at her. No matter what she did, it was never the right thing to do.

Breathing out, she watched more bubbles erupt around her face. Had the squid that had attached her face broken her breathing apparatus? It couldn't have done anything too bad. There was still air.

The squid wrapped around her suddenly fled. Perhaps they realized there was a much larger predator in the water barreling toward them. Fortis hit her hard enough to steal the breath from her lungs and pain flared white hot. She couldn't see anything, couldn't focus beyond the misery that rioted now that he had her.

Adrenaline depleted, all she could do was remain limp in his arms as the salt water burned through her suit and all the wounds decorating her skin.

He said nothing, just propelled them at a speed that was shocking. She'd thought she'd seen him swim quickly before, but he had never moved like this.

Her heart thudded strangely in her chest. All wrong. It was slowing down, she thought, or maybe it had never sped up in the first place. She had a feeling it wasn't right since the first moment those squids had attacked her.

Looking down at her arm, she struggled to lift it so she could see her oxygen levels. That was the most important thing. She was underwater. She had to breathe.

But the squids must have bitten through something important, or perhaps they fucked with something on the back of her breathing unit when that first one attacked her.

"Three percent," she wheezed as more bubbles erupted around her face.

At least Fortis had the wherewithal to look down at her words. "What?"

"Three percent oxygen," she said. Already it felt like the air she was trying to breathe wasn't coming right. The chemical mixture was off. She was getting a little light-headed, and that was not a good thing.

He stared down at her until his expression smoothed out. The confusion that wrinkled his brows was gone, and instead, was replaced with worry that she didn't like.

Fortis paused, stopping so suddenly that her hair floated in front of her face. He smoothed it back with a massive, webbed hand.

"Virago, this is something I wish I did not have to do. I do not have time to explain what it is. We need to move fast because you are bleeding out. Those bites were not kind to you."

She wasn't sure what he was saying. She was just watching the way his lips moved when he talked. "Okay."

"Okay?"

She tried to shrug, but her arm hurt so much that she couldn't. Had they broken the bone? Now that she'd gotten some time away from the squid, it felt like they might have.

The pain swelled over her head again, threatening to drown her. She couldn't focus on anything, not even the slight prick on the side of her neck that was so little compared to all the other pains in her body.

But she struggled a bit when a clawed hand grabbed the oxygen mask on her face and took it off. "Fortis!" she croaked, reaching for it even as he dropped it down into the abyss.

Was he finally going to kill her? Had he given up on her?

"Shh," he murmured, his hand stroking through her hair. "Let me breathe for you, virago."

And then he was swimming again. Darting through the water as everything turned into a blur. Or it would have, if she could see in the darkness. The particles in front of her were like stars moving so fast she could only see the slightest smudge of them as they darted past.

She held her breath for as long as she could, before there was a sudden sensation of air pushing into her body and then... somehow, she was breathing. She wasn't sure how she wasn't drowning.

Even as the pain dragged her into unconsciousness, she marveled that somehow, she wasn't dead yet. Maybe she would be soon, though.

Chapter 26

Fortis had known letting her go alone was foolish. She was an Fachromo, soft and easily hunted. Too many creatures under the sea knew an opportunity when they saw one, and she was certainly that. The shoal of squid had seen her weakness. They were hungry. He couldn't blame them.

Her taste was delicious in the salty brine, and he wasn't the only one who thought so. They had hunted her, bested her, by any right they deserved to get a bite out of her body. But he couldn't let her die. Her own foolish choices were what brought her to this moment, but...

He'd seen her floating there, still struggling against the attack and fighting with every ounce of energy left in her form. Alexia never knew when to stop, and he'd found that remarkable about her from day one. Allowing her to leave him had never been an option.

Looking down at her limp form in his grasp, he had to admit that he felt something for Alexia. He didn't want her to die. That was far more than he could say for a majority of people in his life.

As he darted through the water, holding her tight to his chest, he tried to ignore the scent of blood that coated his gills. She was going to be fine, he told himself. Yes, those wounds were ragged. He could see the vibrant flash of muscle and strangely yellow fat that lined her body in each wound. It was a gruesome sight, but she was stronger than most achromos. She would survive.

But when she said she had no oxygen, he'd nearly lost his nerve. After all that he had done to avoid the achromos, to prove that he did not wish to have them in his life, even as the others took them as their mates... he was now connected to one. He breathed for her, inhaled and exhaled even as she struggled to stay alive. He pushed air into her lungs over and over again, as though his body could tell hers that he would not let her go. No matter how hard she tried to escape him.

Light burst into the ocean as the sun came out. He was close to the surface now, and close to the small village they had built for the other achromos who were working with his people. But now he could see the extent of her injuries and it made him swim ever faster.

Her skin was paler than he'd ever seen it, nearly bone white. Her limbs were limp as he swam, dangling over his arms and fins as though he carried a dead body. She didn't look at him, didn't react to a word he said even when he repeated her name.

This wasn't good, and the realization unsettled him. Fortis didn't want to imagine what her stillness might mean. No, he needed her to be fixed. And immediately.

A movement in the distance to his right warned him that another was approaching. But he didn't even need to guess who might hunt him down.

He and his son had not gone weeks without seeing each other since Aulax had been taken to Alpha. His son was always the first to track Fortis down, and always had been. But he rarely was gone this long.

He didn't slow down, knowing that if anyone could keep up with him, that hunter would be his son.

Together, they blasted through the water as his boy joined him. "I see your hunt was successful," Aulax called out.

"In a way."

"Who is she?"

"A great power in Tau. She has battled me many times and has proven herself to be a warrior we can trust." He didn't want to say too much. She didn't smell like him, at least. That was a small bit of luck, so he didn't have to explain to his son why this warrior woman had been close enough to smell like Fortis.

But it was hard to hide. His fingers clenched her a little harder, dragging her closer to his chest as though his son were a threat. He didn't recognize the response. He'd never cared if any of the other achromo mates were around his people. Why did this one illicit such a feeling?

He was struggling, and he wasn't sure how to address it. Breathing hard, he looked over at his son, who had yet to take his eyes off Alexia.

"She's going to die, father," his son murmured. A flash of bright yellow trailed down Aulax's spine, as though he was sad to say it. "Those wounds..."

"She was attacked by a shoal." He needed his son to know that he had not done this. He needed someone to understand that he was not so lost in his hatred that he would harm a woman like this.

Damn it, she wasn't a woman. She was an achromo. Why were his thoughts so jumbled?

He should give her over to his son. Aulax would take her to the others and ensure that she received the help she needed. But even the thought made him press her even tighter to his chest and his tail flick faster like he could out swim his boy. He didn't want anyone to touch her but himself.

And yet, he knew he couldn't save her himself. Not with wounds like these.

Fortis would have to hand her over, and that would be difficult for him. He wasn't sure why. He trusted these people far more than he trusted her, and still he didn't want to let her go. What if they tried to kill her because of where she had come from? What if they tried to enact some kind of revenge for everything Tau had done?

His mind raced even as the domes came into view. They had done even more work since he had left, and there were quite a few engineers and droids now. What had once been a single, centuries old abandoned dome had turned into a sprawling village of achromos mingled together with his people. The domes were now bubbles all linked through glass and metal tubes. One of the achromos had claimed it looked a bit like a hamster cage. He had no idea what a hamster was, and did not listen when the young man had tried to explain it.

The sunlight glinted off the glass, showing the moving bodies within. Achromos moved inside, some of them working on droids, others programming new schematics for expansion of their village, a few gardening. There were so many things to do within those bubbles that he could hardly imagine how they kept it all straight.

Outside of the walls were the droids. At least a dozen of them, all welding and fixing what needed to be fixed alongside two achromos who were nearly always in the water.

Mira was quick to be the first to jump in with her welder and start building. Arges floated beside her, a massive metal panel in his hands that he held as though it weighed nothing at all. To their people, the metal was surprisingly light. He held it in place for her as she sparked the welder in her hands and started in on the panel. Soon enough, that would be another outbuilding, or garden, or whatever it was that Mira got in her head. She'd been the spearhead of expanding the entire village and never seemed to stop.

The other achromo in the water, Ace, turned as soon as he arrived. That woman had eyes on the back of her head and always seemed to know when someone new was in the area. He didn't see Maketes, but he was quite certain his yellow finned brother would show up soon enough. They all had to stare when a newcomer arrived, and he was certain he made quite the spectacle.

Fortis didn't stop. If they wanted to talk with him, they could do so later. He needed to get her to the infirmary and beg Anya to take care of her. They didn't even have a healing pod like many of the major cities did.

"Father," Aulax said as they sped through the village to the very back. "I think you should prepare yourself that she might not—"

He leveled his son with a look. "We do not put thoughts like that out into the sea unless we wish for her to make them true."

"It is not a thought, but a fact. She has lost too much blood, father. There is nothing you or I can do to change that."

As they reached the infirmary, Fortis had to stop and wait for Aulax to open the moon pool door. And as he floated there, holding her in his arms, all he could think was that he couldn't be too late. Not when he had just gotten her to agree that she would help them. Not when he had finally realized that she was more than just someone who hated his people.

Grinding his teeth, he held still as the doors opened above his head. Aulax reached forward and touched a lock of Alexia's hair, twining it around his finger before letting it float away.

"She must have been a very impressive warrior for you to fight so hard for her," Aulax muttered. "You are not like this with many achromo."

So many words were hidden in what his son said. He stared at the man his boy had become, waiting for Aulax to break and say what he meant. The squeaking doors above them would only provide them a small amount of privacy for so long.

Finally, Aulax cleared his gills with a forceful thwack. "I have never seen you worried about their kind, and you reek of fear, Father. I just want to know what has led you to this point."

"I..." He took a deep breath. "I am impressed by this one."

"That doesn't mean you react like this."

He loosened his hold on her legs and reached forward to touch Aulax's shoulder. Gripping it hard, he stared deep into his son's eyes and prayed that if anyone would understand him, it would be the child who had come from his own body. "I do not have an answer for you. This one is not like the others. She is important and I must... We must keep her safe."

The doors finished opening, and he gave his son a look that promised he would return soon enough. They would need to speak of this, eventually.

He busted through the rest of the moon pool door, scraping off a few scales in the process as he launched himself out of the water fast enough that he could sit on the edge without ever putting her down. Anya was waiting for him, a confused expression on her face, until she saw the woman in his arms.

She let out a gasp and pressed her fingers to her mouth. "Fortis, what is happening?"

Anya always said his name strangely. It was an odd name, and likely one she had never heard before she had lost her hearing. As such, the word was always slightly slurred as she said it.

He tilted Alexia in his arms. Her head lolled to the side, her hair shifting so Anya could see Alexia's face. "She needs help."

"She's lost a lot of blood. I can make her comfortable, but—"

Anya froze at the look on his face. He glared at her with every ounce of rage that made him shake. The look said he would need retribution if Alexia died, and that he would take that retribution out of Anya's own hide if she failed in this.

The water stirred next to him, and he could hear the rumbling of voices in the water. Clearly, Aulax was having to argue with Daios. The male didn't like Fortis much to begin with, and having Anya alone with him? This was likely eating Daios alive.

Good, let the red devil feel a little uncomfortable.

Anya shuddered before stepping closer. "Can I try something first?"

He nodded, though his gaze was narrowed, and he kept his gaze firmly on her. She reached for the breathing tube stuck in Alexia's throat and gently removed it. There was the faintest sound of suction and then... silence.

Her chest didn't rise. She didn't breathe. Without the tube in her neck, she wasn't doing anything on her own.

He couldn't breathe either. Had this all been his fault? Had he somehow done this to her? She didn't deserve to die like this, not when he had just found out what she looked like while she was so fucking beautiful and needy. She was too strong for this. He refused to believe she would die.

Hand shaking, he took the tube out of Anya's hand and placed it back in Alexia's neck. "Do what you can."

"I can't do anything, Fortis. She's been dead for too long, her brain hasn't had enough oxygen. It doesn't work like a switch."

Another achromo walked into the room, looking at a clipboard in his hand. "Hey, Anya? If Bitsy is on, do you mind explaining this request to me?"

But then he looked up and froze. His mouth dropped open, and Fortis could see recognition bloom in his eyes. It was almost like the man knew something that would help them.

With a flex of his tail, he slapped the man into the opposite wall and pinned him to the metal. "What do you know?"

The man wheezed out a long breath, slapping at the scales that held him trapped.

"Fortis!" Anya shouted.

The commotion was sure to bring more achromos. They all were so meddlesome. So he reached for the man quickly, dragging him close enough that he could smell the fear on the man's breath.

"What do you know?" Fortis snarled.

"Nothing much! Just rumors. People in Alpha used to... talk." He scrabbled at Fortis's hands, trying desperately to get away from him. "Let me go."

"Tell me more."

"Genetic experiments. People who were larger, stronger, more capable of protecting important people. I used to work for a few doctors there and they all claimed that it was possible, and that they'd heard of other cities doing it." Another long whimper followed the words. "Please let me go."

Anya's hand touched his forearm, but he knew there was importance in this whelp's words. Doctor. Scientist. Whatever the creature called himself. Coiling his tail around the man, he wrapped the soft flesh in cold, wet scales and forced him closer to Alexia. "Can you save her?"

The man gulped. His eyes were too wide and his heartbeat thundered against Fortis's tail, but there was only a short hesitation before he nodded. "If she's one of them, then she should be able to survive a lot more than this. I can... I can try."

It was good enough.

Chapter 27

The beeping was almost too familiar. How many times had she woken just like this? A hundred beeps, that was what she had always told herself. Count a hundred beeps before she opened her eyes. Then at least she got a few moments to herself.

She always started at her feet. Could she move her toes? Yes. They were moving. Slowly, achingly, but they were moving. Good, she wasn't paralyzed then. Moving up her calves, she felt no pain there either. Her thigh ached. Both of them, now that she was thinking about it. They hurt like she'd gotten sliced into, so that must have been what happened. Maybe a knife fight. It wouldn't be the first time.

Twenty-five... twenty-six...

Moving up past her hips, there were no wounds on her torso, at least. That didn't feel so bad, although there was a strange suction-y feeling when she breathed that might be bad. Her lungs weren't breathing normally, and that wasn't a great sign, but she would take it. Lungs could heal. Hearts couldn't.

Fifty-three... fifty-four...

Her hands and arms hurt a lot more than the rest of her body. Mostly just her biceps, almost as though there was something really wrong with one of them. She doubted that was the case, though. She healed so much faster than other humans, so she must just be a little tired from all the drugs they'd pumped into her body. Nothing a stretch wouldn't fix.

Eighty-seven... eighty-eight...

Alexia had a horrible headache and there was a strange, cotton-like substance coating her tongue. She needed a glass of water, and then a few more meds to kick the rest of this pain. Then she'd be fine. She could go back to guarding or doing whatever it was she'd been doing.

One hundred.

Blinking her eyes open, she squinted them against the searing white light of the infirmary. It wasn't the one in Tau, though. Most of her memories rushed in at that. She'd been attacked by a massive amount of squid who were far too big for their own good, and then Fortis had saved her. At least he hadn't left her to die. She really thought he was more likely to do that, considering the situation was entirely her fault.

But she wasn't dead. So he'd gotten her somewhere with healers who knew how to kick up her body's healing process. She wasn't entirely sure of the science behind it. All she knew was that those with genetic modifications could heal far better than the average human. Alexia had died a few times in her life, only to be brought back with a sharp electrical pulse to the chest and an injection of adrenaline that seemed to make it better.

She blinked the sand out of her eyes a few times, trying to get her bearings. There was glass above her head. Now that her eyes were adjusting, she could see it wasn't all white. The light had just been the sun spearing through the water, although she wasn't certain she would see sunlight for much longer.

There was a thunderhead in the sky. A black cloud that was dark as ink, menacing as it rolled overhead. She stayed quiet as she watched it, just staring up at the coils of darkness.

Tiny drops of rain struck the surface of the water that was probably ten or fifteen feet above her head. Then the wind hit. Soon enough, she couldn't see the sky at all. Rolling waves overtook all of it and then the sun was really gone. It was almost pitch black in the room until the overhead lights flickered on, one by one.

Where was she? Fortis had clearly taken her somewhere safe where she could heal, but this wasn't a familiar city. She'd seen them all with her own eyes, having traveled with Harlow to all of them at some point in her life. This was not a familiar place. Nor were any of the cities close enough to the surface where they could hear the rolling rumble of thunder and the sudden cracks of lightning.

A door opened and closed. The sound was a welcome reprieve to the storm that rolled overhead.

Turning her head to the side, she realized that this room was a dome. She'd only been in a few of these before. Giant metal beams stabilized the whole thing, glass coming all the way down from the ceiling to the metal floor. Plenty of medical equipment was stored in glass faced storage units, and there were two other tables in the room. Not beds. Tables. So perhaps this was more of a surgical suite, although she couldn't imagine why they would have one of these. This had to be a small settlement, something outside of Tau's control.

The door wasn't even connected to any computer. No automatic functions here. Just a real old school door that the young man who walked into her room closed behind him.

He looked up at her with massive eyes magnified by glasses before he cleared his throat. "Oh. You're awake."

"I'm awake."

"Fantastic. I'll get Mira."

Her voice was little more than a croak, but she still made it sound intimidating. "Wait."

The harsh word made the man freeze where he was. She could see his shoulders were shivering with fear as he looked over his shoulder. "Yes?"

"Water, please."

"Oh. Right. Of course. I'm sorry, I forget that morphine can cause dry mouth with some patients. Allow me." He walked over to the corner, where there was a jug of water. He almost dropped the plastic jug on the floor as he shakily poured it into a glass for her and then brought it over to her table. He hesitated before placing it down next to her. "Let me get you a straw."

"I'm fine." Alexia wedged her elbow underneath her and slowly sat up.

"You shouldn't do that." He lunged forward, almost placing his hand on her chest to hold her in place before he froze again. His hand shook. "I just think... You almost died, miss."

Though she coughed as she sat up straight, much to his terror, she didn't feel much worse for it. At least she could sit up straight and drink out of a glass. "I'm fine," she repeated. "Get whoever you said you needed to get."

"Mira. She wanted to know when you were awake first. The others were, of course, interested as well. They have all been popping in multiple times to make sure you were still alive. No one's seen Fortis so…" He trailed off, those eyes somehow getting even bigger. "Right. I'll go get Mira."

She had no idea what had cursed her to end up in this place, but she would never forgive Fortis for bringing her here. Downing the water, she set the glass down and tried to stay upright. If she was going to meet someone important in this place, she damned well wasn't doing it lying down.

Where was Fortis? She tried to look through the water surrounding the glass dome, but the storm above raged so powerfully that it churned at the surface. Foam filled her line of sight, making it impossible to tell if there was an undine out there watching her, or if it was just the nothingness of the sea.

Snorting, she remembered the last time she'd thought there was nothing in the sea.

Speaking of… Alexia looked down at the bandages on her thighs and arms. The squid had bitten into her in quite a few different places, it seemed. She was lucky they hadn't gone for her throat. That likely would have been much more difficult to survive.

She peeled off the bandages while hissing through her teeth. The one on her left arm was the worst, although the muscle was already regrowing. Clearly, they'd given her a good boost of pain medicine for her to not be feeling that nasty piece of work. Her other arm wasn't quite so bad, but it was slightly oozing, which she could only guess meant it had gotten infected somehow. Maybe the mouths of those squid weren't so clean.

But her leg… her leg wasn't good at all. She needed a good dose of nanites to get that to heal. The tiny robots were usually what Tau injected her people, straight into the bloodstream where they could heal. Those squid had nearly chewed right through to the bone with those sharp beaks. Sighing, she shook her head at the mess of it all. If she had just let Fortis carry her back to the ship, nothing would have happened. Her own stupid pride had gotten in the way. She really needed to learn how to manage that emotion better.

The door opened and closed again, this time with a sharper crack that suggested the person entering had a lot more strength than the last one.

Glancing up, she stared at the fire haired woman in front of her. This Mira was strong. She'd been right about that. Muscles bunched up and down her bare arms that she had crossed over her chest. The white tank top she wore was smeared with grease, and her bottoms were a wetsuit that had been folded in half around her waist. There were still drops of water on it.

"You were out in this?" Alexia asked, pointing up to the storm. "Seems dangerous."

"Shit has to get done. So I get it done." Mira leaned against one of the other tables, her eyes seeing more than Alexia wanted her to see. "You took your bandages off, I see. You don't trust our healing?"

"Not a lot of people know how to heal someone like me."

"Yeah, I had the idea of that as soon as I saw you. You aren't human."

The words stung. Alexia had heard them her entire life, but they still weren't great to hear. "I am human, just like you."

"Upgraded?"

"More than upgraded. Created in a lab, perfection personified." She shrugged. "Or at least, perfect for the job they made me for."

Mira's mouth twisted to the side, like she was chewing on the inside of her lip. "What did they make you do?"

"Protect."

"You good at it?"

"Better than anyone here." Alexia glanced around them, trying to decide if she needed to find herself a weapon. Although she supposed she could just kill this woman with her bare hands. None of them would guess she could do that. "I wouldn't suggest testing me."

Mira held her hands up. "I wasn't planning on it. I've seen you lying down. I don't even want to know what size you'd be standing up."

"I need nanites."

"We don't have any of those here."

Alexia frowned. Furrows appeared between her eyes as she took a deep breath and sighed. The sound was a long, deep wheeze, similar to a growl, as she realized she was stranded in the worst of circumstances. "Then I'll need steroids. A lot of them."

"We don't have that many of those, and generally speaking, we keep them safe for those who need them after an infection. You'll just have to heal like the rest of us."

Yeah, she wasn't going to do that. Taking another deep, steadying breath, Alexia threw her legs over the side of the table. The metal dug into the back of her thighs, making the wound on one ache worse than before. Not a big deal, really. She could make it through. That pain wasn't as bad as she'd experienced during her training. Or the last time she'd died.

She'd been electrocuted to death when Harlow had fallen into a pool of water with a live wire in it. Alexia had thrown her Original out of the water and been stuck in it herself.

Wincing, she placed her feet on the floor and shook her head. "This is going to suck."

"What are you doing?"

Alexia shoved herself upright. Her left leg took all of her weight easily enough, although it wasn't a pleasant sensation. She stood still as Mira lunged for her.

"Let's not do that," Mira said, her hands held out as she stared up Alexia's massive height. "Damn, you're a big woman."

"You can try to stop me." She took another step forward, trying out her weight on the right leg, which wasn't as bad as she'd assumed. "But I wouldn't suggest it."

"Where are you going?"

"Getting steroids. I assume they're with all the other medication."

"I told you, I'm not giving you any more medication. I don't know what it will do with everything else the doctors here gave you. It's not like we have a hospital here and you were quite literally dead." Mira tried to grab onto her arm, then released it when Alexia shook her off. "Good lord, you are strong."

"Stronger than most," Alexia replied. She ran her tongue over her teeth as she reached the cabinet and rummaged through it. "What did they give me?"

"I don't know."

Could be worse. She'd had a lot of different drugs in her system throughout her entire life. A lethal dose for a regular human wasn't a lethal dose for her.

Another person walked in, this time a blonde with a droid wrapped around her head. "What's she doing up?"

"Giving herself a steroid injection."

"She can't do that! We had to give her anticonvulsants because she started seizing when we restarted her heart! Steroids could kill her." The blonde woman stepped forward, only stopping when Mira grabbed her arm. "Mira, let me go. She's going to kill herself again."

"I think we let the big woman do what she wants," Mira hissed.

Likely because if she died, all Mira's issues would be fixed. Alexia knew she was a complicated problem to have. None of them trusted her, and she didn't blame them for it.

"Did Fortis tell you who I am?" she asked as she found the box of steroids. They only had six vials. She took three of them.

"Only that you were from Tau, and that we could trust you," Mira replied.

"A man of many words." Alexia stuck the first needle in her thigh, sighing as the steroids immediately started to work. She could feel her body using it to address the wound on her thigh, and could even feel the ragged edges of her wound healing.

She turned toward the other two women, noticing their eyes widened as they stared at her leg. It was visibly knitting together at this point. The perks of being more than human.

"I am from Tau. You can trust me, however impossible that seems. I have no interest in hurting the people here and only want to seek revenge on Tau for all the things they have done to me. What you're watching right now is only part of their experiments."

She stuck the next shot into her left arm, the one with the ooze coming out of it. That one stung, but she just stared as the yellow liquid belched out of the wound before slowing and starting to heal. One last wound.

If she were back in Tau, they would have given her blood. This place didn't have that, though. Or maybe they did, and they just weren't interested in giving it to her. That was fine, too. She didn't expect them to welcome her with open arms.

The two women's mouths had opened as they stared at her, and then a third poked her head in. With dark hair cropped close to her head and glasses on her face, she was so far from anyone who lived in

Tau that Alexia found herself liking her a bit more than the other two.

"What's going on in here?" Her eyes turned toward Alexia and then moved up... up... up... "Oh. Fuck."

Alexia sighed and looked up at the ceiling. "Oh fuck is right. Now where is my undine?"

Chapter 28

Two weeks. That's how long it took for the other achromos to bring her back from the dead, and the entire time Fortis argued with himself that it wasn't necessary to see her. He didn't need to look at her still form, count the breaths that rose in her chest, or linger in the water to make sure she was still alive.

His people had done everything they could to save her. They weren't certain they could do it, but it was better than nothing. They hadn't treated her any differently than one of their own, even though they had good reason to hate her.

He hated feeling so helpless. But he had trusted that his people would succeed. And they had.

She pulled through the pain and the endless torment of death standing beside her, and then he could breathe again. Of course, he couldn't see her after that. She was still healing. He didn't want to get in the way. So he stayed in the water, seeing her only when he was certain she was resting. It allowed him to check and make sure she was alive, but also to know that he didn't bother her.

On one of those occasions, Arges found him. He scented his brother long before the blue fin was in his sight, but he didn't warn Arges away. Some part of him wanted to talk.

No matter how hard such a conversation was bound to be. His feelings were all jumbled, and it was so wrong to even have the thoughts he was thinking of. But also...

"Brother," he said as Arges swam closer. Together, they headed away from the infirmary dome. Fortis found he didn't like anyone else looking at her.

From what he had been told, Alexia had fixed herself. She'd stolen all the steroids they had and then injected herself with them. The drugs had made her flesh heal quickly, but exhausted her. She'd told everyone that she needed some time to sleep, and after that, she would be ready to answer any and all of their questions. He wasn't sure if that was a good plan or not.

Tau was difficult. He knew the others wouldn't understand many of the things she was going to tell them. He didn't want them to think less of Alexia for the life she had lived. She'd fought too hard for his people to judge her.

Arges crossed his arms over his chest as they floated above the abyss together, far enough away from the village for a private conversation. "You have feelings for her."

"Feelings are irrelevant. And I do not." But that was a lie, and he knew it.

Arges knew it too. His brother scowled, obviously disappointed that Fortis denied his feelings. "Fortis. If anyone could understand how you're feeling, it is me. I know my other brothers are difficult to speak with about... well, anything. But I have felt the same thing you are going through."

"And what do you believe I am feeling?"

"Curiosity. The difficult and disgusting experience of being attracted to one of them when you have hated them your entire life. The knowledge that nothing will ever be the same because you found one of them, but that truth also makes you want to claw your eyes out."

That about summed it up, but it wasn't something Fortis wanted to admit. He did hate that he found her interesting, and that was the most difficult part of all of this.

"I do not enjoy achromos," he hissed. "They are a plague upon this sea, and I wish to see the waters run red with their blood. The world will never be the same if they remain as they are."

"I agree."

"You are mated to one, Arges. That has to change things."

"It doesn't, though." Arges shrugged. "I can hate Mira's people without hating her. Is it difficult? Yes, of course. The conversations surrounding how I feel about her people will never be easy. She doesn't like that I want to hunt them and kill them. I don't like that she wants to save them. It'll be difficult, especially considering where yours are from. But that doesn't mean you should shy away from such difficulties."

Grumbling, Fortis shook his head. "I have no interest in her. What more do I need to say to convince you?"

"Give me a reason you don't like her."

He shrugged. "Everything about her is a reason to not like her. She is the enemy. Every interaction with her thus far has been a fight, both physically and in words. It is not the kind of relationship that can be lasting."

"Relationship?"

Fortis glanced over and saw Arges had raised his brow. Clearly, his brother saw something that he did not, and Fortis hated that.

He would not admit that there was anything going on between him and Alexia. He did not wish for there to be anything going on between them, either. These complicated feelings would eventually subside.

He hoped now it would be easier to deny her. She was with others of her own kind, not stuck in the depths with him. Soon enough, they would both forget each other because there were others for them to speak with.

But still, the words bubbled out of his lips. "The ghost of my wife visited me. She told me to live, but I have no interest in doing so."

Arges seemed to think about the words for a long time. The lull in their conversation gave the sea time to swirl around them. Eddies drifted around his body and toyed with his hair, filtering through his gills. It was nice to feel the sea supporting him, as though she whispered whatever he chose would be the right current to follow.

Finally, Arges asked, "How long has it been since you've shown interest in any woman?"

"Since my wife."

"And how long has she been with the ancestors?"

He swallowed. "Many, many years. But I have been faithful to her for all that time."

Arges hummed out a low breath. "You have been faithful and loyal to a memory. It is an honorable thing you have done, but a memory does not care that you are loyal, Fortis. That loyalty was for you. Not her."

The words stung. He had been everything he was supposed to be for his wife, even after he lost her. To hear that, maybe, it hadn't been the right thing to do? He refused to believe it. Admitting all that would mean admitting he was wrong. And that he had wasted so much time in his life when he could have spent all those years being happy.

Shaking his head, he tried to think of an argument that would justify his actions, but then he was saved. Aulax appeared, his lights all flaring in happiness as he approached the two of them. This was just the excuse he'd been looking for.

Clearing his throat, he nodded toward his son. "I need to see to my boy."

"He's a man now, Fortis."

"He'll always be a boy to me."

No matter how old his son aged, he would always be Fortis's boy. That was how it went. Aulax was the most important child in his life, and he refused to see him as anything other than that. Unfortunately, Aulax found that exceedingly annoying.

Was Fortis using his son as an excuse? Yes, absolutely. He knew that. But as he left Arges floating there with more complicated questions that Fortis didn't want to answer, he at least was blessed with a few moments of peace with his son.

Aulax grinned as he approached, opening his arms wide and grabbing Fortis the moment he got close. "She's well enough to see, father!"

"Who?"

Immediately, that grin faded from his son's face. "Your... your woman. The woman you brought back with you on the brink of death? They said we could speak with her today."

"Why would I speak with her?"

It was the wrong thing to say. His son's expression shuttered in disappointment before he pulled himself back together and tried to smile again. This time, the expression was harder to believe. "Because you were the one who brought her here. They thought you would wish to talk with her. While being recorded, of course."

"I don't know what they expect me to get out of her."

"They expect you to get information about Tau. That was why you brought her here. You said she would help us." Aulax cleared his throat. "And I assumed, since you have never shown any concern for any achromo, that you thought highly of her."

"You thought wrong." He was so tired of lying to everyone.

And it appeared his son understood that. Aulax's grin became very, very real as he looked his father over and said, "Then you won't mind if I talk with her? Perhaps she would be more interested in one of our people who is interested in their kind. I'd love to have a long chat with her about whatever it is she wishes to speak of."

Rage burned hot and fierce in his chest. He didn't want his son to talk to her at all. It was wrong to even think of Aulax flirting with the woman he had... had...

Done nothing with. He'd done nothing with her, and therein lay the issue. He wanted to do so much more, and he had not been able to do so.

Frustrated bubbles blew out of his gills before he turned away from the infirmary and toward the area where they usually met with the achromos within their safe village. "Come, son. We will speak with her together."

"As I thought."

He'd fallen right into that trap. Fortis tried to tell himself that he could do this without giving away how he felt. He would meet with her again, see her after she had almost died. He could hold himself together in front of the others who did not think that he would.

The rumors would be over, then. They would all leave him alone, and he could lick his wounds in silence after severing the connection with Alexia.

But then he popped his head up in the meeting room and waited for what felt like forever. She was supposed to come here, wasn't she? She should be here by now.

What if Aulax had been wrong? What if she was still very injured, and no one wanted to tell him? What if she'd taken a turn for the worse and they were all rushing back to the infirmary now?

He couldn't breathe until he saw her shadow moving across the floor. No one could mistake that shadow for anyone else.

And then there she was. Strong, confident, far more than any achromo he had ever met. She had been so limp when he'd brought her here. Her face pale, her features drawn. But now she walked with a straight spine and broad shoulders as she had before.

It made pride swell in his chest. He wanted to grab onto her, to hold her against his hearts and feel her own strange single heart pounding against his own. Fortis hadn't wanted to touch someone else in such a long time. But her?

He wanted to hold her. He wanted just a few moments where he didn't feel guilty for touching her.

Breathing out, Fortis tried not to show how affected he was by her beauty. But the breathless way he asked, "You are well?" must have given him away.

"Fortis," she said, and her voice was soft and quiet. "It's good to see you."

They stared at each other like no one else existed. And in that moment, no one did. It was just him and her, staring at each other, trying so hard to make sure that the other was okay.

His eyes danced over the pulse at her throat, the breath that filled her ribs and lifted her shoulders, the way her hands flexed into fists. And then he looked into her eyes and felt every part of him freeze in wonder. Life burned in that gaze, so beautifully that it made his entire body feel strange.

The gills at his sides lifted, shaking just slightly at her stare. He wanted her to look at him all the time like that. He wanted her to praise him, to breathe out his name as she had before. None of this was possible, though. Not for them. Not here.

Clearing his throat, he tried to pull them both out of this moment. "This is Aulax," he said. "My son."

Her gaze flicked to the younger version of him, and he watched the softness spread even further over her features. "Aulax. I have heard about you and all the fun you and your father got into when you were young."

"Fun?" Aulax repeated. "I don't remember it like that. My father certainly embellished that story."

"I don't think your father knows how to embellish anything."

"You would be right in that." His boy leaned against the edge of the moon pool, looking far too comfortable and flirty. "I didn't realize you were going to be quite so impressive in stature. The others mentioned you were larger than average, but you look like a match for our people. And beautiful at that."

"You are far too young for me."

He was pleased to hear her at least argue with Aulax. Because he was too young for her. That was a better argument than the words that had been boiling on his tongue like, "Get your eyes off her or I will remove them for you."

Aulax chuckled at her words. "Oh, I don't think age has much to do with anything. You came here with my father, and he's an old man."

"I don't think of him as an old man." She looked at him again and his world burst into flame.

Scorching hot heat swelled throughout his entire body. She made him want to grab onto her and see what other passion he could wring from her body.

Every time he thought about it, he knew it was wrong. Devious. He should be better than the others of his people who had fallen under the spell of an achromo. He knew better than to do what he was doing.

His son was still flirting with her. "You should see what it's like with the others. The People of Water have many kinds, but the depthstriders are the most terrifying of the lot. You'll find there are a lot of different people under the sea. All of us are slightly different. There are the waveriders, those people usually live in the shallows. They don't look quite so different from you, to be honest. Although the gills usually give us away. And the tail, of course."

What was Aulax prattling on about? Alexia didn't care about the differences between their people. She needed to give her information about Tau and then move on. That was all this conversation was, and it certainly wasn't an opportunity for her to flirt with his son.

Except, maybe she should meet more of their people. Alexia wanted proof. That was why she had argued with him for weeks on end while he had her trapped. She wanted a reason to go against Tau. And even though she had agreed to help him, that didn't mean she would continue to do so without needing more proof.

A voice in his head screamed he was just trying to get her alone again, but he ignored it. "That is a good idea, son. She should meet the rest of the depthstriders. Perhaps it would be more helpful for her to explain our situation to them than even our own people."

Alexia's eyes nearly bugged out of her head. "You want me to what?"

"Meet the depthstriders," he replied. "In the fathoms of the sea unlike any achromo has ever experienced before."

Chapter 29

It's an insane idea, but not one she was going to pass up. How many people were ever offered to see where the depthstriders lived? Likely no one, as Fortis had suggested.

She would need to be sure that she didn't do anything stupid. The depthstriders were notoriously violent, and they hated humans far more than any other of their kind. Not to mention there needed to be some upgrades provided to her because even she wasn't capable of surviving in those depths.

Alexia might be an upgraded human, but she could still die in pressures like that. There had to be some kind of suit or pod that would withstand the fathoms, but that wasn't a question she could answer. She wasn't an engineer.

As she stared at him, she wondered what had gotten into his head. After two weeks without seeing him, she was certain he was only saying this because he wanted to prove a point. Fortis didn't care about her wellbeing. He'd brought her here, and that was enough for him. He'd done the best thing he could to keep her safe.

But when she'd seen him again, and it was like a live wire had been lit inside of her body. She hadn't realized just how much she'd missed talking to him. Every cell fired white hot, and she suddenly wanted to taste him again. She'd wanted to leap into the water and kiss him a thousand times until he admitted that maybe he'd missed her a little as well.

A voice came from behind her shoulder. "Do you think that's a good idea? She could die. Again."

Fortis huffed out an angry sound that she recognized. "She will be fine. You will make sure she lives."

Mira came to stand beside her, the top of her head just below Alexia's shoulder. "I'm not a miracle worker, Fortis. Pressure at that level would need an entire ship to keep her safe. I can build something along the lines of a pod that you could carry with you, but that would take months of development and testing."

She already knew what Fortis was going to say, and Alexia couldn't stop the grin from crossing her face when he said what she expected.

"You'll have to do a lot better than that. She goes soon. Tomorrow, if we can."

Mira's face turned almost as red as her hair.

Alexia clapped a hand to Mira's shoulder. "Now is a good time for me to fill everyone in on Tau. I think that will help settle this situation."

"You better put a muzzle on that one," Mira muttered as she turned toward the door. "I'll get the others, but you need to get him under control. No one orders me around like that. Not in the city I built with my own damn hands."

She turned to see Fortis talking with his son, and the flirty young man disappeared underneath the surface of the water as well. Then it was just the two of them. Alone. She watched flickering emotions filter across his features and wondered what he was thinking.

How many people even knew what those micro expressions meant? Alexia had spent her entire life surveying people so she would know what they were feeling and what they might do next. She had to know the inner workings of the mind, and apparently that extended to the undines.

But she had no idea what he was thinking now.

He swallowed, his gaze flicking from hers for a moment before he sighed and said, "Come here."

"And do what?"

"Damn it, woman, come here. Let me see that you're all right."

Alexia crouched next to the water, and he reached for her. She had no idea what he was planning on doing, but she hadn't expected him to frame her face in his hands and turn her head to the side. He was looking at her neck, she realized. His hands slid down her arms, feeling for the wounds that should have still been there from the squid bites. Then down to her legs.

Heat bloomed as those strong fingers grabbed onto her thighs with impressive strength and slid down the muscles there. Realistically, she knew he was only doing it because he wanted to feel for the wounds, but her mind went elsewhere.

She wanted him to grab her thighs like he had her ankles before. She wanted him to spread her legs wide and... and...

She didn't know what. But she wanted. And somehow, it felt like Fortis was the only one who could show her.

Still crouched beside the water, she held her breath as his hands slid up her thighs. His fingers lingered there, pausing as though he shared her feelings, before he looked up at her. "You are well?"

"I'm better than I was before. Who knew squid could hurt that bad?"

"I did."

The joke went right over his head. But she still smiled and nodded. "Of course you did. You know everything."

"I do." The two words were so solemn, she knew he wasn't joking when he said them. He stared up at her like the weight of the world was on his shoulders. "I should never have let you go."

There was a lot of meaning in that statement. Alexia had to tell herself he meant only with the squid. He didn't mean it any other way. Fortis wasn't professing feelings for her or that he should have kept her around for longer. That wasn't him. He wasn't like that. He didn't care that she was here or that she... that she almost died.

Because if he did feel like that, then she was so fucked. She was struggling to keep her own emotions separate, and she had never felt like this before. But then again, she'd so rarely felt anything.

Mirroring his pose, she framed his face in her hands. "No, you shouldn't have. But I wouldn't have let you stay, either." She skated her thumbs over his cheekbones. "I am so lucky that you saved me. For that, I will always be grateful, Fortis. You have done more than you know."

His eyes widened at that. And then the gills along his jaw started to flutter a little. She still had no idea what that meant, but she hoped it was a good thing.

He had done more for her than most people ever would in her lifetime. She was used to being the expendable one, but he had saved her life. He had known she was likely to die, and he'd done everything he could to ensure that didn't happen. He had no idea what that did to her. But maybe if she told him enough times, he would understand why it was so important.

A commotion started at the door, and she released her hold on him as he flinched. He didn't want anyone to know that they were even friends, let alone whatever else they were. She respected that.

So she stood and turned long before anyone else entered the room, giving him her back as she faced the onslaught of approaching people. They'd have a hundred questions, and she would answer them all to the best of her ability, but she also knew very well that they weren't going to like the answers.

Multiple people walked through the door. The lean blonde, the shorter woman with glasses, Mira, the young man from the infirmary, another tall blonde who looked like the woman with glasses, and a few more people in the back she couldn't see. A lot of humans for such a small space.

The rippling sound of water had her turning to see other undines had joined Fortis in the tight space. The big blue one pulled himself out of the water to create more room, but a red one, yellow, and Aulax all remained in the water with Fortis.

So many people for such a short conversation. Her lips quirked to the side. "I take it this is everyone?"

"Most," the blue undine said. "My name is Arges."

Then he ran through introductions of everyone in the room. She was already feeling a little overwhelmed. There were so many people here who expected her to have answers for them. She would do her best, but Alexia was bound to disappoint most of them.

Taking a deep breath, she stilled any of the nerves still lingering and opened her mouth.

"My name is Alexia. I am the seventh version of myself that has protected Original Harlow for years. I have been genetically modified every generation to address certain flaws in my genetic makeup, personality changes, and to enhance human abilities. There are many aspects of my body that have been improved beyond the normal human structures, but I will save you all the details of that list."

Mira coughed into her hand. "I think we'd all like to know the extent of those, if you don't mind. Knowing what we're dealing with, even if it's just you, would be appreciated."

"Enhanced strength, lung capacity, faster healing, less oxygen in my blood so I can withstand deeper waters, significant training on how to kill a man with my bare hands, and..." She waved up and down her body. "Obviously I am larger. There are likely more upgrades, but those are the least scientific ones. The rest would have to be explained by a geneticist."

There was a large wall of silence that met her explanation. Clearly, no one knew how to deal with what they were now facing. That was to be expected, though.

She forged on ahead. "Fortis has convinced me that betraying Tau is the right thing to do. To be honest, I have been considering it for a long time. The medication they use to keep people like me in under control ensures that we do what they wish, but even that has been wearing off. Without leaving Tau, I likely would have been decommissioned long ago."

"Decommissioned?" the big red one repeated.

"My kind are only good for what we were bred to do," she replied. "The only reason I would be decommissioned is if I could no longer fulfill my duty in the way I was meant to. I was created to protect Original Harlow, just as many others of my kind were created for others. Years upon years of fixing genetics so that I was the perfect killing machine who was capable of doing everything she wanted. If I could not perform those functions, they would use my genetics to find the problem and then fix it in the next generation."

The words were regurgitated from what she had been told her entire life. But they sounded so wrong now that she had space away from that place.

And maybe she should tell them. Maybe she should reveal that she wasn't entirely without emotion. It was okay to so do here, amongst people who felt deeply.

She didn't expect how hard it would be to open her mouth and say it, though.

"I did not care about my own future. There are... We call them reborns. They are clones of the Originals, used only to heal them whenever they need even the barest of bandaids. Those were the people I couldn't stand to see mistreated as they were. I've watched them wake before. They speak. They have memories they shouldn't have. And the Originals kill them while they are still alive because these clones aren't real people to anyone in that city. I want to see that end."

That was enough, apparently. The yellow undine lifted his fist in the air, pumping it in an eerily human movement. "So that means you are going to help us?"

"It means I want to help you. I don't know how much help I'll be, but I will try my best."

The blonde woman wearing the droid—Anya, she reminded herself—grinned. "Oh, I think we'll find plenty of use for you. All you have to do is keep up with us."

"And that means?"

Suddenly, there were five people all talking over each other. Her training kicked in immediately, and she tracked all the words as best she could.

Ace was already speaking to a few of the droids that had rolled into the room. "Byte? I need you to get information to the waveriders and let them know we have details about Tau, and an informant who will be working with us."

Anya walked over to the red undine—perhaps his name was Daios—and said, "Make sure you check all the weapons we took from Alpha. We modified all of them to fire underwater, right?"

The yellow undine was already talking with Arges. "If she can give us schematics or even just a login into the city, we can use the droids to map the interior. If we have to, attacking them will be easier than we originally thought."

Through all the chaos, Fortis stared at her. Their eyes locked, and she knew without saying anything that he was afraid for his people.

"Fighting Tau will not be easy," she interrupted. "I know you've been planning this for a long time, but that does not mean that you will succeed. This is a city that has run the entire ocean for centuries now. These people are the same ones who made all the mistakes long ago. They are not learning from others. They know every rebellion that has ever happened, every fight that has ever occurred, and they have unlimited resources at their beck and call. They are beyond dangerous. I don't think you understand what you're setting yourself up for."

The mood in the room sobered. She hated that she had to be the person to pull their heads out of the clouds, but it was the truth. They were going to get themselves killed if they barged toward Tau with these few people.

"She's right," Fortis said. "I have seen their city and felt the power of their weapons. It is an impossible thing to attack them and expect that we will win."

"Then why bring her here?" Arges asked, his eyes narrowing.

She wanted to ask the same question. He'd been so adamant that they needed her information, but why would he want that if he knew she could not help?

"Because I believe her information is vital. Because I know without question that she will be an asset we cannot lose. But there is only one way you win." His eyes locked on hers again. "We need the waveriders. The depthstriders. We need everyone. Like my people were used in the fight on Alpha, I believe the depthstriders are the only people who can tear Tau apart."

Arges grunted. "The depthstriders are not easily convinced. They only fought with us in Alpha because your people knew their own were being killed within that city and there was an opportunity to save some of them."

"That is why I must bring her to the fathoms, as I told Mira before. They need to meet her."

Alexia looked over at Mira to see her reaction. She wasn't pleased, but there was a different light in her eye when she looked Alexia over. "Did you say your blood has less oxygen in it?"

"For pressure, yes."

Mira sighed and turned her eyes up toward the ceiling. "All right. Well... Fuck me, this might just work."

Chapter 30

He knew how dangerous an ask this was. And he knew, without a doubt, that she would survive it. He knew they would need all the help they could get from every single Person of Water.

His people were the hardest of them to convince. He knew the depthstriders were not likely to help, especially when it came to Tau. There were too many rumors about the city. So many of his people had experienced painful losses. Tau knew how to find and torment their kind and, if they weren't careful, they could lose everything.

Alexia had the ability to change their minds, though. She knew more about the city than anyone else, and that meant she was capable of giving them details they didn't have now. If he could just convince them to trust her... then it was a start.

As Mira started working on whatever she could to keep Alexia alive that deep in the ocean, he prepared himself for what was to come. Fortis floated in solitude, lingering in the currents as he prayed to all the gods and goddesses of the sea that they would help him convince his pod to fight.

And he felt like the sea was listening. He could feel the tides caressing his sides, as though the sea herself was trying to give him a lingering hug and tell him not to worry so much. His people knew what they were doing. The depthstriders had always been kind enough to trust him. They had supported him for years upon years. They were there when he needed to get his son back.

But a small pit in his stomach wasn't sure if this would work. He knew that they wouldn't want a human in their midst. They were the least trusting people in the sea, especially after Arges had snubbed one of their own.

He smelled his son approaching and told himself that he wasn't upset at the interruption. But this felt like he had limited time to pray, and he needed the sea to hear him. He needed the goddesses to cast pity on a worshipper who had spent his entire life dedicated to them and the memory of his wife.

A memory who did not care if he had dedicated himself to her. And that stung.

"Father," Aulax said, his voice carrying through the water as though he knew Fortis would be angry. "I need to speak with you before you leave."

"Speak quickly. The goddess does not like to wait for anyone."

He regretted the words as soon as he said them. His son had always been better than him, and Fortis knew he needed to listen. But he already feared the conversation that was about to happen.

Aulax had forgiven the achromos, even after everything they had done to him. Fortis had not. And his conversation with Arges hadn't helped.

Apparently, it was possible to have a relationship with one of them and still hate them. He just didn't believe it. Alexia and he fought, that was what they did. Mira and Arges didn't fight, not like two warriors who could tear each other apart. If Mira wanted to fight with Arges, it wouldn't be a fair battle, anyway. Arges would kill her. But when he thought about fighting with Alexia, he believed that given the right training, Alexia might be able to kill one of his kind on her own.

Breathing out, he opened his eyes from prayer and met his son's worried gaze.

"What is it, Aulax?"

"You are bringing her into the depths to meet Mitera, aren't you." It wasn't a question. It was more a disappointed statement that said his son very much did not appreciate what his father was planning on doing.

"I am."

"Mitera hates humans."

"She does."

"She also hates this pod." Aulax gestured behind him like Fortis needed to be told which pod she hated.

To be fair, Mitera hated almost everyone other than the depthstriders.

"Mitera was sent to guide Arges's original pod. She was not received well there for many years until she had finally gotten them to respect her. They all fell in line the way they were supposed to until Arges rebelled against her. The pod she had been given to guide was fractured beyond hope at that point." Fortis breathed out a long sigh. "She holds a grudge for that. I know."

"It's an understandable grudge, but I don't believe she will forgive easily. And yet, you think swimming into her home with a human will correct all that?"

He corrected his son. "Achromo. That is their name."

"They call themselves humans, father. After all they have done to help us, the least we could do is call them as they wish to be called."

He hadn't ever thought of it like that. He'd heard them say the word countless times. But somehow he couldn't bring himself to say the word until this moment.

"Humans," Fortis corrected himself. "There is no love lost between Mitera and the humans. I know it will be difficult for her to believe that their species would rebel against each other."

"It is difficult for her to believe most things. She is not a kind creature."

"Mitera knows what she is doing. Her gift to see into the future is better than any other creature under the sea. She is an impressive woman in her own right and deserves our respect." He hesitated before adding, "If in measured amounts. She hates the humans, and she does so blindly."

"Father, I believe that's the first time you've ever said anything bad about another depthstrider."

"I am not without my faults."

He grinned at his son, knowing that at the very least, he would always have Aulax by his side.

"It's hard to call them humans," he muttered. "The colorless ones have always fit them. They are so... bland."

"They do not come in a rainbow of colors, but I have found there is still color in them. Mira's hair. Anya's eyes. Ace's bright laugh that fills the room with bursts of bright light. There are plenty of colors in the humans, father. We just don't see them."

Perhaps he should listen to his son's wisdom. The boy had matured far more than he was comfortable with. Where was his little boy, who had pulled the tails of visitors and played pranks on those who lived beside them? Now he was looking at a young man, a formidable warrior, and a person he respected.

He sighed, disgusted with himself. "I find it easier if things do not change. I can look at my people and myself with far less... Discomfort."

"Change is good. Change brings about new ages of people and exploration that we might never have tried on our own. I, for one, am very excited for our future with the humans at our side." Aulax grinned at him. "Even if you aren't all that excited."

"I am rarely excited."

"Maybe it's time to start getting excited. Maybe it's time to start feeling all those things that you have refused to feel for such a long time."

But feeling meant he put himself at risk. Feeling the good meant he had to feel the bad too.

Aulax saw far too much, and then his son gently said, "Wasn't Alexia drugged? It made her incapable of feeling things?"

"She told you that?"

"Alexia is very honest if you ask her literally anything. But you remember that part, don't you?"

"Of course I do." It still made him want to rip apart everyone in Tau. She deserved to feel, and feel as gloriously as she had in the abandoned facility with him. What he wouldn't give to go back to that moment before anyone else had seen them together. Before he had all these questions raise in his mind.

"Then maybe you need to consider that while she had medication to hide her emotions, that doesn't mean other people haven't been doing the exact same thing to themselves without the drugs." Aulax flicked his hip fins in agitation. "You've spent your entire life adhering to complicated rules that no one asked you to uphold. You were the one who made yourself live that way, and you were the one who refused to feel anything because you were so afraid of losing someone else like you lost mom."

He stared at his son in shock. He'd always thought Aulax was spared from most of what he was feeling. His son was intuitive, of course. He was more like his mother than not. But he hadn't thought Aulax saw through him that easily.

"I don't know what to say," Fortis rasped. "I thought I had hidden all that from you. I struggled when your mother died, but I never thought..."

"Father, I have known everything from every moment. I was with you through all of it. I just chose to not hide myself, like you did. If I had to hurt again, like I hurt with mom, then it was still worth it. Because I wouldn't trade knowing her for the world."

He felt the fins on his hips shudder in sadness before he nodded. "I understand. But replacing your mother—"

"It's not replacing," Aulax interrupted. "No one is taking mom's place. No one is pretending she didn't exist. She is still in our hearts and our memories, but if I have learned anything through all the pain and torment I have been through, it is that these feelings are worth it. No matter what it costs to feel them."

He hated that his son was so honorable. And loved it, of course. But he hated it at the same time. This wasn't a child before him. It was... Aulax. A man who saw the world more clearly than his father did.

Heart in his throat, he nodded at his son. "You are wise beyond your age. I should listen to you more often, I fear."

"Would that be such a bad thing?"

"Yes. I don't relish taking advice from my son so often when I should be the one giving you advice."

Aulax grinned. "I guess that just means I've grown up, father."

He hated that. It felt like time had passed so quickly when his son was a child only moments ago. He feared he hadn't done enough in the time that he had been given. He wasn't a good enough father. He hadn't taught Aulax enough, but clearly that fear was unfounded.

Fortis quite liked the man in front of him. A lot.

Now, he would bring Alexia to his people, he would get them to fight, and then he would destroy the city that had caused so much harm. To his people, and to so many others.

Even if it meant changing how he saw the world around them.

Nodding, he asked, "How is Mira doing? She needs to work faster if we are going to do this. The depthstriders will be difficult to convince, and I wish to move sooner than later."

"Mira knows you're in a rush. She's doing the best she can with the time that has been given. She just doesn't want Alexia to, you know, die."

The sarcasm. He was going to smack his son upside the head if he kept talking like that. "I'm sure she doesn't want Alexia to die. Neither do I. But I think everyone needs to understand that there is far more at stake here than just Alexia's life."

"Are you willing to risk it?"

"No," he growled. "I just want it done faster."

"Then you need to learn patience, father. There is no faster." Aulax flicked his tail. "Pray to your gods. I will return when they are ready for you."

He only hoped it wouldn't take forever and a day. He knew how much of a perfectionist Mira was. But perfection had no place here.

Fortis wasn't sure how long he floated, praying to the sea and existing just beyond the edge of reality. His mind wandered into the future of anything that passed by him. Some People of Water got too close, and he watched as their lives warped and changed. Some of them were going to have children soon. Others were going to die peacefully, some in tragic ways. But most of these outcomes were things he would never tell them. Even the fish that passed by showed him snippets of a future in the sea.

Bright flashes of color, of sunlight burning through the waves. Some of the fish would see weapons firing all around them, and they wouldn't make it. Their lives would be cut short very quickly by the anger of humans. One of them in particular saw a battle between the humans and the People of Water, and he knew very well what that fish saw. Unfortunately, it died far too early for him to guess who might win.

The sea did not want him to see that ending. Perhaps because he was going to die long before it happened. Because he could feel his death coming soon.

Which was why he was rushing. The end barreled toward him, and he feared what that meant. He had to do everything he could before he lost all of his chances of helping.

"Father?" Aulax's voice broke through his reverie many hours after he had seen his boy.

Blinking his eyes open, he wondered if it was daylight because it was the same day, or if he had meditated away hours on end.

"They are ready for me?" he asked.

"As ready as they're going to get. Mira isn't happy, but Alexia isn't letting her do any more testing. She said it was good enough, and that you don't like to be kept waiting." Aulax's lips quirked to the side. "She's a lot like you."

"One of the reasons I appreciate her presence," Fortis replied.

He flicked his tail and swam past his son, heading back to the small human village. At least there he would be able to get this journey started.

He had no idea what waited for them. Surely Mitera had seen that they were coming. The old woman saw more than most, and she would know without a doubt that they were coming for her. She'd prepare a show that would try to scare Alexia away from that deep abyss.

Alexia wasn't one to get scared easily, though. As he approached the village and saw her lowering into the water, he prayed one last time to their gods that she wouldn't break at the sight of his people.

Chapter 31

The suit wasn't entirely bulletproof, but it would have to do. Sliding into the water, she affixed the head piece a little tighter. The fibers of the suit were made from iron, and they were so thin, they almost appeared like threads. The idea had come from research they'd stolen from Tau. She had to give it to Ace and her people, the droids they built were useful when it came to hacking.

It had taken little Byte only a few moments to splice into the mainframe and download a significant amount of data points. Nothing that was protected, of course. Tau wasn't so arrogant that they didn't ensure their most important files were hard to get. But they didn't put as much care into making sure it was hard to find suit protocol for the deep ocean excursions.

The suit was air tight, reinforced in multiple ways, and the headpiece shouldn't crunch in the pressure. It would also help her breathe oxygen with tubes inserted directly into her airway through her nose. It would make talking a little difficult, but she could still do it.

She'd had to insert the tubes herself. Anya had nearly thrown up a couple times before Alexia had grown too angry with how long it was taking and did it herself. Alexia had medical training, to make sure she was prepared just in case anything happened to Harlow while she was on duty and no medical professionals were available. Inserting a tube was easy enough, even if it was nasty work.

The water was cold, but she couldn't feel it through the suit. That was good. While Mira was worried about structural integrity and its ability to maintain pressure changes, Alexia had been worried that it would be cold. Metal and all that. She had feared the heating units wouldn't work like her exoskeleton had.

It was working well enough for now, at least. Hopefully, she would get through this without dying.

If she didn't, well, it would be an adventure that she wouldn't regret. No human had been into the abyss before, and certainly not with a depthstrider. Not even in a ship. The opportunity to do so burned in her chest. She wanted to see it with her own eyes, even if it was just darkness.

A rush of water pushed her forward before an undine circled her. The flash of deep purples, lavender, and bright yellow lights gave away who it was long before she saw his face.

"Every time I'm in the water with you, I am shocked by your size." She spun with Fortis, looking along the massive expanse of his tail until she reached his chest. The bulging muscles there flexed with every movement and made her mouth water.

She wanted to drag her hands all over those muscles, and it killed her that she hadn't gotten the opportunity to do so yet. She wanted to rake her nails down his chest, bite down on those incredible pectorals, and then lick her way between the valley of his abs. None of these thoughts were safe for what they were doing right now, but she couldn't help herself.

She knew the moment he smelled her arousal. His dark eyes seemed to sharpen on her, and a wicked grin spread across his face. "No, Alexia. We have things to do."

"I hate it that you can smell me so easily."

"And yet, I love that I can."

The deep rumble in his voice sent shivers throughout her entire body. She hated that she reacted to him like this when there were other things for her to focus on. She needed to get her head on straight. But all she wanted was to ask him to take her somewhere else so she could experience the pleasure only he seemed to give her.

"Are you ready, Alexia?" he asked, jolting her once again from her thoughts.

Taking a deep breath, she nodded. "As ready as I'm going to get."

He looked around them as though he were making sure no one was going to see him, and then he swam closer. In a sudden rush, his hands grabbed her around the waist and pulled her to his side. With a delicate touch, he ran his finger down the side of her throat where her pulse rapidly beat.

"It is a shame Mira found a way to let you breathe on your own. I quite liked doing it for you. My tentacle inserted into your neck made me feel... strange." His gaze didn't move from her pulse. The thudding of her heartbeat clearly captivated him, and for a moment, he looked like he had the first time he'd scented her arousal in the water.

But then he stiffened and moved away from her, and she saw that another undine approached them. Clearly, she wasn't someone he wanted to be seen with. Not yet, anyway. Why did that sting so badly?

She swallowed hard and pulled herself together. Even Fortis seemed to swirl the water around them, yet another way he hid the scent of her desire.

It made her feel foolish. To him, this was just curiosity. A way to satisfy a need… But here she was, pining over this undine who did nothing but disappoint her.

Arges approached them with a grim expression on his face. "All right, there's not much more I can do to prepare everyone. You two head out, and I'll make sure that I get everything situated here. There are plenty of people willing to fight with us, but almost everyone is waiting to see if the depthstriders agree to help. Then they'll make their decision."

"This is why I wanted to hurry," Fortis scolded.

This time, he reached for her without hesitation. A quick grab, and a sudden flick of his powerful tail, and they were off. Flying through the water as though rage powered him to be even stronger. They darted past the rest of the village that she'd seen from the inside, then over the edge of a drop off that descended far into the darkness. The light faded, and the entire time she watched his colors fade as the light stole them away.

It was easier to stare at him than look at where they were going. After all, the depths were still terrifying. The last time she'd been down there, the squid attacked her. She could still feel their powerful jaws gnawing on her body and sawing through muscles. But this time, she had him.

As his muscles moved between her legs, sending them careening into the darkness without an ounce of fear, she felt very confident that he would keep her safe. What creature in the ocean would be mad enough to attack him?

"Stop staring at me," he muttered.

"Why?"

"Because it's unnerving."

She shook her head and chuckled. "You can't see anything, anyway. There's no light down here."

The darkness had snuffed out the sea. Now it was just her and her own thoughts, existing in the nothingness of bleak dark. If she was still staring in his direction, it was entirely without her knowing. She was just looking where she had been moments ago when there had still been light.

He snorted. "I can see just fine. You and your human eyes are just weaker than my peoples'."

There was a long pause before she repeated, "Human eyes, huh?"

"My son has reminded me that even if I do not trust your people, you still deserve respect. If you wish to be called humans, then I can... learn." He ground the words out like he was angry.

Of course it would be Aulax. The young man had popped in to visit her multiple times. And while he had been sweet and understanding of many things, he hadn't exactly seemed to realize the danger they were all in. He wanted everyone to see the use in each other, that much she could understand.

But it would take more than that. Humans were terrified of the undines, and for good reason. With creatures as large as them, it wasn't foolish to wonder what would happen if a human pissed one off. It was just basic survival.

"Well, your son does seem to have a streak of kindness in him that I don't see as easily in you." She snorted. "Actually, your son is a lot more kind than I've ever seen you be. He's a good person."

"You don't think I'm a good person?"

"You're..." Alexia hesitated. "You're like me."

"Which means?" He turned them, twisting them in a spiral down into a current that would help propel them deeper into the water.

She could feel their speed pick up. He seemed to have successfully pushed them deeper and deeper into the ocean, and she was already feeling the pressure change squeezing her. The suit seemed to hold, though, and she would take that as a win. Even if it meant she did have to explain her thoughts to him.

Alexia licked her lips and hoped she was explaining this well enough. "I don't think either of us is necessarily good or bad. I think that answer is a lot more complicated for someone who has fought their entire life for people who have pointed them at an enemy and fired. Whether you believe that you are the same as me or not, I see it in you."

His arms tightened around her. Carefully, he took her feet and tucked them against the warmer hip gills that would help keep her from freezing. "I do not think we are that different, virago."

"Why do you call me that, anyway?"

"It is customary to give names to those you respect." He obviously didn't want to say anything to her about this. Every word was ground out through his teeth, like he was embarrassed to admit it. But perhaps they both needed this moment.

Even if she couldn't help but joke with him. "Like a pet?"

"No, not like a pet," he replied, perhaps a little harshly. "It is a gift. A name that means something. A respect that is shown as a way to tell you that I see into your soul. I see who you are and I have named you from what I saw."

"Ah." Another long silence that was only broken by the sound of his fins slicing through the water. Then, very quietly, she said, "Are you going to tell me what virago means, then?"

He took a long time to reply. "It is a warrior woman. A fighter who is recognized by another fighter, and a woman with... heroic qualities."

She slapped her hands on his chest. "But you've been calling me that for a very long time."

"I have."

"Before you even realized I was going to help you."

"Yes, virago. I knew even before you agreed to help our people what kind of person you were. It is not such a strange thing to admit." His lights flickered on, some of the yellow illuminating his face in ghostly light. "The depthstriders you are about to meet might frighten you. They will touch you, most likely. Do not fight them. They are only glimpsing your future."

"You're changing the subject because you're uncomfortable, aren't you?" she asked.

"Yes."

"Why?"

His arms tightened a little more around her before she felt him sigh out of his rib gills. "Because I do not know how to have this conversation with someone I admire, Alexia. I haven't had to do this in a very long time, and I will admit, I am suffering because of that."

He... admired her?

That made parts of her light up that she hadn't even realized could glow. She wanted to grab onto his stupid face and kiss him. She wanted to tell him that she felt the same. She'd never met someone so admirable, and that he'd taught her what that even meant.

But then she felt a hand on her ankle. Flinching, she tried to stay still like he said, but it was hard when a hand reached out of the darkness and grabbed onto her.

"Don't," he growled. "It is an insult to deny them."

"An insult?" she grumbled in response. "It is my future. Should I not get to tell them whether or not they see it?"

"You will never know what they see unless you ask them to reveal it to you. They are in control here, and always will be. You are in their home."

Another clawed hand passed down her back, smoothing over her shoulders in a caress before darting away. Another toyed with the edges of her helmet, as though threatening her that at any point, they could pull it loose. Another hand, this time touching the spots on her thigh where the squid had wounded her. Another hand, this time slipping between her and Fortis and moving along her belly.

Fortis growled at that, and the hand immediately retreated.

"You are doing well," he said, though his voice was pinched. "Just let them keep doing this. We're nearly at the center of their home."

"Their home? Not yours?" She flinched again when another hand came out of nowhere and trailed down her spine in such a delicate touch that every muscle in her body twitched.

"I haven't lived here in a very long time." He cupped the back of her head and drew her tighter to him, almost as though he was afraid one of them would grab her and rip her out of his arms. "Most of these depthstriders have never seen a human in their life. They have spent countless years down here, living in the deep while seeking out the future. It is a difficult life, and I chose a different current when I was very young. I chose adventure rather than future seeking, although I am very good at that as well."

"Ah."

Alexia stared over his shoulder, where she swore there were lights flickering in the distance. Bright little flecks of white light that immediately called her gaze, trying to convince her to follow them. Only then she realized they weren't actually far at all. Those lights were the tiny ones that decorated the chests of countless depthstriders who were so close to them. All she could see were the rolling masses of their lights flickering as they reacted to her future.

Their tails were all tangled together. A ball of them knotted around her and Fortis as they moved through the sea. They were all massive, so big she wondered if Fortis was even the largest of them. Their bodies were decorated with powerful muscles, dark colors that were nearly ink black, and bright specks of light created to lure in the weakest of prey.

Then their voices rose. All of them at once in a deep whooping call of the depthstriders, all echoing throughout the sea and making the surrounding water vibrate with their anger. They must have realized she was a human. And they didn't like the snippets of her future that they had seen so far.

What had she gotten herself into? This place was cursed, and if she wasn't careful, it was where she would die.

"Easy," Fortis reminded her. "I won't let anything happen to you."

But could he really promise that?

Chapter 32

Fortis had known this would be difficult, but he hadn't realized just how bad it would be. His people were ruthless in their pursuit of knowing everything about her. They grabbed onto her shoulders, arms, back, legs, anything they could get their hands on as they tried, desperately, to see into her future.

And in some way, he'd been tempted as well. He'd fallen into her future with them, even though he promised himself he wouldn't do that without asking. Her future was just too intriguing, even to him. But the future they all saw together was muddy. There were too many currents she could take. Too many opportunities for her future to split.

He hated looking into futures like this, because it was always harder to guess what people like her might do. Fortis knew her better than the rest of the depthstriders, and even he couldn't follow the currents that would allow him to guess where and when she was going to be. He didn't know if she was given the opportunity to betray him, whether or not she would.

Eventually, light bloomed in the distance. Mitera had never been one for darkness, and soon enough, he could find the homeland of all the depthstriders.

He tried to see it through Alexia's eyes. She was used to metal cities that burst through the sea, forcing everything around them to bend to their will. But this city was built out of the sea itself. Silty towers of mud that had been hardened by deep-sea vents, where multiple depthstriders leaned out of carved homes. Their tails were still deep within the tunnels, leaving them to appear almost human-like as they watched them pass.

Lights illuminated from the many bioluminescent plants. Usually these species wouldn't survive in the sea the way they were, but they were protected by the depthstriders themselves. Lights were useful this deep, and it was exhausting for his people to constantly light themselves.

And then there were the patterns. Swirling stones in rippling circles that spiraled in on themselves, marking where certain families lived. Each of those swirls had a meaning. Some patterns were directions, some were family markers, others were areas of the village they were in. His people had done all they could to make this a home, even in the deepest of the sea.

They had created an inspiration of architecture out of the stone and mud, spires that twirled around themselves, homes that were deep winding paths and kept the families within safe.

"Is that... a farm?" she asked, her voice catching as another depthstrider grabbed a handful of her hair and tugged gently.

He looked, but he already knew what she was referring to. They had been cultivating fish for a very long time. The woven nets were made of sea fronds that had been dried in caves before returning them under the sea and weaving them into a braid that was then used to create nets. All of these contained massive amounts of fish, living intentionally and without too much concern for their wellbeing. It helped this deep in the ocean. There were very few hunting grounds here, and most of them, if not all, were taken up by the wild animals that lived deep in these waters.

"It is a farm. But don't look around too much, Alexia. The depthstriders won't like it that a human knows so much," he murmured.

The knot of depthstriders around them dispersed, although he could hear them murmuring. She wasn't natural. She shouldn't be here. What was he thinking bringing her into the heart of their home?

He had been thinking this was his last chance, and none of them seemed to understand how meaningful that was. Soon enough, they would know how little of a chance they had left.

He had seen it. And he was certain the rest of them had seen it as well. They knew their ocean was threatened. They knew that the humans were so close to destroying everything they all held dear.

They were running out of time. Or perhaps his real fear was that he was running out of time. His death barreled toward him and Fortis's use would soon come to an end. At least this he could still do this.

Mitera drifted out of her home, floating before them with that billowing jellyfish like hair that always looked so beautiful. All her iridescent coloring, floating around her head and undulating with her movements, used to captivate him. Just looking into her pale white eyes was to see every color that had ever existed. She was the most powerful of them, seeing into the future further than any other.

He hoped he wouldn't even need to argue after bringing Alexia here. Mitera would see the future clearly, as she always did. She would know, without a doubt, that he wanted them to fight for the right reasons.

But from the expression on her face, he knew he'd been wrong.

Fortis murmured under his breath, "That is Mitera. She is the oldest seer, the mother of us all."

"She's your mom?"

"Not biologically. She is... somewhat of a wise woman, you could say. She is the oldest and most practiced of us all. We trust her implicitly. This is the woman we need to win over."

"Understood." She swallowed hard, and he knew that his words hadn't helped to settle her fears. If anything, he'd only made it worse.

"Fortis!" Mitera's voice called out. The sound erupted from the water like whale song, or perhaps the voice of a goddess herself. "You have returned to your people and violated our greatest law."

"It was necessary to do so."

"There is nothing that could give you the right to bring one of their kind here." Mitera's hair turned a vibrant shade of red, only barely visible this deep even with all the surrounding light. "She has no right to be here. Not in our home. Not even in our sea."

"She is from Tau."

Angry hisses rose around him, all the people surrounding them enraged by what he said. Because if she was from Tau, that meant she was part of those who had hurt them, maimed them, killed them. She was part of the evil they had never been able to exact revenge upon.

Exhaling bubbles from his gills, he hugged her a little tighter before turning her around to face Mitera. Alexia had been looking over her shoulder, of course, but she would want to face her opponent directly. He knew his virago well. She would battle until her last breath.

"She has agreed to help us," he called out, trying to get his people to see reason. "She has left her city, knowing that she would betray all those she had once lived with. Their city is worse than we ever imagined, and that means she deserves to enact her revenge. She has just as much reason as we do."

"Reason?" Mitera hissed. "She has no reason to be here. If she is going to fight with us, then let her fight with Arges and all the others who can stand to be surrounded by their stench. Leave that life to those who are foolhardy and see no issues with how her people live. This is not the way of the depthstrider."

"There is more we can learn from the humans than you give them credit for, Mitera. I would see that she is taken care of, and that we use the knowledge only she can share." He took a deep breath, knowing his next words would not go over well. "I am here to ask the depthstriders to fight with us. Attack Tau with me, take the information that we have been given by this woman, and we will destroy the city once and for all. Then we can rebuild this sea with the humans. Together, we will learn how to live with each other after we cut the head off the achromo cities."

Mitera stared at him like he'd lost his mind, and every other depthstrider stopped moving. Not even a flicker of a hip fin stirred the water surrounding them as they all realized he wasn't joking. He hadn't brought Alexia here to be punished.

He wanted them to work with humans to destroy humans. And he already knew they were going to deny him even that.

But he would not give up. Wrapping his hands around Alexia's waist, he gave her a little squeeze. "Talk, virago. Give them a reason to believe us."

She took a deep breath, and for a moment, he thought she would deny him. After all, she was not the perfect person for this. She had been a warrior her entire life, and while they would respect that, they would not praise her for it.

"I hate them as much as you hate them," she finally said. At their hisses, she lifted a hand for silence. "I know that is hard to believe. Perhaps there is a part of you that thinks that if I lived there for so long, that surely I agreed with what they did. But they manipulated me, they genetically enhanced me, they created me for everything they wanted me to do. I had no choice in anything that happened."

Mitera's hair flared wider, making her look like one of the massive jellyfish that absorbed all its prey. "I care little for your story."

"And yet, it is a story you will have to listen to. The people in that city don't care who you are, what you are, or why you want to go against them. Greed is the only language they speak. They have lived for hundreds of years. Countless of them, the original people who destroyed our world above and then decided to take over yours. There is no fixing what they have done. There is nothing humans can do. But you cannot truly believe that all of my kind deserves death."

A sudden, long silence was her answer. He felt her ribs expand in a shocked breath that she let out very, very slowly.

"Oh," she whispered. "You do believe we should all die."

"I don't care what you do with yourselves," Mitera said. "But you will not stay here in our ocean, ruining everything for the rest of those who live within these waters."

"We have nowhere to go."

"It's not my task to keep humans safe. There are others who I am certain can do that just fine."

Alexia's shoulders straightened, and he could smell her rage on the water. The others would soon smell it too, and they would rise to the challenge she had no idea she was issuing. "The people who are supposed to look after us are corrupt. They are the ones who have harmed you as well. They are the people none of us can trust, yet you expect me to go back to them?"

Mitera's hair alternated between putrid yellow annoyance and bright red rage. "It is not my responsibility to convince your people that empathy is worthwhile."

"That's rich coming from a creature who won't even offer help to those who need it."

Oh.

That wasn't the right thing to say to Mitera, but he could hear the rumblings from a few other depthstriders. They were all thinking the same thing. Why shouldn't they help the humans? Clearly, help was needed, and they were uniquely qualified to offer it.

But Mitera had never been a forgiving woman.

"We will not help the achromos. We've tried to fight Tau before, but your people are as slippery as eels and as deadly as the greatest of foes. We have lost more lives to your city than you could imagine. Your people deserve what they have been fighting to get for centuries now. If that requires the loss of all your lives, then it is just the will of the sea." Mitera gave her one more look up and down before tsking. "You waste all our time."

He knew before Alexia even spoke that she was going to do something stupid. He could feel it bubbling up inside of her. Fortis tried to smack his hand over her lips, but it was too late.

She called out, "Then look into my future! You are the best of them, are you not? What the others could not see, you should be able to find easily. Look into my future and see what it is that I will do."

It was a temptation even the greatest of them could not deny. Someone asking a depthstrider to look into the future gave them so much more ability to see even further. There was always a fight when the person was unwilling. The future seeker had to wade through all the things the person was afraid they would see, or perhaps even just walls they hadn't realized they'd put up. It was a struggle to see the future of a person who did not wish them to see it.

But this? This was offering up an entire future on a platter and begging Mitera to peer into it.

Their leader looked at Alexia again, this time with a clear and direct threat. Fortis tensed, not sure what Mitera would ask.

Their mother replied, "I will look into your future, willingly and gladly. But I request you allow me to show everyone here that future. If you are so confident that you will not take part in the destruction of our people and our sea, then I would have everyone confirm this confidence."

Fortis couldn't let this happen. "Mitera—"

"Fortis, keep your mouth shut. This is her choice."

Alexia was all too quick to reply. "Let them all see."

But that was dangerous. She shouldn't just let anyone peer into her future when he knew what her future was.

Death only waited there. So much death, and Mitera would see it too quickly.

But Alexia had already wriggled her way out of his arms. She approached Mitera and the two of them collided with a rough embrace. He didn't have time to stop it, because Mitera's colors swirled in a rainbow of patterns, and then all he could see was Alexia's future. He saw himself returning her to Tau. He saw the plan they would make, all the details and hidden secrets she would reveal.

It was good. Though he couldn't see the details, he knew without a doubt that it would work. He saw the hope that blossomed amongst his people. The feeling that they could do this. For once, they were going to destroy the people who had threatened them. They were going to win.

And then he saw white walls, just like his wife had seen. White walls, bright lights, and dark hair sliding over his features. He wasn't sure what the others saw. Perhaps they saw the future from the perspective of someone else in the room. But for him, all he could see was what he was going to see.

The calm. The peaceful relaxation of death. And the knowledge that he was finally returning home.

Although this time, he also sensed that there was some hesitation in him at leaving. He wasn't ready to go. All the other times he had seen this future, he was always ready to seek out his wife in the afterlife. But this time, he wasn't. There were reasons for him to stay and he was sad to go. He didn't want it to happen so soon.

Each depthstrider rumbled with anger. He could hear their frustration and rage at what was revealed. They didn't look past that moment, though. They didn't seek out what happened after his death and he wanted to scream at them because they needed to look past that. They needed to look into the future further, because maybe she killed him for a good reason.

Instead, they stopped there. Mitera pulled back from Alexia with a pleased expression on her face. Even she knew this meant the depthstriders would remain in their safe darkness while the rest of the sea boiled.

"You will kill him. A dear friend of our people, a male who has proven himself worthy time and time again," Mitera said. "Why would we ever help you do that?"

Chapter 33

She... What?

Who was she going to kill?

Alexia looked around, confusion making it hard to think about what the creature in front of her had said. She was going to kill someone? Well, that wasn't new. She'd killed a lot of people in her life, and very few of them deserved it. But she knew that this was important. They weren't going to work with her because of who she killed and that... didn't feel right.

She looked around and realized they were all staring at Fortis. There was pity in their eyes, as though they knew something about his future made her pause. And then she realized they were talking about him.

They thought she was going to kill Fortis.

She shook her head. "I'm not going to kill him."

"You are going to kill him. The future is set in stone. There is no way for you to change what is coming."

"There's always a way to change what is coming. I am not the person I was when I first met him, and I have no interest in killing this man." She actually laughed because it was so ridiculous to even think. "I would sooner cut off my own arm than kill him. He has shown me so much in this world, freed me from the chains of my own people, and given me the chance for revenge. Why would I ever want to hurt him?"

"It is a question you need to ask yourself. Because you are going to, my dear. That much I know without question. And I have no interest in helping you if that is how it is going to end." Mitera turned away from them. "You have asked for our help, and I tell you now, we will not give it."

Alexia couldn't believe this was how it was going to end. They'd come all the way down here, and all it took was a single look into a future and then this person was certain that Alexia was the enemy?

It couldn't end like this. Not when she had tried so hard to get to this point, and she'd given up everything that she was. Everything that she had become.

"I won't take no for an answer," Alexia called out. "Your people deserve to choose on their own. They should help us if they want to. That's how this works. You don't get to make the final decision, and you don't get to tell them how to live their lives. If that's how you run your people, then you are no better than Tau."

Fortis's hand came around her waist, that broad palm bracketing her waist and nearly spanning her entire stomach. He tugged her back to him, his arm around her a clear warning to everyone who surrounded them. Alexia had never been more proud. She knew it wasn't easy to make this show of claiming, but he had done it. Even though he likely didn't want them all to think that they were... whatever they were.

"This woman has earned my respect," he said, his voice thunderous and loud. "And I trust what she says. Tau can be defeated. We can overtake that kingdom of people who have plagued our lands. But I will not accept help from you if you are unwilling to see the future as it is meant to be. We will work together with the humans to create a better home for all of us, not just ourselves."

A voice came from the crowd, and Alexia looked over to see a pale female depthstrider pushing through the others. She was lovely in the way that many of them were, graceful with tiny filaments spreading off all her fins with tiny glowing lights. But this female was delicate where many of the undine were not that at all. "She's going to kill you, Fortis. Why should we trust her at all?"

Fortis merely pressed his hand to her spine, rubbing his thumb along her hip. "Because I know she is going to kill me. I have known for many years. I knew almost the first moment I met her who she was. My wife saw my future, as many of you know. I recognized this woman for the person she would become, and I still trust her. I still believe she is the key to bringing about a new age where we are all safe. Not just the People of Water, but the humans as well."

Another murmur rose through the crowd. Perhaps some of them were surprised he had called them humans, because that was not the way of things with their people. But she knew Fortis would not back down. This was important. He would not change his words or mince them to make others more comfortable.

"We must move forward," he said, his tone softening into something most of these people had likely never heard before. "We need to acknowledge that the future cannot be the same as we have always planned it to be. Yes, that will be difficult. No, I don't think we will always choose the right current to buffer us through the sea. But I do believe with both my hearts, mind and spirit, that the sea wants us to do this. She has chosen our safety to meld with theirs."

They deserved to make this choice on their own. Alexia wanted to tell them that. She had been the person who had all of her agency taken away her entire life, and having someone make decisions for her had never been easy. Even when she'd been told that was the only way to live.

Mitera's colors kept rioting through all the rainbow, as though she had no idea what to do or say. Perhaps she wasn't used to people challenging her world views. This would be difficult for her to accept.

Especially considering the depthstriders seemed to mostly agree with Fortis. There were plenty of them looking around at each other and nodding. They wanted to help. She could see it. But there were too many people waiting for Mitera's decision.

And then Alexia realized she had to do what she had always done in Tau. She had to put her own safety aside and take the risk of a lifetime.

She pushed out of Fortis's grip and moved so everyone could see her. Kicking her feet to stay floating, she raised her arms and struggled to stay floating before them. "You can see me for what I am. I'm sure some of you look at me and think I am very weak. But Tau took me and changed me. They didn't even let me be birthed by a real mother. I am not the same as the humans you have come across before, and there are more like me. I am begging you to help all those who are still trapped in that city. I am begging you to see reason."

"Begging will get you nowhere," Mitera said, hissing out the sound as though she needed to convince other depthstriders that she was right. "You have no place here and never will."

But the pale, beautiful creature who had spoken before moved a little closer. "Wait, Mitera. Perhaps we should hear her. Fortis trusts her."

Fortis leaned down and quietly murmured, "She is the sister of my wife. At her death, she watched Aulax for many months until I could take my son back again. I mourned my wife, and she took care of my family."

So she was compassionate. Alexia nodded before addressing that woman directly. "There are a lot of people you can save in that city. So many who have never breathed on their own. Tanks of people who were created just to be a bandage for wounds. I know that doesn't make sense to you, but they're killing innocents in there so that they can live unnaturally long."

A man pushed forward in front of the others. The massive creature was covered in scars, and far larger than the others. Perhaps even as large as Fortis himself. "You ask us to save this city that has done nothing but threaten our lives and kill our people? Some of us have no mercy for them."

"I'm not asking you to save the city," she argued. "I want you to destroy it. Two cities are more than enough. We can rebuild in places where you agree we can go, not where it is most convenient for my people. But Tau is filled with evil. That darkness seeps into the sea and taints it. I ask you to have pity on the weak, but to destroy all those who have harmed so many. I want to see the ocean run red with their blood just as much as you do.

"Tau has always been a fortress. First, you could not find it. Those who did would soon find there is a shield around it. I will tear that down for you. Then it is just like any other city. You've already destroyed two of them. I want you to come in through the doors I will open, and kill everyone inside."

Voices lifted, arguing with each other. She could only pick out a few snippets of what they were saying. Quite a few of the depthstriders wanted death. Offering them a chance to get into the city that had plagued them for years and to kill all who stood in their way? It was a battle they had been asking for. Others were more interested in saving those who could be saved.

She heard some people mentioning that if they saved people in that city, then many achromos would be indebted to them. And though she didn't want to argue that point, they weren't wrong. She could use that to her advantage.

"My people would owe you their lives!" she shouted, and everyone quieted again. Even Fortis seemed to hold his breath as he waited for what she would say. "I cannot control them. But I can promise you, they will not forget that you saved them, or that you granted them a chance. There is so much here that you do not understand, but I want you to see it. I want you to make connections with my people, and I desperately need there to still be good people in this world who still want to fight for what is right. I believe we all need to remember that."

More rumblings, more arguing, but she kept her eyes on Mitera. The woman was looking at all her people and Alexia knew what was going through her mind. She was going to lose them if she didn't side with the humans. They would rebel against her, just as Arges and his people did. She was making choices that her people did not like, and if she didn't change and move with this new path, then she would be left behind.

A flash of dusty grey turned her billowing hair into something ghostly.

"What does that color mean?" she asked Fortis.

His voice was quiet and hesitant as he replied, "She is afraid."

Alexia knew that feeling. "Can you bring me closer to her?"

"Of course, virago."

He flicked his tail, and they glided closer to Mitera. The woman's eyes widened even further as they approached, and that fear was so prominent even Alexia could see it now.

Quietly, so they wouldn't be overheard but by the closest depthstriders, she said, "I know you want to keep your people safe. But I will give all the information I know, and it is a lot. Everything that has ever protected that city, every exit, every entrance, every weapon that Tau has — I know almost all of it. There is very little that would surprise me and, therefore, little that would threaten your people that they were not prepared for in advance."

"How can you promise that?"

"Because I helped to build all of it. Every generation of me has worked with those in Tau to keep everyone in it safe. If there was anyone who knew how to get in and out of that city, it would be someone like me. Because they have worked with us for years to make sure that nothing could ever go wrong. Our opinions, our thoughts, all of it was controlled by that city. But I broke free. I should be dead. They would have killed me if they realized my thoughts had wandered, but I got away before they could."

Mitera seemed to think about her words before finally giving a small nod.

Fortis's hands clenched down on her and he whisked her away from Mitera. She could feel the excitement coursing through his entire body and all of his gills that fluttered around her. Even his fins were shaking with anticipation.

"I call for war, then!" Mitera shouted.

The massive undine who had asked for bloodshed screamed at the words. It was a haunting call, the sound of a hunt being summoned as he looked to Fortis.

"You," the big one said, pointing at Fortis. "When will you need our warriors?"

"I will send my son to collect you. Be ready. We do not know when we will fight, but it will be soon and it will be bloody."

"We will be ready for death, and look forward to killing as many achromos as we can." The man thudded his hand against his chest and then opened his mouth. A massive tongue escaped, licking at the sea as though he could already taste the bloodshed.

And with that, Fortis fled. Alexia grabbed onto his shoulders to stay in his arms, feeling the water pressing her back down into that darkness. But soon, the light from the city faded and all she could see were the bright, flickering lights of the depthstriders who followed them. So many of his people, just lurking in the darkness. The only thing that gave them away were the glowing dots on their bodies that flickered on and off like a strange strobe.

It made the entire sea feel like it was alive. The ocean was boiling and she could do nothing to stop it or the fear that burned in her chest.

"Why are they chasing us?" she asked, her voice whipping away from them as they moved through the water.

"Because we have made a deal. They get blood, and we will either provide it for them, or provide our own." He swam faster, harder, his entire body undulating with the movements and rolling between her thighs. "They will chase us until we are far enough away to no longer be a threat to their people."

"They think I'm a threat?" she asked, then laughed at the mere thought. "Look at them! How could I even remotely hurt one of them?"

He laughed with her. "You're going to kill me, virago, I'm sure they believe you could kill them as well."

That was a sobering thought. Alexia still didn't know what to think about that impossible future. She didn't want to kill him. There was no future she could imagine where she would even try.

Alexia wanted to treasure him, she realized. What a terrifying thought when she had never even attempted a relationship with anyone else.

"I'm not going to kill you," she said. "I won't let that happen."

"You don't have a choice. You'll kill me, and I will join my ancestors in the next realm." He held her a little tighter. "I already forgave you for it."

But could she ever forgive herself?

Chapter 34

He was surprised they'd done it. For a while there, it had felt like touch and go. But his people had seen reason, largely because of her arguments and because of his belief that the future was right. He knew they were fearful that Alexia was going to kill him. But he also didn't care.

Fortis had made peace with his future long ago, and now he was lucky enough to see it come to life. He knew what was going to happen, unlike so many people who did not. He knew where he would end and how it would end. Life hadn't always been that easy.

But now, he was just elated. After all that he had done in his life, and all the things he would leave behind, he had completed the greatest deed. He had brought his people to glory. Soon, they would battle with Tau and with the depthstriders' help, he was certain they would win. Tau would fall. The most evil of the human cities would tumble into oblivion, and the rest was in the hands of those he trusted.

Already Mira and Anya had figured out ways to work with the humans in the cities, to convince them they could trust his people and that there was plenty of use in a partnership. They were ready to work with each other. Even the depthstriders.

A laugh burst free from his lips as he soared through the currents, disappearing into the sea as the other depthstriders were left far behind them. He hadn't felt this free in such a long time. He hadn't known what it was like to feel the weight of all his responsibilities and fear of the future disappear from his shoulders.

Was this what others felt like near the end? The elation of giving up the weight of life? It was maddening and so perfect.

"What are you laughing about?" Alexia asked.

"My end is near," he replied with another chuckle. "It is a good feeling."

"I have never met someone so excited for their own death." She shook her head, her hands moving against his arms as they smoothed across his biceps. "Do you really believe I'm going to kill you?"

"Yes, of course. It has been seen by many people. My story has always had an end, and I've known it for many years now. It was odd to see you after so many years wondering who was going to be the one to end my life." He squeezed her a little tighter, turning away from the village and heading out into the deep sea. "I'm glad it's you. If it had to be anyone, I'm quite pleased to know that you are the one who will hold the blade."

She frowned up at him. "I know you have proven to me a great many impossible things. But I find it so hard to believe that I would ever hurt you. I haven't believed in your ability to see the future before, and I don't intend to believe it now."

"Maybe you won't have a choice. In your belief or your ability to prevent my death." He could see that happening. Her people were dastardly, and their plans often hurt many people. "If you have to choose between me and everyone else in the sea, then you must kill me. If it will stop the plan that we have spent so much time building, then you have to do what it takes. Yes?"

She took a deep breath. "I suppose. But I don't want to kill you."

"You are strong enough to do so. Maybe that's why you were brought into our current and why the sea believed you could help us." There, in the distance, he could already see the facility he had brought her to before. It felt right to bring her to this place where he had realized just how serious he felt about her, and how much he wanted her.

"I don't…" She paused, and then nodded. "If that's what it takes."

They both knew that they would never be together for a long time. He had to believe that to be the truth. Fortis had done everything in his power to keep himself separate from her. She deserved to not mourn him after he left, at least not for a long time. If he was capable of learning this lesson to live when loved ones were gone, then she was capable of it as well.

He entered the area where the ships would have sailed through, his fins trailing along the bottom as he gently propelled them into the space. Then it was so easy to lift her out of the water and sit her on the edge of the facility with all that glass and cool blue light behind her.

Alexia was quick to remove her helmet. The braid of her dark hair was freed, swinging against her face and playing on the harsh edges of her features. She was right here, in that strange metal suit, waiting for him to do whatever he wanted.

Fortis planted his palms on either side of her hips, leveraging himself out of the water so he could loom above her.

"You told me that if you knew you were going to die, you would want to live as much as you could before it happened. Now, I bring you back here to ask..." He paused before correcting himself, "To beg you to indulge me."

"Indulge you?" she asked, her pupils blowing out until her eyes were as black as his. "What do you want me to indulge you in, Fortis?"

He didn't have the words to say it. He wanted her to know that he was obsessed with her. That after their moments here, all he had thought about were the little moans she had made, the way her waist would fit so perfectly in his hand. He wanted to lick every single scar that covered her body and slide his tongue between her thighs.

Fortis wasn't sure how to ask for it, though. He hadn't explored his desires in years. He knew women were complicated, no matter what species they were. There was a lot he could ask of her, and there were ways he could ask without touching her.

Seeing the heat in her gaze helped. She looked at him like she wanted to eat him alive, and she'd been looking at him like that like that for a while now. All he had to do was trust that the two of them were more compatible than he thought.

"Take off your suit," he said, his voice little more than a growl. "I want to see you again, virago. But this time, I want to see all of you."

"Are you certain about this?" she asked. "Even if I'm the one who is going to kill you?"

"I've never been more certain of anything in my life."

It was the truth, and he hoped she could hear that in his voice. He wanted her to know that he desired her beyond reason, beyond any of his training or understanding of how he should feel. He'd spent so many years hating her kind, and especially the people from her city and yet... One look at her and he was weak.

Alexia pushed back from the water and stood. The suit was easier to take off than he thought it would be. She hooked her fingers into deep grooves on the sides and slowly took off first the chest plate, then the arms. They thudded onto the ground hard in harsh clangs that echoed around the room and bounced off the glass. Then she leaned down to take the same armor off her legs, leaving her in nothing but a tight fitting wetsuit.

His gaze feasted on the strength of her thighs and the broad power of her shoulders. Every part of her showcased the power that filled her form. There was no reason for her to be so strong, especially after all he had done to her. Starvation might have made her slightly more weak, but it did not show in the way she stood there, staring at him with heated eyes.

Then she lifted her hands and peeled off the wetsuit. Fortis had to grip the edge of the floor so he didn't lunge across the room and devour her. She revealed pale, strong shoulders with mounds of muscles on them. Dotted with scars, she was a vision of power. Then that fabric revealed her breasts as well.

He had forgotten how captivating they were. She was beyond stunning, with those small breasts peaked with blush pink. He'd only seen coral that color before, and even then, they were never so tempting to lick.

More skin, more hard edges and long lines. Her abs were as defined as his own, although they were mottled with scars and what looked like scorch marks. He'd not seen those when he had been coaching her through fingering herself, but he also realized that his attention had been elsewhere.

Already, he could feel himself hardening behind his scales. His body wanted to surge forward, foreplay be damned. He wanted to plunge himself into her and know what it was like to be inside a woman as warm and wet as she had described herself.

He wanted her, plain and simple. And the sight of her leaning down to peel that wetsuit off her legs, the profile of the hard mounds of her glutes, nearly made him lose all reason.

Why was it he felt like an animal with her? He'd never been like this with his wife. He'd always been able to separate what they were doing and the reasoning for it. Oh, there had been some pleasure, but never like this.

Never had he felt desire gnawing at his mind, surging through it like there was another beast within him. The logical side of his mind told him to ease her through this, as he had before. To tell her with his lips and teeth and tongue that he wanted her beyond anything else on this planet. But the beast inside of him wanted to leap out of the water, grab her neck between his jaws, and rut into her until they were both screaming.

Taking a deep, shuddering breath, he kept his gaze on her as she stood.

He could see the hesitation in her eyes. She didn't want him to think that she was lesser because of how she looked. And that broke his heart.

"You are beautiful," he murmured, the words aching as his throat seemed to close around them. "So incredibly beautiful."

She clearly didn't know what to do with her hands. Alexia smoothed them down her stomach, perhaps a way to ease her nerves, but for him all it did was draw his attention down her hairless body. She was perfection personified. How did she not know this?

"Virago. May I touch you?"

Her throat worked in a swallow. "What are you going to do when you touch me?"

He could feel the heat flare through him at those words. Then every gill on his body stood up straight, fluttering with all the energy and need within him. "Everything, Alexia. I'm going to do everything."

Her cheeks turned bright red, the color spreading down her chest. "Oh, well, if that's all you're going to do."

He didn't have any patience for her sass right now. Pulling himself out of the water, he slid across the floor and grabbed onto her. Gently, he tumbled her onto the cold tile so he could loom above her.

Icy droplets of water fell from his shoulders, and each one of them rolling across her skin like pearls. Fortis leaned down to catch one that pooled in her collarbone, his dark tongue tracing along the soft skin there as though he had found his own treasure in the movement.

A low groan echoed through his chest. "You taste so sweet."

And she did. Like spun sugar and smoke, that made him want to taste more of her. So taste he did.

She had given him permission, and he took what she offered. And more. He wanted everything that she knew she wanted and everything she didn't know she wanted. He moved down her chest, licking and sucking at her skin until he finally reached the pebbled peak of her breast. Licking around it, he reveled in the sound of her moan that echoed through the room.

She didn't care if she was loud, and he loved that about her. The song of her passion let him know what she liked.

"Has anyone ever touched you here?" he asked, even though he knew the answer.

"No. Only you."

"Good. We're going to find out what you like, Alexia. And if I remember correctly..." He bit down on her nipple, hard enough that she let out a little squeal and arched off the floor.

But when he looked up into her shocked gaze, she was staring at him with even more red on her features. She'd liked that. She'd enjoyed the slight edge of pain.

Good, she was going to likely feel it once he figured out how to put them together.

Fortis took his time playing with her, alternating between her breasts as he bit and licked and sucked. He had her writhing underneath him in only moments, but he wanted more than that.

Gliding webbed hands down her sides, he felt for every place that made her whisper out a, "Don't stop. Right there. Yes, that feels so good."

Finally, finally, he allowed himself to slide his webbed fingers between her folds and seek out that warm, wet heat she had described. Fuck, she hadn't been wrong in that descriptor. She was dripping between her thighs, and though that felt very strange to feel, he couldn't help but want to touch more of it. Leaning down, he licked his way up her neck all the way to her mouth.

"Kiss me again, virago. Like you did in the sea."

She wasn't hesitant about her pleasure. Alexia ground herself against his webbed hand, and he had to make sure his claws were nowhere near her. He could easily cut her, and she wasn't looking out for herself. But then she wrapped an arm around his neck and drew him down for a vicious kiss, and it was hard for him to think of anything else. Her tongue tangled with his, rubbing over the ridges and bumps that covered it.

She moaned into his mouth, riding his hand toward her own oblivion. "You feel so good."

"I'm going to feel much better soon. I wanted to ease you into this, but I cannot wait to taste you."

"Taste me?" She was breathing hard, staring down the length of her own body as he suddenly moved until his face was between her legs.

Ah, her scent here was divine. Thick and earthy, feminine, just as he knew she would be. All his to devour. Fortis licked his lips, staring at the deep pink and red of her folds before he dove in.

Why describe to her what he was going to do, when he could just show her?

Her flavor exploded on his tongue, and he groaned into her flesh. The ridges of his tongue slid along her slit, finding a nub at the top that seemed to make her arch more than the rest.

Even though she was larger than the average human, he knew she was going to be tight. He had to make sure she was prepared to take him. He had to make sure she would survive this encounter, even though it might hurt a little.

Humans were delicate, he reminded himself as a haze appeared in front of his eyes while he tongued her. His jaws ached to open even wider, draw her deeper into his mouth until he was coated with the taste of her. He wanted to spread her across his chest, bury her beneath his scales, so he would never forget this moment as her thighs trapped his head between them.

It wasn't enough. It wasn't nearly enough.

Grabbing onto her hips so hard his claws drew blood, he looked up at her and waited until her gaze met his. "Breathe," he reminded her, before plunging his tongue deep inside her pussy.

Chapter 35

She wasn't sure what was even happening to her body. Everything was on fire and somehow ice cold at the same time. She couldn't focus on anything other than the feeling of him between her thighs. His ridged tongue, with all those bumps, was doing things to her sanity. She was breathing so hard it was like she had gone on a run.

Then his hands came up along her sides, and those claws scraped her skin. She saw stars as he suddenly sank his tongue inside of her. She could feel every single one of those ridges as he pulled his tongue back out and then sank back in again.

"Fuck," she whimpered. There were no other words. Just the incandescent feeling of her body tightening, coiling, just as he had taught her it could do before. It spun tighter, even more impossibly needy, no matter what he did. His tongue rolled, his fingers pressed that button at the top of her slit, which had been so pleasurable when she'd touched it herself.

Then one of those clawed hands reached up and grasped her

breast, his thumb toying with her nipple while all the other sensations made it hard to even breathe.

And then it all turned white hot, just as it had before. She knew, without a doubt, that he was going to make her come. She'd done it before, and now it was happening again. But somehow, it was so much more when another person made her feel this way. The out-of-control sensation just kept going, building more and more until she thought she might break from it.

She came with a harsh curse and a gasp that made her chest ache. Every muscle in her body tensed as she rode the wave of pleasure and ground down on his face. He groaned into her and she knew it was because he was enjoying her pleasure just as much as she was. And that made it last even longer. She couldn't breathe. She could barely exist. This was all because of his doing, the first and the second time, and she was just...

Incapable of speech, Alexia realized as she spiraled down from that high.

This time, though, she hadn't felt the splatter of his release as well. And when she opened her eyes, she could see that he hadn't come as she had expected him to. Instead, all she could see were the twin cocks that were harder than she remembered them being the last time. They looked painful, pale in coloring, but still so solid they must hurt.

"I want to touch you," she rasped. "It hasn't been fair that you've only touched me so far."

She could see the argument in his head. He didn't want her to touch him, because he was clearly enjoying himself. But desire won over. He slid his hands underneath her arms and lifted her as he rolled onto his back. So easily. All it took was movement, and suddenly she was on her hands and knees over him. He was still between her legs, but now she was at eye level with his cocks and the flexing muscles of his abs.

Now that was a sight. Alexia hadn't ever thought she would be attracted to cocks. She'd seen human cocks plenty of times in her life, and they were always rather disappointing, flaccid things. The way they hung between a man's legs or their size when they were hard had not intrigued her.

But these? These were impressively large, with a tapered end that made her certain she could make them fit, even if it was her first time. All she would need to do was take it slow.

Licking her lips, she tried something she had seen Harlow do many times. Swirling her tongue around the head of his cock, she took just the tip into her mouth. In truth, that was all she could do. Swirling her tongue, she hollowed out her cheeks and sucked as hard as she could.

His hips bucked, and he grabbed the back of her head, fingers lacing in her hair as he tugged her back. "Easy, virago, or this will be over far too soon."

She liked the sound of that, though. She wanted him to be incapable of thought, just like he had made her. She wanted him to be incomprehensible because of the things she did to him with her hands and tongue.

Wrapping both her hands around the base of him, she moved them up and down his impressive length. "Is this better?"

Their eyes locked, and she could see how close he was to losing control. "Careful," he murmured. "I don't know what I'll do if I lose control."

"Hopefully something incredible," she murmured, before sucking him back into her mouth.

Fuck being careful. Fuck his feelings of taking this slow and savoring the moment. Alexia didn't want to do either of those. She wanted him to pound into her. She wanted those claws digging into her skin and drawing blood while he sank between her thighs with these cocks. He'd already made her come. Surely he knew that she wanted more than just that.

So as she teased him, tormented him, licked and sucked until she had already gotten herself even more soaking wet than before, she tried hard not to think about what he was doing.

Because he'd sank his tongue back inside her. He swirled it, stretching her muscles as though he were trying to prepare her for what would come. His fingers weren't quite enough, she knew that. The webs that were between them would make it hard for him to insert anything more than a claw and the first joint. Not enough to prepare her for these cocks.

Which she wanted him to use. Now. Sooner. Why were they still waiting?

Moaning around the thickness of him in her mouth, she finally pulled back. A string of drool connected her lips to the tip, and she realized she had never seen anything so viscerally sexy.

He drew back to stare at her, and she was certain he felt the same way. His abs flexed even more, his lips parting as he fought with himself to gain any semblance of control. But she didn't want him to have control.

So she darted out her tongue and licked away the string, leaning down to press her tongue against the small hole at the tip of his cock.

"Fuck," he groaned, and suddenly she was moving. She had no idea how he made her feel so small, but he lifted her as if she weighed nothing. Fortis spun her, so she was seated astride his tail with his cocks between her legs and her hands braced against his powerful stomach. Looking at him, she tried her best to keep her wits about her.

But she couldn't stop herself from leaning down and licking the groove between his abs, just like she'd been wanting to do for such a long time.

He groaned, and those abs flexed against her tongue as he shifted forward to grab onto her hips. "Please don't make me wait any longer, virago."

Oh, she loved the sound of his begging. It was music to her ears, and she wanted to hear more of that.

Hissing out a breath, she flexed her thighs and lifted herself all the way above his cocks. This was daunting. She'd done a lot of scary things in her life, but never something like this. She'd even put her body at risk countless times, but this was different. This had a meaning and a purpose. It wasn't pain she sought. That was easy to find. Pleasure was much harder.

She notched the head of him between her folds, feeling the strange slickness of him. She hadn't really thought about the smooth texture of his skin when she'd had him in her mouth, but he was so smooth. So warm.

Rubbing him back and forth past her entrance, she coated him in all of her own wetness, hoping it would make all of this a little easier. And then, with a deep breath, she sank down on the tip of him. The strange sensation of fullness immediately hit her. It was like something had speared her, but she didn't mind that it had. She held her breath, sinking down a little further, feeling the strange burn as he pressed against muscles that had been tight her entire life.

But then his clawed hands grabbed onto her hips, stilling her motions. "Easy, virago. You don't have to take it all in one go."

She inhaled sharply, looking up to see his expression had gone from creased pain to a softness that she rarely saw from him. He didn't want this to hurt her, she realized. Somehow, that made all of this even easier.

Nodding, she let his hands guide her. Sitting up slowly, she let him pull back before gliding in again. Inch by ever so tantalizing inch, he stretched out her body. Not in one long go like she had intended, but in many glides that opened up her body to him until he was able to thrust inside of her without any resistance.

It took time.

Patience.

Aching need as they both struggled to remember to breathe while they sought out a pleasure that felt like it might be earth shattering.

"Good," he praised throughout all of it. "You're doing well, virago. Just a bit more. Look at you, you're doing amazing. Just a bit more. You can take a bit more."

As her eyes rolled back in her head, he lifted her sharply off that cock and then... Where was the ease? Where was the glide? Suddenly she was pressed back down on a cock that wasn't coated in all her slickness. Eyes bulging open, she looked down to see that he had moved her to the second cock. The first now pressed against her clit as he started the process all over again.

Her muscles clenched, her stomach seizing at the tiny movements that somehow weren't enough to bring her to the edge but also felt so impossibly good. She just wanted to know what it was like to explode around his cock, and he was withholding that from her. With every movement, every shift, every inch that he stuffed inside of her, she wanted more.

More movement. More friction, more than what he was giving her right now.

"Fortis," she moaned. "Please."

"You're not ready yet, virago."

She slapped her hands down on his chest and glared. "If you don't fuck me like you mean it, then I will get off of you and finish what you started."

He glared at her, both of them suddenly realizing that this was a battle and neither of them wanted to lose. She saw his jaw grinding, the muscles in it working as he gave her a sharp nod and thrust up into her with one sharp movement.

She saw stars.

The thickness of him pressed against every inch of her body. Her inner walls fluttered around him, the beginning of an orgasm that she knew would bring about her end. Could she die from this? It felt like she might. Then he pulled out, so fast she almost gasped, only to shove back in and thrust all the air from her lungs with the movement.

His hands gripped her hips a little tighter, lifting her off his bottom cock and impaling her on the top. Though there was more friction with this one, it was still easy to take. She could feel the texture of him, the size, the shape of the tip that suddenly bottomed out inside of her as he reared up and cupped the back of her head.

Fortis devoured her lips, hungrily licking and biting while he shifted her up and down with his free hand. He controlled every moment. His powerful biceps flexed with each movement, drawing her up and down his cocks until he would suddenly shift her to the other. Over and over again, she was moved along each individual cock as she chased that high.

"Yes," she hissed, reaching between them to press her fingers firmly against her clit. "Yes, please."

"Are you going to come for me?" he asked, his mouth moving down to the junction where her shoulder and neck met. He bit down there, hard, and it somehow made her even more tense.

"Fuck," she ground out as her muscles tensed.

And then she felt him come. She felt his cock twitch hard inside of her and then a burst of heat that filled her near to bursting. She'd never thought it would feel like that even as her muscles tensed and she came with him.

Throwing her head back, she hissed out a long breath as she rode the waves of her orgasm. And as she slowly wound down, she realized he was still playing with her clit. Toying with her with the edge of one of those impossibly sharp claws.

He stared at her, those dark eyes seeing too much. "Again," he growled.

"I can't."

"You can. Give me three, virago. At least three."

She stared at him, feeling the empty ache as he withdrew his cock from her channel, only to plunge back in with the other one. It was still hard. His second cock was still so hard.

As she bounced, completely at his mercy, she realized she could come again. If he kept doing this, if he kept up this pressure and the mesmerizing touch of his fingers, she wouldn't have a choice.

And she did. Embarrassingly fast. She clenched around him and he threw his head back in a groan she felt all the way to her core. Together, they disappeared in this secret place, surrounded by the ocean as their voices echoed through the empty chamber.

She'd never felt more loved or more connected to another person in her life. And yet...

As she panted and laid her head down on his chest, she couldn't help but feel empty. Even with his cock still twitching inside her, she feared the future that was coming. He was so certain she would kill him.

Alexia feared he was right.

Chapter 36

Fortis would have luxuriated in that cave for the rest of his life. Having her draped over his chest, pressed against his hearts that now thundered for her, it was an experience he wasn't likely to forget. Unfortunately, they both knew this was the only chance they would get.

Their time was limited, not just because of his death, but because of what they had to do. Soon enough, they would find themselves in the depths of a war, and they were both integral parts.

So he woke her when she drifted off to sleep with quiet words and even more quiet touches. He pressed lingering kisses to her shoulders, breathing in the scent of her skin before he helped her put on the suit. Not that she needed it, but Mira would want it back now that they all knew it worked.

As he swam back toward their village, he felt a pit in his stomach open. He didn't want this to end. That was the hardest part of all of this. Fortis wanted to stay with her and live for a little while longer.

He'd known about his death for such a long time, but nothing had prepared him for a moment when he didn't want to go. He'd been so ready for such a long time, and now? Now he wasn't even remotely ready. All he wanted was to stay just a few more days.

What if the depthstriders changed their mind? They were only fighting for revenge. Once he died, would they change their mind? It wasn't entirely out of the question. They were a fickle bunch, and they preferred to help their own rather than anyone else. They could decide that they would not fight, and there would be no one left to argue with them.

The other part of himself, the less anxious side that floated through the sea with her in his arms, wanted to see what happened with the sea. The humans and People of Water working together, after all this time. He wanted to swim through the cities they would build, and he knew they would be great. He wanted to see Anya and Ace lead a group of humans toward fixing the land above. He wanted to see all the beauty that would come from the partnership between so many who had hated each other for so long.

Just before they reached the village, Alexia reached up and cupped his jaw. He stopped swimming instantly, and looked down at the strong, capable woman he somehow was lucky enough to have in his arms.

"Fortis?" she asked.

"What is it, virago?"

"I just want you to know that my time with you has been the best part of my life. I don't think I ever even knew how to live before you showed me, and I want you to know how grateful I am for it. No matter what happens."

He wanted to kiss her. He wanted to drag her back to the facility with all that glass, and watch as she arched her back as she came. There were so many more things he wanted to try with her, but time was not on their side.

Sighing, he ran his hand down her back and looked at her instead. "I will never forget you, virago. Not in this life, or the next. You have changed the way I see this world, and for that, I am also grateful. I am lucky that you were kind enough to not kill me the first moment you saw me."

She snorted. "You're lucky you're a fast bastard, or I would have."

They grinned at each other, the threats of the past long forgiven. And he would have stayed forever, smiling at her with all the hope he could feel in his hearts, but they did not have the luxury of time.

"Father!" Aulax's voice called out. "We're ready."

What did he mean they were ready? They couldn't be ready, not yet. There were still many things for them to do, and figure out, and they needed to plan. But by the time he coasted them into the village, he could see there were plenty who had already planned without them.

"How much did you tell them before we left?" he asked, heading to the main meeting area of the village.

"Everything," she said. "I gave them all the access codes I had, and every single map I could remember. I gave them access to Tau's inner workings and changed the codes in one of those droids to make it look like it was coming from my ship."

He blinked down at her. "You did all that in such a short amount of time?"

Again, she looked at him like he had lost his mind. "I am very efficient, Fortis."

And so she was. He just hadn't realized how efficient and how difficult that would make things for him.

Exhaling, he brought them both into the main room for them to be accosted by a hundred people trying to talk all at once. Perhaps a hundred was an exaggeration, but it felt that way.

Alexia was yanked out of the water by multiple hands, all of them grabbing at her and dragging her into the fray. There were so many humans wandering around in the room, each of them trying to talk over another as they moved in small groups toward their own goal. He didn't know what that goal was; it was hard to hear any of them speak over the massive noise they were making.

A red hand grabbed his arm, urging him back under the water so he could speak with the others. But his eyes were only on her.

She pulled the diving helmet off her head, her long braid swinging free like a whip as she approached the crowd without fear. She was easily a head taller than even the tallest man in that room. Alexia took over any space that she was in and commanded attention wherever she went.

Daios again tugged on his arm, this time forcing him to dip underneath the water.

"What is wrong with you?" Daios muttered.

Everything.

Nothing.

He had lost his mind because a warrior woman had barged into his life and now she seemed to believe he could exist without her. She was able to shake off all that they had experienced together, and he wasn't sure he liked that. He wanted her to be consumed by thoughts of him, incapable of thinking of anything else. Especially this close to their encounter.

Daios smacked him in the throat. Hard. "Get your head back on straight, Fortis. Listen to me. There are plans and you have to follow them, and you can't do that if you're mooning over some woman who you already know is going to kill you."

Fortis glared at him. "How do you know that?"

"I know a lot of things. You forget, I have worked with the depthstriders most of my life. You're not the only one I know, and many of your people are talking about how you are siding with the woman who is going to kill you." Daios frowned. "Why you are doing that, I will never understand. But it is not my job to understand you. It is my job to ensure you have your head on straight enough that we all get this done the way it has to be done."

Fortis understood the meaning behind his words. They were on borrowed time.

"Why are we rushing?" he asked as they swam to another section of the village. "I assumed we would return and have to make as many plans as we could before all of this was happening."

A depthstrider swam past them with his arms laden with weapons. Three droids followed him, each of them already equipped with more weaponry that would likely be used in the upcoming battle.

Daios shook his head. "Before Alexia left, she gave them all the idea of what the plan should be, and it was a good plan. She'll return in the ship, pretending to lick her wounds after she lost you. It'll be a two month long story that they'll need to get out of her, and she knows enough about them to lie well. Her Original will believe her, because Alexia has always been a soft spot in Harlow's armor. It gives her a chance to reestablish connection and then let us in."

"This is a terrible plan. You're all leaving it up to fate that they trust she hasn't been compromised, or that they wouldn't decommission her at first sight."

"This is the plan she suggested, and we are trusting that she knows what to do with her own people."

But she didn't. They'd already established that truth. She had fought her entire life to get out of from under the rule of Tau, and now they were all trusting that they wouldn't kill her for it?

Daios's brow furrowed. "Unless you fear they will get her back under their thumb?"

"No, I fear that she will do something foolish and get herself killed." And therein laid the problem. Alexia was so angry at all of those people, and he knew it might not be reasonable to expect her to withhold that anger.

With a slow exhalation of bubbles through his gills, Daios nodded. "I believe the only thing we can do now is to trust her, Fortis. We have shown Alexia what it is like to be with us, to support us, to do all the things that we have been doing for countless months on end. We have to believe that she will do the right thing, even if it is hard."

"Like kill me," he muttered, before shaking his head. "Understood. What is the plan?"

"We have manufactured another battery for her to attach to her ship. The maintenance droids we stole from Beta also went to the location she revealed to ensure the ship was still viable, and the system is ready to go online as soon as you place her in it. She will return to the city in the same ship, with the knowledge that she will need to undergo vigorous testing to ensure she is still the woman they believe her to be. Once that is completed, she will open the locks on the city one by one. We will enter that way and kill as many people as we can."

"And if they retaliate?"

"We leave through the same vents that she is opening. But we will also have many warriors taking down their exterior ships with the droid enhancements Alexia provided us with. Between our people and the weapons on these droids, we should be able to be safe outside and in. Inside, we kill a few people at a time, continually attacking through the new vents she is opening and then leaving before they are closed."

They made it to Mira's workshop, where he had assumed the battery would be. "They will realize it is her. No one else would make the mistakes like that. They have had hundreds of years to perfect the protection of their city."

"That's where the depthstriders come in. Alexia is dropping the shield around the city as soon as she can, and the depthstriders will work on dismantling the city's exterior. Apparently, there are glass structures that stand between the water just outside of Tau. Once those are removed, the entrances into the city are vast and many." Daios shrugged. "The depthstriders will puncture through the windows of the city. One by one."

As far as plans went, it wasn't that bad. Tau had never been attacked outright. Which meant although they had prepared for years, their protections had never been tested before.

They approached Mira's workshop and were greeted by a wall of droids. The flashing lights and bleeping sound of their language filled the water with red hues and strange echoes. Droids always made him uncomfortable.

Mira was already out of her workshop in a silver wetsuit. She had her rebreather over her face, swimming around a familiar battery. She barely acknowledged them, but did at least look over her shoulder at their approach.

"It looks good to go," she muttered, but there was a pinch to her expression that Fortis found familiar at this point. "I don't know. It's not the same battery the ship used before, and I'm afraid that will make it pretty fucking obvious that it's been tampered with."

"Just tell Alexia. She'll make up a reason for it. Perhaps she had to dock at an old facility to make her return."

"Not a bad idea. But you'll have to be the one to tell her." Mira shrugged. "She's already coming this way, anyway. They should have briefed her by now."

Already? Surely not. There were countless reasons they needed to take their time, and yet... He turned and there she was. Swimming over to them in that graceful way she always managed. Flippers on her feet, a mask securely around her face, and her hair braided into a higher, slicker ponytail.

Damn it, this was really happening. No matter what he did to slow it down.

Determination turned Alexia's expression almost into something unrecognizable. "Oh good, you already have the battery ready."

Mira nodded. "I'm concerned about the look, though. They'll know this isn't the same battery you were sent out with."

"I'm sure they'll expect that. I have been gone for two months. They know I didn't have enough power to sustain me that long. I'll think up something." Alexia waved a hand, then looked at him. "Think you can carry both of us, big guy?"

This was his moment to say no. He couldn't, actually, carry both of them. It was a valid reason to not be able to bring her anywhere. He'd need someone else to go on this suicide mission with him. Clearly.

But his stupid mouth said, "I can carry both things just fine, virago."

Daios and Mira shared a look before his red finned brother cleared his throat. "Once she's in the ship, you are supposed to head back to the other depthstriders. They have a plan for you to fight with them, and considering your fate, I'm sure Mitera knows where you are supposed to be and at what time."

He hoped she did, because he sure didn't. Fortis knew that these were the last moments of his life, though, and he would not linger in the worry and fear of what might happen next.

"Tell Aulax that he was the son I always dreamt of," he murmured. "And if my boy can find me near her ship, we will have our final moments together."

He gathered Alexia in his arms, grabbed onto the handle of the battery, and headed out.

They said nothing on the journey. But there weren't many things left to say. She knew how he felt. She knew that his life had been forever broadened by her actions. The only fear he had was what would happen next, and how soon it would occur.

It didn't take them nearly long enough to get back to her ship, or perhaps it took the same amount of time and he had just been lost in thought. But far too soon, he saw the ship on the ledge right where they had left it. A fine layer of dust now covered it, but there were marks where the droids had landed.

"The droids made quick work of fixing your ship," he murmured as he brought them to the ground in front of her ship.

"Mira told me. She said they made sure it would start once the battery is in place."

They both were far too hesitant to let each other go. Neither of them wanted to say what was going to happen next, and he didn't want to leave. Not yet. He wanted to make sure she was safely inside. Then he would let her go.

"Just make sure they don't catch you—" he said, at the same time as she spoke.

"Don't take any unnecessary risks."

They both chuckled, and he cupped the side of her neck, drawing her in close to him. "Be safe, virago."

"Same to you, Fortis. We'll see each other again."

He knew they would. But, as she headed into the underbelly of the ship and left him alone in the sea, he feared the next time he would see her would be the end. As he plugged the battery into the top of her dusty ship and watched the lights all turn on, he told himself he had been preparing for this moment for years.

He still wasn't ready.

375

Chapter 37

She hated being back in this ship. It felt so wrong. She'd come so far from the person who had first chased him down, and yet, all Alexia could think about was who she used to be.

Soon enough, she would have to pretend to be that woman again. She would need to convince the people of Tau that she was the same Alexia who had left. She would need to be emotionless, capable of anything, unaffected by the world around herself because she knew that a little drug would take away any fear or anxiety she might have.

An icy feeling trailed between her shoulder blades. She'd have to take the drug again. Bracing herself against the control panel, she stared at the dusty glass at the front of the ship. She breathed out, seeing the steam of her own breath.

Of all the things she had prepared herself to do, she hadn't thought about the injections. That's the first thing they would do to her. A quick jab in the side of the neck, just to keep her calm and make sure that everything moved forward normally. She hadn't had the drug in many weeks, at least as far as they knew. All the scientists would want to poke and prod at her. No one knew how someone like her would react to not having their "medicine" regularly.

The geneticists didn't realize the people who were enhanced could even have feelings like she did. They chose not to believe because it was so much easier than the truth.

Taking a deep, steadying breath, she started hitting buttons on the ship to wake it up. The first thing she heard was the sound of the computer coming back online.

"State your designation."

"It's the same person as before, computer. Alexia, personal guard to Original Harlow. I have completed my mission and would like to return home."

"Running diagnostics."

Of course it was. She could hear the soft clinks of droids attaching themselves to the top of the ship. They got to work in no time, drilling into pieces of the ship where they would implant trackers, so Mira knew where she was at all times.

And of course, there were the droids in her pockets. Tiny droids the size of beads, made by Ace. She said they would do what no other droid could. They'd get in and out of the city, making sure to film every single detail so that the undines who entered the city would know where to go by sight and not just by reading a map.

These people had thought of everything, and now it all came down to her. Could she betray her own people? Absolutely. She needed her revenge like she needed breath. But whether or not she could convince the Originals she hadn't changed, that would be the greatest and most difficult task of her life.

"Ship online," the computer stated. "Protocol is to remain until the guard has completed duty."

"I told you, I already did," Alexia muttered as she started hitting override buttons.

"The nets and transport holds are all empty. Please seek out the target again."

Fuck, she hated computers. They were always arguing at the worst of times, and she needed to go. "Ace, why didn't you send me with a droid that could override this talkative bitch?" she muttered as she tried to get into the main system.

The problem was that she had to show up with something. A large squid, or perhaps a small whale would trick the computer to let her return to Tau, but she wasn't sure how she was going to find one of those. They didn't have a lot of time. The depthstriders were already getting antsy.

She couldn't think with the damn glass covered like it was. She needed breathing room and space and all the other things that were required for her mind to think. Even if that ended up being a few moments of her staring into the abyss before she figured this out.

Maybe she needed a few moments with the darkness. Just to get her head back on straight.

"Computer, clear the front glass of all debris."

A loud rumble started throughout the ship, and then it shook itself. She hung onto the back of her pilot's chair and waited for the dust to settle.

There was something out there. Lurking in the gloom. Alexia could barely make out the shape, but it was there. Waiting for her to see it. Unsettled, she reached for the button that would flick on the headlights.

The lights came on and illuminated the massive undine in front of her ship. She gasped, already berating herself for having any sort of reaction when she should be practicing for Tau. But then she realized it was Fortis.

"You didn't leave," she said, a little stumped as to why.

But then he swam a little closer, those dark eyes seeing far too much. "I couldn't let you go alone, virago. You know you're going to need me."

"Fortis, it's too dangerous for you to come back with me. I know that. You know that. It's just not safe."

"You need a reason to return. They won't let you back into that city without a good reason." He raked his fingers through his hair. "I've been thinking about this plan and why it made me nervous. It ends with them trusting that you didn't leave for your own reasons. They won't believe you. They won't trust you. The moment you walk into that city, they are going to put a bullet in your head."

He wasn't entirely wrong. The risk was there. But she couldn't have him coming with her and risk himself as well.

"They will tear you apart," she said. "The only way to make sure there is no suspicion at all when I return is to come back with you, Fortis. Not with you following me. Not with anything other than your dead body, or your incapacitated being ready for them to dissect."

His head tilted to the side, a curious gesture that she recognized all too well. "You knew this."

"I did."

"You didn't tell the others because you didn't want to risk my life." He almost looked angry. "I thought we'd already talked about this. You know you are supposed to kill me."

"And I'm willing to do everything I can to not kill you, you stubborn bastard." She gripped the back of her chair so hard the leather squeaked. "I don't like being painted as the villain in your story."

"You are not the villain! You are just the end." He reached out his hand and touched the glass. "I am going to leave the living realm, Alexia. You are going to be the weapon that takes me out. I have come to terms with this and I am comfortable with it. But you cannot fight fate. It's not possible."

"I don't want to see you get hurt."

"And it is something you cannot stop from happening. Let me do this last thing for you. Let me know that in the end, I helped to keep you safe."

Her heart twisted at the words. She knew why he wanted to keep her safe. She understood that he was struggling with this as much as her, and that part of her knew she couldn't fight fate, just as he was saying.

But she didn't want to see this happen. She wasn't sure she would survive it to see them tear into him like they had all the other undines they had in their grasp.

Taking a deep breath, she readied herself to tell him no. That she would have to disappoint him and he would have to keep living, even though he wanted to see his dead wife. She hated to be the person to make him live, but he had to.

"Alexia," he said, his tones almost begging. "Do this for me."

She hated every second of this and she hated even more knowing that she would let him convince her. Because that meant she was one step closer to having to kill him, and here she had been, thinking she could avoid all of it.

Taking in a shuddering breath, she nodded. "Your last memories of me are not going to be good. They're going to be of the person you worked so hard to get me to no longer be. I hate that you won't even be able to see the real me while all of this happens."

"I will always know who you are, virago. I will see you struggle to do what is right and be victorious. I know, without a doubt, that you will lead our people toward a better future." He planted his hand flat on the glass, waiting until she did the same. "I adore you, Alexia. But even more than that, I believe in you."

He couldn't have said a worse or better thing.

"Damn it," she hissed. "You foolish, wonderful man. I will never forget you."

Because there wasn't much more she could argue. She had to slam her hand down on the computer, and said, "Computer, lock target in front of ship. Net him."

The ship came alive at that. After all, it was a ship meant to hunt and to maim. The net speared through the water, making it almost impossible for Fortis to even try to dodge it. Not that he did. He remained still, ready for anything to happen as it wrapped around him and dragged him toward the belly of the ship.

At the same time, all the engines fired. Her small ship lifted through the water so that it could gather him up with metal arms against the belly, and then they were off. That easily.

She hoped the droids had time to put the trackers on the ship. Alexia would need those later.

Her stomach churned, though. As they hurtled toward Tau, all she could think about was how difficult this would be. She didn't want to hand him over to them. She was signing his death warrant, and it would be a painful death.

"Computer, approximate time until we reach Tau?"

"Six hours and twenty-three minutes."

So they hadn't been that far from Tau. Fortis had led her on a multi day chase, but that didn't mean that Tau had ever been out of reach. She was only a six-hour journey away. They could have found her at any point, and yet, they hadn't.

Settling into the pilot's chair, she started working through all her training to keep her emotions in check. What she wanted to do was lash out, though. The Originals had done everything they could to make her an asset and then they left her to rot at the bottom of the ocean? How dare they? She was a fucking person, and they didn't give a shit!

"Computer?" she asked, her breathing already a little ragged. "Can you please play whale sounds?"

"Affirmative."

With that sound in her ear, she tilted her head back and tried to meditate for the rest of the journey. All she had to do was believe good things could happen. She was going to go in there, the plan was going to work, and everyone would realize that Tau was the villain after all. The cities would thrive without the added influence of evil people who had been alive for far too long, and this would work.

All she had to do was sell this as a believable entrance.

It took her all six hours to calm herself. And when the computer announced they had reached Tau, she was ready.

This would be fine. She was going to give the performance of her life.

Grabbing the headset where it hung on a hook above her head, she brought it down to her ears and turned it on. "Alexia to Tau. Alexia to Tau."

There were a few moments of crackling silence before another voice said, "Alexia? Confirm Original name."

"Harlow."

More silence, then crackles as though someone on the other

side was trying to get a higher up. Then came a voice she recognized. "Sargent Russell here. Are you claiming to be Alexia?"

She sighed. "I am returning with the undine. My apologies that it took so long. He was a wily bastard. Took me all over the ocean before I finally got him."

That would stump them. They certainly weren't sure what to do with that, and she knew for damn certain that they were going to try to figure out a way to deny her entry.

But Harlow wanted Fortis. And if an Original wanted something, the entire city did what they could to provide it.

The Sargent came back online. "Please head to the scanning dock. You must understand, we didn't expect your return."

"Affirmative. Heading to docking bay four now."

She hung the headphones up and told herself everything would be fine. This was the only way any of it was going to work. She could do this.

But as the bright green scanning lights hovered over her ship, checking to make sure that everything was exactly how she said it was, she wasn't all that certain that she was ready. What if she lost it? What if she fought with them to keep Fortis safe? She should have made the infuriating man go get the damned drugs that he had dropped into the ocean and she could have injected herself with it to start.

"Alexia?" She could just barely hear the voice on her headphones, but quickly grabbed them again.

"Here."

"Why is there an unrecognized battery on the top of your ship?"

"You know our batteries wouldn't last me two months, Sargent. I found another one in an abandoned facility. Damned lucky it had any juice in it, and only enough to get me home. The undine tore one of the other ones off my ship." She covered the mouthpiece with her hand, then took a steadying breath and continued. "Sargent, I have been without my medication for too long. If your scanning is complete, please collect the undine and bring me back inside. I need to be reviewed by medical. I have completed my mission and I will not be treated like an animal."

That seemed to do it. The docking bay door opened over her head and she readied herself to let him go. It was how it had to be. He would die so everyone else could live.

"Fuck," she whispered as tears burned her eyes. She needed to get her shit together, and fast.

The doors of the ship opened, and she squared her shoulders. She would be fine. This was for the betterment of all people, not just herself.

She turned with a cool expression to face the army of scientists and soldiers. Six guns were pointed at her, and already there were medical staff ready to stick her with whatever they could.

She lifted her hands with a wry grin. "What a welcome home."

Chapter 38

Fortis knew he had to make a show of this. The humans who would bring him into this city were not going to be happy with just capturing him. They did not expect a creature of his size—one who had already attacked their city—to come quietly. If he wanted her to live, then he needed to prove her right.

He listened to their conversation, hearing the way the scientists didn't trust her. He knew the moment she was given the injection. The sound of her sigh likely reassured them that she was waiting to be treated, but he knew the sound for what it was.

She was disappointed. Embarrassed. There was even a hint of guilt in that sound, as though she had been the one who had made a grievous mistake in coming back.

This had to be done, however. She had to make it through this city and unlock at least a few of those hidden entrances, or none of this would work. They needed her to betray her people and to do that; she had to make this believable.

And so did he.

So when the doors opened and a rush of soldiers appeared towards him, he made it look real. He fought and struggled against the net, ripping at it with his teeth and baring those sharp fangs for everyone to see. He snarled at them, writhing over and over until they had no choice but to fear him.

"If this net was not here, I would have already torn you limb from limb," he growled. "There is nothing I love more in this life than tearing into human flesh and tasting your blood on my tongue. I wish to see you destroyed in every way you can imagine, and then suck the marrow from your bones."

Fortis assumed they could understand him, just as she could. He also assumed that no matter what he said, they would believe it a threat, as they should. But they did not know that he was going to die today, just as he did not know how she would kill him.

The soldiers pointed their laser weapons at him, ones he knew would sting if they fired. He wasn't afraid of those, though. He had taken many of them to the chest and tail throughout his years. What he did fear, however, was the scientist who walked into the room with a handful of needles.

No, this wasn't right. They weren't supposed to kill him before she could.

"We won't make the same mistake as last time. What I gave you should have incapacitated a whale," the scientist grumbled before barking, "Make sure he can't move."

Multiple soldiers lifted the net out of the water and then pinned him down onto the floor with it. The net was nearly impossible to wriggle in now, although he tried. His fluke slapped against the floor and four more humans arranged themselves around the edge. There were at least ten of them holding him down now, perhaps more that he couldn't see over his shoulder.

Eventually, he pretended to tire. Fortis let his fins flip to a dramatic final thwack and then heaved a giant breath as he laid quietly for the scientist to approach him. He had to believe in the vision, and trust that Alexia would be the one to kill him. He knew his end. He knew his future. And his future was her. It always had been and always would be.

The prick of the needle warned him that soon, he would feel the effects. If they gave him double what he had been given the last time, he wasn't sure how awake he would be. The drug would eventually make it hard for him to be aware of his surroundings.

The drugs took over quickly. He wasn't faking the way his muscles went lax and how even his breathing was. His mind was only barely aware that he was still in this room. He could see the white ceiling above him, and hear the murmurs of the humans surrounding him, but he wasn't all that concerned about what they were saying.

"Just kill it and get it over with," one of the soldiers said. "I don't understand why you'd keep it alive. The beast is more trouble than it's worth."

The scientist sighed. "Because we cannot study them or harvest their organs if they are dead, you moron. The specimens need to be alive for as long as possible. Besides, Harlow wants to be present when this one dies, considering he took her favorite guard away from her. What would you do if you were in her position?"

Something slid underneath his body. Two metal arms that were strangely sturdy as he was lifted off the ground. The same soldier who had asked the question walked beside him as they moved, and that man grumbled under his breath, "I'd want the creature who nearly killed our most skilled soldier dead. That's what I'd want."

So there were intelligent achromos. Humans, he corrected himself, and then would have laughed if he had been able to do so. He'd always assumed the humans were stupid creatures, but one of them was actually able to make a joke that he found funny.

How interesting to discover such a thing when he was about to die.

Soon enough, what he saw melded into the vision he had seen from his wife. The white ceiling that rushed past him, the flickering of lights that he realized now weren't lights turning off and on, rather that he was moving underneath them. Rows of lights that started and stopped as they moved through Tau.

The journey brought him closer to many more humans. There were gasps of shock as they realized who was being transported among them. Some of them hissed out words like, "Impossible. That one is too large! Surely it isn't from the sea?"

So many voices that all overlapped with each other. Voices that he would bring with him to the grave and hoped that he would soon return to haunt.

He was wheeled into the room where he knew it would all end. Just as his wife had predicted and just as she had shared his future with him. He recognized the lights on the ceiling. He knew this place like he knew his own soul. How many times had he watched this very moment? Knowing the bright white lights above him would start to go blurry and how he would struggle to keep his eyes open?

A sense of peace blossomed in his chest. He had been waiting for this for so many years, now that it was here, he could let all of that fear and aching unknowing go. Soon she would arrive. Soon, he would be prepared for the end.

But there were details that he hadn't expected. The sound of clanking metal as the scientists prepared themselves for the extraction of his organs and parts. The mutterings of the men and women who surrounded him, each of them speculating on the differences they would find within him, and what they were going to do with the organs.

"They are stronger, and far more capable of surviving under the water than us. What I want to know is how the pressure doesn't affect them. Even deep-sea fish are incapable of coming up from the depths like the undines do." The female voice was soothing and quiet, even though she spoke of things that no human had the right to understand.

"I think our own curiosity is not worth wasting all this time and effort. We know there are healing properties in their skin. We should be using this specimen to discover how they heal so much faster than us, and how we can adapt that knowledge so we don't waste so many resources on creating more reborns." This time it was a man's voice, much harder and clipped.

He'd known the humans were experimenting on his people for a reason, but he hadn't thought it was for this. They were so curious about his kind, they didn't even realize that it should have been much easier for them to research what his people could do.

They could have just asked. All these years wasted, and all they'd had to do was work together. He had seen that it could work. Look at the village Mira and Arges had built. They could have been working together for years and the ocean they could have cultivated would have made so many happy, wealthy, healthy. All the things that these people wanted, but they were so bound and determined to do it on their own before they would ever deem it worthwhile to ask another for help.

He couldn't wait for all of this to be over, but anxiety churned in his stomach. What if he had made a mistake? What if they were never able to do what he believed their people could do?

Anxiety spiked the longer he was alone with these people. His heart rates picked up, and he could hear the little blips of whatever monitor they had hooked him up to as it went faster. He couldn't think of anything but the sound of his own rioting hearts. They knew he was nervous, and that was the biggest shame of his lifetime.

Breathing harder, he struggled to open his eyes. She should be here soon. She was meant to be here. Why wasn't she?

"Ah, Harlow! You've arrived." One of the male scientists said.

If the Original was here, surely that meant Alexia was too. Unless they had killed her. Unless they had decided that it wasn't worth the risk to keep her around, and they could make another of her so easily. They didn't care if she was gone.

But he did.

Damn it, he cared if she was gone and he could only just barely blink his eyes against the bleary light. He'd thought he was ready. He'd been at peace with what was happening, but he wanted to see her again.

Just like the vision had promised him.

One last time.

And then there it was. The sight of her dark hair blocking out the blinding light that had been so painful to look at. The darkness of her was the same comfort as staring into the abyss. A lovely and welcome sight after he'd been so exhausted. Breathing in deeply, he stared up at her with all the love that he felt in his heart.

Had he told her that he loved her? Not in so many words, but he thought with his actions that he had.

It was kinder that he hadn't admitted it. She didn't need to know how much he loved her when they were going to be parted for all eternity. But maybe the drugs had gone straight to his brain, because he regretted not telling her. She deserved to know that someone loved her.

"So, this is where you brought him?" Alexia asked. Her voice was a welcome balm compared to all the other voices he didn't recognize, nor did he have any interest in hearing them speak.

"He's going to go into processing. But we thought Original Harlow would like to see him first." That was said by the female scientist who had wanted to tear him apart to understand how pressure didn't affect him like it did humans.

"Ah," Alexia said. Her hand landed on his shoulder, and he knew it must look like she was there to lay claim to him, but he could feel the comfort in her steady touch. "I don't think we're going to experiment on this one."

"We are."

"No, you're not." Her voice hardened. "This is Harlow's prize. I hunted him down for her, and I brought him back. I don't care what experiments you were going to choose, and I don't care about your petty interests. This is her undine."

He had been warned that she would be cruel, but it was still hard to hear her say all this. He wanted her to tell them all to fuck off, and protect his prone body while he could do nothing by lay there and take whatever they offered.

But it was also his time. And no matter how hard his mind wanted to fight to live, he knew that this was the only choice he had.

Another voice spoke up, and this lilting tone must be the Original Alexia had spoken of. "I don't care what they do to him, Alexia. I'm just pleased you did what I asked."

"I understand that, Harlow. But you also sent me on a mission to kill this creature and I did not do it yet. I wanted you to be here, so that there was no question that I do your bidding and let nothing stand in my way." Again, her voice turned to something like steel. "I know there are rumors that I couldn't possibly be the same guard I was before I left. Though I am on medication again, I find I resent those who believe I will not serve you until my dying breath."

The sigh that echoed in the room was nothing short of lovesick. As though Alexia had said something that was truly romantic. "Oh, you sweet thing. You always know just the thing to say to me. Go on then. Kill him and we'll tell them all to stuff it. You were always the best of them, even if a few emotions slip through here and there."

And then Alexia turned toward him. All he could think about was her standing there, looking down at him with those dark eyes filled with regret. She held her hand out. "Give me four hundred milligrams of neurotoxin. The one we pulled from the diatoms."

"Alexia, we cannot just kill him. The information within his body is too valuable to destroy a specimen like this!"

"I will make you if I have to."

The scientists rushed. And all the while, she looked down at him. Surely they all thought she was looking at the greatest prey she would ever catch in her life, but he saw the brightness in her gaze. He saw the way her eyes were already watering even as she struggled with herself to not cry.

A needle and vial were handed to her, and she carefully drew the neurotoxin out of the bottle before handing it back. Her hand dropped out of view, likely to his arm where he knew, without a doubt, she would kill him.

But then she hesitated. He could see she wasn't going to do it. There was a flare of rebellion in those dark eyes, and he had to stop her. This was both of their destinies as much as it hurt.

Struggling through the drugs, he lifted his hand and press it to hers. With his hand on hers, he guided the needle into his flesh.

Whispering so no one would hear what he said, he quietly told her, "It's all right, virago."

A single tear rolled down her cheek and dripped onto him. He felt the heat of it splash against his neck at the same time as he felt her inject him. His entire body seized for a moment, every muscle stiffening in pain until he felt it all let go. All of his body was so loose, so at ease. He hadn't thought it would feel like this. Like nothing had ever been wrong and everything was going to be all right. He hadn't realized that sinking into death would be so... peaceful.

And the last thing he saw was her beautiful, sorrowful eyes filled with tears.

Chapter 39

These fucked up people. Alexia would never forgive them for this. Never. He didn't deserve to die, and they had taken the only good thing she had.

She just wanted him to live. That's all. She didn't want to beg for it or ruin the mission that she was on, but she wanted him to live so that she didn't have to lose the only thing that had ever made her feel like a person.

He was everything to her. And as she watched his gaze slacken and his body go limp, she could feel herself dying with him. The person he had brought into this world, the version of herself who was soft and kind, died a long, sorrowful death. She went with him, wherever he was going, because she damn well wasn't going to be that soft Alexia here.

It wasn't safe to be soft in this pit of vipers, where everyone wanted to see others in pain. They were testing her. She knew that. They were testing to see if she really was the person that she had once been, and if killing an innocent undine would make her slip up.

Well, they had no idea what she was going to do to them now. She would tear them apart with her bare hands, show them all exactly what the undine had taught her. She would be the nightmare that brought this place to its knees and she would bathe in their blood, just as Fortis would want her to do.

Straightening, she wiped her expression clean of all the thoughts she was having. They couldn't see her anger. They couldn't see the hatred bubbling underneath the surface of her being.

So when she turned, she looked just like her old self. The woman who would take quite literally anything from anyone as long as Harlow was happy. "There. Dead."

Harlow clapped in glee. Her face had already creased into a bright smile, wrinkles forming at the edges of her eyes that she would surely kill a reborn to fix very soon. "Delightful! Now, I have a surprise for you. You got back just in time for it, and I cannot wait for you to see it."

"A surprise, Harlow?" She followed her Original and told herself not to look back. Don't look at the body of the man she had fallen so deeply for. But she did. She looked back at the scientists and narrowed her eyes on them. "Don't fuck with that body. It's not yours. Dispose of it."

They glared at her, but she could see they were going to follow her instruction. They wouldn't desecrate his body, at the very least. Now, she just had to shake Harlow for a few moments and get this plan rolling.

As they strode through the blinding white halls, Alexia found it harder and harder to not let anger overwhelm her. She'd seen Harlow's picture on that wall. She knew this woman had been there at the start of the end of the world. And now, she acted like it had never happened. Like it wasn't a big deal that humans were down here, experimenting on each other and everything else in the sea.

As they walked toward one of Harlow's private quarters, Alexia had to make sure she wasn't breathing hard. Already, the sound of her anger was perhaps a little too obvious.

She needed to distract herself before she did something stupid. Like angrily rage that this woman had made her kill the only man she loved. Or just outright murder the woman for everything Harlow had done.

Not that they wouldn't just bring her back. Alexia was sure the Originals had a plan in case someone assassinated them as well.

"Harlow?" she asked. "Please fill me in on everything that I missed."

"Oh, nothing much. There was a grand party. Everyone was there. I surely missed you while you were gone, though. The guards who were to be your replacements were all so dull. I didn't like them."

Boring. All of this was so boring. None of it actually mattered, and she didn't understand how these people managed to live like this for hundreds of years. Who cared about a party or the people who attended? Who cared that someone had worn something so out of fashion that it was so last week?

But she played along. She kept herself in check, all the way to the back room where Harlow usually worked out whenever she got the idea that she might want to do that. The mats were still on the floor, dark blue, so they didn't offend Harlow's eyes. And then there were the tall glass windows, each one of them about as wide as Alexia was, stacked next to each other like dominos to look out into the dark sea beyond. Exterior lights illuminated the speckles of dust in the water and the nothingness that was out there.

"Good, we arrived just in time." Harlow said. She spun in a small circle before sighing. "Listen. You've been gone for such a long time, and I wanted to do something special for you. I have appreciated your companionship, and you truly are the best person to walk through life with me."

She didn't like where this was going. "Thank you, Harlow."

"Now, I understand that there are going to be people who talk. You have always been a bit different from the other guards, but I liked that. So I let you be. Unfortunately, many of those people have a lot of power here and I need them to like me." Harlow walked over to another door and hit the locking mechanism. It unlocked, and a person walked through. "So this is my gift to you."

A person? What did she want with another person?

But then Alexia really looked at this stranger and stared into her own dark eyes. She traced the outline of her own dark hair, pulled back in a tight braid that made her features look even more severe. This version of her was slightly broader, a little heavier set with muscle, but this was... her. Except she was dressed in a pale grey suit, far more rigid than anything Alexia would have worn. This suit had black buttons down the center, and the new genetically enhanced version of herself started to unbutton them as they stared at each other, revealing a white tank underneath the blazer.

Alexia was standing in front of herself, looking at a woman who shouldn't exist and yet, they both knew what had happened.

"Alexia?" she asked.

"Alexia the eighth, to be specific," this woman said.

Her eyes were so dead, Alexia realized. No emotion in them at all, as though she wasn't really alive.

Harlow seemed to realize what Alexia was horrified by. "Ah, yes. That. There's always been a flaw in you, unfortunately, and it usually relates to emotion. They said if I wanted to keep you, I would have to fix that."

"How is this a gift, Harlow?" Alexia moved as the other version of her moved, making sure the woman wouldn't get behind her. She knew what personal guards were meant to do. This creation would attack her at any given chance. That's what this moment was for. Without a doubt, they were going to kill her.

"Because you get to meet your replacement! I thought you'd want to know that I am going to be well cared for. Your entire life has been about making sure that I am happy, and now, after your death, you can be rest assured that I will be fine." Harlow lifted a hand and dabbed at her eyes, as though she was teary-eyed just thinking of it. "I'm going to miss this version of you. But time moves on and sometimes we make mistakes."

"Harlow," she hissed, but the Original was already walking to the door.

"No, no. I simply can't stand it. Alexia the eighth, make sure your predecessor is dead before you come back out of this room." Harlow took a deep breath and nodded. "This is the right thing to do."

The door closed behind her, and then it was just Alexia and the newer version of herself.

"You don't have to do this," she said, starting to circle the other woman. "They want us to kill each other, but we can both get out of here alive."

The eighth version of herself pointed up. "They're filming everything. You know even saying something so stupid is a bad idea."

Sure, they were filming. Who cared? She was going to be out of this room before any of this footage got out. "You really don't want to fight me," she replied, ignoring the warning about the cameras. "You may have been training to serve Harlow, but I have lived far more than you."

"They made me better than you for a reason."

"They made you numb. Emotions are nothing to be feared. They are to be embraced."

They circled each other, all while the eighth version rolled up her sleeves like that was going to help her fight. All it took was a twitch of muscle, and Alexia reacted. The two of them lunged for each other.

They came together in a clash of power and weight. She knew this version of herself would have more muscles than she did, but Alexia was now wiry and strong from swimming. She also had the added advantage of something to fight for, which this other version did not have.

Grappling with the bigger woman, she managed to get her in a headlock. "Listen to me, they have done something terrible to you. You need to snap out of it. The drugs in your system can be bested."

"You need to die." The eighth reached back over her head, grabbed a handful of Alexia's shirt, and dragged her over her shoulder.

She hit the ground hard enough to knock the wind out of her, but she had to move or be killed. Rolling, she just barely blocked herself from a boot to the ribs.

Alexia stood, making sure to shake out her hands before she landed a punch square in the face of the other woman. The punch made her hand ache, but it felt good to do it. So she did it again, and again.

But then her hand was caught on the fourth strike, and the eighth yanked her in close enough to wrap her arms around her. She squeezed so hard it became hard to breathe.

The eighth was breathing hard, but ground out, "You are an anomaly. They are fixing the problem with me."

"Yeah," she wheezed. "I never did anything they wanted me to do."

And then she head butted herself.

Fuck, that hurt. The hard front of her skull connected with the eighth's nose, and it cracked immediately upon impact. She felt it break against her skull, and damn, it felt good to do. The eighth reeled back from her, blinded momentarily by pain and blood that gushed out of her nose.

A perfect opportunity. Alexia might have waited before, pride in her own fighting skill giving her opponent a chance to collect themselves.

But she wasn't going to do that. Not when everyone's lives were on the line.

Sweeping out her leg, she took the other Alexia onto the ground and crawled on top of her. Like Fortis had done to her so many times, Alexia locked her limbs around the other woman. Keeping the eighth's arms pinned with her strong legs, she wrapped her arms around the woman's neck tightly.

"As you die," she snarled, struggling to keep her grip, but managing to pin the other woman. "I need you to know this. You are capable of far more than they tell you. You are strong, able to do whatever you want to do. Your emotions were never meant to be taken from you. They did that, and I will exact revenge for all of us. For every version they are still growing, and all the ones who came before us. They will die for what they have done."

Finally, the last wheeze rattled out of the eighth Alexia's lungs. She kept her hold for a few minutes more, making certain this version was dead. And for good measure, Alexia then snapped her neck.

"That feels so wrong to do," she muttered as she finally released the dead body. It flopped away from her, and she stared down at her own dead body while telling herself that this was fine.

She knew she was going to have to kill people. She'd killed many other people before.

She just... had never killed herself. Or a version of herself. Or was this woman even her? They'd had completely different experiences throughout their entire life, so this really wasn't her at all. It was just a stranger who wore her face.

"Still weird," she muttered before reaching for her shirt and yanking it over her head.

Alexia made quick work of her pants too, tugging all the fabric off before she started stripping the dead body. All the while, she muttered apologies. "Really sorry about this. You don't deserve to be treated like this, but... well. Duty calls. If anyone could understand that, it would be you."

Somehow, staring down at a nude dead body that looked exactly like hers was even worse. And dressing one? That was particularly awful. She never wanted to do this again. Not in her life. This was wrong. So wrong.

"I don't even know why I'm talking to you. You're dead," she muttered as she yanked pants on over the eighth Alexia's legs. "But being in a room with a dead body that looks an awful lot like yourself is really, really terrible. I wouldn't wish it on my worst enemy." She hesitated. "Or are you my worst enemy?"

Alexia shook her head and finished swapping their clothes.

"I'm really losing it. First Fortis, now you, and then the rest of the sea. I just have to figure out what to do next." Straightening, she smoothed her hands down the blazer and then started buttoning it.

If she was a completely emotionless robot of herself, then she would not be seen without her jacket buttoned up to her throat. And for a moment, she let herself cry. Tears streamed down her cheeks and silent sobs made her shoulders shake as she donned new clothes and a new persona.

She had known this would be hard. Nothing about this had ever suggested that it would be easy, but she hadn't realized just how awful it was going to be.

Her eyes went to the windows, and she unconsciously sought him out. Because her mind still swore that he had to be there. He had always been there. If she just kept looking, then soon enough, she would see that purple tail, or a flicker of yellow lights out in the depths.

But she was all alone now. Just standing in a room, staring out at the sea, with the dead version of herself at her feet.

And she was running out of time.

She needed to get her shit together and get out there. Someone would eventually look at the footage from this room. They would see that the wrong Alexia was walking through the city. She needed to get out, convince Harlow she was that emotionless version of herself, and then... off she went. Infiltrate the city and kill almost everyone inside.

Alexia leaned down to empty her old pockets of those tiny bead droids and dropped them all onto the floor. They knew what to do now that they were released. Each one of them zipped off in different directions, and they'd find the control room soon enough.

Taking a deep breath, she headed out the door into the hallway, where Harlow waited. Her Original looked her up and down, and then asked, "Was it grisly?"

"She put up a fight." Alexia tried to keep her voice completely emotionless. "It is done now."

"Good. Oh, the poor dear. I did really like her, you know." Taking a deep breath, Harlow shrugged. "But there are so many of you. Killing one isn't going to make me lose sleep. Now, do you mind picking up my laundry? I had my new dress dry cleaned, and he always irons it wrong."

"Right away, ma'am." She turned away from the woman who had made her life a living hell, and promised herself the next time she saw Harlow, she would kill her.

Chapter 40

They were all idiots, Alexia realized. Rich idiots who thought that the world was something they could manipulate and control. As she strode past the laundry room, ignoring an order from Harlow directly, she realized every single Original in this entire city was a fool. But they thought they were geniuses, and that's where the problem began.

They had power, and they had it for a very long time. That power had given them the feeling that they were better than others, even though that simply wasn't true. They thought that with power and money, their minds were better than everyone else's. But all of these people had just been lucky. Lucky to get a few funds more than others, lucky that a business had done better than their competitor, or had been looked upon favorably by fate throughout all of their lives because they already had a leg up.

History would not look upon them kindly. As she walked through the halls toward the armory, Alexia knew she would be the first person to destroy all the reputation they had built for years. She would tell every story that would make them seem less a god and more the fragile beings they really were.

She would make sure everyone knew that they were incapable of brushing their own teeth without someone reminding them. She would tell stories about how often she had to clean up their messes, or how they cried often because someone had hurt their feelings. They were human, not gods, and hundreds of years of life hadn't changed that.

A group of soldiers walked toward her, and she placed her hands behind her back to mimic their posture. Spine stiff and straight, she walked past them without another look, as though she belonged here.

And they did the same to her. Because everyone who worked for the Originals didn't exist. They were drones in a hive. No thoughts, no feelings. If they started to exist, they were just replaced. Like they had already done to her.

She turned right down the hall and entered the armory. It was mostly deserted this time of day, considering all the guards were heading to the mess hall to get their food before training. Everything in this room was deadly, because it didn't matter if they trained with live weapons. It wasn't a big deal if someone like her died.

There were no windows on these walls, just racks full of guns. More and more of them until she got to the sword section. Then the blunt objects, like clubs and all the other items that would hurt if someone was hit with them. She took a deep breath and started gathering all the items she would need.

Striding to the back wall, she grabbed a stun gun and shoved it into the front of her pants. This was a good weapon for up close. Then she grabbed what looked like an assault rifle and slung it over her shoulder by the strap. It fired large energy balls that would clear a room out quickly, and that's what she needed. Two more stun guns went into the back of her pants for when the others eventually ran out of power.

Good enough. This would get her started. She took her long braid and coiled it on top of her head, tying it in a knot so it wouldn't get in her way.

A small tap at the door had her slicing her gaze toward it, only to see one of those little droid beads on the ground. They'd found the control room, which meant everything was ready.

She bent down to grab it and pressed it against the back of her ear.

"You hear me?" a voice came through. Mira's, it sounded like.

"Loud and clear."

"Ready?"

She swung the rifle into her arms and turned the safety off, feeling the familiar weight and heft of it. "Oh yeah, I'm ready."

This hallway led toward a complicated network of halls that would lead her to the control room. But there were bound to be people who stood in her way. Too many people lived here, and every single one of them would see her, armed to the teeth, and they would try to stop her.

Good. She needed to let off some steam.

The first person who rounded the corner was one of the Originals. She thought his name might be Donatello, although she'd had little interactions with him. He always traveled with two guards, as he was a paranoid individual who went through more reborns than the average person. She took that rifle in her hands and blew a hole straight through his chest.

There was a stunned moment of silence as he looked down at the gaping wound that oozed blood and then staggered to the side. Considering he had a hole in his chest the size of a goblet of water, she had no idea how he was still standing.

One of his guards reached for a weapon and the other ran for Donatello. She shot the one who reached for his weapon first. The energy pulse hit the massive man straight in the forehead, and he went down hard enough to shake the floor. The other had already gathered the Original up in his arms, likely heading for the med bay where they would sacrifice another person to keep this ancient being alive.

"He should have died a long time ago," she snarled at his retreating form as he made his way away from her down the hall. "Let him die."

The guard hesitated for the briefest moment. He even looked over his shoulder at her and then heaved a long sigh. "I cannot let him do that. You know it as well as I."

She shot him in the back, a killing shot that would make sure he didn't feel too much pain before he went into the afterlife. It weighed heavily on her shoulders as she stepped over the first dead body, and then the other. She looked down at the Original's face, seeing the man in the picture on that island. He had been so young, and still appeared so young now. He'd been nervous then too, though. She'd seen it in his eyes on the picture.

Nervous like he was now, with those wide eyes telling her he was terrified to die. But he wouldn't die for too long. Soon enough, someone would find him. As long as there was the merest chance that electrical activity in his brain could continue, they could bring him back. She'd seen it happen herself.

Taking a stun gun out of her pocket, she leveled it on his head. "You should never have lived this long. Humans weren't meant to survive hundreds of years. That is why we were given an expiration date. Look at what you and your people have done in all this time. Nothing of use, and everything just to satisfy your own needs without caring about anyone else."

She shot him in the head so no one would be able to piece him back together. The first real death of an Original, at least that she knew about. He was dead and gone and no one was going to piece together those splattered bits of brain.

Unless they could do a brain transplant.

Fuck.

She hated this. But for good measure, she shot him six more times in the head until there was no way to even tell who he had once been, and where that head had gone. She knew for a fact that they had never successfully managed a full head transplant. She'd been there when they had tried, and she was quite certain this man in particular had been the one leading the charge on how to do that.

Finally, she ran through the halls, keeping out of the way of anyone else. She didn't want to fight more people until she absolutely had to. Like in the control room.

Reaching that room, Alexia pressed herself against the wall and took a few deep, steadying breaths. She could do this. They had built her to kill, after all, and now that was exactly what she was doing.

They just had never thought they wouldn't be able to control her. Taking another deep breath, she turned her head to look at the control room.

"Mira?" she asked quietly.

"Still here. I heard gun shots."

"You're about to hear a lot more. There's fifteen people in the control room at all times. I will clear it out and start opening what I can until the alarm blares. Then I need to get out of here, and I'll start opening the other doors that are manual overrides. Send them in now."

"Now?" She could hear clicking, like Mira was trying to type at the same time as talking to her. "The shield is still up, though."

"It won't be for long."

A ghost of longing shivered down her spine. Fortis would rush into this room with her, all teeth and claws. He would have loved to have seen this moment where she would destroy all the people who had haunted both of them for such a long time.

He deserved to know that she had done the right thing. And beyond that, he deserved to know that she had made them bleed for him.

Baring her teeth in a very undine-like snarl, she slapped the button to open the automatic door and ran into the room, guns blazing. She knew this room well. There were six massive monitors, all lined up in three neat rows. There would be two people at each of them, and that was twelve accounted for. The other three would be stationed on her right and left, and then directly ahead of her. Though the one ahead would be looking out at the water, because the guard liked to watch the lights and the fish.

As expected, there were fifteen people all at their stations making sure the city ran like a well-oiled machine. She shot the nearest two at their desks, watching as they slumped over the control panels. But that was all the time she would get to make it easy.

The two on each side of her were already holding guns. Shots flew, and one of the massive monitors was caught in the crossfire. She dove for cover, taking out another one of the scientists at the monitors as she fell onto her side and hit the floor.

Sparks flew over her head, landing on her shoulders and in her hair. She smelled singed flesh where it was already burning through her skin, but that didn't matter. She didn't matter.

Glancing over the top of the monitor, she watched as one of the guards tried to get three scientists to head to the door while he opened fire on her. She didn't care if she got shot, though. She wasn't trying to hide. Alexia shot all three of them until one of the guard's blasts caught her in the shoulder.

Dead. The arm went limp. He'd cut right through the tendon in her biceps and the rifle dropped onto the floor.

That wasn't good. She really needed to use that more. She'd only killed six of them so far.

Breath shuddering in her lungs, she reached for the stun gun at her waist. More manual work, but at least they would drop.

The guards were trained to protect. So they'd ushered the other six scientists into a group at the back of the room, thinking they could keep them all safe with covering fire.

They couldn't.

She stood and headed right for them. The stun gun made quick work of the remaining scientists, and she happened to catch one of the guards unaware as well.

But then pain bloomed in her chest. Wincing, she looked down at the red spreading through the blazer. Not good. Not good at all.

She had a job to do, a job to finish, and she would do it. With a harsh yell, she threw the stun gun at the head of one guard and spun for the other who had shot her. They assumed she was out, but she still had another stun gun in the back of her waistband, and she pulled that out quickly. One blast. Right in the head.

Spinning, it felt like the world slowed as she took her next shot. An answering shot rang out, and she jerked back as it struck her in the chest a second time.

They stared at each other, both breathing hard. She could feel her heart sluggishly complaining about the lack of blood. But then the guard staggered to his side, dropped onto his knees, and then fell to the floor.

Swallowing hard, she shuffled to the nearest console. "Computer, activation code xi rho tau."

"Original Harlow access granted."

Perfect.

She got to work. Tapping the screen, she left bloody fingerprints smeared across the glowing green as she dropped the shield first. Sparks flew down from the ceiling and a wire dropped through a damaged panel that crackled with white hot electricity.

"Shield's down," she said to Mira. "Send them in."

"They're already going. Which door?"

She opened three of them before the room went red. "Two in alpha quadrant and one on the eastern side."

"You sound hurt."

"Doesn't matter." She hit one more release, but her access had already been revoked. All those bloody fingerprints would give her away too easily. They'd know exactly where she had opened the gates .

Stepping back, she fired her gun and shattered the computer screen. Smoke billowed out of this one, and then flames burst to life. Soon enough, water would rain down from the ceiling to protect what little was left.

"Alexia, if you're hurt, we need to abort the plan." Mira almost sounded frantic. "This won't work if you die."

"I'm hard to kill," she hissed. She grabbed two of the guards' rifles as she limped out of the room. Turning, she fired at the door control and watched as it left a black hole in the wall. It would buy them some time before anyone could get into the room. "I don't have to survive for this to work. I just have to get enough doors open."

"Alexia—"

"Thank you, Mira. Your opinion has been noted. I will be working counterclockwise from here. All the gates I can manually open, will be open."

And then she dropped the earpiece on the ground. The little droid rolled away from her, slipping underneath the damaged door to hack into the mainframe and do whatever it was the droids could do. Maybe they would open more doors, but some of them had to be opened manually.

The acrid bite of smoke filled her nose as she headed toward the first manual lock. Two guards careened around the corridor, but she shot them before they even realized what had happened.

She left a smear of blood on the floor behind her, but she reached the first hatch. It was a manual lever, and she needed to use her entire body weight to turn it. But it finally gave, and with a deep breath, she opened the hatch.

A gilled head appeared through it almost instantly. It was the yellow finned one. Maketes. She knew his name. She just... her mind was wandering.

He gave her a feral grin. "You look worse for wear."

"Just get in here and kill some people, will you?"

"Sure."

He crawled into the hall and flared all his spines wide. The deadly spikes gleamed in the white overhead lights. "Stay alive, Alexia," he said.

"I'll do my best."

With her bloody hand on the wall, she started her process toward the next hatch, listening to the wet slaps of a hundred undines entering the only home she had ever known to bathe it in blood.

Chapter 41

Life is a funny thing.

Sometimes, it is lost far before it is meant to be lost. Sometimes, it is given back when it shouldn't be.

Lights blinked in and out of existence. Wasn't it supposed to be a void of darkness? Instead, the glimmering lights appeared to be caused by the power grid of a city turning on and off. As though they had... won.

Was he dreaming? Or perhaps his soul had returned because he needed to know the end before he left to greet all his ancestors. Fortis knew it was to be expected that his spirit might want to linger, but he could still feel his body.

He could flip his fluke. He could feel the bruising where she had injected him, and he knew there was far more strength in his body than there should have been after she'd poisoned him. Surely that wasn't right. He had died. That was his destiny.

But as he felt life fill his veins and reality hit him hard, Fortis understood that he had not, in fact, died.

Sitting up, he pinned his gaze to a man in the corner. The human was a weak-looking thing, shivering the moment Fortis's gaze caught him where he stood. He lifted his hands as though begging a monster to not hurt him.

"Please, please no. She sent me. Alexia sent me."

Why would Alexia send anyone to greet him? She should have made certain that he was really dead before she left, because that was his fate.

"What happened?" he snarled.

"My name is Doctor Barker. I have been a friend of Alexia's for many years. When she approached me after returning and told me about you, I thought she was mad, but the more she talked, the more I believed." He twisted his hands together in a move that betrayed how nervous he was. "She asked me to be here when you woke, and told me to tell you that the future is never concrete. And that sometimes, we have to choose our own path even if someone else told us what to do."

"That makes no sense."

"She said you would say that." Doctor Barker seemed to hesitate before adding, "She also said to tell you that whatever future you saw might not have been the whole truth. That maybe you saw her, but she never killed you after all."

That dastardly woman. She'd changed his fate.

He didn't know whether to be furious or joyful. Because he hadn't wanted to go yet. He wanted to stay alive. With her. Fortis wanted to spend an entire lifetime dedicated to learning every sound she made. To explore the world that she had never seen and to see all the wonder in her gaze every time he showed her something new.

And he wanted to make her happy. He wanted to see her smile more often. He wanted to hear that horrendous laugh and watch as she experienced new things. He found her amazing and wonderful and he'd never told her that.

This doctor was now standing in his way, though. Fortis rolled off the table, landing on his forearms hard and wincing at the impact. Maybe he wasn't entirely at his best, but soon enough, he would be. And then he would find her.

Leveraging himself upright, he looked the doctor in the eyes and growled, "Where is she?"

"I don't know."

"Then why did she send you here?"

"To make sure you were alive." The doctor swallowed with clear nerves. "She wanted to... well, she wanted to make sure you were taken care of. The others would have experimented on your body and they would have realized very quickly that you weren't, in fact, dead. That's why I took you here."

Here? He looked around and realized this wasn't even the same room he'd been in before. That complicated things.

"I was awake when they took me into the other room. I knew where they had taken me and how to get back." Frustrated now, he crawled to the wall so he could lean against it and pull himself higher than the doctor. Glaring down at the man, it did at least ease his anger to see the man's trembling begin again. "How do I find her?"

"I don't know that either. She didn't tell me anything of her plan, but there has been sounds of fighting out there for hours now." To punctuate his words, a resounding bang echoed outside of the door, as though someone had fired a gun and then a loud silence that came after.

Of course they had been fighting. Fortis had missed all the fun.

He headed for the door, only to pause and look back at the doctor.

"If she's hurt, how do I fix her?"

"You bring her back here. I have everything I need to make sure she doesn't die." A troubled expression crossed his face. "I hope she isn't hurt, though."

So did he, but he also knew Alexia and knew all the choices she would make. She risked herself every single day to make sure that others were well. He wouldn't be surprised to find her injured, especially if everyone else was fighting.

With a sharp nod, he headed out into the hallway and closed the door behind him. Hopefully, the doctor would remain in there. He doubted any of his own kind would harm the man, but he would spread the word as soon as he found the other People of Water.

It didn't take him long.

He headed down one blood smeared white hallway to find his first depthstrider. The female was bloated with rage, her spines all lifted and her body larger than it would be when she wasn't so angered. She turned toward him with a hiss, and he could see that a blast had caught her across the face, cutting through her lovely pale lavender cheek.

"All is well," he said as he crawled past her on his forearms. "Where is my human?"

"Fortis?" the depthstrider breathed out. 'But you're meant to be dead."

"I did not die."

"But fate said..."

"The vision was wrong. I did not die. I was meant to be here, and the sea saw to it that my soul did not yet flee. Alexia saved me, regardless of how my future was interpreted." And he would never forget that she had saved his life even when he told her not to.

"I have not seen her. But there are others roaming the halls. Some of the achromos still fight us, but their numbers have dwindled. Soon, they will all be dead but those we have chosen to spare."

He found that he didn't care. There were bad people here, yes. He wanted them dead just as much as anyone else, but he wanted... Her.

Alexia had become so much more important than getting his revenge on these people. He'd spent his entire life wanting to harm this city, to destroy them for what they would do to him, but now he just wanted to be with her. Who cared what his people did to this city now?

Nodding, he went in the direction the depthstrider pointed, quickly finding familiar faces. Mira stood at the end of one hallway, a gun loosely held in her hand while she talked with Arges. He was surprised either of them were standing around when anyone could have attacked them. Was the battle really that close to finished?

She caught sight of him and her eyes widened. "Fortis! I didn't know you were..."

"She didn't tell you? The damned woman didn't kill me."

A slow grin spread across Mira's face. "I didn't think she had it in her to lie to you like that, but look at her, surprising me at every turn. Welcome back to the land of the living, I guess."

"Where is she?"

Arges moved into his line of vision, the gills on the sides of his neck flat with serious emotion. "We were just talking about that. We're not sure where she is, Fortis. We expected to find her at the last open hatch, but she must have moved on to the next."

"And someone was sent to retrieve her?"

The other two looked at each other before Mira winced. "No. We've been fighting for our lives here. Tau had more people in it than we thought. Most of them are holed up in the same room at this point, but we can't get into it. We're not sure if there's an escape pod attached to it, but there's about fifty people in there."

"That doesn't answer my question."

"No one has looked for her, Fortis."

His gills flared wide with an angry hiss. "Fine, I will go."

"We could use you here, brother," Arges said. But there was no real emotion in his voice. Clearly Arges expected him to go.

So he did. Fortis headed down the nearest hallway, following the path she should have taken. There was so much blood on the floor, he slipped as he moved. He ended up crawling through the red streaks on his forearms, only reminding him just how much he hated not being in water.

The first five hatches were all open, and the sound of the water splashing against the edges was the only thing he could hear. But then he came to the sixth, and he smelled her blood. There hadn't been many people here, or if there had been, they were all inside. So now he could follow her blood on the floor, only hers. She'd been dragging her feet as her life force spilled out.

Here she had slipped. There was a smear of blood down the wall where she'd fallen, a pool of it where she'd rested for a moment before she continued going.

Hearts pounding in his chest, he finally found her on her hands and knees past the seventh hatch. She was nearly at the eighth, crawling her way towards it.

Alexia didn't even look at him as he approached. All her attention was on her labored breathing and words he could just barely make out. "One more. Just one more."

He made it to her side and gathered her up in his arms. She fought for a few moments, but then stilled when he pressed his lips to her forehead.

"You brave, stupid woman," he breathed against her. "What did you do?"

Her entire body went limp in his arms. He took all of her fear, her exhaustion, as she dropped her head onto his shoulder with a heavy thud. "I saved you because you wouldn't save yourself."

"You saved all of us, Alexia. The fighting is over. The battle is done."

Her breath hitched. The sound was so similar to a sob, he wasn't sure what to do with it.

"Good," she whispered. "I'm glad."

"We need you with us." He grabbed her jaw, forcing her head up to look at him. "What were you thinking, letting me live?"

Her features were so pale from blood loss. There were multiple smears of blood along her jaw, like she'd touched her hand to her face while trying to keep herself going. A bruise was already forming along her cheekbone and there were strands of red in her eyes. But she was alive. She was still looking at him, still fighting as he had always known that she would.

She lifted a shaking hand, still covered in blood, and gently touched his cheek. "I freed you from your prophecy, Fortis. No more expecting death. No more waiting for the end to come. I just want you to live."

He leaned forward and kissed her. His people didn't do this, but he now knew how badly he needed to kiss her. Her lips still tasted sweet, even if there was a metallic hint.

"You should have left me to die," he murmured against her skin. "They would have killed you if they found out that I was still alive."

"I figured they'd do that anyway."

"Alexia…" he breathed, before he pressed a kiss to her shoulder. "I never got to say how you fill my soul. Every day with you has proven to me just how valuable you are. I've heard other humans say I love you, but the words simply don't feel like enough."

She hummed against his skin. "I love you too. I just hope it's not too late."

Then he realized she was worse off than he thought. To him, Alexia was always a strong pillar of a warrior who could not be stopped. But now he could see how weak she was. She'd been crawling to the next hatch, not even realizing she could stop fighting.

But now he was here.

"I'm going to take care of you," he said as he lifted her more firmly with one arm. "Doctor Barker is waiting for us."

"Oh good, he survived." Her head lolled against his shoulder as he started dragging her back the way he came. "I didn't think he would, to be honest. He's not a fighter."

"He was there in the room with me when I woke." Fortis frowned as he maneuvered her over some bodies that had been left in their way. "How did you not poison me? You asked for the neurotoxin."

"I didn't give you the neurotoxin. I hid it underneath your arm. I stole a different drug from them, one that I knew would make you sleep and seem like you were dead." She sighed, but the sound rattled concerningly. "Doctor Barker should have it now. I'm sure he will use it to protect himself if he needs to."

"You dastardly woman."

"I always have a plan," she whispered, her voice growing far too quiet. "Always. That's who they trained me to be."

Her cheeks were far too pale. They were white as a pearl, and he didn't mean that as a compliment. He was concerned she had lost too much blood, but if there was anywhere in the sea that could save her, it was this place.

So he brushed his hand over her head, dragging her a little faster and a little harder. "Rest now, Alexia. I'll make sure you're safe."

At the first sight of another person he could trust, he called out for help. Two of his own people and one human ran for him. The young man he had seen in Mira's village before, although he'd never interacted with him. Between the group of them, they moved Alexia much faster.

Doctor Barker was waiting, and if he lifted a needle when they entered, Fortis ignored it. Together with the others, he laid Alexia on the table he'd just been lying on and then turned to the doctor with a snarl on his face.

"Save her," he demanded.

The man had already dropped the neurotoxin and was putting gloves on his hands. With a snap that filled the room, the doctor nodded. "I'll do my best."

Chapter 42

Doctor Barker hovered over her a little too much. The man was incessant that she be completely healed before he even let her out of his sight, which she knew very well had to do with the massive undine hovering just behind him. It was like Fortis thought if he left her alone for even a moment, then she would die.

She wasn't going to die. Alexia had survived worse than this.

"I really am going to be fine," she reminded Fortis, as she leaned back on the hospital bed and looked up at the familiar ceiling. "I survived a stabbing where they cut into every single one of my major organs before I killed them."

Doctor Barker hummed low under his breath. "I remember that one. That was a squabble between Harlow and one of the other Originals, wasn't it?"

"Lester, I believe."

"Right, Lester."

Fortis leaned into her line of vision, his voice a storm cloud of anger. "Why were you stabbed by this Lester?"

"Oh, Lester didn't do the stabbing. None of the Originals get their hands dirty. He had his guard stab me fourteen times for a slight from Harlow. He didn't like her, she didn't like him. They were always fighting about something. I took the stabbing that was meant for her, and they considered their differences settled for the day."

She winced as Barker wove a thread through her sensitive skin. Usually stitches didn't hurt this much, or maybe she was just better at handling them while she was on emotion manipulating drugs.

Fortis snapped his jaws at the Doctor. "Careful with that."

"S-sorry," Barker stuttered, but then the damned man's hands started shaking. "I'm not used to stitching people with an audience."

She sighed and reached for the doctor's hands. Gently holding them in one of her own, Alexia gave him a little squeeze and a soft smile. "You are not used to working on people who can feel as much as I can now feel. It's all right, Doctor Barker. Do your best. I have endured far worse pain than this."

He stared at her, his eyes widening and his pupils blowing out until his eyes were little more than black. "I don't know how to respond to this kind version of you, Alexia. You were always so practical and so insistent on doing your job and nothing else. It is hard to look at you like this and see the same person."

"I'm not the same person." Though that didn't sit right after she said it. Alexia tilted her head to the side, looking at Fortis while Doctor Barker started stitching her back together again. "Or I guess I'm more myself than I ever have been before. I'm the same person, just... allowed to be me now."

She stared into Fortis's dark gaze the entire time Barker worked on healing her. She didn't flinch again, because she didn't need to be afraid of any pain while her depthstrider was here.

It didn't take very long. There was medicine that accelerated her healing and was designed to work with her body. The genetics they poured into their guards were designed so that she could be injured a thousand times and wouldn't take that long to be back in fighting order. She could endure more than the average person, but now, as she looked into her future with this massive sea creature, she knew she wouldn't have to be as prepared to hurt.

Not, at least, unless she wanted to defend the people she now called family.

Doctor Barker held up a needle, but then froze when Fortis bared his teeth and all his gills flared wide.

"Alexia?" Doctor Barker asked, his voice once again shaking. "These are the steroids that should speed up your healing. Would you like me to inject you?"

"Yes please."

"You don't have to," Fortis told her. "You don't have to take anything again."

Oh, this sweet, sweet man. He clearly didn't trust that Doctor Barker wouldn't inject her with all manner of drugs, or even try to kill her. Or maybe he feared that the doctor would try to put her back to the way she had been before, and that she wouldn't be able to make decisions for herself anymore.

Alexia reached for Fortis this time, grabbing onto his hand and drawing it to her cheek. "He's not going to hurt me, Fortis. They're just steroids."

"I don't know what that means."

"It'll help heal me faster, just like after the squid attack. It's not the first time I've taken this, and it certainly won't be the last." She nodded at the doctor and held Fortis's gaze as the needle pressed through her skin.

The steroids always worked fast, and these would be even faster than the ones she'd taken from Mira. Soon, she would be well enough to see the others. Because she could feel the apprehension in the air.

They'd done it. They'd taken over Tau, even though right now it was a tenuous hold, and now they weren't sure what they were going to do with it.

She pushed herself upright and swung her legs over the bed, taking a deep, steadying breath. "Doctor Barker, do you ever think about how delicate this city really was? For all those years, we thought it was entirely impenetrable. No one would ever destroy Tau, even if it was the only city left in the sea. And now..."

"Now we live to see it fall," he murmured. The Doctor slumped in his chair and then ran his hand over his face. "I believe our folly was always in believing it was strong. There is no certainty in life, and no certainty in this. We created beings in these walls, manipulated our own genetics, played god for so many years, it was hard to imagine that it would last forever. I... I am glad to see it end. Even if it was far easier to tear it all down than I ever believed it would be."

She smiled, but it was a sad expression at the same time.

Mixed emotions boiled through her. She was so glad no one else would get hurt. Thrilled that the reborns and genetically enhanced children would now have a chance to live a real life, one where they weren't changed or tormented or torn apart for research. But this building, full of all its secrets and horrible endings, had been her home. It was the place where every childhood memory had been built, good or bad. And now, everything was going to change. All because of what she had chosen.

It was the right thing to do, and she was thrilled to have won. But that didn't mean there wasn't some part of her that was a little sad too. Not for herself, but for the future that could have been. The future that should have been, if this place had been filled with good intentions and not people who wanted to tear apart the world to satisfy their own curiosity.

Gently, she pushed herself upright. She had to grab onto Fortis's arm to steady herself, but she could already walk without feeling like she was going to fall over.

She nodded at Doctor Barker. "I'm fine. Thank you. I think you should stay here while we meet with the others, though. Just in case. I'll explain who you are and all the things you could help them with, but... You know."

"I appreciate any kind word you can put in for me."

Alexia wasn't all that certain her word would mean that much to these folks. They barely knew her. Yes, she had helped them take down their enemy and perhaps a little easier than they had expected. But at the end of the day, their bond was just as weak as with anyone else in Tau.

As she walked out into the hallway with Fortis yanking himself across the floor beside her, she looked at him and said, "You know they all owe you their lives, right?"

He seemed confused. "Who?"

"Your people. The humans that were helping you. All of them. They owe you their lives."

He shook his head as they turned a corner. "I don't know what you're talking about, Alexia. They don't owe me anything."

"You were the one to convince me that this life was worth living, even if it was hard to shake off what they had trained me to be. You were the one who proved everything to me was worthwhile. And if they didn't have me, they never would have gotten into Tau. This city would have ruled for another two hundred years while the Originals lived an unnaturally long time. Nothing would have ended. It would have been countless years of fighting until all of our kind was entirely wiped out. All of that changed because of you and no one else, Fortis."

He didn't have time to answer her, because they rounded a corner to see the others gathered together. All were faces she now recognized. Mira, Arges, Anya, Daios, Ace, Maketes, even Aulax who had somehow joined the battle, even though she was sure Fortis would be angry about that.

Glancing over at the massive undine beside her, she was pleased to see she was right. His face had warped into an expression of rage as he glared at his son.

Aulax just grinned and waved at him. "Sorry, Father. You were supposed to be dead."

"That excuses your choices, how?"

"I am an adult now."

"And I'm still bigger than you," Fortis snarled. "We will have words about this soon enough."

Right, they were going to get into a bigger argument if she didn't step in. So she strode between them, toward Mira and Ace, who were both still muttering together in front of a large glass window.

Alexia knew where they were. The window looked down into the lower level where the mess hall was. The Originals had likely never been in it before, but there were plenty of guards who knew how fortified it was. There was food as well, and that would give them time to negotiate.

Ace said, "It doesn't look like there's an exit from the room, but I wouldn't put it past them to be figuring out how to make one. I know they aren't going to give up easily, so we need to consider that this room may have an exit."

"Let them run! Where are they going to go?"

"Beta. There is a section underneath it that we discovered where people from Tau were working, remember? The same with Gamma. They could disappear and then take over another city. It's a goose chase we don't want to get into, Mira. What if they survive? What if they convince others to follow them again?"

Alexia stood beside them, crossed her arms over her chest, and surveyed the room beyond. There were around fifty people in there. Some of them were more familiar than others. It appeared they had taken quite a few scientists and guards with them, but not as many as she'd thought. Really only one guard for each of the twenty-four Originals, and then a handful of extra scientists. They had run, but they hadn't been able to gather as many people as they expected.

"This whole city is a blood bath," Alexia murmured. "We're going to have to clean the whole thing up for months to get it working properly."

The two women behind her paused, but it was Mira who said, "Excuse me?"

"The city. You're going to take it as your main base, I assume. Your village will remain standing, of course, for those of you who want to be closer to the sun and the storms. But this city has everything you need. It has contact with all the other cities, and can control nearly everything that they get from a resource standpoint. All the programs here are how we get food and where it comes from. Not to mention you can work with the leaders of the other two cities much easier from here and could force them with the direct threat of the weapons that are stored in Tau." She took a deep breath, her lips pressed into a firm line as she caught sight of Harlow down there. "Ace, hit that button on the wall beside you."

Though there was a small amount of hesitancy, Ace did exactly that. She hit the button, and Alexia knew the people down below would hear her.

"It's like shooting fish in a barrel. Which one of you should I kill first?" she snarled.

"Alexia?" Harlow's voice echoed through the speakers on the upper portions of the walls. "Alexia, how are you up there? Did you trick them? Kill them all and release us."

"I'm not going to do that."

"I just created you. You are the perfect version of yourself!" Harlow stamped her foot. "Alexia, you are required to listen to me!"

"Alexia the eighth is dead, if that's who you're referring to. I killed her when you locked me in that room and waited for only one of us to come back out. All of you knew what you did, and what guilt you carried on your shoulders. You're the reason the world ended, and still here you stand, assuming you're owed something by the people and the planet you destroyed."

There was a long moment of silence and fifty faces staring up at her in shock.

"How do you know that?" Original Lester asked, his voice shaking with rage.

"I saw the museum you left as a cock stroke to yourself. You're all idiots, you know that? You think you are so smart, creating a way to control the weather. But you just ruined the only home you had, and now seem to think that the sea is yours as well. But you've just been ravaging that too. All you know is how to destroy."

The Originals started talking amongst themselves, but Harlow didn't move. She stared up at the window, and Alexia wished she was closer so she could see if that was sadness or rage in her eyes.

"Alexia, you're like a daughter to me. I've been with you through seven generations of your being. What would you have us do?" She widened her arms, as though waiting for a hug. "Seven generations of your life, and all that effort to make you the perfect being that you are. Surely that proves how much you mean to me?"

"That's not good enough," Alexia interrupted. "You made an eighth, Harlow. You were going to kill me."

"Only because the others made me."

"You want me to see you like a mother? Well, I do, Harlow. I spent my entire life looking up to you, dreaming that you were the woman I wanted to be, loving you as much as I could with all those drugs running through my system. You are my mother."

She was done with all this. Done with the expectation of the people down below that she would help them. Over the expressions of the people surrounding her, who worried she would help those they had just defeated. But neither group expected her to reach for the old school gun at Mira's waist. This one had bullets in it, and that was more than enough.

Arges reached for Mira at the same time she turned. All the undines lunged for their mates, grabbing the women like they thought she was going to harm the people around her, but she wouldn't do that.

No, she spun and put a perfect bullet hole through the window, and right out through the glass above all the Originals. It was too high for any of them to patch. They'd never reach it time, anyway. Water gushed in, cracks forming around the hole as the pressure of the ocean compromised the entire room.

Screams echoed from the room as the Originals and their guards ran for the door. They all pounded on the sealed entryway, their cries of begging and pleading unanswered as water quickly filled the room.

"What did you do?" Mira hissed.

"I ended this." Calmly, she handed the gun back to Mira and then reached for a droid that had been rolling around Ace's feet. She held it up to the glass in front of them, and immediately, the droid started heating a tiny rivet gun and melting the glass. It would patch the hole long before the water reached their level.

And the entire time, she made sure to watch as all the Originals drowned. One by one.

"We could have used their knowledge," Mira murmured.

But Alexia shook her head. "They had more than enough time to fix what they broke. It's our time now."

Chapter 43

He could see the others were angry. And in some sense, he understood why. A lot of knowledge had just drowned in front of them. But as he stared at those floating bodies, he couldn't feel bad for them. They had gotten what they deserved, and the more he thought about it, the more right this felt. She'd needed to heal from all the things they had done to her, and this was the best way for her to do so.

Alexia had gotten her revenge. Finally. She'd cut all the ties to the people who had weighed her down for years now, and she shouldn't feel guilty for choosing her freedom over their influence.

He touched a hand to her shoulder, drawing her toward him where he was propped against the wall. "We're leaving for a bit."

Mira's head whipped around toward him so quickly he thought he heard her neck crack. "Excuse me? You're not taking her anywhere. She's the only one who knows how to get around this place."

He was ready to argue on her behalf, but Alexia replied, "Ace's droids have already mapped the place. You'll need to go room by room to make sure anyone left alive either agrees to join us or kill them. Just make sure you aren't going into sector twelve."

Anya stepped forward, tapping on the droid attached to her head. There was likely a map already on the glass that descended over one of her eyes. "What's in sector twelve?"

"The experiments. There should be quite a few genetically enhanced children in those rooms. Some of them will still be in stasis, so waking them up needs to be done carefully. And beyond that are the rooms with all the reborns. They are genetic matches for the Originals."

Daios slapped his tail on the floor. "Shouldn't we destroy them?"

"They aren't the Originals. They're clones. And they deserve to have a life just like we do." Alexia's voice had hardened, but Fortis already knew a threat when he saw one.

He moved in front of her, glaring at Daios until the red finned bastard backed down. "We're leaving. Clean the city up. All of you. If this is to be your new home, there is no reason for it to be filled with corpses."

And then he turned, gathered Alexia in his arms, and headed for the nearest hatch.

She looped her arms around his neck and didn't complain in the slightest when he attached the breathing tube to her neck and dove into the water with her. He knew it would be freezing for her, and she had just been injured, yet his brave and wondrous woman did not even hesitate to disappear with him.

His soul filled with happiness, knowing that he had finally found someone who would allow him to let go of all his chains.

They'd survived. Both of them.

As he raced through the waves to the one place he wanted to show her more than anywhere else, he let out a laugh that echoed out of his chest. Happiness, like this, was so rare in life. He wanted to enjoy every single second.

She looked up at him and bubbles exploded out of her mouth as she started laughing, too. Perhaps they were both delirious as they realized they were free now.

Soon enough, he found the cave system that had always captivated him. Not for the lights that hung from the ceiling in little blue glow worms and not for the water that splashed up in it. But for the hole in the ceiling that the sun and lightning would flash through, revealing all the carvings on the walls.

Carvings from People of Water, of their own kind swimming through the waves. Whales and squid, sharks and small schools of fish decorated the walls in such detail, they looked almost alive. Hundreds of carvings, all done by his people.

Alexia pressed her hands to her mouth, staring at each of them with wide eyes before she crawled out of the water. "What are these?"

"I don't know. A bored artist's escape, I imagine." He pulled himself out of the water as well, brushing his hair back as he looked with her. The depthstrider carving beside him was so detailed, he could run his claw along the texture of its scales. "I thought you would find it beautiful."

"I do," she breathed, but she wasn't looking at the carvings anymore. Now she was looking at him.

Some uneasy feeling relaxed in his chest. Finally. This is what he had been waiting for. A moment alone with her, where he could indulge himself without the fear of death looming over both of their shoulders. He knew what he wanted to do with the time he'd been given back.

Perhaps he shouldn't lick his lips while staring at her. Apparently, that gave him away.

She took a few steps back, her hands already going to the bloodied jacket she wore. She peeled it off, revealing a soaking wet white shirt beneath that did nothing to hide the muscles of her stomach flexing as she moved, or the tight peaks of her breasts. "You've been given years back, Fortis. So many years when you thought you might be dead."

"I have." He crawled after her, corralling her toward a flat stone in the center of the cave. "So many years."

"What do you plan to do with them?" The back of her knees hit the stone, and she looked back at it in surprise.

He used that opportunity to leverage himself upright. Grabbing the roof of the cave with one hand, he waited for her to turn back and gasp as she realized he was now far above her, holding onto a rock with one hand and waiting with the other to grab her around the throat.

He curled his claws around her thundering pulse, forcing her up to look up at him. "Take off your pants, Alexia."

She complied. It was likely a little difficult for her as he held onto her neck, but she wriggled out of the wet garment and tossed it aside. Only then did he lower her onto the flat stone that looked like an altar. She was laid out before him, covered in salt water that dripped from her collarbone and pooled in the hollow just below her ribcage.

Leaning down, he cut through her shirt with his claw, leaving it in two tattered pieces and then peeling it back to reveal those breasts he so adored. "I intend to feast upon you for hours, Alexia. That's what I'm doing with my years."

He descended upon her like a man in a frenzy. The taste of her skin was enough to make his mind fracture. He'd always held back from her, at least a little, because he knew how large he was and how new she was to all this. But she'd taken both of his cocks the last time, and surely she could take them again now.

Alexia hooked her arms around him and drew him down. Their tongues tangled with each other, exploring the taste of their passion even as his claws found her nipples. He couldn't stop touching her. Couldn't help that he wanted to drag his fingers down her sides, likely bruising with such a harsh grasp. But he wanted to crawl inside of her. It was a need, a frenzy, that overtook his entire being. He wanted her, that much was certain, but he needed to be closer to her than he was right now.

"I missed you," she said, nipping at his lips. "I need you inside me."

"I need to taste you first."

A low whine vibrated in her throat. She was as desperate for him as he was for her, but he had to be the reasonable one here. She might have a little more experience than before, but she needed far more than a few kisses and a breast grope before she could take him.

Trailing down her body, he pressed kisses to every part of her that he could find. And then slowly he turned, rolling them on the rock until she was on top of him with his lips sucking at her breast. With a soft pop, he drew back and stared up at her.

"Ride me," he said.

"You want me to what now?"

She might not have any idea what he meant, but he could damn well show her. Grabbing onto her hips with his hands, he slowly rocked her back and forth across his tail. The scales gave her the texture she was desperately seeking, and he could indulge himself in her for a bit.

Darkness fell upon the cave as night turned the room to silver, with the meager beams of moonlight coming from the hole at the top of the cave. And as he watched her rocking, finding her pleasure on him, he committed this moment to memory.

She was stunning with her dark hair still coiled in a braid, some strands coming out and loosening around her face. The silver moonlight barely showed much of her at all, just giving him an impression of flexing muscles where she braced herself on his stomach. Both of her biceps were strong, bulging with power as she moved. Her abs flexed, little mountains that he knew many other women didn't have. Not like Alexia.

And then came the rain. Soft droplets even though he knew it would be a deluge outside of this cave. But the raindrops had to wind down through the small hole at the top of the cavern, dripping onto her body in little icy beads. Bumps rose on her flesh, a sign that she was cold.

Her face scrunched as it always did when she was close, and he knew now was his moment to join her. Fortis hesitated, though. Just one more moment as lightning turned the entire room into a bright white glow. She reached her peak without his help, her head thrown back and all her muscles tightening in an impressive display of strength and power.

"By the gods, you are beautiful," he murmured as she slowly opened her eyes. "Beyond beautiful. A goddess who has taken flesh and blessed me with her presence."

"Shut up and fuck me," she said with a soft laugh. "You're looking pretty good yourself, undine."

He surged upright, shifting her forward so she could feel the pressure of his cocks between her legs. "Are you done waiting, virago?"

"I've been done waiting since the moment you realized you didn't die." She hooked her hand behind his neck and used that to pull herself closer.

She teased him on her knees, using her free hand to slide the tip of him through her folds. Back and forth, she made sure that he knew every texture and every sensation of her on his entire length before notching him and pushing down.

They both groaned as he slid into her, the feeling so sublime it was almost hard to breathe. Inside of her was home. It was everything that he'd been searching for for nearly twenty years until this moment with this woman resting on his lap, taking him deep inside of her body.

"Fuck," she breathed, drawing the word out long and slow. "You feel so good."

"Perfection, virago. Now move."

"I don't want to."

A surprised laugh burst out of him, and then he palmed both of her hips. "You've had a trying day, dear one. Allow me."

He lifted her up and down. Even though she was heavy with muscle, he could still show her how to move for the both of them. Slowly, he eased inside of her and then drew her back up. He wanted to feel every bit of her surrounding him before he lost his mind.

It was hard to breathe like this, though. He kept his pace deliberately slow, slower than it needed to be, as his breath sawed in and out of his lungs. His control was going to snap soon enough.

Alexia pulled upright herself, still clutching his neck and forcing him to lean back so he could support her. And then she dropped back down on his other cock. Hard. Hard enough that he slid right to the base and both of them groaned with the force of it. Then she lifted herself again and dropped back onto the other one.

Just like he'd done to her before. But this time it was her doing it. Her using all the weight of gravity and her own body to take him. Over and over again, she toyed with him. Teasing him as he had just teased her.

"Virago," he breathed, trying his best to stay sane while she continued her rhythm. "Come for me."

"You first."

"Damn it, woman. Come for me!" he barked, and then she shattered.

He could feel her clenching around him, each muscle coiling around his cock until it was too much. He came, both of his cocks exploding at the same time. One inside of her and the other splattering the stone behind her as he yanked her close to him.

Fortis pressed his lips to the top of her head, holding her against his hearts as they both came down from a high that felt almost impossible to have reached with one of her kind. And yet, he had.

This woman was everything to him and more. And he hadn't told her that before dying.

"I will never forgive myself for thinking I should die without telling you how marvelous you are. How much you changed my life and how dearly I would have regretted never telling you that you are the other half of my soul. I love you, virago. More than I thought possible."

She pressed her lips to his chest, turning her head so that she was tucked beneath his chin. "I know you do, Fortis. I am obsessed with you. I hope you know that. I love you more than anything, and I don't think I'll ever regret giving up my life for you. The one we will make together will be so much better than any future I might have had otherwise."

He liked that.

Leaning back on the stone, he stared up into the stormy sky and breathed out the last bit of tension that still existed within his heart. "A future," he murmured. "I like that."

449

Chapter 44

They returned without hurrying like they might have once before. Alexia wanted to indulge herself in him. And for the first time in her life, she didn't feel like she had any duties to return to. After all, she had completed her mission. She had brought back an undine of impressive power and she had saved the world with him.

Let the others figure out the rest of it. She wasn't the person to ask about relocation or how other people might feel. She was a soldier. Always had been, and always would be.

So she fought a battle of a different kind with him. Fortis fought with lips, and teeth, and tongue, learning each other's bodies anew as it felt like the two of them were different people. Like they were allowed to be who they wanted to be for the first time.

But eventually, reality set in. They needed to return to Tau, at least for a little while. Fortis gathered her up in his arms, a low growl rumbling through him as she wrapped her legs around his tail and her arms around his neck.

"Don't look at me like that," he rumbled, pressing a kiss to the side of her neck. "We won't leave."

"You and I both need to eat something more substantial than fish you caught in the ocean." She laughed at his antics, though.

With him, she felt like she was his world. And that was a blessing. It was more than she ever thought she'd get in this life.

He sighed and pressed their foreheads together, soaking her in one more time as he placed the breathing tube in her neck. It was an easier insertion these days. He'd done it so many times, she finally had that small bundle of goo that kept it from resealing as she healed, just like the other undine mates.

"Fine," he grumbled. "But the first moment I can steal you away, I intend to."

"Of course you do."

And she wouldn't stop him. Together, they swirled through the waters until they approached Tau again. She had expected to at least see some bodies floating in the water, but there was nothing around the city but suspiciously clean water.

A bright flash of yellow approached them, and at first she thought it was Maketes. But then she realized the light was a bright glow, and she knew it wasn't any of the undines who were more used to shallow waters. This was a depthstrider.

Aulax raced toward them and let out a whooping call before he finally reached their side. "And here I was thinking you'd be gone for at least a week!"

Fortis shifted her over and reached for his son.

She hadn't expected to be greeted with a hug. When was the last time that had happened? Had it ever happened? And it wasn't like they moved her out of the way so that Fortis could have a moment with his son, either. Aulax grabbed her and wrapped her up in the hug as much as his father. The wall of undine wrapped around her, tugging her deeper into their family unit and she...

She didn't know what to do with this. Was she meant to hug them back?

Aulax ruffled her hair with his hand and tugged her even harder until she was sandwiched between the two of them. "You're overthinking it. Just be hugged and hug back."

This would take a lot of getting used to. But she snuggled into the surprising heat of the two of them and let herself relax. Maybe it was new and uncomfortable, but it was also hers. And that was something she valued.

Finally Aulax drew back and with another tug at her hair, he guided them back to Tau. "When you offered the city to Mira, I think at first she wasn't going to take it. There are an awful lot of ghosts in this city, but also I think she was excited. The more contacts she made, the more she thought it was a good idea. Of course, many of the people from Alpha aren't trustworthy to be left alone yet. Not in a city like this. But there were plenty of families in Beta who have been working for a very long time and haven't gotten the space they need to grow. This facility could be a home for them, unlike any other."

That had always been Alexia's hope. They spun in the water around one of the coiling hallways and then up into one of the few moon pools in the city. This was where ships usually had at least two check points before they were let into Tau. Now, all the doors were open.

A few undines swam in the spears of light that illuminated them from the city. A couple of them had tablets in their hands, holding them up to scan pieces of the city that might need to be repaired after the fight. Droids were also in the water, some of them zipping past with what looked like vital seeds or food. Maybe they were bringing some of these resources to the other cities who desperately needed it.

She liked that idea. They should be doing something along those lines. Spreading the wealth and ensuring the longevity of each city.

"Mira wanted to talk with you," Aulax said, looking at her and not Fortis. "I think about that room full of bodies."

"The drowned ones?"

"No. The people who haven't woken up yet." He scratched the back of his neck. "No one else will deal with them, I'm afraid. The People of Water don't like... them."

Right. That made sense.

Fortis grabbed her arm, making her look at him before she left. "Do you hear that?" he asked.

"Hear what?"

"The voice."

She furrowed her brow and tried to listen as hard as she could. "No, Fortis. I don't hear any voice."

He looked troubled by that fact, but then he shook his head as though to clear the thoughts from his mind. "It's fine. I forget that the sea talks to me, at times. It is just..."

"A new voice," Aulax interrupted. "Why is there a new voice?"

The two of them stared at each other, and she feared she was missing something very, very important.

"Boys?" she asked, slowly. "Why does that sound bad?"

They remained looking at each other, and then she realized they were listening. Intently. Their eyes were fogged, and some of the other depthstriders had also stopped moving. They were all staring into the distance as though listening to something or someone who she could not hear.

Swallowing, she sat down on the edge of the moon pool and waited. Soon, Mira joined her as well. The two of them remained quietly looking at all these frozen undines, even though some of the higher water ones moved around them. As though it was normal to see the depthstriders all freeze as one.

"Have you ever seen this happen before?" Alexia asked.

"No. But Arges said it's nothing that's hurting them, so we shouldn't worry too much." Mira put her hand on her shoulder and squeezed. "Perhaps we should leave them to it. The depthstriders are closer to the ocean than any other of their kind, and sometimes it talks to them. Like a goddess."

"They said it was a new voice."

She looked over her shoulder and up into Mira's troubled expression, but the redhead quickly wiped that look off her face the moment she saw Alexia looking at her. "We'll deal with it when we must. But first, I would have your opinion on those rooms full of people."

Standing, Alexia headed off with her, but stopped into one of the guard rooms to change her clothing. She was wet and covered in only a jacket and pants that had certainly seen better days. If Mira reacted to seeing her so unclothed, the other woman was very good at hiding it.

Finally, she headed off toward the room where all of her nightmares had begun. When she walked into the area for genetic enhancements, she was pleased to find none of the children were there.

Mira waved at the empty tubes where some of them had still been growing. "Children, we know what to do with. Even though they are going to have different needs, we already reached out to Beta and many of the people who were relocated from Alpha. Quite a few of them have experience in childcare, and they have been informed that these are slightly different children than they are used to. I'm certain with enough time and love, they will be just like everyone else."

"That's... nice." Alexia didn't have the right words for the relief that poured through her. These kids, who were just like her, were going to have a normal life. People weren't going to hate them or fear them or try to put them in little boxes like that was a normal thing for children to suffer through.

She was going to see them grow into people. Just like they were supposed to be. Even if they were a little stronger than most or if they were a little more capable, they were not going to be looked at as different.

They were just kids.

Mira smiled at her, as though she understood the meaning underneath those two words. "Your Doctor Barker has offered to be their personal physician throughout their lives. He's already quite concerned about the genetic enhancements and what that might mean for children or breeding with the rest of us. He thinks you all might be the future of humanity. Even if the origin of where your bloodlines came from is a little unusual."

She grinned. "I hope they make up the most ridiculous story about where we came from. I'm going to tell the children we're aliens who came from Above."

"You just might be. Doctor Barker has made suggestions that your people might be able to survive on the surface, or at the very least, be hardy enough to manage it." Mira shrugged. "Who knows? Maybe someday we'll make a trek up there and discover other people already living there."

Wouldn't that be a surprise?

Alexia strode through the room that had inspired all her personal nightmares, and into the frigid room where all the reborns were stored. Her breath fogged in front of her mouth as she stood there with Mira, looking at all the hundreds of tubes filled with people. Each of them were identical to the others. A perfect match. A clone of all twenty-five people who had ended the world.

It was strange to look at them. She walked a few feet forward and stopped in front of a woman suspended in front of her. She was a clone of a lesser known Original. The woman had been a social recluse.

"Clara," Alexia said. "This one is a clone of Clara, one of the scientists who headed the genetic program."

"Oh, so some of the Originals were actually useful, then?"

"Some of them. Most were intelligent folks back in the day. Scientists, doctors, Harlow was a physicist. But hundreds of years of life had made everything boring and some things she knew would never have answers. Why we were here, what lives beyond our planet, all of that knowledge was taken from them the moment they couldn't get off this planet and had to come underneath the sea." She laid a hand on the ice cold glass, fractals of frost spearing between her fingers. "But these people are not them."

"That's why we wanted you here. We have a bit of a problem. Waking them all and sending them to the cities underneath the sea is going to be difficult. Swarms of the same person walking around isn't going to be good for... anyone." Mira ran a hand down her face. "Logically, we all understand these aren't the same people. They've never been awake. They don't even have memories. But they need to have a decision made about where they are going and what we are doing with them. Frankly, I don't feel like I should be the one making that choice."

Of course they couldn't just wake them all and unleash every single one of them into general populace. There were hundreds of them. So many clones in varying states of age.

She headed out of the icy cold room and booted up one of the computers. She brought up the life chart for Mira to see. "There are eight hundred and fifty-four clones currently in this room. Half of them have already been used. The reborns are frozen and put back in stasis if some of their organs have been harvested, but there were more organs that still be used. Essentially, if they only removed a kidney or a liver, they would keep the reborn alive just to take more organs and have less waste."

Mira's face twisted in disgust. She didn't have to say anything.

"I agree. But it was the only way they could make sure that every body was appropriately used and not wasted." She typed in a few more things and then pointed at the screen. "That leaves us with four hundred and twenty-seven. Half of which are still in the zygote phase. They can be terminated without feeling any guilt. They are still growing."

"So that ends up being..."

"Two hundred and twelve. Just about eight versions of each person left. I would suggest that a set of them who are capable of existing on their own as adults, be put in separate cities. They're unlikely to ever meet." She pointed to a count. "It's essentially two of each person that are always available for some sort of need."

"One can go to Beta for now. I can have someone there show them the ropes and how to be people. The other can remain here."

Alexia pointed to a few more numbers. "And there are six more each that are babies. Two could be brought out into the world as twins."

Sitting on one of the chairs near her, Mira blew out a long breath and puffed her cheeks. "So there's a hundred more. That still leaves us with what? A hundred and twelve people in stasis?"

Alexia nodded. It didn't settle right, but that was where they were. "We can't just wake them up now. They'll have to remain as they are and slowly be added into the cities."

"We could do the same here. It's unlikely that Beta and Tau will mingle, but there's always the chance."

"A hundred people that we're choosing to keep asleep." Alexia shook her head. "It feels wrong."

"There's nowhere else to put them, unless you want them to go to the prison city."

"I don't," Alexia snapped. "I know it's the right thing to do. They will wake up eventually. I just... I wish I could save them all."

"You did save them all." Mira scooted her chair closer, pointing at the numbers once again. "If you weren't here, these people would have been used for god knows what. Now, they have a chance at a normal life. Alexia, you have to take that as the sign that it is. Without you, they would have all suffered a much worse fate than waiting a few more years to wake up."

Alexia nodded and tried to get that through her head.

"Listen to me. You're saving four hundred and twenty-seven people. Not to mention countless others that Tau was controlling and using to distract from what was going on here." Mira grabbed her hands and squeezed them. "Take the time you need to let this settle in. I'm sure it's not easy to believe. But it's the truth."

The truth.

Alexia bit her lips and nodded. She could believe it. Someday.

But for now, she would help get these reborns to homes where they could live. Really live.

Epilogue

Fortis slowly came back into this world. The voice had been the one he'd heard in that tomb. The deep voice of reckoning had warned them all of what they had done.

"You have all entered a time where humans will now be part of your life. Whether you wished them to or not. I have been asleep for centuries. Waiting. I know what you face and what you will soon see. And it is I who will help guide you."

And then all depthstriders were shown the same vision at the same time.

He wasn't sure what they were meant to get out of it. Humans swimming alongside their own kind. New cities, ones that incorporated his people into them. He saw entire rooms where the People of Water had the ability to swim up into tubes and rest in entire homes that were accessed by droids for them. Metal arms that brought them food allowed them to work with the humans in massive spaces filled with people making decisions with each other. There were children, too. Children with smaller tails, two tails, children that looked like humans and his people mixed together.

It was a good future, but one he knew many of his kind would fear. This would fundamentally change their lives. No more would the People of Water have to avoid humans or expect to be fought with. They would be... enmeshed.

When he could finally see the surrounding world, he looked at his son first. Aulax had a bright grin on his face and so much hope in his eyes. "That is our future, father?"

"I believe so."

"I cannot believe..." Aulax let out a shocked laugh. "Then it worked. Everything we did. It worked."

So it had. More than any of them could have expected, it had worked. They had created something that had changed the very fabric of time itself. And he, for one, was so excited to see it come to fruition.

"And I get to be here to experience it with you," he murmured, before throwing his head back and laughing.

Together, he and his son rejoiced in the future that would come. He knew there were some, like Mitera, who were terrified. They did not know where they fit into this new future, but he knew exactly where his family fit. Right at the heart of it all.

Alexia returned with Mira, and he knew that his life had only just begun with her.

"We're moving some of the reborn. The droids are already preparing their transport, but we'll need some of your people to guide the ships," Alexia said. "The droids can get where they are going, but I'm concerned they won't get there safely. The reborns are important."

"Were are they going?"

"Beta, for now. There are fifty pods that need to be moved, twenty-five adults and twenty-five children."

He nodded, but then reached for her. "Come with me. We'll guide them together, and you can see them in their new home."

Fortis knew how much that would mean to her. She had nearly given up her entire life to see these people safe and sound. She would need this closure, to know that they had made it to their destination, and that they were waking up to welcoming arms. He knew because he would need the same if he were giving up his son.

She leapt into the water without hesitation, and he made sure she could breathe before they were off. Aulax joined them, his son filling her in on the vision that the newly awoken god of the sea had seen.

"Another god?" she asked Fortis, not interrupting his son as the young man continued to tell her a more complicated tale with every moment. "Should you be worried about that?"

Faintly. A part of him wasn't sure who was talking to them, and he feared what kind of creature would have that sort of power. "The sea is mysterious. I do not know what awoke in the bottom of the sea, but I do know that its purpose is similar to our own. It wants humans and the People of Water to work together."

"Then it can stay." She rubbed her hand along his forearm as he dragged her toward the transport.

It was a strange beast of a droid. It looked more like a ship than he'd expected, as the creation was made to harvest the pods. A few arms at the edges were plucking the pods out of the city and depositing them like egg sacks on the sides. There was a deep sea creature who looked like this, he was certain.

Wincing, he watched as the last of the pods were loaded up before it started heading out. The ship coasted out over the abyss, carefully moving until one lone pod shifted. He couldn't help but notice the glowing egg sack drifting down into the abyss, its lights flickering before it went out.

"No!" Alexia gasped, before she grabbed onto his arm. "We have to go get her."

But then he heard that deep, aching voice rumble in his mind again.

"Her," it called, and there was so much interest there.

A flash of a vision appeared in his mind, but then he realized it wasn't a vision at all. He was seeing what the god at the bottom of the sea saw. A sealed tomb, one that had been closed for centuries and one that he deeply hated. The entrance was dark, and covered in scratch marks from centuries of trying to claw his way out. But he never had been able to until this moment.

Now there was a light at the edge. A crack where a massive, green, clawed hand could wedge a sharp claw into the side and start to pry it open. Bit by bit, that claw wiggled and forced the opening larger and larger until it finally snapped open.

Fortis fell with the god, feeling the weakness in his body and how large he was. He was massive. Bigger than Fortis had ever felt in his life, with a tail that was tattered and worn. And as he looked down at his hands sinking into the muck, Fortis realized his skin was nearly translucent. He could see right through to the bones beneath.

The god flexed his fingers, curling his hands into fists and suddenly all those bones glowed. Fortis could see his skeleton through his skin, and he knew whatever this creature was, it was not one of their own kind. But it also wasn't a god.

He had been trapped for years. Centuries. He had been stuck in a tomb that humans had made, but he didn't want to destroy them all for it. No, he wanted one singular person to pay penance for what everyone else had done.

And that pod, falling into the abyss, was his opportunity to seek amends for centuries of pain and torment.

As the vision fell from his eyes and the pod drifted ever deeper, Fortis held Alexia a little tighter to his chest. "The sea demands reparations for what was done to it."

"The death of the Originals wasn't enough?" she snarled.

"No. The sea requires someone alive." He looked at the pod with pity, and then turned toward the rest of the ship and continued onward with it. "There is nothing we can do now. Whoever that was will awaken as a servant to a god."

Alexia nodded, perhaps believing his strange words likely for the very first time. And together, they turned toward a brighter future, knowing that enough sacrifices had finally been made.

Follow me on socials or Amazon to keep your eye out for the next book!

Acknowledgements

What an insanely wild ride between all of these creatures. I have LOVED dearly, deeply, and immensely writing in the Deep Waters series. This book has renewed my love of…. Everything, I guess? Just writing and being creative and the relationship I get to have with all of you. It's all so wonderful and exciting and freeing.

So thank you to each and every one of you who started this series and said you were cool with fucking fish men.

You're literally the best humans on the planet.

About the Author

Emma Hamm is a small town girl on a blueberry field in Maine. She writes stories that remind her of home, of fairytales, and of myths and legends that make her mind wander.

She can be found by the fireplace with a cup of tea and her two Maine Coon cats dipping their paws into the water without her knowing.

For more updates, join my newsletter!
www.emmahamm.com